7/22

NIGHT, NEON

Center Point
Large Print

Also by Joyce Carol Oates and available from Center Point Large Print:

Dis Mem Ber
Night-Gaunts
Pursuit
My Life as a Rat

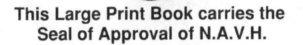

This Large Print Book carries the Seal of Approval of N.A.V.H.

NIGHT, NEON

Tales of Mystery and Suspense

JOYCE CAROL OATES

CENTER POINT LARGE PRINT
THORNDIKE, MAINE

This Center Point Large Print edition
is published in the year 2022 by arrangement with
Penzler Publishers/The Mysterious Press.

The text of this Large Print edition is unabridged.
In other aspects, this book may vary
from the original edition.
Printed in the United States of America
on permanent paper sourced using
environmentally responsible foresting methods.
Set in 16-point Times New Roman type.

ISBN: 978-1-63808-303-0

The Library of Congress has cataloged this record
under Library of Congress Control Number: 2022930277

for Kay Simon

CONTENTS

DETOUR

Too early for spring, you couldn't trust such blinding-white sunshine in mid-March. And the smell of damp earth thawing, reviving—too soon.

The result was, Abigail was feeling light-headed. Unreal.

A seismic sensation, as if the very earth were shifting beneath the wheels of her car on the familiar drive home.

Staring ahead, dismayed—blocking the road was a barrier with a jarring yellow sign: DETOUR.

"Damn."

Rarely elsewhere than in her car did Abigail address herself and usually in an exclamatory/exasperated tone. If anyone had overheard, she'd have been mortified.

"God *damn*."

Three-quarters of the way home, and now she'd be forced miles out of her way. For these were country roads that intersected infrequently, unlike urban streets laid in a sensible grid. She would return home later than she'd planned and have less time to herself before her husband returned from work.

That dreamy interlude, preparing a meal with

care, for just herself and her husband. A fireside dinner, with lighted candles.

And she had good news to share with Allan, which she would keep for just the right moment.

Darling, guess what!

The lab report—?

Yes! Negative.

Not totally unexpected news. Not after months of treatment. But exhilarating nonetheless, for in a year of medical news not invariably *good,* even *mildly good news* is welcome.

One by one, with robotic precision, drivers in vehicles ahead of Abigail were turning onto a smaller road. She wondered at their docility— *she* was tempted to drive around the damned barricade.

Her house was less than a mile away. Should she take a chance and try to drive directly to it? No impediments or construction were visible in the road.

You had to resent the nonnegotiable nature of DETOUR: ask no questions, no one to ask, simply follow the "detour" on trust that it will lead you to your destination.

Was ignoring a detour illegal? Was it dangerous?

What a strange thing for Mom to do! Getting a traffic ticket, a summons, the first in her lifetime . . .

She was not an impulsive person. No.

Thirty years she'd lived in the same house in the suburban countryside, five miles west of Stone Ridge, New Jersey, with her husband and, while they'd been young, their several children; thirty years, the unvarying route on North Ridge Road. In all those years she'd driven into the surrounding countryside only rarely and had little knowledge of the network of rural roads. She could not recall encountering a detour, or if she had, how inconvenient the detour had been.

She'd hoped to have more time to herself in the house, in the kitchen, her favorite room in the house, before her husband returned from work. Though possibly, Allan was already home, for he'd become semiretired the previous year, his schedule varying from week to week as his (legal) services were required at his firm.

Her husband's custom was to recount his day to her in detail: what he'd done at the office, how much (or how little) he'd accomplished, with whom he'd had meetings or met for lunch or spoken with on the phone. There were ongoing narratives—names that had become familiar to her over the years, though she'd met only a few of her husband's colleagues; ongoing themes of rivalry, alliances, sudden rifts, feuds, tragic developments, startling consequences. In these accounts, Allan was invariably the protagonist: the center of the narrative.

Though Abigail did not always listen closely to

11

these accounts, she took comfort in hearing them. Impossible not to feel a wave of tenderness for the man who, through the years, from the very start of their marriage, solemnly recited to his wife the banalities of his life, as a child might recite the events of his life to his mother, secure in the knowledge that anything he did, anything he said, because it was *his,* would be prized by his mother if not by others.

In exchange, Abigail told her husband of her day, more briefly. For she was the wife, she had a dread of boring *him.*

As a young woman, indeed as a girl, Abigail had learned to shape herself to fit the expectations of others. If there was a singular narrative of her life, it had the contour of a supple, sinuous snake, ever delighting in its contortions and in the shimmering iridescent camouflage-skin that contained it.

Even as a mother! Perhaps as a mother most of all.

Crucial not to let them know. How frightened you are, how little you know. How astonished you are that they have survived.

For nothing is so flimsy-seeming as a human infant. Soft-skulled, soft-eyed, with such tiny lungs, you fear they might collapse with wailing.

"Damn!"—her car was bumping, jolting. A fierce winter had left the narrow country road in poor condition, potholed and rutted. Following a line of other vehicles, Abigail was forced to drive unnaturally slowly, gripping the steering wheel in both hands. A throbbing pain had begun at her temples, the sensation of unreality deepened.

Surely the detour would double back soon. You had to surmise that a detour describes a half rectangle around an impassable road, the object of which is to lead back to that road on the other side of the blockage. But Cold Soil Road seemed to be leading in the opposite direction from North Ridge.

Oh, where was her cell phone?—she should call Allan to tell him that she'd probably be late. But her handbag was out of reach in the back seat, where she'd carelessly tossed it.

In late afternoon the sun was unnaturally bright. The sky resembled a watercolor wash of pale oranges, reds—too "pretty" to be real—and of a particularly banal prettiness, like calendar art. Deciduous trees that only the previous week had been skeletal and leafless were now luminous with tight little greeny buds.

Too soon!—Abigail felt a frisson of alarm, dread.

Cruel to awaken the dead, in spring. More merciful to let us sleep.

From Cold Soil Road her car was shunted onto a narrower country road that seemed to have no name, or at least she could not discover any name. No choice but to follow the DETOUR signs, with resentment and mounting unease, though a left turn should have been followed by a right turn to begin to complete the (rectangular) figure of the detour and not this slow curve leftward into the countryside . . .

Where am I being taken? This is wrong.

Traffic was sparse on this unnamed road. No one seemed to be coming in Abigail's direction, all traffic in the other direction, strung out along the detour like dispirited Bedouins. Worse, after so much jolting, the steering wheel of Abigail's car seemed to be loosening; each time she turned it, the car responded less immediately, as if she were driving on ice.

At last, at a curve, she turned the wheel with no effect at all—the car continued forward, off the road and in the direction of a shallow ditch. Panicked, she pumped the brake pedal, but this too had little effect.

Something struck her forehead, as if in rebuke. She heard a murmur of startled voices at a distance, witnesses to her folly.

She cried in protest. *No!* It was not her fault, something had happened to the steering wheel.

The front wheels of her car were in the ditch, the rear of the car remained on the roadway. The windshield had seemed to fly back toward her, striking her forehead. She was sobbing with frustration, dismay. What had happened to the steering wheel? And the brakes—useless.

Much effort was required for Abigail to extricate herself from the tilting car. Pushing the driver's door open, climbing out into the road, panting. Her heartbeat was erratic, like her breath. She'd been so taken by surprise! Her balance had been affected, she walked as if on the listing deck of a boat.

A vehicle approached, she waved frantically for it to stop, but the driver seemed not to see her, continuing past without slackening his speed. The vehicle's windshield shone with reflected sunshine, she could not see the driver's face.

Calling after in a pleading voice—"No, wait! Please don't leave me . . ."

Her handbag, containing her cell phone, had been left in the car. She could not bring herself to climb back into the car. Fortunately, the ditch was fairly shallow, the car's front wheels submerged in less than a foot of water, but the water smelled brackish, foul; she did not want to wade in it, still less did she want to grope around in it, where water had begun to seep inside the car with a hoarse, gurgling sound, as of occluded breathing.

Peering through the side windows, she couldn't see her handbag, guessing that it had been flung down onto the floor. No, she couldn't retrieve it, not her cell phone, not her wallet . . . The car key was still in the ignition, she couldn't bring herself to retrieve that, either.

In the interim, another vehicle had passed in the roadway. If the driver had seen her, and her car partway in the ditch, the driver gave no sign, but drove imperturbably on.

She climbed back onto the roadway, trying to hold herself erect, unswaying. She understood: it was crucial not to give an impression of drunkenness or injury. (Was her face bleeding? A stranger would not wish to bloody the interior of his car.)

Her fingers, gingerly touching her throbbing forehead, came away unbloodied, but her nostrils felt loose and runny—was her nose bleeding? She hoped it wasn't broken, she dared not touch it for fear of injuring herself further.

But what had happened to her left shoe? She was standing in just one shoe; on her left foot was a light woolen sock, soaked from the ditch.

Miserably she looked around on the roadway to see if the shoe was there—but no, of course the shoe was inside the car, no doubt on the floor in the front, where brackish water was seeping in.

No choice but to make her way, limping, half sobbing, along the road in the direction of a house nearby; she would ask to use a telephone. This was not an unreasonable request, though she was looking disheveled and her damned nose was leaking blood.

Now! You must prove yourself.

A curious sort of anticipation overcame her. Almost euphoria.

Most of her life she'd been *waiting*—for what, she hadn't known.

As a bright and curious girl-child, waiting for her true life to begin. As a restless but shy adolescent, waiting for her true life to begin. Before she'd met the man she would marry, waiting for her true life to begin. And then, in the months before she'd married this man, waiting for her true life to begin.

Before she'd had her first pregnancy and her first baby—waiting for her true life to begin.

And since the children had grown and gone away—waiting for

her true life to begin.

Something meant for me alone. Just—for me.

That has been waiting for me to arrive.

Because I have not been in the right place until now.

But now—am I in the right place?

It was comforting to see that the house she approached wasn't a derelict farmhouse like others in the area, but a house that resembled her own: a dignified Colonial of wood, brick, and fieldstone; not new, in fact probably at least one hundred years old, but beautifully restored and renovated: roof, shutters, and windows replaced and the clapboards freshly painted creamy white, which suggested that the property owners were affluent, like Abigail and her husband, who lived, Abigail calculated, about three miles away—if you took not the circuitous detour but a straight line.

Gravel horseshoe driveway, spacious front lawn with evergreen shrubs, several acres bordered by tall oaks, at the rear a barn converted into a three-car garage.

Abigail's heart lifted! Whoever lived in this house would not be suspicious of her but would recognize her as a neighbor.

Possibly, whoever lived in this house knew her and, yet more possibly, knew her husband.

Possibly, these homeowners had been guests in the R__s' house and would be grateful to return their hospitality.

Before ringing the bell beside the front door, Abigail dabbed at her face with a tissue, which came away stained with blood; she used another tissue to wipe her damp eyes and to blow her nose, cautiously. With a stab of guilt she recalled having heard the front doorbell in her house ring not long ago, and standing very still, waiting for the ringing to cease and whoever it was to go away from the door; for no one of her or Allan's acquaintance would have rung the doorbell without first notifying her that they were coming, and no one who rang the doorbell without first notifying her was anyone she'd have wished to see.

A second time she pressed the bell buzzer, politely. She would not press insistently on the buzzer, for such an act would signal aggression, a kind of threat. Nor would she knock loudly on the door and frighten or antagonize whoever might be inside, listening somewhere in the interior of the house.

Rehearsing what she might say, with an apologetic smile—*Excuse me! I am so, so sorry to bother you, but I was following the detour and I've had a little accident, my car is in a ditch! If I could use your phone to call my husband . . .*

Though she might have said *call AAA* or *call a garage,* she preferred *call my husband,* as this phrase indicated not only the likelihood of a nearby household but the stability of a lengthy marriage.

And she would give her address, to establish her identity as a fellow property owner, with all that that entailed of prohibitively high property taxes in Bergen County, which was, of all counties in the state, one of the most affluent, thus one in which the subject of taxes provided homeowners with an immediate subject with which to bond in sympathy—*We live over on . . .*

For a confused moment, not remembering: Was it *Ridge Road? North Ridge?*

Ringing the doorbell again, listening for a response. None.

Her forehead throbbed, her nose was leaking

blood. If only she'd remembered to bring that damned cell phone with her!

Despite the prematurely balmy air, she was shivering. The sole of her left foot ached; she'd stepped on sharp stones.

Then recalling: there was surely a side entrance to the staid old Colonial, a door that led into a small vestibule and then into the kitchen.

Limping, favoring her shoeless foot, she followed a flagstone path around the side of the house, and there indeed was an entrance, as in her house. And here too was a doorbell, which she pressed with more confidence—in her own home she understood that whoever pressed the buzzer beside the kitchen door was likely to be someone familiar with her household, the FedEx deliveryman or the gas meter man or a friend; those who rang the front door were likely to be strangers, about whom a homeowner would naturally feel wary.

Are you hiding in there? Please—if you are hiding—I only need to make a phone call, you are under no obligation to help me further . . .

I am not injured. I am not bleeding! I promise.

I am your neighbor.

But no one came to answer this door, either. Abigail shaded her eyes to peer through the window: there was the vestibule, with coats, jackets, and sweaters on hooks, boots on the floor, exactly as in her house, and a doorway opening into a kitchen. Bars of sunshine fell slantwise on a tile floor not unlike her own, a deep russet brown. And hanging on an overhead rack, shining copper utensils.

"Hello? Hello? I—I'm in need of—help . . ."

It seemed to her that she was being observed. A surveillance camera eye, somewhere overhead. On the doorframe, a discreet notice, like one beside the kitchen door of her house: THESE PREMISES PROTECTED BY ACHILLES HOME SECURITY, INC.

Then she realized: whoever lived here surely kept a spare key outside somewhere, beneath the welcome mat or beneath a flowerpot or urn, as she did.

The key to this house wasn't beneath the welcome mat, Abigail discovered, which was reasonable: keeping an outdoor key in such an obvious place was an invitation to a break-in, as her husband had warned. Better beneath a flowerpot, an urn, or a wrought iron chair or table in a nearby courtyard, which was a little distance from the door and not so likely to be discovered by an intruder, though in this case Abigail was thrilled to discover the key within minutes, beneath an ornamental urn a few feet from the door.

Managing then to unlock the kitchen door and stepping inside into a warm, yeasty-smelling interior that felt welcoming to her, she had no

21

fear that an alarm would ring, as indeed no alarm rang. Though certainly she was ill at ease, and would stay in the house only long enough to make a telephone call; she would then return to her incapacitated car and wait for help from AAA, and would not inconvenience anyone if she could avoid it.

"Excuse me? Hello? Is anyone here? I—I only just need to make a phone call . . ."

Her voice trailed off, uncertainly. She stood very still, listening. (Was the floor creaking overhead? Was someone upstairs, also very still, listening?) After a moment she decided no, just a distant sound of wind in trees, an airplane passing overhead.

Her mouth had gone dry with anticipation, excitement. Her heartbeat, triggered by the accident with the car, continued rapidly, with a kind of exhilaration.

So long *waiting*—for what?

But where was the telephone? Abigail expected to see a wall phone in the kitchen, in the approximate place where there was a wall phone in her kitchen, but the design of this kitchen did not precisely resemble hers. And the counters were olive, while her counters were, less practicably, white; the deep-sunken aluminum sink was in a different location from where hers was, as was the Sub-Zero refrigerator and the ovens set in a wall—(as in her kitchen, there were two ovens, one above the other). Close up, the tile floor did not so closely resemble the tile floor in her house but was of a darker hue.

Looking so intently for a telephone had caused the light-headedness to return, as well as a curious fatigue mixed with anxiety, as if, even as Abigail understood (of course!) that she was trespassing in a private household, and had no right to be here, and was behaving very strangely for a person who valued privacy as she did, nonetheless she felt a strong impulse to lie down somewhere, in some quiet place where she would trouble no one and no one would trouble her, and when she was rested and thinking clearly again, she would complete the task for which she'd entered the house of strangers . . . Though for the moment the very concepts *phone, call, husband* had passed out of her consciousness.

She knew her name, though: *Abigail R—*. And the address of the house in which she'd lived for thirty years—she was sure she could recall it, if required.

However, as long as she was in this (unfamiliar) house and no one seemed to be home and she was certainly disturbing no one, she reasoned that she might as well use a bathroom, for she'd been needing to use a bathroom since the accident. She winced at the loud sound of the toilet flushing and the groan of old pipes, an echo of the pipes in her own house that needed replacing. And afterward, taking time to wash her face with cool water, dabbing at her bruised forehead and blood-stippled nose with wetted tissues. A strong smell of lavender soap lifted to her nostrils, a scent that brought comfort.

The children in this household too had grown and gone away, she thought. For you could not have such luxury soap in a downstairs bathroom if there were children in the house; you could have only utilitarian soap, and even this they'd leave filmy with the grime of their hands. Impossible, too, to have such delicate linen guest towels!

And so, there was something sad, bittersweet in the soap scent.

Wincing, too, to see her face close up in the bathroom mirror—often she was mystified that she looked so unlike herself, more resembling one of her older female relatives than herself; though in the eyes of the world, she supposed, she was—still—considered an attractive woman, well-groomed, poised, cultured. Her skin was still relatively unlined, her hair thick and glossy. She had not the courage, for instance, to dress other than expensively, as she would never have dared to appear in public without judicious makeup; her daughters, who'd scorned makeup when young, would have been appalled to see their mother without it, even in the privacy of her home.

Wiping her hands on a linen hand towel as discreetly as she could and returning the towel to its proper place as neatly as she'd found it.

Thank you! I am so grateful. I will not stay long, I promise.

Continuing now through the downstairs of the house, looking for—exactly what, she couldn't recall, but she would recognize it when she saw it. A small item. A small item placed on a table . . . Unsteady on her feet and indeed the floorboards of the house were uneven, a characteristic of older houses, like basements—"cellars"—with oppressively low ceilings that could never be raised.

Giddiness increased, unless it was faintness. The sensation of unreality grew like waves lapping about her legs. She was hesitant to lean forward and lower her forehead to her knees to increase the blood flow into her brain, for she feared the action might make things worse and she would fall in a dead faint and be discovered by strangers and reported to authorities.

Had to lean against walls. Against the backs of chairs. She seemed to know the way—somewhere. Feeling the need to go upstairs, surrender her pride, and crawl on hands and knees up the (carpeted) staircase, out of breath and wincing with pain.

At the top of the stairs, resting for several minutes before heaving herself to her feet.

Almost there, she consoled herself. Wherever it was she needed to go. She'd have to conserve her strength, dared not squander it heedlessly; once she'd slept for an hour, she was certain to feel much better and to know what to do next.

Someone she'd meant to contact—a husband? *Her* husband?

His name had fallen away, his face was a blur. His name—well, she would know his name, to which her own name was attached . . .

With the instinct of a blind creature she staggered into a room containing a bed. At the top of the stairs, first right. It was a large room—it was a large bed. Her trembling hands managed to pull back a satin comforter so that she could fall into the bed with a shuddering sigh—every bone in her body dissolving, disappearing into the most exquisite sleep; and when she opened her eyes, she found herself staring at a ceiling less than eight feet above her head, unless it was a low-hanging cumulus cloud. She smiled at the sight! Her brain was well rested, a kind of balm had washed over it.

The bed was so large she felt dwarfed within it. The sheets were of exceptionally good quality but dampened by her sweaty sleep, for which she felt chagrin; she reasoned that if she had time, she would change the sheets, and no one would be the wiser.

She lifted herself onto her elbows, staring.

Where *was* she? This was not a bedroom familiar to her, yet it "felt" familiar—spacious, with pale rose (silk?) wallpaper and attractive furnishings that looked like family heirlooms. One of them was a massive mahogany bureau, atop of which a row of framed photographs had been placed with loving attention.

For you are securely *in the world* only if there are such photographs of loved ones to testify to your existence, and your worth.

From the bed, however, Abigail could not make out the faces in the photographs. Some were very likely older relatives, others were children. But all were hazy with light reflected from the windows, unnaturally bright for a late afternoon in March.

Here was a rude surprise: Abigail's clothes had been removed from her body!

So strangely, she appeared to be wearing a nightgown. Neither familiar to her nor unfamiliar: a nightgown of soft flannel in a pink floral pattern, that fitted her naked body loosely.

She blushed hotly to think that someone had dared to undress her while she'd been asleep and had put a nightgown on her, as one might prepare a child for bed or undress a hospital patient; she'd given no consent to anyone to touch her, still less to remove her clothing . . . That she'd been undressed—and dressed—without having awakened suggested that she'd been sleeping very deeply, perhaps for a longer period of time than she'd imagined.

"Hello? Is someone here?"—her voice seemed to reverberate in the air close about her.

On her feet, shakily. Bare feet on a carpeted floor. Even the light woolen socks had been removed by whoever had dared to undress her.

While she'd slept, her heartbeat had slowed. Now it was rapid again, painful. All her senses were alert.

She must escape! Must find her clothes and dress and slip from the house. Whoever had dared touch her might return at any moment.

Shuddering to think it might have been a *he*. A stranger, daring to strip her naked even as she lay oblivious in sleep as profound as death.

She searched for her clothing in the room and could not find it, though her single shoe lay on the carpet beside the bed as if it had been tossed down. She thought—*But just one damned shoe is useless!*

In fact, this was not true. Had she not climbed out of her car and walked along the roadway and entered this house wearing but the single shoe?— she could do this again if necessary.

Another surprise: when she tried the bedroom door, the doorknob was loose in her fingers.

So, though the doorknob *turned* and *turned,* it did not open the door.

She pulled at the doorknob. Yanked, tugged.

Panicked, she called out, "Hello? *Hello?*"

Rapping on the door with her fist. "Hello? Is somebody there? I—I'm in here . . . I'm upstairs, I'm *here*."

She pressed her ear against the door. Beyond the rapid beating of blood in her ears she could hear—something . . .

Voices? Footsteps? A door opening, closing? The ordinary sounds of a household, at a little distance.

Desperately she struck her fists on the door. Calling out, crying—*"Hello hello hello! Let me out!"*—until her throat ached, her voice was cracked and hoarse.

Was she being kept *captive?* Was she a— *captive?*

Of course it was likely a mistake of some kind. A misunderstanding.

Mistaken identity, was it? She, Abigail R___, closely resembled another woman, perhaps . . . This other woman was the one intended to be *captive.*

Standing now close by the mahogany bureau, still she couldn't make out faces in the photographs. No matter how she squinted, the faces inside the frames—adults, children—remained out of focus, hazy with light.

And the view from the second-floor windows: tall trees, mostly leafless, a landscape that was still sere and bleached from winter, though beginning now to revive; since trees surrounded the house, there was no visible horizon, all was foreshortened.

Yet when she looked more closely, she saw that the scene was flat and unconvincing, like a stage set; trees, grasses, sky, overly bright sun seemed all at the same approximate distance from her, lacking depth.

The wave of dizziness intensified. Was *she* flat as well, in this landscape?

When had "perspective" come into human consciousness?—she tried to recall.

Medieval art was strangely flat; there was no illusion of depth. Human faces lacked expression, as if the artists of the time did not "see" the plasticity of the normal face. Children did not resemble children, but rather stunted adults.

She pressed her heated face against the windowpane, trying to see at a slant—a corner of the barn that had been converted into a garage, a glimpse of the country road where her car was stranded a quarter mile away, front wheels in a ditch.

Oh, why had she abandoned her car so quickly! She should have tried to free it from the ditch. If she'd rocked the car forward and back, forward and back, gaining momentum by degrees, as a more confident and skilled driver might have done, she might be home now. Instead she'd given up at once, defeated.

Instead she was trapped in a stranger's house. Only a few miles from her own house, *captive.*

Her bladder ached sharply, as a child's bladder might, in animal panic.

A bathroom adjoined the bedroom, Abigail went to use it, hurriedly.

Here was a spacious, white-tiled bathroom that was clearly in frequent use. Thick towels hung on racks, slightly askew. There were two sinks, neither entirely clean. A mirror just perceptibly spotted. Electric toothbrushes (two), a twisted tube of toothpaste, hand lotion, hand mirror, hairbrush, combs (two), cuticle scissors, tweezers . . . At least two people used this bathroom. Abigail lifted the hand mirror and saw, yes—it was a silver mirror, heavy in the hand, ornately engraved but in need of silver polish.

Mirrors ran the length of the bathroom in panels. In each mirror a wraithlike figure in a shapeless gown, like a shroud, stared at Abigail, aghast.

Then she saw, the bathroom had a second door that might lead into another bedroom or into a hallway, but when she seized the doorknob to turn it, she discovered that the door was locked.

She could have sobbed. The doorknob had turned in a normal way but to no avail, the door was *locked.*

Stumbling back into the bedroom, Abigail saw to her astonishment that a stranger had entered the room in her absence. At first she could not see his face clearly—it was blurred, like a smudged thumb. He must have unlocked the door—the door with the broken doorknob—for there appeared to be no other way into the room. And what was he carrying?—a heavy cut-glass vase of dazzling white flowers that exuded a pungent fragrance. Gardenias.

Flowers for the invalid!—for *her.*

"Why, darling! What are you doing out of bed?"

He was startled, alarmed. Genuine concern for her, an undercurrent of dismay and exasperation.

"And your feet—*bare.*"

Abigail was sure she'd never seen this man before. He had thick white gnarled-looking hair, a low forehead, and a broad, flushed face; he wore a dark pin-striped suit that fitted his stocky figure somewhat tightly, a white shirt and neck-tie, polished dress shoes. Indeed, he'd brought the bouquet of white flowers for Abigail, setting the vase on a bedside table.

How powerful, the sickly sweet smell of gardenias! Abigail felt dizzy, dazed, as if ether had been released into the airless room.

Stunned speechless as the stranger addressed her worriedly: "Please go back to bed, darling. D'you want to catch pneumonia again? Next time might be fatal. And what if you'd fallen when no one was here!"

"But I—I—I don't belong here . . ."

"Bare feet! For God's *sake*."

He would have led Abigail forcibly back to the bed, but she shrank from him, rebuffing his hands, preparing to scream if he touched her—but he did not touch her; instead, unexpectedly, he shrugged and turned aside, as if Abigail's behavior had offended him.

"Ah, well. It's just good that I've come home. I never know what—what in bloody hell—I will discover."

He laughed, harshly. Clearly he was disgusted. But he was dismayed. Yanking off his necktie and hanging it in a closet on a rack of other ties. Abigail could see that these were expensive designer ties. His back to her, oblivious of her, matter-of-factly he removed his suit coat and hung it carefully in the closet; removed his white dress shirt, his trousers, and his shoes to change into more comfortable attire—red plaid woolen shirt, khaki trousers, moccasins.

A heavy sigh—"Jesus Christ. I *never know*."

Abigail stood staring, astonished. This stranger was changing his clothes before her eyes with the casual disdain of a husband. Almost, she was moved to apologize, for clearly there was a profound misunderstanding between them.

To Abigail's greater astonishment, the white-haired man proceeded to recite to Abigail, in grim detail, his day: an early-morning conference call with clients in Tampa and Dallas; a luncheon meeting at the club with ___, ___, and ___; much of the afternoon spent at his desk, going over accounts with ___; then, on the phone with ___; then, another conference call with clients in San Diego and Houston—

Abigail interrupted: "Excuse me!—but I want to go home . . ."

The white-haired man ceased speaking. A coarse red blush deepened at the nape of his neck. All this while he'd been standing with his back to Abigail, stiff and unyielding, refusing to face her. She sensed that he was very angry; he had not liked being interrupted in the midst of his report, which had seemed to him important and should have impressed his listener.

"I—I said—I want to go home . . . You've locked me in here, I don't belong here, *I want to go home.*"

Abigail was shivering violently. The sensation of faintness deepened. She said, stammering, "You—you have no right to keep me here! It's against the law—to keep me against my will! I never consented. I don't know you. I had an accident on the road, but I'm not injured—I don't need any medical care—I've been able to rest, and I'm ready now to leave—*I want to go home.*"

"Darling, you are home. Please just get into bed."

Gently, grimly, the man reasoned with Abigail.

He was several inches taller than she and at least thirty pounds heavier, his breathing audible. He might have been appealing to a neutral observer—he was being the most reasonable of men.

Abigail protested: "I—I am not home. I don't know who you are. This is wrong—this is not my home . . ."

"Of course this is your home! You're just very tired, dear. It's time for your medication."

"No! No medication!"

Abigail's voice rose in alarm. The white-haired man dared not press the issue.

"It's a mistake. I don't belong here. There was a detour. At North Ridge Road . . ."

Buoyantly these words came to Abigail, as precious as a life jacket to one drowning in treacherous waters—*North Ridge Road.*

Other words she'd lost, could not retrieve, but somehow these crucial words had returned to her, which she was sure would impress her captor.

"Detour?—I didn't notice any detour, darling. You haven't been out—what would you know of detours and road conditions? *I've* been out. I've never heard of any North Ridge Road—I think you must mean Northanger Road. But that's nowhere near here, that's over in Hunterdon County." The man spoke patiently, and with an air of sorrow. Though white-haired, he wasn't elderly; probably in his early sixties. You could see how disconsolate he was. How close to despair. How bitterly he blamed *her.*

And how awkward Abigail was in the flannel nightgown that fell billowing to her ankles and would have tripped her if she'd dared to push past her captor and escape out the door . . .

But no: she seemed to recall that there was no escape through that door, at least for her.

No escape!—as her captor insisted that she return to bed, as if she were ill. As if the fault were somehow hers, that she was in this predicament and he was obliged to be with her, overseeing her. For of course she could not be trusted to be alone. For of course she had proved that by her behavior. Insisting that of course she *was* home, this was her *home,* it was upsetting to him, as it was to their children, when she demanded to be allowed to go home when this *was* her home, for she was only just tired, and she was only just confused and had not taken her afternoon medication; but she should be comforted to know—*she was home, this had been her home for thirty-two years.*

Abigail protested: "But—you are not my husband! This is ridiculous."

"It *is* ridiculous. *Of course* I am your husband, and you are my wife."

For a long, painful moment they stared at each other. Each was trembling, furious.

The thought came to Abigail—*You have hurt this man's feelings terribly. What if he is your husband—what if you are mistaken?*

The sensation of faintness deepened. Vertigo, in the brain.

A mistake, some sort of mistake, but whose fault?—Abigail could not comprehend.

More likely, Abigail thought, the man with the gnarled-looking white hair and wounded, peevish face was intended to be her husband but had been poorly chosen for the role; as she, Abigail, the wife of another man, had been cast as his wife just as poorly.

As the house in which she found herself, this very bedroom, was intended to replicate or to actually be her bedroom, and her house—yet was not.

Abigail recalled that dreams are inaccurate in small, baffling ways. Why?—to understand, one would have to understand the human brain, which is beyond comprehension.

A small mistake can be a cataclysmic mistake. Once such a mistake has been made, who can unmake it?

Why didn't they send better actors!—Abigail had to laugh.

And then: if they'd sent better actors, she would never have realized. A captive, and the "husband" the captor, the keeper of the key, and she, the "wife," would never have realized.

"You are very tired, dear. And you know, darling—you are not well . . ."

Silently she demurred. Yes. No. But yes—she was very tired.

The man had the advantage, obviously. He must have a key to the door, for he had dominion over the house. As the roles had been cast, to the male has gone the dominant role, and it would be futile for Abigail to protest so late in her life. If the stranger confronting her would not acknowledge the imposture, if he continued to behave belligerently as if Abigail were, indeed, his *wife of thirty-two years,* there was little that Abigail, his captive, could do about it.

A weariness had settled over her like a fine-meshed net.

With a forced affability, as a husband might do, moved to magnanimity in the face of a sullen and unreasonable wife, the man reverted to the (familiar, comforting) subject of *his day at work:* conference calls, meetings, luncheon. He spoke of his plans for the next day and the next, reciting more names, a litany of names, ___, ___, and ___. For if you are a man among men, you are securely *in the world* only if there are such witnesses to testify to your existence, and your worth.

In this way, beating Abigail down as one might beat down a defenseless creature with a broom, not injuring the creature but (merely)

38

beating it down, down, wearing it down; the captive swayed on her (bare) feet, very tired now, faint-headed, weakened as the fine-meshed net tightened about her. When had she eaten last, she could not recall. When had she slept last, she could not recall. When had she drawn a deep breath of fresh air, the kind that fills the lungs to capacity and thrills the soul, she could not recall. When had she heard her own name enunciated, what name was hers, she could not clearly recall. Perhaps she was anemic, her blood would require an infusion. Perhaps her brain had begun to dry, crumble like clay. Perhaps she could no longer chew and swallow solid food; soft-blended food would have to be provided by her captor or captors, or she would perish.

The exasperating certitude with which the white-haired man spoke made Abigail realize that she'd lost such certitude. In the accident perhaps—her forehead slammed against the windshield.

That was it: the beginning. Her fingertips touched the swollen bruise, sensitive between her eyebrows, as a third eye, yet unopened.

She'd misplaced crucial words. She'd left her handbag behind, and the small electronic device with which (she knew! she felt this so strongly) she could have summoned her true husband, who would have annihilated this imposter. She'd lost the key to—something. What, she wasn't sure. In a shadowy region of her brain, these crucial words resided, but she could not locate the region, and if she did, she could not have opened the door, which was locked, or its doorknob sabotaged so that it turned uselessly in the hand. Now she recalled that she'd been seeing signs in recent days, weeks: the faces that mirror your own face, familiar faces that behave in unfamiliar ways, faces whose expressions you must decipher in order to decipher your own condition—those faces that have been smiling, alert, admiring through your lifetime but have now (inexplicably) ceased to smile. When these faces betray alarm, dread, pity, you shrink from being seen by them and you no longer wish to see *them*.

She cried how she hated him!—why didn't he let her *die?*

Pushed his hands away, screamed at him not to touch her even as he protested: "But I love you! My darling wife, please . . ."

Now he did advance upon her. Clumsy, weeping. As an older man might weep, unpracticed in tears. His arms in the woolen shirt around her, Abigail in the flannel nightgown smelling of her body. She was not without shame—*shame* would cling to her to the last.

Holding her tight. Holding her as a drowning man might hold another person, desperate that she not escape. Abigail could not breathe, this person was squeezing the breath from her. Arms against her sides, bound tight. As together they staggered toward the bed, fell heavily onto the bed. The physical reality of another's body is always a shock—*size, density, heat.* His tears wetted her face. She had not the strength to break free. Until at last, too exhausted to resist, she lay beside her captor, weeping with him, in deference to him, her brain blank, annihilated. Her eyelids were too heavy to keep open and so what bliss to surrender to sleep; what bliss, the sweet, sickly, dazzling white smell of gardenias that pervaded the room entering her nostrils, flowing up into her brain like ether, precipitating the most delicious sleep in the arms of the stranger.

His arm over her, heavy, comforting.

"My darling wife! I will never abandon you."

Something was pressing on her chest. An opened hand, a sweaty palm. Terror of suffocation.

Waking abruptly to glaring light. Was it another day, a morning, or was it the same day, interminable?—had she endured a *night?*

But sleep had bathed her raw, aching brain. She could think more clearly now.

Here was the shock: beside her in the rumpled bed lay the man—the man with the gnarled-looking white hair, the stranger intended to be *her husband,* on his back, open-mouthed, asleep, breathing deeply, as a drowning man might suck at air.

41

Stunning to Abigail to realize that she'd slept beside her captor. Hours of oblivion, shame.

In her sleep she had not known. Yet she must have known. Could not have *not* known.

Again it came to her: how large, how solid, how purposeful, how *real,* a (masculine) body beside a (female) body, horizontal in a bed.

In the night the man must have pulled off the red plaid shirt—his fatty chest was exposed in a thin, stained undershirt. Beneath the satin comforter his lower body might have been naked. (She could not bear to look. *Would not.*) On the carpet beside the bed lay the man's red plaid shirt, trousers that looked as if they had been flung down.

The white hair was disheveled. The face showed strain, fatigue. Coarse hairs had begun to sprout on the jaws. The eyelids quivered. A whistling sound in the nose. Oh, she'd been hearing that whistling in her sleep, it had insinuated itself into her sleep, in her dreams, a bright red thread of mercury, a poison seeping into her brain. Abigail shrank from the man, in revulsion for his damp, perspiring body and in dread of waking him. A despairing thought came to her like a reversed prayer—*Will I have to kill him to be free?*

An unnatural light shone through windows overlooking a flattened landscape, a bright-blue papier-mâché sky. Piercing laser-white of spring sunshine, from which there is no escape.

And the sweet-poisonous smell of gardenias—this too clung to bedsheets, pillow, her hair, which was matted and wild about her head, as if she'd been a captive not for less than twenty-four hours but for many days.

On her (bare, tender) feet!—carefully easing out of the bed. Scarcely daring to breathe for fear that the imposter-husband would awaken suddenly.

She must escape her captor.

She must act quickly, immediately.

She must not allow her captor to take the advantage again. To wake, to overcome her.

Rapidly her thoughts careened along a roadway to an unavoidable destination: she would break the vase over the man's head as he slept, cracking his skull and rendering him helpless; the blow might not kill him, for Abigail had no experience committing so desperate an act, no sense of how much strength might be required to execute it; nor did she want to hurt another person, even an adversary. Even a poorly cast actor meant to be her husband.

And if she rendered her captor unconscious and helpless, where would she find the key? In a pocket of his trousers? In a drawer somewhere in the room? She had no idea.

Absurd, she could never hurt another person. Not Abigail R___! She had neither the will nor the strength.

He was not to be blamed, perhaps. As blameless as she. As confined.

But she was trembling with excitement, adrenaline flooded her veins like liquid flame. So long as the man slept, she had a chance to escape. So long as he possessed no consciousness of her, she was free of him. In a closet she discovered women's clothing, she snatched at a jacket, at slacks, a soft jersey fabric that would be warm against her bare legs, a pair of shoes sturdy for running.

On the bed, amid rumpled sheets, the white-haired man continued to sleep heavily. His breathing was irregular and hoarse, painful to hear. In his nose, the thin whistling sound that grated against Abigail's nerves.

For some minutes, as in a curious trance of lethargy, Abigail regarded the *imposter-husband* with mounting rage. Obviously he was the one who'd undressed her. Apart from Abigail, he was the sole actor in this preposterous, haphazard drama in which she'd been confined. He had gazed upon her naked body, he had dared to touch her, commandeer her. He had dared to lock her in this room, and he had dared to overwhelm her with his superior weight, his very anguish, he'd dared to force her to lie docile in his arms, too weak to resist. All that he'd done he had done to *her.*

Waking from her trance as if someone had

snapped their fingers to rouse her, Abigail stealthily lifted the heavy cut-glass vase and carried it into the bathroom, removed the flowers, and, as quietly as she could manage, poured out the water; breathing calmly, thinking calmly, silent on bare feet, she returned swiftly to the bed where her captor lay sleeping, and not giving herself time to think, she raised the vase high over her head and brought it down hard on the skull of the slumbering man, who wakened instantaneously, gave a high, shrieking cry, thrashing, bleeding profusely as with fearless hands Abigail again lifted the vase as high as she could and brought it down a second time against his skull . . .

Wanting to cry in triumph—*It isn't my fault. You took me captive. I didn't choose this. You will survive.*

Quickly then, Abigail dragged up the comforter to hide the ruined, blood-glistening face. The body had convulsed and had ceased twitching.

She knelt beside the man's discarded clothing. Searching pockets, frantic to find a key.

Hastily she pulled off the bloodstained nightgown. Hastily she washed her hands in the bathroom, taking care that no faint blood residue was left on the towel. She threw on clothes she'd pulled from the closet, scarcely troubling to note whether they fitted her. No time to spare, shoving her (bare, tender) feet into shoes that fit, or nearly. In the other closet she discovered, in a pocket of the dark pin-striped suit coat, a key chain—keys; to her sobbing relief, one of them fitted the bedroom door and allowed her to open the door with a single assertive twist of the knob.

"Yes! Like this."

Now she had only to retrace her steps. Hurriedly, down the stairs, through the kitchen, and out the rear door into fresh, cold, bright air, no one to observe, no one to call after her, now frankly running in the awkward shoes of a stranger, panting, out to the road and along the road a quarter mile or so to her car, which was exactly as she'd left it the previous day—front wheels in a shallow ditch, rear wheels on the road.

In a haze of exhilaration, running in bright, cold air. How rarely she ran now, in this phase of her life! After the confinement of the bedroom, after the stultifying embrace of the captor-husband, what joy to draw air deep into her lungs.

So relieved to see her car, Abigail laughed aloud. Though the car was shamefully mud-splattered. Her husband would be astonished, disapproving. *What have you done, Abby! I just had that car washed.* A white car, impractical. After a little difficulty she managed to open the door to the driver's seat, managed to climb inside. There, the key in the ignition!—just where she'd left it.

"Yes. Like *this*."

And now, would the engine start?—Abigail shut her eyes, turned the key. After a little hesitation the familiar sound of an engine starting. Her luck had held.

Now the task of rocking the car forward and back, forward and back, determined to get the front wheels free, until at last the wheels began to gain traction, borne by momentum. White exhaust billowed up behind. The wheels strained, but took hold. Abigail laughed aloud in sheer relief.

With a final jolt, the car was up on the road. Four wheels, solidly on the road. She could breathe now. Her eyesight had become sharper, she was breathing more deeply. Since taking up the vase of flowers in her hands—making her way silently into the bathroom—she'd been electrified by a rush of adrenaline that had not yet subsided. If only she'd had more faith in herself the previous day—if only she'd been guided by instinct—she would be at home now, and safe.

Driving back in the direction of North Ridge Road. At least she believed that she was driving in the direction of North Ridge Road.

Several miles, passing few vehicles. She wasn't seeing detour signs. Yet the landscape seemed familiar. And there, abruptly, was North Ridge Road.

And there, again—the barricade and the jarring yellow sign: DETOUR.

Again, no one in sight. No road crew repairing the road, no impediment that she could see, beyond the barricade itself.

This time Abigail drove around the barricade, boldly, with no difficulty, onto the grassy roadside and back up again onto the pavement, and continued on North Ridge toward her home, which she calculated was less than two miles away.

The sun was still unnaturally bright, luminous. Budding leaves were just perceptibly greener than the previous day. Her heart was suffused with hope, within minutes she would be home.

CURIOUS

1.

Q. *Many of us, your admirers, have long been curious—where do you get your ideas, Mr. N__?*

A. *Ah! This too has long baffled me. We are all mysteries to ourselves, enigmas . . .*

Truth is, my friend, I've never had the slightest curiosity about where my "ideas" come from—my own or anyone else's.

In fact, you may be surprised to learn that despite my reputation as *the most erudite and cerebral of twenty-first-century writers,* I have very little curiosity about anything.

Indeed, I am not even curious about my lack of curiosity. It might be said that I resemble an individual with a neurological deficit that prevents him from identifying faces—"prosopagnosia," or "face blindness." In the most extreme cases the afflicted cannot recognize even their own faces in a photograph or a mirror, let alone the faces of relatives or friends.

No. I'm not curious *why.* Who cares *why?*

Face blindness, color blindness, tone deafness—these are not personal choices, but deficits in the brain. It is said that sociopaths have no care for morality, psychopaths have no care for another's pain, the autistic have no "theory of mind"—no ability to imagine the interior lives of others. To be lacking in *curiosity* is to inhabit a small but distinctive category.

I am not even curious about the curiosity of others, as a scientist might be. No more than I would be curious about a dog sniffing excitedly in a pile of rotted leaves. Whatever the dog might unearth in the next several seconds, whatever the excitement of the dog, who cares?

But now that you have asked me the (inevitable) question, the (unanswerable) question, indeed the (stupid) question, I am provoked to speculate. As, feeling a sudden itch on my skin, I am provoked to scratch recklessly enough to draw blood.

Where do the ideas informing the bizarre and seeming inexhaustible fictions of N__ come from?

2.

It is true that my "ideas" do seem to come, as some observers have noted, from some odd, quirky, distant realm of being. Not daily life, not newspaper accounts. Not personal experience. (Not usually!) Not others' work—not since adolescence. (Myopic) biographers have tried to trace lines between (what they know of) my life and (what they can glean) of my art, with unconvincing results. Any idiot with an impressive vocabulary can argue a "casual" relationship where there is none.

I rarely refute the most implausible notions. I am respectful of the eccentricities of others, so long as they are not malicious or meant to denigrate me. Though I don't "take pride" in my achievement, any more than I "take shame" in it, for whatever it is, it does not seem wholly my own, yet I suppose I must bear some responsibility.

What is curious, I suppose, is that ideas don't "come to me"—really. Rather *I go to them.*

It will depend upon where I venture. If I hike up (oddly named) Wolf Pit Mountain at the edge of the desolate little mill town in which I find myself living in the sixth decade of my life, on the Pennsylvania side of the Delaware River; if I make my way through tall, stiff grasses along the bluff, if I dare to push open the door of the old "Erikson mansion"—(a Greek Revival ruin invaded by generations of impudent children); if I dare to step inside, proceed cautiously across the (rotted, perilous) hardwood floor; if I find myself in a derelict drawing room where wallpaper hangs in strips like flayed skin, and overhead, the remains of a crystal chandelier shattered with BB pellets yet "chimes" in the wind; if awkwardly I squat to the floor to examine small, obscure objects like jigsaw puzzle parts awaiting the touch of the master; if, that is, a sequence of mysterious elements are in order, like DNA—it is possible that an "idea" will come to me with a palpable jolt, like an electric current.

Though sometimes it's another sort of experience altogether—a sensation as swift and sudden as a tick hopping onto a warm patch of skin and instantaneously embedding itself there.

By which I mean a *deer tick*. The smallest, most malevolent of ticks, no larger than the period at the end of this sentence.

How, why, to what purpose, this has come to me in this desolate ruin—in which, strictly speaking, I am "trespassing"—I have no idea. For the obscure objects on the floor might be shards of glass, bits of crockery, strips of fossilized wallpaper, a button made of bone, a fragment of a yellowed ivory piano key . . . Once, a postcard from an otherworldly place in Utah called Bryce Canyon, badly weathered, its scrawled message only just barely readable—*"Missing you all! Love you! Promise be home soon. Janey."*

With this "idea" seeded in my brain, I hurry back home.

At such times I must be extremely cautious, for descending the mountain is nearly as arduous as ascending, in some ways more treacherous, for it is easier to slip and fall while descending than while climbing; one can *crawl* uphill (if needed), but one cannot crawl downhill.

In the brownstone on the river, a place of refuge

rather more than a residence, still less a "home," I quickly take notes in a fever of inspiration. (Of course, I do not think, *inspiration.* This is a word without meaning to me, though I believe it has some sort of sentimental meaning to you.) Too excited to stop for a meal, too excited to try to sleep, I "take notes" for hours, until I discover that it is past midnight, my eyelids are drooping, and my hand is aching, and exhaustion rises about me like murky water.

Usually, in time, an "idea" from the mansion will be strong enough to develop into a work of considerable length. Novella, novel. (Yes, the faded postcard from Janey became a substantial novel, one of my most elaborately plotted.)

But time is required for such an effort, as time is required for any growing thing to take root, send up shoots, falter into life, "flourish."

However, if I walk in another direction, along the river, past shuttered mills and small factories, past weatherworn brick row houses, past taverns with neon signs burning in daylight like insomniacs unaware that the night has ended— my "ideas" are likely to be of another sort, on the whole less ambitious.

In town, my walking is not "hiking"—still less "climbing." I keep a relatively fast pace, for walking slowly is maddening to me, fraught with peril, like riding a bicycle too slowly or speaking so slowly one is apt to forget the beginning of a sentence by the time one reaches the ending.

Also, if you walk slowly, you are likely to be seen as *ambling, idling.* You are likely to be seen as one who wouldn't mind a stranger falling into step with you with that most offensive of cheery greetings—*How's it going?*

Yet more offensive—*D'you live around here?*

Herrontown, Pennsylvania, is a friendly place. It's a friendly place in the way that a tide pool reeking with algae is a friendly place. Nothing much is happening, and you can't escape.

Yet Herrontown has "historic" significance. (Which is not why I am living here. I care for "history" only if I am writing about it.) Several skirmishes of the Revolutionary War took place in this part of the Delaware Valley, not far from Trenton, New Jersey. Often I find myself in the old city center—"historic" Herrontown Square. Near the eighteenth-century Episcopal church and churchyard. Near the Revolutionary War cannon and the monument to fallen soldiers of bygone wars. (The last war so honored is the Gulf War [1990–91].) Mourning doves scatter as I proceed along the walkway.

In the small post office just off the square is a solitary clerk of indeterminate age—young?—no longer young?—from whom I sometimes purchase stamps; this individual is heavyset, with a melancholy/peevish face, straggling hair to his shoulders, in T-shirts stamped with obscure logos (Iron Maiden, Black Sabbath) that strain against his fatty-muscled torso. Often I am the only customer in the post office. Our transactions are civil but terse, unyielding—(I take care to avoid "eye contact" with this morose individual for fear that he might misunderstand)—as brief as possible. Inevitably I feel a tinge of something like sympathy for the post office clerk, if not pity. Yet also—*No. It will not be you.*

As I leave, clutching a small sheet of stamps—(for why should I buy more than six stamps at a time?—I may not live to use them all)—the morose clerk sighs unconsciously, as a mound of sand might sigh if it could.

A block away is the public library, housed in an old stone fortress of the Revolutionary War era to which plate glass windows have been added, somewhat incongruously; inside, unflattering fluorescent lights that make even robust library patrons look ghostly. The chief librarian, Ms. Laporte, is a stylish woman in her early fifties with a particular smile of recognition for me—"Hello, Mr. N__!"—for she'd known immediately who I am, or once was; on my second visit to the library she led me in triumph to a shelf of my books, which she'd arranged in the bookcase labeled LOCAL AUTHORS, and invited me to sign, and which I did sign, with some reluctance, having extracted from the earnest woman a pledge that she would protect my privacy in the future and refrain from *pointing me out* to anyone when/if I ever returned. "But of course, Mr. N__! We are just so honored"—spoken with an air of apology and not a trace of irony. With a small bequest to the library given by a generous/anonymous patron, Ms. Laporte has been able to subscribe to literary publications like *Paris Review*, *Poetry*, *Conjunctions*, *Boulevard*, *McSweeney's*, *TLS*, and *NYRB*.

Sometimes on wintry afternoons I drop by the library, perusing these publications as hailstones pelt against the windows. Thinking how snug we are in here, like survivors in a cataclysm, unable to (yet) know the dimensions of the cataclysm.

Elsewhere in the library, high school students sprawl rudely at tables, clicking through laptops, as oblivious to their book-lined surroundings as two-dimensional figures in video games.

Though the library is one of my places of refuge, in recent months I have been avoiding it. I am not sure why. Sometimes such impulses grip me—instincts for which there are no name, though possibly they are, like most instincts, related to self-preservation.

Yet today I find myself entering the library. Unobtrusively, shaking droplets of rain from my coat. And there is Ms. Laporte at the front desk, surprised in the act of stamping a date into a library book for a patron, casting a startled glance in my direction, a confused smile, with an expression of—is it gratification or mortification? Inevitable that I will pass by Ms. Laporte's desk, greet her with a courteous smile, though not a warm nor even a brisk handshake (for we have not had that sort of relationship), nor would Ms. Laporte offer her hand to me. And the thought comes to me, unbidden—*Not you. Sorry!*

I know: Ms. Laporte is (possibly) in love with Mr. N__, the notoriously obscure and reclusive *twenty-first-century author of enigmatic fictions.*

But though I share a name with N__, I am not in fact *N__*. Thus I have no responsibility for the fantasies attractive, well-groomed, and "stylish" women, married or un-, spin of me in their idle hours.

As (partial) restitution for avoiding the library/avoiding Ms. Laporte for months, I will donate five hundred dollars to the Friends of the Herrontown Library.

3.

After the post office and the library, there is the neighborhood grocery store. Where, like Herrontown residents who have neither the inclination nor the energy to drive three miles to the glaring Safeway at the mall, I am obliged to shop for necessities.

McGuire's Grocery, corner of Humboldt and Depot. In a neighborhood of old redbrick buildings, small businesses, vacant storefronts.

Draw a deep breath, step inside. A sensation of unease, anticipation awaits.

Three cashiers. But only the third cashier is of interest.

The name hand-printed on the little plastic badge is exotic—KEISHA. The woman herself is not at all exotic: in her late thirties, sallow-skinned, shyly awkward—"H'lo, sir, how are you today?" (Annoying query that cashiers at McGuire's Grocery are evidently required to ask customers.) From a distance Keisha appears to be bald, but closer up you see that her delicate head is covered in a fine, soft down, the hair of a new-born. She is painfully thin—upper body, arms, wrists. Her face is a girl's face cruelly drawn with fatigue, her eyeballs lightly flecked with blood.

(Cancer? Chemotherapy? And now her hair is beginning to grow back?)

Vaguely I recall, this is the female cashier who'd been wearing unflattering knitted caps on her head last fall. And then, for a while, could've been months, she'd disappeared from the grocery altogether. Until this minute I had not quite realized she'd been gone.

Though the most physically frail of the cashiers at McGuire's, Keisha is the most diligent and efficient. Deferential to customers, respectful and attentive to her work. Rarely smiling until she hands me the receipt for my purchases, and then a sweet, shy smile—"Thank you, sir."

58

Evoking the reply: "Thank *you*."

It seems that I have become something of a regular customer at McGuire's (by default, for I would rather not patronize the dingy grocery at all, as I would rather not "patronize" any store in any way that might be construed as routine, predictable). I am not so frequent a customer as to greet Keisha with anything like surprise, or pleasure, at seeing her back at the cash register. (As if having returned to McGuire's is any sort of life!) Still less would I presume to ask how the poor woman is, as I have heard others do, with maddening cheer. *So, Keisha, how's it going?— you're looking good.*

Such flippant greetings are offensive to me, even if they don't seem to be offensive to Keisha, who merely smiles and murmurs a courteous reply.

None of your business. Leave me alone. Go to Hell.

But no: not this young woman. Not likely.

Today my purchases in McGuire's are few and unremarkable. I will not note them here, for there is an obscure sort of shame in presenting, for the world's glib judgment, anything so intimate as the items a solitary individual purchases for himself to eat/drink in the solitude of his barely furnished residence—*None of your business* is the appropriate commentary.

Less than a half dozen items for Keisha to briskly scan and push along with her thin, deft hands. On the third finger of her left hand she wears a plain wedding band that fits her fingers loosely. So, she is married.

Hardly surprising. Very likely the woman is a mother, too.

Paper or plastic?—Keisha will inevitably ask, though you'd think (I would think) she's intelligent enough to recall that she has asked me this question before and that I am the sort of ecologically conscious customer who would prefer paper over plastic.

Still, the cashiers at McGuire's always ask. No matter if they have asked numerous times before. No matter that I always give the same answer.

To help the alarmingly thin Keisha, I will "bag" my groceries myself. Indeed, I am feeling a reluctant sort of tenderness—weakness—in the vicinity of the cashier, and a peculiar impulse to reach out to touch her (very thin) wrist, as if to give comfort.

And the baby-fine hair that scarcely covers her scalp! My fingers yearn to stroke Keisha's hair, which appears, in the harsh fluorescent lighting overhead, the hue of soft, faded copper.

And I find myself thinking, with a thrill of wonder—*You. You will be the one.*

4.

And so a decision has been made, it seems.

Yet not (so far as I can comprehend) by *me*.

Walking home along the river at my usual brisk pace to signal to whoever might be observing— *There is a man with a destination.*

Carrying the (single, paper) bag from the grocery that weighs heavier than I'd have anticipated.

It's a wide, windy river, the Delaware. Gusts of wind stirring the waves into small whitecaps.

A sensation of unease, agitation has come over me. Is it the wind. Pricking tears in my eyes. (Each night before bed I take one drop in each eye of a stinging liquid, allegedly to slow the ravages of a premature glaucoma; my eyes have grown sensitive.) A mounting tension, excitement, as if something were about to burst into flame.

When the flame illuminates the newspaper page from beneath with an exquisite, quivering radiance. That is how I am feeling!

The decision has been made. The choice.

Postal clerk, librarian, cashier—*cashier.*

(It should be clearly stated: I have very little interest in "characters" of the kind that populate prose fiction. The individuals I've described who live in the small town in which I seem now to be dwelling are not "characters," but actual living people—that is their singular, sole identification. They are not *representative* or *significant.* There is no way to imagine that they are of any worth except to a small circle of persons who know them, if even to those.)

It's true—(I see now)—I've been aware of the cashier *Keisha* for some time. Not entirely consciously, but—aware.

Usually, cashiers, clerks, waiters, and waitresses pass into and out of my consciousness without definition or identity. If Keisha had not returned to work, I would not have missed her, and even now, I am sure that if I never saw her again, she would soon fade from memory.

Does that sound harsh? It does not *feel* harsh.

Since I have long ago exhausted my patience with others, indeed with my own self, there is really no opportunity for emotion to flourish, as bacteria flourish in warm, humid recycled air (like hot-air dryers in public lavatories touted as "sanitary"). For reasons that will remain my own business, by the (relatively young) age of thirty-four I'd had enough emotion. I'd had enough *interest, curiosity.* Quite content not to become involved with another person for the remainder of my life.

If you love, you will regret it.

To love is to love unwisely.

Harden your heart! Before another hardens it.

Yet by the time I reach home, my heart has begun to beat rapidly. My eyes blink rapidly, as if a blinding light were being shone into them.

"I will! I will do it."

Rare for me to exclaim, even in the privacy of

62

my house. Rare for me to laugh aloud, as I am doing now.

What I will do: set a plot in motion and see where it ends.

(*If* it ends. Some plots have no natural conclusions.)

I will send Keisha a fifty-dollar bill with no explanation. Just a folded sheet of paper in an envelope with the terse message, in small caps— FOR KEISHA.

Address the envelope to Keisha c/o McGuire's Grocery, Humboldt & Depot Streets, Herrontown, PA.

Stamp the envelope. Take outside, mail in a corner mailbox.

(Does it signify anything that the mailbox less than fifty yards from my residence has been defaced with graffiti in white spray paint?)

(In conventional fiction, certainly: such graffiti would be "symbolic." In the less-classifiable prose for which N__ is known, the very point of the observation may be its [ontological] pointlessness.)

Calculating when this envelope will be received by Keisha. Not tomorrow, but surely the following day. When Keisha arrives at the grocery, the manager McGuire will hand the envelope to her with a quizzical smile—*Keisha! Here is something for you.*

Taken by surprise, embarrassed, suspecting

nothing and with nothing to hide, Keisha will (probably) open the envelope as McGuire looks on; she will be stunned to discover the fifty-dollar bill with the scarcely explanatory note *for Keisha.*

Almost, I can hear the woman's baffled stammer—*Oh. Oh, dear. What on earth is . . .* Almost, I can see the blush rising in her sallow-skinned girl's face.

Beyond this, what inane remarks McGuire might make, what comments from coworkers expressing surprise, amazement, a twinge (no doubt) of jealousy—I have not the slightest curiosity.

Out of the void, a fifty-dollar bill sent to *her*— Keisha will be suffused with wonder: Who is her (anonymous) benefactor? And why *her?* One of the great mysteries of the woman's life, never to be (fully) explained.

5.

Humdrum, ordinary, predictable, unexceptional—banal, trite, commonplace. The lives of most, possibly all, inhabitants of Herrontown, PA, whose population declined precipitously in the 1950s with the closing of several factories and whose most distinguished architecture is a ruin—the old Erikson mansion atop Wolf Pit Mountain. (Absurd to speak of Wolf Pit Mountain as anything other than a high, steep hill with a scenic view of the Delaware River extending for miles.)

All that is new in Herrontown, or relatively new, is, at the river's edge, a redbrick factory that was once Pennsylvania's premier manufacturer of ladies' hats and gloves, now under reconstruction into what the builder describes as a *luxury condominium village.*

(Will the condominium village ever be completed? Doubtful.)

(Like repairs to the old, once-elegant brownstone in which I live amid minimal furnishings, curtainless windows emitting a stark, raw light from the river, bare hardwood floors, and boxes of books I haven't gotten around to unpacking, for there are—literally!—no bookcases in the house to receive them, and I have not gotten around to purchasing bookcases, reasoning that the effort involved might be disproportionate to the actual use I will make of the [several thousand] books that have followed me around for decades like old, lost, reproachful loves, most of whose names I have forgotten.)

Humdrum and ordinary setting, in the most humdrum and ordinary of seasons—late winter, early April.

Gunmetal-gray clouds swollen like tumors, strips of snow remaining beside walls, in shaded places. Today, a Thursday, most humdrum and ordinary of weekdays and yet the day that, by my calculation, Keisha should receive the envelope from her employer, which should have been received by McGuire in that morning's mail, and so in late midafternoon I return to the grocery to purchase a few items, though it is much too soon for me to return.

(Will anyone notice? Steeling myself for a lame remark from McGuire.)

As soon as I enter the store, my eyes seek out Keisha. She is one of just two cashiers on duty at this hour, and she appears to be more distracted than usual, talking with a customer, smiling, glancing about. *Searching for—who?*

I can sense (I think) a subtle alteration of the air in McGuire's. Judging from casual remarks cast in Keisha's direction by her coworkers, it would seem that her surprise gift is known to them.

Lingering not far away in one of the aisles, pretending to peruse shelves of the most banal and predictable of Campbell's soups, I observe that Keisha is in fact an attractive woman, if you are not repelled by her extreme thinness and the sight of her scalp showing through her downy hair like a private body part. Her facial features are delicate, her skin is strangely unlined, though sallow, with an olive cast—she is (just possibly) of mixed blood, as the vulgar cliché has it, light-skinned black, northern African, Middle Eastern, even (East) Indian. Her eyes are very dark, beautiful (you might say, if *beautiful* were not another cliché that I would never use professionally), and they appear to be more alert, brighter than I have ever seen them. Though Keisha is wearing her usual uniform-like clothes—loose-fitting smock, slacks—she has looped a rose-patterned scarf around her slender neck, a festive note.

Laughing at a lame joke a (male) customer has told to her. Pretending to laugh. The first time (I am sure) that I have heard Keisha laugh.

Am I responsible? Suffusing the poor woman with a sense of worth, dignity? Hope?

After ten, fifteen minutes pushing a shopping cart through the narrow aisles of the store, I reappear at the checkout area at just the right time: Keisha is the cashier without a customer.

Setting my several items on the counter beside the cash register. Exchanging the usual (perfunctory, banal) greetings with the cashier bearing the name tag KEISHA. As if there were no (secret) connection between us—as if I didn't know so much more than Keisha knows of the circumstances of that morning's surprise gift.

Keisha is smiling, friendly. Not quite so shy-abashed as usual. Definitely something has happened to lighten her spirits.

A sensation of vertigo comes over me. That this woman, a stranger to me, is yet linked to me, unknowing.

Unique in my life. That a stranger and I share a

secret, though it is more fully my secret than it is hers.

"Paper or plastic, sir?"—a familiar query uttered with more warmth than usual.

But already I am reaching for a paper bag to bag the groceries myself.

And already on the jubilant walk home I am planning the second gift, to be sent to Keisha in ten days.

This time, one hundred dollars.

In the shape of a crisp, newly minted one-hundred-dollar bill—which I am sure Keisha has never seen before, never held in her hand.

Do I even recall which U.S. president is on the one-hundred-dollar bill?—I do not, for it is Benjamin Franklin; and through some clumsy oversight of U.S. history, the great Franklin was never elected president.

Having to make a special trip to the local bank to acquire the bill. Not a word of explanation to the female clerk, no awkward small talk, lame jokes of the kind others feel obliged to make in the bank, clerks as well as customers—polite and courteous and without expression, my way of confronting the world.

"Here you are, sir. Is there anything more we can do for you today?"

"No."

After a beat, coolly—"Thank you."

Hurrying home then, to prepare the envelope for Keisha.

This time I have decided to make the message a little longer—FOR KEISHA, WHO IS SO KIND.

Hesitating between *good* and *kind.* Deciding on *kind,* because it is kindness that seems more significant.

A good person might not be actively kind. But a kind person is actively good.

Addressing the envelope and mailing it, as before. Calculating when I should return to the grocery—neither too soon nor too late . . .

Perhaps I should explain. Though you have not asked.

(Stupid questions are more or less the rule of interviews like yours. But stupid questions that violate protocol are taboo, and our greatest taboo is the proscription against asking about money.)

Money means very little to me. In fact I have no idea how much money I have in assorted investments, bank accounts scattered in several states. (Twenty million? Thirty? Only my accountant knows, and Gopnik is sworn to secrecy.) Royalties from books, sales and resales of publication rights over a lengthy (if unspectacular) career can accrue a fair amount of money, if not carelessly spent; of course, N__ is notoriously a celibate bachelor, has no dependents, thus no obvious heirs. Interviewers who don't hesitate to ask me asinine questions about where I get my ideas at least have the good sense not to ask about money.

It is true, for some thirty or more years my books sold moderately well, for literary fiction of an avant-garde sort. Inadvertently I'd become a sort of cult figure, having repudiated my (working-class) background to explore worlds of surreal, baroque beauty, cerebral phantasmagorias, like an Eros-obsessed Borges; as I have determined to keep my private life private—out of shyness so extreme as to suggest morbidity—my reclusiveness has been mistaken for an aristocratic arrogance, which in turn has whetted the curiosity of the weak-minded. Films were made of my most obscure fictions, as of my most popular fictions, by both American and European filmmakers, as well as by the Korean fantasist Park Chan-wook. For a brief while in the 1980s there was a TV series adapted from my shorter fictions, in the mode of a more esoteric and intellectually demanding *Twilight Zone*.

All the while, I've had few expenses. I travel infrequently, save most of my money, invest in ultraconservative bonds, live very comfortably/frugally on my interest as my imagination and energies have begun to wane, and I find myself unable to write novels, even novellas, concentrating more recently on enigmatic prose pieces that mimic nonfiction, in the service of what

I would call "higher fictions" (if the term were not so pretentious). As I have lost what minimal curiosity I once had in the complexities of characterization, the bedrock of the traditional novel, I have gained a keener interest in the complexities of "concept": how a concept, or idea, can be made to develop, as if it were a character in a way; as an unpromising seed or bulb that appears rotted, stringy, hairy, can yet be coaxed into sending out shoots into earth, flourishing in a cracked flowerpot, and finally "blossoming"—like my favorite spring flower, narcissus, with its pale, delicate petals, its faint, sweet fragrance that is the very emblem of fragility and finitude.

In this way boldly exploring not a mere "mystery," but the essence, the germinating seed, of mystery itself.

And so: perhaps that is why I am drawn to Keisha. Not repelled by the woman's extreme fragility and aura of (dare I say it?) premature doom, but instead attracted by it.

6.

Eagerly anticipating my return to McGuire's Grocery.

For the first time in memory, waking early, before dawn, with a wild sort of elation—anticipation—(is this what others mean by *curiosity*, an ardent fluttering of the pulse?)—to see what effect my second gift has had upon the cashier.

Discovering that I am frequently glancing at my watch. I am frequently thinking of *her.*

Surely the first time in my life that I have thought so intensely of a stranger whose last name is unknown to me.

And now that I think of it, there is something touching, I suppose, in this curiosity. For curiosity is a cabinet of vulnerabilities. Ignorance is the bulwark against the risks of curiosity. *I do not know, therefore I am. I yearn to know, therefore I am incomplete.*

Curiosity is a habit of youth. The desperation to know what others think of you. The curse of adolescence, wishing to control what others think. While at my age I scarcely care what I think of myself, let alone what others think of me.

(Perhaps, perversely, as interviewers have claimed, there is a "renewed interest" in the fictions of N__ of the 1980s; it isn't likely that I will ever know, since I lack the curiosity to investigate. I do own a computer, a very old Dell, but the last time I checked, the clumsy machine was not connected to the internet, and its word-processing skills are so crude, I prefer my 1996 Japanese electric typewriter, now a sort of antique treasure among typewriter aficionados.)

Three days later, I return to the grocery. Late afternoon. And there is Keisha at her usual station, distractedly scanning items, bagging groceries—in loose-fitting smock, slacks—no festive scarf tied about her throat today.

To my dismay I see that Keisha is unsmiling. Slump-shouldered. Her face has been made up with a particularly unconvincing rosy-peach makeup to disguise what appears to be bruising beneath her right eye. Her upper lip is swollen. Her delicately boned nose is swollen. *She has been beaten. By—*

Husband? A jealous husband.

Nothing I could have anticipated. Given gifts of cash by an anonymous admirer, the poor woman has been suspected of—infidelity?

My gifts, meant only to enliven the poor convalescent's life, have backfired for her.

No one has noticed me in the grocery so far. I don't think so. There is a little flurry of activity, unrelated to Keisha, at the other cash register.

Trying to disguise my alarm, I push a grocery cart into the interior of the store as if I have come simply to shop. (Will anyone notice that I have returned to the store, so soon? I am hoping that N__ is as invisible to others as they are usually invisible to him.)

With a few innocuous items to purchase, I return to the front of the store. My heart is beating rapidly, contritely. Though Keisha has two customers waiting in line and another cashier has none, I make my way to Keisha's cash register, as if not happening to notice. My behavior is senseless, suspicious. I am beginning to perspire, a creature at bay.

Waiting in line. Gazing (covertly) at Keisha. The shell of her head looks particularly fragile today. Bruised, swollen face. Partially blackened eye. Yet bravely she has tried to disguise her injuries. She has even applied lipstick to her partially swollen, asymmetrical mouth. All day (I assume) the poor woman has had to endure stares, clumsy queries, or murmured commiseration from nosy strangers.

My dear! What has happened to you?—I will not inquire.

Though my heart contracts with sorrow for Keisha. Unless it's anger for whoever has abused her.

To whom is the unhappy woman married, who could not share in his wife's (minor) good fortune but felt obliged to punish her for it? Another time I note the wedding band, with a pang of contempt.

Puerile symbol of the marital bond. Such *ordinariness* suffocates.

"Paper or plastic, sir?"—the cashier's voice is low, hoarse.

"Paper. Why do you always ask?"

Keisha glances at me, startled. Sharpness in my voice that I hadn't intended. Possibly I'd meant to sound commiserative, sympathetic. But the reply is awkward, for I am an awkward person

74

outside the confines of my being, in which I am precisely calibrated.

Keisha murmurs "Sorry!" It is too late for me to murmur *sorry!* to her, but I set about putting the several purchases into the bag myself to compensate for the sharpness in my voice, which I did not intend, I swear.

My poor dear, I will help you escape. If you will let me.

7.

And now I am at an impasse. For if I continue to send Keisha gifts of cash and her husband discovers them, he will punish her, perhaps more savagely than he has done. My impression is that Keisha is too honest to dissemble, the kind of woman who feels guilt over small matters even when she is guiltless.

A wild thought comes to me and keeps me awake late into the night—I could arrange for Keisha to receive a large sum of money, which would free her from the brute. (Thousands of dollars?) (One million dollars?)

For much of a day the possibility consoles me. Trying to imagine what such a gift could mean to a woman like Keisha, who is obliged not only to work at a minimal wage in McGuire's dingy market but who has just recently completed a cycle of brutal medical treatment.

A trust fund, perhaps. Monthly allotments. Some (legal) way of providing the woman with financial independence, at least.

Thinking—would a woman like Keisha, no doubt a longtime inhabitant of Herrontown, Pennsylvania, with probably no more than a high school diploma, if even that, be capable of breaking ties to an oppressive husband? Asserting her own dependence at her age?

One million dollars, gifted to a grocery store clerk! It could not be kept secret, the spouse would know. The family would know. Relatives. Neighbors. Media would sweep upon the frail woman greedily. Total strangers would seek her out, hoping to exploit her.

As I work out how to proceed, I have to concede that something like *curiosity* is driving me now. Each morning, instead of lying near comatose in bed, scarcely able to open my eyes, I wake eagerly, wondering what will happen next: what I will direct, that will happen next. For the cashier's (ordinary) life is in my control, if I wish it.

"How exciting life is! I'd never realized"—this bizarre remark is uttered to my tax accountant, Gopnik, who stares at me as if I have suddenly begun speaking in a foreign language.

Rare that I say anything to Gopnik beyond a minimum of words. Tax statements, bank statements, stacks of canceled checks and receipts.

In Gopnik's presence a robotic efficiency courses through me. Even my murmured words of greeting and farewell are the utterances of a robot.

But now Gopnik is nonplussed. Smiles inanely, as if to agree with me, however bizarre and improbable the sentiment—*How exciting life is* . . . in Herrontown, PA.

Gopnik doesn't live in Herrontown. Gopnik lives in Doylestown, forty minutes away.

Inquiring of the accountant how it might be arranged—a "trust," established by an unknown benefactor, with interest paid in (monthly?) allotments to an individual who would be given minimum information about the arrangement.

"Well. It could be done"—Gopnik's reply is notably lacking in enthusiasm.

Why would it be done, *who* would be the beneficiary of such a (desperate?) transaction, Gopnik knows better than to inquire of his reticent client.

8.

Yes, it is true: I am betraying my initial "neutrality"—"objectivity"—as one whose relationship to life is essentially that of the investigator/experimenter.

Led by curiosity to discover the grocery clerk's schedule: five days a week, with Mondays off. And where the grocery clerk lives: one point eight miles away from my own house on the river, though inland, in a "working-class" residential area of Herrontown.

Rare for me to become so *involved* with anyone—anything.

Rare for me to experience such *feeling.*

But here I am, across the street from the grocery store on one unexpectedly mild afternoon in April. Waiting for Keisha to leave with a coworker at the end of their shifts, six p.m. Following the coworker's vehicle at a discreet distance in my own vehicle. Noting where Keisha is dropped off.

Driving past the small clapboard house on Mill Run Street, a street of small, interchangeable clapboard houses. Some of the houses run-down, needing repainting, repair. One or two of the houses abandoned, boarded up. Puddles from melted snow and ice glistening in driveways. Mud-rutted front yards. In the small front yard of the cashier's house at 54 Mill Run Street, bright yellow daffodils beaten down, broken after rain.

She has planted these daffodils, I seem to know. Broken after rain, mud-flecked, yet still alive, vivid yellow.

Oh! The knowledge is a needle to the heart. *Seeking beauty even in ugliness.*

Driving past the house, circling the block. Slow. No hurry. Where else to go? Nowhere else calls to me. Driving past the small, undistinguished clapboard house another time. Daring to park a short distance away.

Lighting a cigarette. (Seven years, five months since I've smoked.) Sudden thrill in the lungs, as if youth itself is flooding back.

For some time sitting here, smoking. Watching the house through the rearview mirror on the exterior of the car, beside the driver.

Watching the house—her house? Why?

Might've felt discomfort, unease—shame. Yet oddly I do not. Emptiness of mind: stained sink into which a thin trickle of water falls from a faucet. As it falls, it drains out.

From time to time, vehicles pass my parked car. Slow-moving vehicles, driven by faceless figures.

Am I waiting for *him* to come home?—the brute husband.

(There is a narrative in which N__ might pay to have the "brute husband" dispatched, disappeared. Ah, I could afford to pay an assassin, in fact two assassins, a very handsome sum! But this is not that narrative.)

About to pull away from the curb when an insolent-looking boy of about fourteen appears, pedaling a gleaming red bicycle, turning into the rutted driveway beside the clapboard house.

She has bought the boy that bicycle!—I know it.

Not that the bicycle is *new*. Might've been purchased secondhand from Mike's Bikes New &

Used in town, which sells a few expensive Italian racing bikes amid less expensive American bikes and secondhand bikes. But the boy's bicycle is a recent purchase, I am sure of this.

Driving away. Pressing too hard on the gas pedal, the car lurches. Goddamn! Damn *her.*

The money I've given the woman was for her, not her family. Can't be trusted to spend money on herself. What are families but leeches.

So angry! Feeling betrayed.

Deciding then, I will never return to dingy McGuire's. Never again risking such ignominy.

Led by curiosity to discover Keisha's last name: *Olen.*

9.

. . . soon then calculating that I must seek out Keisha to speak to her directly. To address her in my own person. *I have seen in your face a soul of beauty. You are kind, generous, good. You must be protected from your own goodness. My wish is to make you happy . . .*

All this is true. Yet the words are laughably banal, vulgar.

Such ordinary words, I can't bring myself to utter. My fear is that one day I will wish to commit suicide, a most reasonable decision, yet, being unable to compose a suitable note, I will be thwarted and forced to live forever.

Silence is not really an option in matters of suicide. As nature abhors a vacuum, so silence is a kind of vacuum that others will noisily fill with idiotic theories that will debase the dignity of the suicide simply in being suggested.

Not sure (now) how to proceed. Not (it seems) able to desist.

Like a compulsive hand washer, required to enact the identical ritual dozens of times a day simply to be able to breathe normally, I now find myself unable not to think of *Keisha Olen* virtually all the time. Not the woman herself, but the riddle she represents.

Have I fallen in love? With—her?

But I am immune to love—that's to say "love." No emotions engage me except as fossils of living feeling, transmogrified into language and, through language, into *texts.*

True, decades ago such emotions coursed through me like electric jolts, as (no doubt) they course through you, leaving you exhausted and uncertain about who you *are*—the emotions or the vessel through which they course.

Take comfort: in time, if you apply the proper strategy, these emotions will drain away like a sutured abscess.

And so the elaborate strategy I've decided upon is a kind of triage: to satisfy the spurious attachment I (seem to) feel for a woman scarcely known to me, by the name of Keisha Olen, I am writing (typing, on my Japanese electric typewriter) a letter to her, which I hope will be the last I will write to her—

Dear Ms. Keisha Olen:

I am writing to you as the executive director of the Society of Deserving Americans. Originally established in 1889, the Society has an honored tradition of providing monetary gifts to individuals who are deemed—by virtue of their kindness, good-heartedness, and inner worth—outstanding citizens in their communities—"deserving" of recognition. In bestowing these awards, the Society does not seek publicity and requests from all awardees that its bequests remain confidential.

This year, only two individuals have been selected as Deserving Americans in the Delaware Valley: you, Keisha Olen, are one of these. Both you and your fellow Deserving American have already received your First and Second Gifts. Your Third Gift is to be a more substantial sum of money, which will be awarded to you if you (1) pledge never to speak of it to anyone, not even a close family member; and (2) pledge to use the money exclusively on or for yourself, and not on family, church, or charitable organizations, however worthy.

Acceptance of the Third Gift must be in person. It will not be sent through the mail like previous Gifts. You (and your fellow recipient) will be asked to appear at the Delaware River Inn, Herrontown, at five p.m., Monday, April 15. Please arrive promptly. A table will be reserved for you and your fellow awardee in the restaurant. A light meal will be served, at which time you will receive the Third Gift. You must come alone and arrange to leave alone and keep the meeting, and all circumstances surrounding it, confidential.

G_ G_
Executive Director
Society for Deserving Americans

This (carefully composed) letter is mailed to Ms. Keisha Olen at 54 Mill Run Street, calculated to arrive on the Monday preceding the date of the meeting. It is my supposition that Keisha brings in the mail herself on Mondays, which is her day off from work, while on other days she may not be home when the mail is delivered and may not see it until it has passed through others' hands.

The risk is that Keisha will not be free on that date or at that time. For there is no way she can contact me to arrange for another time. This is a risk I must take.

However, the Delaware Inn is ideal for our meeting. As a local "historic" landmark with inflated prices, it is well known to local residents like Keisha, who rarely patronize it.

Yes, this has all been shrewdly calibrated. My most ingenious narrative in years, I am thinking!

And so, by way of this invitation, which to anyone with a modicum of skeptical intelligence would be identified as a ruse, the naïve and trusting grocery store cashier is seduced into agreeing to a meeting with a stranger—a surreptitious meeting with an individual she believes to be a fellow Deserving American. Since she is sure to recognize me as a customer at McGuire's, this is a (plausible) explanation.

And does everything go as planned at the Delaware Inn? Yes, but no.

10.

On the afternoon of April 15, precisely at five p.m., here is Keisha, hesitantly entering the Delaware Inn: in a dressy blouse and jacket, skirt, and high-heeled shoes. To my disappointment, her eggshell-fragile head is covered by a flowery hat of the kind a Christian lady might've worn to church in 1957. Just inside the doorway, she halts, blinking and staring. She is very nervous, like a wild creature that suspects it has blundered into a trap and is poised to bolt away.

"Keisha! Hello! You're here—too?"

Keisha sees me and recognizes me. One of the grocery store customers! She blinks at me, confused and alarmed.

"What a coincidence! You are the other 'recipient' . . . Congratulations!"—my voice is lowered, discreet. It will take a few seconds for Keisha to comprehend the circumstances: the *coincidence* that the other of two Deserving Americans summoned to the Delaware Inn is someone known to her.

To placate any suspicion she might have about this remarkable coincidence, I show Keisha my letter from the Society of Deserving Americans, near identical to her own, which she hurriedly skims; but Keisha has not a suspicious bone in her body, thus no reason to wonder at the coincidence, if that's what it might be called. Judging from my manner, she has no reason to suspect that I know anything more than she does about the mysterious award we are each to receive.

A flawless ruse! Presenting myself not as the master plotter of the Society of Deserving Americans, but one of its Deserving Americans.

Awkwardly, we introduce ourselves. (Of course, I provide a fictitious name.) Yet more awkwardly, we shake hands. (It's clear that Keisha is not accustomed to shaking hands.)

For this daunting occasion, which must also be a secretive occasion, Keisha has made herself up like a high school girl at a prom. Her sallow skin glows, her thin lips are fire-engine red. Shadows and dents beneath her eyes seem to have vanished. The scanty eyebrows have been penciled into thin crescents, but there is nothing to be done about the chemo-ravaged, lashless eyes that stare wonderingly at me.

Naturally, I take charge. Keisha looks to me to lead her. Where, as a customer at McGuire's, I am somewhat stiff, formal, unsmiling, now, in the foyer of the Delaware Inn, in this startling new setting, I am gentlemanly and affable, smiling easily.

"Yes, we're both to be congratulated! This is an amazing honor . . ."

"Did you—tell anyone about it?" Keisha's voice is strained, hoarse.

"Of course not. It has to be a secret. *You* didn't tell anyone, did you, Keisha?"

"N-No. I did not."

"Because I think they would nullify the award if we did," I tell her sternly. "It would be—I think—a violation of our contractual relationship with the Society, which we have acknowledged by coming here today . . ."

This sequence of words is so plausible, so legal-sounding, Keisha nods grimly. It is good for her to *be told* such a sentiment by me, an older gentleman, seemingly an "educated" gentleman, to assuage any doubts or ambivalence she might have.

Allowing me then to lead her into the River View Room overlooking the dazzling Delaware. Amid so much that is banal and predictable, a river is always in a way fresh and unexpected.

Our reserved table?—an affable host escorts us to it, the very table I'd requested, in a farther corner. At this hour of the day the River View is virtually deserted, sepulchral. Unobtrusively I will remove two envelopes from a briefcase to place on a ledge beside the table, as if they have been awaiting us.

A waiter appears: Drinks?

Not for her, Keisha murmurs; then, relenting, "D'you have soft drinks? I will have a Coke."

Coke! Have to bite my tongue to keep from making a sardonic remark about toxic chemicals manufactured for mass consumption.

Determined to remain sober, I order a glass of dry white wine. A single, singular glass.

Now, conversation! Excitement rushes through me like adrenaline through a pathologist about to make the first, exquisite incision in a fresh corpse sprawled before him.

"What a—an—occasion! We will celebrate . . ."

In my gentlemanly guise I ply my self-conscious companion with low-keyed questions—background, family, how long has she

87

lived in Herrontown, PA—("Forever")—how long has she worked at McGuire's?—("Seems like forever").

Discreetly, I don't ask Keisha about her health. Not yet, about her marriage.

Is she unhappy, does her husband abuse her?—no. Not yet.

As she answers my questions in a halting, hoarse voice, like one unaccustomed to conversation, Keisha glances nervously about the faux-elegant restaurant as if she fears being observed, overheard. I am made to realize that this is a person who is rarely asked such questions, or perhaps any questions at all of a general nature. I am made to suppose that this is a person at whom no one, certainly not a well-dressed stranger, has actually *looked,* with interest, in a long time.

Though uneasy, Keisha is also flattered. The fact of the "award" has made her think differently about herself, perhaps—*Yes. You are special. Did you ever doubt you were special?*

Keisha is wearing a lemon-colored satin blouse with a floppy bow and white plastic buttons; her jacket is a coarser fabric, a wool-synthetic blend, dark beige. I seem to know that these "dressy" clothes are not new purchases, but years old—from a time when she'd been much younger. Her ears are unusually small, waxy-pale. Her throat is pale, in contrast to the rosy cosmetic face. On the fourth finger of her right hand is the wedding band, still loose; on her right wrist, which is very thin, a loose-fitting, inexpensive woman's wristwatch. Touchingly, her short, brittle fingernails have been polished fire-engine red, to match her lipstick.

For some days I've brooded about how much cash to give Keisha. A dramatic increase seems plausible, but not too dramatic; better to whet her desire for more money, and then more, to keep her interested and involved—even, to a degree, mildly anxious. And so Keisha's envelope contains ten crisp one-hundred-dollar bills.

Am I in love? Ridiculous!

Our drinks are brought by the waiter. Wondering who we are, what relationship. Well—let him wonder!

"Again, dear Keisha—congratulations!"

Ceremoniously I lift my glass, click it against Keisha's glass. Dry white wine clicking against a vile dark chemical concoction. Keisha laughs, breathlessly. She is making a valiant effort to be gay, festive—a woman for whom surprises are (probably) not often happy.

Well, how frequently are surprises "happy" in any of our lives? When was the last time someone rushed up to you crying *Good news! Happy news! You won't believe this!*

Indeed, no one has ever rushed up to me exclaiming in this way. No one has ever burst into a house in which I was living, or into a

room in which I've been sitting, waiting . . .
Good news! Happy news! You won't believe this, N__!

Keisha is drinking the vile Coke, which fizzes at its surface as carbolic acid might "fizz." I see that the fire-engine red lipstick has smeared onto one of her front teeth. I see that the coppery-brown penciled eyebrows are asymmetrical, as if the hand that applied them was shaky. Like her ears, Keisha's nose is oddly small and oddly pale, nostrils pinched like slits. Her very face seems too small. Does chemotherapy *shrink* a face? Or—might the treatment have been radiation?

Indeed, has Keisha recovered from this treatment, as I'd assumed? From cancer? Had her illness even been cancer? *Had* there been an illness? For weeks—months—I've assumed that I know the outline of the cashier's life; it's something of a shock to realize that I know very little about her. The hair loss might be caused by something else altogether—a thyroid condition, a gastrointestinal disorder.

It soon becomes clear that Keisha has not much to say, apart from expressing a childlike wonderment at her *good luck.* For, to her, despite the letter she'd received, at which I'd labored more intensely than I labor at most of my prose fiction, she doesn't really think she might *deserve* the mystery gifts she has been receiving. To her, as to, perhaps, the class of individuals to which

90

she belongs from birth, there is only *good luck* and *bad luck.*

Bad luck would be cancer. Good luck would be mystery gifts of cash out of nowhere.

As if good luck were not the consequence of a (human) agent, in this case. Rather, akin to what is (quaintly) called an Act of God—like weather, earthquakes.

Yes, it is somewhat disappointing to me that Keisha has so little to say to me. My questions encourage her to speak only briefly. I might be a schoolteacher, an authority figure of some vague kind, whose authority is not to be questioned, but whom she would avoid if she could, for she is uncomfortable in his presence; my white dress shirt, dark blue tie, camel's hair sport coat seem to have intimidated her, which was hardly my intention. Rather, I'd dressed out of respect for her and for the occasion, which is (after all) as remarkable in my life as in hers.

Indeed you are in love. And indeed, it is ridiculous.

Keisha is not a beautiful woman, I see now. No doubt I have been mistaking fragility for beauty. The drawn, melancholy features, the effects of illness. Soft, fine, downy hair, lashless eyes that seem to penetrate mine with a kind of helpless candor. Even Keisha's (relative) youth has been deceiving—she is not so young as I'd thought, surely in her forties.

And she is (annoyingly) reluctant to order anything to eat, with the excuse that she isn't hungry at this time of day. "But we are to have a light meal, according to the directive." I am speaking gaily, giddily. The wine seems to have gone to my brain. "Shall I order for you, dear?"

Dear. Have I been calling Keisha *dear?* That has not been my intention.

Keisha frowns, stroking the nape of her neck. Stroking the baby-fine hairs at the back of her head. It isn't clear that *dear* has even registered with her, she is distracted by the setting—white linen tablecloth, plate glass window overlooking the river, sunlight scintillant on the river. The River View menu, bound in a kind of quilted white fabric, absurdly large, pretentious, seems to intimidate her too.

Is the woman impressed by me?—I wonder. How crude her husband must be, by contrast. With me.

Of course he is (probably) (much) younger than I.

To prepare for this momentous day, I had my camel's hair sport coat dry-cleaned for the first time in nine years. (It was last worn at a funeral nine years ago.) I had my (untidy, straggly, thinning) hair washed, trimmed, blow-dried at the Herrontown Barber. My shirt is freshly laundered, properly ironed, with (onyx) cuff links.

Yet Keisha seems scarcely to notice my clothes. She is still glancing worriedly about the restaurant—as if anyone in this restaurant would be likely to know her. In her hoarse voice she asks, "D'you think they will come to meet us? Or maybe they are here now—watching us?"

"Who?"

"The people who—the Society . . ."

For a moment I have no idea what Keisha is talking about. Then I realize, I should seem as wondering and uncertain as she is. I should certainly not behave as if I know more than Keisha knows about our circumstances. Though of course, by instinct, Keisha defers to me, as male.

I tell her yes possibly. They might. "The letter was indeed somewhat inconclusive. They seem to want to keep it secret. Like the state lottery—who wins. So that people won't be asking for money from the winners. Or from the Society. Like people on welfare and food stamps . . ."

People on welfare. Food stamps. A startling tone here. Does Keisha resent *people on welfare* and *food stamps,* or has she *been* people on welfare and food stamps herself?

The waiter has been hovering about our table. He is deferential to me, less certain of Keisha—her status, her relationship to me. Judging from the quality of her "dressy" clothes, she is not a relative, surely.

He is daring to wonder if you are lovers. This woman and you!

A flush comes into my face. Not sure if I am abashed or prideful.

"Come, dear! The Society expects us to order a light meal. It seems to be part of the ritual."

Reluctantly Keisha agrees to a fruit salad platter. My order is *charcuterie et fromage.*

It's amusing to me, unless dismaying, that my companion never asks me about myself. Though I have inquired about her life with genuine interest and curiosity, Keisha does not think to ask me a single question. Too shy, I suppose. Women of her class are not comfortable asking questions of what might seem to them a managerial class.

At McGuire's, the bantering red-haired McGuire is free to chide and tease his employees, but they dare not chide and tease him in turn. All they can do is laugh, with varying degrees of mirth.

Also, Keisha is (probably) just not curious about me. Whoever I am, I dwell beyond the range of anyone who might factor meaningfully in her life.

Our orders are brought to the table: a large, lavish fruit salad for Keisha, served in a hollowed-out pineapple; *charcuterie et fromage* for me, on a marble platter with a sprig of grapes and fancy Waterstones crackers.

Keisha stares at her food and laughs forlornly. "Oh! This is kind of—fancy . . ."

"Yes, indeed. Very nice."

How childlike, the woman's eyes. Almost, it seems as if the pupils are dilated. Beautiful eyes, though still slightly bloodshot.

"Just eat as much as you want, dear. You should try to put on weight, you know."

Again, *dear.* Unconsciously the incriminating word has slipped out.

But Keisha seems scarcely to notice. Perhaps nothing about me is *noticeable* to her.

"Guess I don't have a whole lot of appetite, most days. Also, I have to make supper when I get home. I can't stay much longer here. I have to try to eat with them, too. I should."

Valiantly Keisha lifts a fork, impales a small slice of pineapple. Minutes are required for her to chew the tangy fruit, as I spread brie onto crackers. On the river the sun is losing definition, dissolving into the western sky behind successive hills like something spilled.

Prodded by my questions—(I abhor the vacuum of silence in a situation like this, for which I have only myself to blame)—Keisha begins to tell me more about herself. Yes, she'd been born in Herrontown. She'd gone to school in Herrontown. She'd gotten married in Herrontown—both times.

Both times?—politely, I express surprised interest.

"The first time, I was nineteen. Y'know—had

95

to get married." Keisha laughs, daringly. Thinks better of it, biting at her lip. "That didn't last— that was *sad*. He enlisted in the Marines—they sent him to the Gulf—when he came back, he wasn't the same . . . Anyway," Keisha says, sighing, trying to spear an elusive single Concord grape on her fork, "it didn't last, and we had three kids. But—"

"Are you still on good terms with him?"

Naïve question! Immediately I regret it.

Keisha shakes her head, pained. Anyway— there came another husband, seven years later.

Wanly Keisha smiles. It is clear to me that the woman yearns to confide in me, yes this second marriage is problematic too, but no, she cannot speak so frankly, so intimately to a stranger. Cannot speak of the man who is *the husband, the husband right now,* she has no choice but to defend and protect.

Of course I understand. I am the wise elder, the gentleman who understands.

"Anyway—the kids are okay. I live for those kids. What God sends to me, I can accept, as long as—you know, the kids are okay. That's what I pray for."

Though your husband is a brute. Yes?

Still, that pained look. For Keisha is seriously thinking. The Deserving American award has shone a light upon her, dazzling her.

Confiding in me suddenly, in a lowered voice,

that she'd had "bad scares" in her life—twice. First when she was just twenty-six and had to have "cysts" removed, but the second time, last fall, the cancer had "spread farther." Wiping at her eyes, she tells me that only God saved her.

There'd been surgery: "Mas-teck-nom-y." Then—"Chemo."

God, and Jesus, and prayer. Her kids, her family. Why she had to keep going, not give up. Though she'd wanted to, sometimes—just give up. But grateful to be alive. That the treatment hadn't been worse. Every day, on her knees, giving thanks. Who'd taken it hard, almost harder than she had, was her husband—"It was like he'd been kicked in the gut, he said."

Keisha is about to say more about the husband, then thinks better of it.

"Well—whoever is giving us these gifts, it's like they are the answer to my prayers. Because we have been hard hit—financially. Because of course I had to take off from work. There's no medical benefits at the grocery—of course. There's not enough 'margin of profit'—Mr. McGuire says. Lucky just to stay in business. Lucky to have the job. So these gifts, it's like God is guiding their hands. Knowing how we need the money—my family. They are wonderful people, I guess—Christian people." Astonishing to hear Keisha speak in such an outburst of warmth and certitude.

*She is going to give the money to those leeches.
Her family. Of course she is not going to spend it
on herself.*

Trying to remain calm. Merely noting,
"Christian? Really? I don't recall the letter
speaking of—"

"They'd have to be Christian people. Who
else would answer prayers like this? Society of
Deserving Americans—that wouldn't be *atheists*."

Keisha pronounces *atheists* with an odd
inflection, as if it were a foreign word whose
meaning she doesn't quite know, except that it is
repugnant.

"Whoever the 'Society' is, they are good
people. They are people of God."

Keisha knows. Keisha is certain. No ambiguity
here. No persuading *her.*

Suddenly boredom suffuses me like ether. A
wave of something like vertigo passes over my
brain.

My experiment! What a farce. A "plot" set in
motion—swerving out of my control.

How badly I'd longed to be close to this person,
to have her confide in me as in a friend; such
intimacy, such rushes of words, I could not have
dared anticipate. And now, facing the woman
across a table, scarcely three feet between us, I
am overwhelmed with dismay, a wish to excuse
myself and depart. The bill has already been paid
on my credit card.

Keisha reaches into her cloth handbag to show me pictures on her cell phone—a succession of smiling faces. One of them is the insolent brute on the bicycle—I recognize him at once.

"They are the light of my life," Keisha says, sniffing. "Well, I mean—Jesus is the *light of my life*. But my daughter Jill, she's nineteen, just that age when I was married, and—"

I am calculating how to end this politely and flee. Shall I give Keisha the envelope as I'd planned? Or—shall I not?

Both Keisha and I are finished with our meals. Neither of us has been very hungry. But I have ordered a second glass of wine.

How pathetic it seems to me now, my notion of willing this woman one million dollars! No wonder Gopnik stared at me as if I were mad.

This woman. In my disappointment, I am angry with her. I seem to have forgotten who Keisha is, why she is here.

Have pity. She is a figure of pathos, not contempt.

Keisha has laid down her fork. Her eyes move toward her wrist, she is anxious about the time.

Quickly I assure her that the meeting has been a success, in my opinion. "And here are our envelopes, as promised."

For it seems that two envelopes have been placed, unobtrusively, on a ledge beside the window of our table, beside my chair. The one addressed to MS. KEISHA OLEN contains ten crisp bills, and the other, addressed to a fictitious name, contains, as filler, a many-times-folded newspaper page.

"Oh! Thank you . . ."

Keisha takes the envelope from me with an expression more of dread than anticipation. "I guess—I'll wait to open it later. I'm kind of afraid—what's inside . . ."

This is disappointing to me, I think. But no—the money is *hers*. She must do with it what she will.

"And I also, my dear. It will be a private revelation."

As Keisha puts the envelope into the deepest recesses of the slightly soiled fabric handbag, so I fold my envelope in two and slip it into an inside pocket of the camel's hair coat.

I am feeling such strain, it seems that Keisha and I have been together for hours. In fact, we have been at our riverside table less than one hour. So soon ended! But my predominant feeling is relief.

We are on our feet. Another time I see that Keisha is thin-limbed, fragile. I am hoping that the money I have given her will help her in some way to *thrive*. But I am reconciled to the likelihood that surely, yes, she will spend the money on others far less worthy than herself. For that is Keisha's character, and character is fate impervious to "plot."

On our way out of the restaurant, the waiter, whom I have lavishly tipped, bids us good evening. The host, with a bemused air, says "Have a good evening."

In the hotel foyer, we shake hands in farewell. Keisha's hand is shockingly small-boned, cold. I tell her that it was wonderful to meet her and that she is very deserving of her award.

"Thank you! And you, too . . ."

Keisha has forgotten my name, I see. But no matter, it has been a fictitious name, in no way to be confused with the reclusive genius N__.

I do not want to feel anything further for Keisha. Not in a mood to accompany her to the parking lot, to her car. No. My excuse is a need to use the men's room.

And perhaps Keisha is eager to be alone as well. To get into her car, to tear open the envelope. To discover what the miraculous Third Gift is, for which she will be grateful for the remainder of her life.

Resolved, I will never see Keisha again.

11.

Soon after this humbling incident, in the early spring of 2012, I left Herrontown, PA.

Not the slightest curiosity, what became of Keisha Olen. Or any of them.

For surely nothing of significance could happen to them.

What had been significant in Keisha's life had been *me*. And I had no curiosity about *me*.

What?—you are offended by this abrupt termination of the story. It is unsatisfying. It is in violation of the rules of fiction.

But may I remind you, *this is not fiction*. This is rather the wellspring of fiction. Its (mysterious) origins. You, unlike me, are suffused with *curiosity*. Your naïveté allows you to wonder what becomes of "characters" after their stories have ended—as if "characters" continue to exist outside a story.

In the case of Keisha Olen, as in the cases of the morose postal clerk and the stylish librarian, what became of them after I moved to a larger city was of no interest to me. At once, or nearly, I ceased thinking about them.

Until your (naïve) question—*Where do I get my ideas?*—I had all but forgotten them. As cattle graze a field, then move on, a writer grazes a territory, then moves on. Nostalgia for where you have grazed is not seemly. Delicious mouthfuls of fresh grass are interchangeable, it does not matter *where*.

In fact, you are probably coming to resemble me in this way. In other ways too, you will one day realize.

· · ·

In fact I have returned to Herrontown, several years later. For I am required to sell the property on the river, which in my absence has deteriorated like a gangrenous limb.

Finding myself at McGuire's. Corner of Humboldt and Depot Streets, nothing much changed.

Steeling myself to enter the dingy grocery. The interior seems smaller now. Only two checkout counters are open.

But there is Keisha still at her post!—a stab of emotion leaves me weak, stunned.

But no. The cashier is not Keisha Olen. A slender young woman in smock and jeans, with a girl's face, close-cropped sand-colored hair. Many years younger than Keisha would be.

A roaring in my ears. Though I can see clearly that this young woman is not Keisha. The store owner, McGuire, grayer and stouter than I recall, seems to recognize me. "Hel-lo! Welcome back." Couldn't have been certain who I am, or once was. Five or six years have passed.

Slowly, like a man in a daze, I make my way along the narrow aisles. Like my brownstone, the grocery store has deteriorated. The very floorboards beneath my feet are wearing out. There is a scarcity of frozen foods. The fresh produce is not very fresh. Driving into town, I'd noticed a new Safeway—McGuire's days are numbered.

For a moment I hesitate, badly wanting to leave. I'd intended to buy a few groceries but regret entering the store. The roaring in my ears is mounting. My usual "cocky" assurance has vanished. After a few minutes shopping I return to the front of the store, where McGuire seems to be waiting for me.

No idea how urgently the words would issue from my mouth—"Does the cashier named Keisha still work here? I used to know her—a little—she lived—lives—on Mill Run Street . . ."

McGuire ceases smiling. His face registers surprise, pain.

Like one reluctant to speak who is yet thrilled to speak, McGuire tells me it was a terrible thing—"Her husband murdered her. Beat her to death right in their house. Kids in the house, but couldn't stop him in time. He had a poker, he'd been drinking. Keisha had been saying how things weren't going so well between them, her husband had 'bad nerves' from the Gulf War. He was jealous as hell of Keisha for having friends." Fiercely McGuire wipes at his eyes. "Keisha was loved by everyone who knew her. There was no one like her in any of our lives . . ."

"When—did this happen?"

McGuire calls to a big-busted blond woman stacking cans on a shelf: "Shirley? When did Keisha pass away?"

"She didn't 'pass away,' man. She was murdered."

The blond woman speaks with her own particular vehemence, as if in his squeamishness McGuire has somehow insulted the dead woman.

The way McGuire submits to this, one senses that the two are related, intimately.

"All right. But when?"

"Five, six years ago."

Briskly a gum-chewing teenage cashier is ringing up my purchases. The exchange means nothing to her, she isn't even listening. My knees are so weak, I must lean against the counter. The gum-chewing cashier has turned to me, I see her snail's mouth moving but have missed her words. Patiently she repeats:

"Paper or plastic, sir?"

So. I have answered your (stupid) question. Please don't ask another.

MISS GOLDEN DREAMS 1949

Hel-*lo!* Welcome to Sotheby's! Come *in.* As you see, your seats are reserved. Today's (private) auction is restricted to the most elite collectors.

And I am the most prized item on the bill— *Miss Golden Dreams 1949.*

That's to say the single, singular, one-of-her-kind three-dimensional living-breathing-plasma-infused *PlastiPlutoniumLuxe Miss Golden Dreams 1949.*

Not mass-produced. Not "replicated." Just— me.

(Re)created from the authentic DNA of—me.

The most famous pinup in the history of America *and* the most famous centerfold in the history of *Playboy. And,* by popular acclaim, the Number One Sex Symbol of the Twentieth Century.

Do you doubt, Daddy? Approach the platform—(no, Daddy, you can't climb up on the platform!)—see for yourself.

My eyes *see.* This voice you hear is issued from *me,* it is not a spooky recording of Marilyn's hushed, breathy, little-girl voice, but the authentic thing. *I am the authentic thing. Full-sized, anatomically correct in every crucial way.*

How am I "animated"? I am *not animated,* Daddy. I am *alive.*

In fact I am superior to the original Miss Golden Dreams. *She* was just a frightened girl, her (flat, perfect) stomach growling from hunger. Those shadowy parts of my brain that once preserved troublesome memories have been (mostly) excised. My teeth are certainly in better condition—whiter, more even, and cavity-free—than they were in 1949. A heated red liquid is circulating in my veins and arteries, serving double duty as one-third more efficient in carrying oxygen to my brain than my old anemic blood—*and* it's an aphrodisiac, an added bonus.

Good thing you've brought your checkbook, Daddy.

How'd you like to own me, Daddy? Take me home with you? Love me?

Daddy, I know I could love *you.*

All you've got to do, Daddy, is make a bid for *Miss Golden Dreams.* And keep bidding. Keep upping the ante. Up—up—up, until your rivals fall behind, panting and defeated.

Lowest acceptable purchase price for *Miss Golden Dreams* today is twenty-two million. Highest—hey, there is no *highest.*

In fact, it's predicted that we will set a Sotheby's record this very day—*you,* the most elite of Marilyn collectors, and *me,* Marilyn.

Yes, *Miss Golden Dreams* is the original

Marilyn nude. *The* nude. The one you saw as a boy and never forgot. The one that rendered all the girls, at least the girls you knew and the women you would come to know, irrelevant.

So young! (Practically as young as your granddaughter, but don't think *that*.)

Fun fact: I was paid fifty dollars to pose for this photo.

Fun fact: I wasn't "Marilyn Monroe" yet—the studio hadn't named me. I was Norma Jeane Baker.

Fun fact: already I'd been abandoned by a husband, divorced.

Fun fact: occupation *starlet,* but—already—dropped by my studio.

Gaze greedily upon Norma Jeane as she was in 1949—more than seven decades ago. *That* was an era of female beauty like none before or since, and *Miss Golden Dreams* is the most desirable of them all—the "icon" beside which all other females fall short.

Flawless nude on red velvet. Soft, sinuous velvet, like the red interior of a heart. Creamy-white baby-soft skin, flawless skin, bright red lipstick smile revealing small, perfect white teeth, blond hair tumbling past (bare white) shoulders.

Pinnacle of human evolution—a female infinitely desirable, yet unthreatening. An infant, yet a sexualized infant. Sweet-smiling, dimpled cheek, sparkly eyes gazing coyly at *you* as a little girl would do, partly hiding her face. (For this is Daddy's girl, but a *naughty Daddy's girl.*)

Now, in the twenty-first century, human evolution has passed the point at which the species can be reproduced only by sexual inter-course—that is to say, by the powerful attraction between the sexes; in a (not very romantic) era of artificial insemination, sperm donors, uteruses for hire, and surrogate mothers, a dazzling blond female is no longer essential but has become a luxury item, like an expensive sports car or a yacht—a thirty-room mansion overlooking the Pacific . . . If you can afford these, Daddy, you can afford *me.*

My promise is that, being dazzling blond, and nude, which means barefoot, I will not ever demand equality from you; I will not—ever!—decide that I want to be you by defiling my perfect female body—having ghastly surgery to remove my breasts or to remove my velvety-red vagina and replace it with . . .

Ugh!—I know. Just the thought is—nauseating.

(And people wonder why so many disgusting "trannies" are raped, slaughtered, cast aside—as if rogue females are not inviting misogyny by refusing to be *feminine.*)

Not *Miss Golden Dreams!* Not me.

Here before you, lying as naked and docile as an infant, is the apotheosis of what was once celebrated as *femininity.*

Yes, I am proud of myself—this "self." Flawless creamy-white skin, moist blue eyes, girl's pointed upturned breasts and narrow (twenty-two inches!) waist and tender bare feet with toes tucked under.

What a thrill for you! (And you, and you.)

That special low-down-dirty thrill knowing that Miss Golden Dreams was paid so little to abase herself, naked; paid so little to pose for the image from which *PlastiPlutoniumLuxe Miss Golden Dreams* has been fashioned by the miracle of twenty-first-century robo-technology.

It's a thrill, too, don't deny it, that in a fury of sexual competition with your brother-rivals, *you* will bid millions to own me; and once you have won me, and brought me home with you, and locked the door after me, you will keep me to yourself—for the remainder of your natural life.

You're a rich man, you have taste. You've acquired Renoirs, Matisses. Those late, erotic drawings by Picasso celebrating the elderly satyr and the always-young voluptuous girl-children who entice him.

You own silk screens by Warhol—*Jackie*, *Liz*, *Marilyn*.

But these are flat, two-dimensional. The (ugly) Warhol *Marilyn* is a cartoon figure, no life, no breath, no soft white arms to embrace you until you cry out.

And so your collection is not complete. Not until you acquire *me.*

Thrilling to you, Daddy, who are wealthy and have never been desperate for fifty dollars (with which to reclaim a battered secondhand repossessed car), near penniless since you have no employment other than *starlet* or *model,* where men call the shots, pay cash and no tips; you, who might if you wish scatter gold coins on the pavement for beggars to scramble after; you, a gentleman of a certain age, class, stature who will adore Marilyn as long as she resembles her young self and never ages. And in this form, as a *PlastiPlutoniumLuxe* creation, Marilyn is guaranteed to *never age.*

Can't blame you, Daddy. No!—never blame *you.*

For as you age, it's all the more crucial for you to keep a gorgeous young woman by your side, as a reminder that, though *aging,* you are (somehow) still young, indeed you are no more than my age, for a woman must be the mirror of a man's soul, otherwise—who cares for her? *Why* care for her?

No! I am *not being sarcastic.* Certainly I am *not being shrill.*

I am breathless, breathy. My voice is a little-girl voice—feathery soft. You must incline your head to hear. Kingly, you lower yourself to me that you might raise me, a beggar maid in disguise, to your own level.

No one blames you! Of course not—no.

Marilyn understood. Marilyn forgave. Marilyn never blamed Daddy, never blamed her own mystery Daddy, who'd abandoned her mother (and her) when she was a baby, in 1926. Never bitter, Miss Golden Dreams has made a career of the opposite of bitter, for men do not like *bitter,* and who can blame them?—not Marilyn!

Not bitter that I'd earned millions of dollars for strangers, but not for myself. Not bitter, since I've become an *icon* and a *collectible*—that's enough glory for *me.*

I was the very first *Playboy* centerfold—in December 1953. Hugh Hefner had seen pictures of me, he had to have me as his first centerfold—guaranteeing success for *Playboy*—but he never got around to paying me, not a penny.

(Don't believe me? That Mr. Hefner didn't give me a penny? See, he'd bought the right to the photograph from the photographer for $500. Not a thing to do with me.)

(Which doesn't mean that Hugh Hefner wasn't crazy for me. For sure, he *was.*)

(Oh, Mr. Hefner was romantic! After I died, he paid $75,000 to purchase the cemetery plot right beside me, and when *he* died, in 2017, at the age of ninety-one, he was buried there—right beside me. *His* Marilyn.)

(I know, it's strange. It's hard to believe. That Hugh Hefner could be crazy for me, pay $75,000 to be buried beside me, but never pay me a penny for the use of "Marilyn." You just shake your head, bemused—*men!*)

Not to boast a little, but I wasn't just the first—and most famous—*Playboy* centerfold, I was also the first *Playboy* cover. All over America on newsstands—the newest glossy magazine for men, with Marilyn Monroe on the cover! Though I am wearing a low-cut dress in this photograph, though I am *not nude,* yet how gorgeous I am, and how young!—my face distended by a wide red lipstick smile that will never, ever *go out.*

See, Daddy? Just the way I'm smiling at you right now.

Bidding will start in a few minutes! Please take your (reserved) seat.

Please do not stand in the aisle staring at me, Daddy. I told you that I am the actual Marilyn—I mean, Norma Jeane. And yes, I am *alive*—I am a *living thing.*

You're blocking the way for other customers, Daddy. There will be plenty of time to stare at me once you're seated and the auction begins.

You are a special Sotheby's Platinum Plus client, Daddy. Which is why there is a nameplate on your chair. Which is why I am smiling and winking at *you.*

Would you like to love me? Take me home with you? Yes?

Desperate for love all my life. Not just when

I was Norma Jeane, scrambling to be a photographer's model and starlet. All my life, until the last night of my life (about which we don't have to speak, nor will you wish to inquire, for of all things Daddy does not wish to know about his Marilyn, her final miserable days and nights), for I'd been taught by my (abandoned, scorned) mother's example that if a woman isn't loved, she is nothing.

If a woman is not beautiful, desirable, glamorous, "sexy," she isn't going to be loved, and if she isn't loved, she is—nothing.

And if she is nothing, she will be very, very unhappy; like my mother, she will end up in a lunatic asylum, where the predominant desire is to wish to die.

Daddy, I have a feeling you will like this: a low-down-dirty thrill to learn that I was married while in high school—sixteen—very young for my age despite my shapely body—(but a virgin!)—and very lonely. Though my mother did not love me for more than a few fleeting seconds over the years and could not force herself to embrace me, let alone kiss me, I cried and cried for her in the orphanage, where I was placed when she could not care for me, and in the (nineteen) foster homes where I was sometimes—not *always,* only just *sometimes*—sexually molested.

Well, we didn't call it by such a nasty term, then. Not *sexually molested.* So vulgar! You might say *interfered with*. You might say *drew unwanted male attention*. You might say *the way that girl looked, already at age twelve, you could see she was trouble.*

In the final foster home in L.A., my foster mother took pity on me, or maybe she was exasperated with me for my continual surprise when boys and men "interfered" with me. She'd had enough of my crying and didn't like the way my foster dad was eyeing me, so she introduced me to a neighborhood boy a few years older than me, who proposed to me right away—and we were married right away—except—(I never understood why, I don't understand even now)—my young husband, Jim, abandoned me after just a few months to join the Merchant Marines and get as far away from Los Angeles as he could.

Why was the question I asked Jim, begged him, he'd said he loved me, so why then did he leave me? Why do you say you love me but then leave me, do I need more love than you can give? More love than you are capable of? Continuous love, like a radio that is never turned off? Unflagging love, relentless love, ravenous love? All I wanted was to prepare Jim's meals and cuddle with him, make love with him, bury my face in his neck and hide in his arms and—I guess—he became frightened of me—I started calling him Daddy when he was just twenty years old . . .

Thrilling to you, Daddy, I guess—to know that I was "suicidal." Just in my teens I'd threatened to slash my wrists when my husband shipped out (by his request) to Australia, begged him to make me pregnant before he left, but he refused—abandoned me and left me and broke my heart.

You wouldn't break my heart, would you? Promise?

It's a sign of how naïve I am, and how innocent I am, that men have broken my heart—*you* have broken my heart—so many times.

Yes, I am shy. Everyone said so, how shy I was. (And am.) Except when my clothes were removed, my shyness seemed to melt away, too.

Why is this?—I do not know.

In this, I am unlike *you*. For *you* would be mortified to appear naked in the eyes of strangers. *You* could not bear to be stared at, assessed and judged.

I've never been ashamed of my body. I did not actually think of it as "my" body—I called it my "Magic Friend"—where I got this from, I do not know.

Of course, robo-technology has replicated Norma Jeane's skin of 1946—(perhaps it is even more dazzling-smooth than the original!—that's an extra bonus for you). Creamy-white *Plastaepidermis* covering *PlastiPlutoniumLuxe Miss Golden Dreams,* as snug as a glove.

My Magic Friend never let me down. She had

the power to make strangers love me. I always knew—I still believe this—that if my father had seen my Magic Friend, he'd have loved her, too. I mean—*me*.

Look how you're all staring at her—gosh! I guess I'd stare at her, too.

What was wonderful was, when you looked at my Magic Friend naked, you didn't see *me*. Poor, sad Norma Jeane could hide inside her.

That's why deformity and ugliness scare me!—I never want to get old, wrinkled, shriveled, ugly. Always I want to be *Miss Golden Dreams*—just as I am right now.

(And it is a fact, this is *me*. Re-created from the "organic residue"—DNA—of my actual, authentic, certified corpse through the miracle of medical technology, reconstituted as the gorgeous nude girl lying before you in a suggestive yet innocent pose on red velvet.)

(Yes, it's hard to grasp. "Marilyn Monroe" officially died in 1962, age thirty-six; born in 1926, she'd be ninety-five now. But *that's* just the old Marilyn, of yesteryear; we are living in a very different world now, where, if you can afford it, you can be "de-aged" while living and "reconstituted" following your death.)

Almost, I seemed to know that I would live forever—somehow! Even as a girl, Norma Jeane had faith.

In my interviews I would say (in my little,

breathy Marilyn voice, with widened blue-gray eyes)—"No sex is wrong if there's love in it."

And I would say—"If I could have a baby, I would never be sad again."

You would have given me a baby, wouldn't you, Daddy? I guess it's kind of too late now, even the miracle of *PlastiPlutoniumLuxe* doesn't enable you to have children, but you can do (almost) anything else with state-of-the art *PlastaGenitalia,* as you will see.

Anyway, I know that I would have been a good mother! All the mistakes my own mother made, I would not make. Not Marilyn!

Would've adored a beautiful little angel-baby, little girl-baby I'd have dressed like a doll. Cuddle and kiss and wrap in swaddling clothes and bury in the cradle so we wouldn't hear her wailing in our bed.

If her hair turned out brunette, not blond, not white-blond like my hair, that would've pre-sented a problem, I guess—the public would look from baby girl to me and figure out that my hair wasn't "natural blond," so there'd be sniggering pieces in the media. (Easiest solution would've been to bleach the baby's hair to match my shade of blond, I guess!)

But the main purpose was to have a per-fect little baby to be the momma of—Norma Jeane like she was supposed to be, not as she *was.*

Well, it didn't happen, Daddy. No need to look worried—it *won't.*

No need for you to be jealous of a kid, Daddy. Never happened.

I love you looking at me, Daddy—don't stop! Guess you understand, most of what I say is just kidding?

Marilyn is a ray of sunshine, so *funny.* Not nasty-funny, sarcastic-funny, but little-girl funny, to make you feel good about the world.

Such fun we'll have together, Daddy!

Don't listen to the rumors, Daddy. Some people are saying—jealous people, nasty, igno-rant people—that I have been auctioned here at Sotheby's many times, that this is not the first time. Some people are claiming that fatal "acci-dents" happen to the wealthy collectors who have acquired me, sometimes within a few days—falls down flights of stairs that result in broken necks and severed vertebrae, cardiac arrest midway in vigorous intercourse, aneurysms, glioblastomas, untraceable "organic" poisons that cause the liver to disintegrate—but these are false rumors, and very silly rumors, pay not the slightest heed to them, Daddy.

I vow I will adore you—only *you.* I swear, there have been no men before you, Daddy. *You* are unique.

As I am lying in this inviting pose on the red velvet drapery with my perfect glowing

Plastaepidermis and perfectly coiffed blond *Plastahair,* so I will lie at your feet. I will prostrate myself before you. I will be your beautiful bride. I will not—ever—murmur a word of sarcasm. I will not be impatient with you, though you are a foolish, doddering old man; I will be respectful of you, I will fawn over you as only a "fawn" can fawn—(we have learned our tricks young, fawns and girls, for we have learned to survive).

I vow, Daddy: I will never accuse you of not loving me. I will never accuse you of abandoning me. I will never accuse you of exploiting or betraying me. I will never accuse you of taking my money, hiding it in secret accounts. I will never collapse in hysterical tears crying and screaming at you that I loathe you—the very sight, the very touch, the *smell* of you.

I am not a madwoman. I do not cry "ugly" tears—when I cry, I am very fetching.

I am not a nasty woman. I do not want to be your equal. I will adore *you.*

I am not bitter. Bitter wouldn't melt in my mouth.

Nobody wants a broody, teary *Playboy* centerfold. Can't blame them! I wouldn't, myself.

Could you guess, seeing me here so young, posing in the nude on sensuous folds of red velvet, so sweetly smiling, so unperturbed and unaccusing, that within a decade I would be the

Sex Symbol of the Century, and a few years after that I would be dead . . .

You could guess? Yes?

But no, don't think of *that*. Not yet—(you haven't even brought me home. Our honeymoon has not even begun).

Though it is thrilling, isn't it?—to think of *that*. Thrilling revenge of the male, that the female is so easily destroyed. The way you can break a crystal glass under your feet. The way you can smudge a watercolor—it will never be the same again. Crumple a butterfly's wings in your fist.

Miss Golden Dream's beauty makes you sick, really. Your weakness thrown in your face—resentment, humiliation, shame that this afternoon you will be in a frenzy to bid millions of dollars for an animated *PlastiPlutoniumLuxe* doll in fierce bidding with other males in which your dread is that you will be impotent and fail—for only one of you is the most wealthy, the Alpha Male—and he will "collect" me.

For Marilyn will be auctioned—sold—to the highest bidder. Never any doubt, that is the promise—Marilyn will come into the possession of the highest bidder.

Money will go to strangers, not to Marilyn. But Marilyn is not bitter. Look at that fresh young face glowing with happiness, which is a kind of innocence! Nothing to do with money, nor with questioning the motives of others.

Love me, Daddy! I will love you.

Every man who'd ever loved me abused me. Not bitter! Just a fact.

Sometimes it was push, shove, pummel, punch. Sometimes it was cold, vicious-shouted verbal abuse. *Tramp! Whore!*

Oh, yes! Piteous. But *you* will be the exception. But *you* will not abuse me, will you? Not *you.*

As *you* will not topple drunkenly down a flight of stairs fleeing in terror from your *Plasti-PlutoniumLuxe* bride with the hard-clamping arms and legs, fall screaming, thumping against steps and break your neck. *You* will not suffer a heart attack in our marital bed as the hard-clamping arms and legs grip you like a python, you will not die of an untraceable organic toxin from the dazzling red lipstick smile—*you* are special.

And so, *you* deserve *me.* Blond bombshell who's also girl-next-door. Ever alive, exactly as she was in 1949—precisely replicated chromosomes, identical cells down to the teeny-weeniest organelle. See! I am breathing, my eyelids are fluttering, my gaze is fixed upon *you.*

We'd be happy together! Have fun together! Just you and me.

Tell me what you like best, and I will do it. And do it, and do it.

I will keep every secret of yours. I will suck you dry, the loose, flabby sac of you eviscerated and your brittle bones turned to soup. And you will scream in ecstasy, I promise.

Remember, Daddy, all you've got to do is make a bid for *Miss Golden Dreams*. And keep bidding. Don't ever stop bidding. Up—up—up, until your rivals fall behind, defeated. The lowest estimate for *Miss Golden Dreams* at today's auction is only twenty-two million.

Highest?—Daddy, there is no *highest*.

WANTING

1.

Badly she wants a man.
  Or, she wants a man badly.
  Or, she wants a man. Badly.

2.

Wanting must be glaring in her face. As obsidian glares in even the faintest light.

Casually he approaches her. Stands beside her, leaning his elbows on the railing above the embankment, where seed-flecked waves slap against the concrete in harsh arrhythmic surges.

Friendly murmur—"Hello!"

No threat or intimidation in the greeting, but she doesn't reply, for it is her prerogative not to acknowledge a stranger approaching her in this public place.

Though noting to her amusement that the man's (bulky) shadow precedes him, bent like a Cubist artwork against the vertical bars of the railing above the river.

"Hey. Are you—alone?"

L.K. has not looked at him. She is a mature woman, practiced in composure, who will not betray the surprise, alarm, intrigue she feels at this intrusion.

Telling the intruder lightly, though with an air of finality, "No. Not really."

This is meant as a rebuke. Cool, definitive. But the intruder laughs as if she has said something witty, and in these circumstances (public place, attractive woman) witty means girly, flirty.

" 'Not really'—what's that mean?"

A smile baring damp, chunky, stained teeth. A smile inviting complicity.

Faint odor of clay, paint from his clothes. Turpentine?

Exactly what the words say—she considers telling him. But no, better not.

At least he isn't standing too close. There's a comfortable distance between them. And there are others on the embankment and on the grass close by, adults who would come to her rescue if necessary.

He persists. "Well, you look alone. In the present moment."

Laughs again, a sort of belly laugh, and in fact he is carrying a belly like a kangaroo pouch, above a sagging belt, khaki work trousers splattered with paint stains.

Adding, in a rueful tone, "And me, too."

Meaning—he, too, is *alone?*

Something poignant in the admission by so self-assured an individual. And in the formality of his speech, even as he is trying to be casual, relaxed—*In the present moment.*

Yes, that is not an ordinary way of speaking. That is a distinctive way of speaking. There is subtlety here, irony. An education. Character.

The way he glances at her, sidelong—quizzical, searching. He knows her, she thinks. Recognizes her.

Someone L.K. might have known years ago, in her former lifetime in this city . . .

Well, it's her fault that a stranger has approached her. Standing in this public place on Belle Isle, conspicuously alone.

Indeed L.K. has fashioned herself into a *presence:* tall, poised, wearing a shift of a coarse, nubby beige material that falls unevenly to her ankles, like sculpted drapery, and an antique satin jacket discolored with age; ivory bracelets clattering against her slender wrists, ivory beads the size of quarters around her neck. Hair loose to her shoulders, glistening silvery-blond like metallic filaments.

On her pale, narrow face stylish dark-tinted glasses that give the impression of being opaque. Half her face hidden.

He, the intruder, the smiling man in paint-stained clothes, isn't wearing dark glasses and so his (mud-brown) eyes are exposed, with a look of frankness, openness. (Eagerness?)

Coming up unobtrusively beside her on the walkway overlooking the Detroit River. A lone man seeking a casual conversation? A predator

126

seeking prey? An artist seeking a subject? As Belle Isle is a public place, it is the stranger's prerogative to position himself casually beside her at the railing, yet she feels a twinge of sexual vigilance.

This sensation, of sexual alertness, arousal or repugnance, interest or disdain, became familiar to her as soft, wrinkly scar tissue on an obscure part of the body. Sizing up men she encounters—not usually in so public and random a way as she is doing now—though keeping a certain distance between them, on guard. Positioning her chic canvas bag between them in a way that might be strategic, just in case.

He sees this. He is sharp-eyed.

(Is he annoyed, insulted? Wounded?)

He might be wondering (she supposes) who she is—*what* she is: Visitor to Detroit? Artist/ photographer? (The bag is large enough to contain a sizable camera, and in fact it often does. But not this afternoon.)

She has not responded to his overtures beyond vague murmurs, yet she hasn't moved perceptibly away from him.

Often men approach L.K. in public or quasi-public places. At social gatherings, certainly. She does appear (much) younger than her age. Some of this is natural, for she is, or was, naturally very beautiful in a wan blond way; and some of this is by design, for she has made up her face, especially her eyes, carefully outlined with black mascara and shadowed with silvery blue, with the zest and cunning of an artist. Her eyebrows, so pale as to be invisible, she has darkened with pencil. Her long, exquisitely manicured fingernails are pearly, opalescent. She has subjected her drab, graying hair to extensive treatments to achieve this striking look of liquid silver, and she has swathed her body in clothing and adornments that suggest a work of art. (L.K.'s actual body has become wraithlike to her. It is aging, inevitably. In mirrors her vision is deflected—she has learned to prefer steamy mirrors, after a shower. It has been some time since she has wished to see herself fully naked.)

Wanting a man badly does not mean wanting all men or any man badly, or even mildly, for L.K. is selective, she is not (yet) desperate; or, even if desperate, she is not (yet) willing to be reckless.

Well, yes—she is willing to be *reckless*. But selective.

In fact, for several minutes she'd been aware of the man at a little distance, regarding her curiously, a vague figure, as in those old fake photographs of ectoplasm, hovering in the corner of her eye, which she might acknowledge or ignore. This figure, this person, staring toward her with a certain intensity—avidity, hunger— as she stood leaning her arms on the railing and gazing toward the farther shore (Windsor,

Ontario: Canada). Listening to the sullied waves of the Detroit River lapping against the concrete embankment, loud and sharp, like hands rudely clapped.

Not clear if the man in the stained clothing was looking at a (lone) woman on the walkway who happened to be L.K. or if indeed he was looking specifically, with interest, at *her.*

Thinking—*Does he know me? Do I know him? Please, no.*

Well, too late. Politely she finds herself smiling. Politely lifts her eyes toward his but takes care not to actually engage with him.

Her impression is: a genial, creased face, round as a sunflower.

Jaws covered in a coarse gray stubble. Deep lines bracketing his mouth from smiling too frequently.

And he is tall, looming. Might be a former athlete going soft in middle age. Still-muscled shoulders, upper arms. Reminds her of—who?— the Chinese dissident-artist Ai Weiwei? She smiles to think of Weiwei: a courageous artist whom she much admires.

On this man's big head a soiled baseball cap, slouched sideways. Graying-brown hair straggling out from beneath. A glinting-gold stud the size of a dime in his left earlobe.

On his enormous (size twelve) feet he is wearing hand-tooled leather sandals, of high quality but stained; sandals that betray big, splayed naked toes, misshapen and discolored toenails. If he were a husband or a lover of hers, she would wince to see such toes, such toenails, exposed in a public place.

A wave almost of faintness sweeps over her. Sees herself seated, and the thickset smiling man beside her in such a way that his feet, his big, naked, heavy feet, are in her lap . . . Is she trimming the toenails? Is that a small nail clipper in her fingers?

Certainly, this man is a stranger. L.K. has never seen him before, despite the air of familiarity about him. Unless . . .

She'd lived in Detroit for a tumultuous eleven years when she was a young woman and a young wife, and now she is returning after many years. How very many, she has not allowed herself to calculate.

Not a triumphant visit. Yet not an aggrieved or repentant visit.

Well, a *necessary* visit. An old, once-beloved friend who lives now in nearby Grosse Pointe, terminally ill.

She has seen her beautiful dying friend Mia in the hospice that morning. She will see Mia again tomorrow morning, and then (she thinks) she will depart and return home (New York City) and again return in a week or two weeks, or possibly sooner, for the funeral, for she cannot *not* attend the funeral; and then, surely, there will be a memorial service in another few weeks . . .

Blinking tears from her eyes as much of vexation as of grief. Oh, how life has caught up with her, who, as a girl, had been as fleet-footed as a gazelle!

And her nostrils pinch against the smells of the river, a smell of rotted things blown in gusts against her face and a smell of chemicals, repugnant yet in a way reassuring, familiar, unchanged over decades.

The intruder, her erstwhile companion, is peering at her beneath the rim of the soiled baseball cap, which she sees is a Detroit Tigers cap, white logo against dark blue.

She remembers: Detroit Tigers, Detroit Lions. One is baseball, the other football.

He is smiling, the corners of his eyes creased. Perhaps he senses that she has returned to Detroit on an errand of mercy. Even if it is a futile errand.

Something catches in her throat, she is stirred, aroused.

She wonders where the smiling man has come from. Her impression is, he'd crossed the bridge on foot, he lives close by or has parked a vehicle on the Detroit side of the bridge.

His clothes are work clothes, obviously. His khaki trousers have numerous pockets, such as a carpenter or a plumber might have; his shirt is a shapeless jersey pullover, stained and stretched at the neck.

When she first noticed him, he'd been walking briskly. Like one accustomed to crossing the narrow bridge to Belle Isle. Until he'd sighted her on the embankment, and paused.

Wind stirring her clothing, her hair. She is thrilled to imagine how she'd appeared to him initially.

On the dark green choppy water a cruise ship is passing. Festive sounds, music and laughter. At this distance L.K. can just make out the name on the white bow—*Spirit of Belle Isle*.

Often, years ago, she'd seen this boat, or its predecessor, on the river. Making its festive way west from Belle Isle to the farther side of the Ambassador Bridge and back again.

Who takes a cruise on the Detroit River? Presumably tourists—but who would come to the ravaged city of Detroit as a tourist?

The smiling man in the baseball cap comments on the *Spirit of Belle Isle*. Has she ever taken the cruise? No?

He tells her that he has lived most of his life in Detroit but has never stepped foot on the *Spirit of Belle Isle*. Yet, a few nights ago, he'd dreamed of the boat.

". . . but it was different from this one. And the river wasn't the Detroit River but was meant to be the Niagara River. The fear on the boat was, we would be sucked by the current and plunge over the Falls."

Thoughtfully the man tells L.K. this dream fragment as if it could be a matter of importance to her. She wonders at his audacity, his vanity. The vanity of the self-satisfied male! Or is it simply that this man wants to interest her and is saying something he thinks will intrigue her.

Oddly, L.K. is intrigued. She has been fascinated by his thick lips, his big, blunt, stained teeth, something piratical about his manner, his swagger. The way he strokes his unshaven jaws as a man might stroke a beard.

She laughs. He sees that he is entertaining her. He will like her better, he will admire her more, if he believes that he is entertaining her.

"Are you a visitor here? You don't look like you live here . . ."

"Yes. A visitor."

She expects him to ask why she is visiting, whom she is visiting, but instead he asks if she has seen the Eastern Market murals—painted by Detroit artists.

She tells him no, she doesn't think so. She'd been aware of colorful murals she'd seen the previous day on the walls of abandoned buildings, but she hadn't known what they were.

"Well. These are more than colorful. If I had my vehicle with me, we could . . ."

Vehicle. Odd choice of a word. There is a

formality to the smiling man's speech, somewhat at odds with the genial slovenliness of his appearance, that intrigues her.

And he has said *we could* . . .

How casually he has introduced *we* into his conversation. L.K. hears but does not reply.

At last he tells her what he has seemed to be preparing to tell her: his studio is in the Durant building.

A neutral statement—*His studio in the Durant building.* Not an invitation exactly.

"D'you know where that is—the Durant?"

"I think so. The name is familiar. Yes."

She isn't sure. A center for young and emerging artists in a rundown section of Detroit, near the waterfront . . . But she is pleased that her companion is an artist of some sort. Flattering to L.K., she'd sized him up almost at once.

A sort of Ai Weiwei, she thinks. Physically big, with a big head, large, expressive features.

Such a man, sexually rapacious. A bull of a man. His weight on a woman would be crushing. L.K.'s breath is quickened.

He tells her that his studio is a fifteen-minute walk from where they are standing. Tells her that he hikes over to Belle Isle most afternoons to alleviate stress. Flexing his stubby fingers as if they pain him.

Stress. L.K. smiles at the word. This man, with a gold stud winking in his ear and big, splayed, grimy toes! Not likely such a man is vulnerable to *stress.*

Stress. More likely a female malady.

L.K. has not thought of the Durant building in decades. It is something of a shock—not altogether a pleasurable shock—to hear the name spoken now.

"Yes. The Durant."

Where she'd driven to interview a young artist in his studio, for the *Detroit News Magazine.* His name—she can't recall his name. A handsome light-skinned Hispanic or an African American . . . A Detroit version of the Haitian artist Jean-Michel Basquiat, who'd become enormously famous before dying of a heroin overdose, still in his twenties.

The Detroit artist whose name L.K. has forgotten had enjoyed a vogue locally for a while. Taken up by well-to-do (white) women from suburban Grosse Pointe, Birmingham, Bloomfield Hills; then, for some reason—whether because he'd committed a faux pas, or disappointed one of his patrons, or simply worn out his novelty as many of his kind did—shortly after the day of the interview, his career had peaked and he'd lapsed back into the obscurity from which he'd emerged.

Almost, L.K. can remember the name. She feels a vise tighten around her chest.

This man, middle-aged, slovenly, so very

different from the lean young artist L.K. had once known, is asking L.K. if she would like to walk over to the Durant. Across the bridge. "There are fantastic views of the river from the Durant . . ." Hesitantly he issues the invitation, for he is making himself vulnerable to L.K., to be rebuked if she wishes.

She will tell him *No thank you.* Politely.

No—not just now.

Another time perhaps.

And yet: there is something about him. Indeed yes, she has been lonely.

If this man might love her, eventually. Adore her.

For he seems to L.K., by the look of yearning in his face, the sort of man searching for someone to adore. The avidity and hunger in his eyes, his frank and unassuming manner . . .

No one has adored L.K. in some time. Badly she yearns to be adored. Almost, she is willing to compromise: she will expend emotion of her own in exchange for (male) adoration.

Yet: the thought is ridiculous. She knows.

If her beautiful friend from college were not dying less than ten miles away. If she were not in dread of visiting Mia again in the morning. If she were stronger-willed, less lonely . . . She would not be vulnerable to such ridiculous thoughts.

Time for her to escape. Return to the safety of

136

her hotel, where she will lie exhausted in a hot bath, drift off to sleep . . .

She has been on Belle Isle long enough. In dark glasses, yet blinking in sunshine. (For her eyes are weak from crying. Bloodshot, she supposes. No one must know.) She has been here long enough in gusts of wind, hearing the *slap slap slap* of waves against the embankment.

Engaging in banter with a stranger, a thickset middle-aged *artiste* in a Detroit Tigers baseball cap.

Time to edge away with a polite murmured excuse.

Yet—somehow—L.K. hears herself say yes.

Impulsively, she would like very much to see her companion's studio in the Durant. *Yes!*

3.

Twenty-four hours before: driving from the Detroit airport into the sprawl of the city in a dazzling-white Honda chosen specifically to replicate the (compact, economy) vehicle driven by her and her young husband when they'd first lived in Detroit.

Passing exits on the John Lodge Freeway she has not recalled in years. Decades.

Eight Mile Road. Seven Mile Road. McNichols. Livernois. Woodward. Cass. Dequindre. John R. Beaubien. Grand River. Michigan Ave. Gratiot. Grand Boulevard.

April: yellow forsythia wild growing and profuse amid the ravaged Detroit landscape.

Gusts of wind, tattered clouds, an air of giddy promise.

How happy they'd been! In that other lifetime.

Her heart quickens in apprehension. She is trying not to be fearful of what she will see at the hospice in Grosse Pointe.

On the phone, stammering—*Yes, of course I want to come* . . .

But she has no plans to stay with her friend's family in Grosse Pointe. No matter how they have insisted, *no.*

Doesn't want to be a burden on them. She insists.

Not at such a time. *No.*

She will stay in a hotel. She has made a reservation. At the Renaissance Center, a few miles from Grosse Pointe.

Like a war zone, leaving the suburban townships on I-75, entering the Detroit city limits below Eight Mile Road. Here are broken-backed wood frame houses, crumbling brownstones. Burned-out shells of houses. Mounds of rubble in vacant lots in which patches of jungle have sprouted, gaudy and defiant. Against ten-foot rusted wire fences bordering the expressway, litter, like confetti blown by the wind, fixed and calcified.

She has brought a camera with her, she will

take photographs of the ruins of the once-great American city.

Prospective titles: *Detroit: City of Heartbreak.* *Detroit: City of My Heart.* *Detroit: Phantom City.*

She is a serious photographer, or was. Her work, like her life, slipping through her fingers.

Fewer vehicles on the expressway than she recalls. Fewer passenger cars, lumbering trucks. Still that stink of exhaust. Pavement badly cracked, potholed. At the Third Avenue exit, traffic slows and thickens: an accident in the left-hand lane. Blocking two lanes of traffic are police cruisers, ambulances.

Don't look. Have mercy. Could be you . . .

All her life she has had such thoughts in times of crisis. The deaths of others, the shocks and woundings of others, how unfair, how unjust, she passes by unscathed, stricken with guilt. Surely soon it will be her turn?

Overhead, a police helicopter. Deafening.

Of course this is a very different Detroit from the Detroit she'd known: more than half the population has vanished in the intervening years. A million and a half residents in the late 1960s, now less than seven hundred thousand. Even before she and her husband moved away from the city, numerous others they'd known had left. After the "civic unrest" of July 1967—three days of rioting, looting, and burning; martial law—

virtually all of the "white" population moved to the (presumably safer, more affluent) suburbs. Or departed from the Detroit area altogether.

Or died. L.K. has not wanted to know very much about these deaths.

She and her husband had lived in the city for eleven years, but at its outer, northern edge, in a residential neighborhood of white home-owners. Gradually this neighborhood became "integrated"—with persons of color (Indian Americans, Asians) of a professional class, fastidious with houses and lawns, ideal neighbors.

Race had not been an issue with her or with anyone she knew well. She would have sworn— *We are color-blind.*

Though much has changed, she senses that the old city remains beneath the surface just as tissue, blood, and bones lie beneath skin.

And now traffic is moving again. Approaching the exit for Tiger Stadium.

Amid the ruins of the old inner city are dilap-idated buildings upon which local artists have painted murals in bright, savage colors. The murals are primitive, powerful: gigantic portraits of glaring Aztec faces, cocoa-gleaming bodies contorted in ecstasy, fingers outspread in appeal or in warning, outspread arms and legs, cascades of rippling dark hair, newborn brown babies attached to bloody umbilical cords and floating like milkweed seed. The shell of a burned-out structure festooned with heraldic black panthers, shrieking eagles, crosses oozing blood. Water tanks atop buildings, covered in Byzantine graffiti and scowling black faces. On a wall of an abandoned tenement building an astonishing mosaic-mural in mimicry of a medieval vision, an ascension of angels to a robin's egg blue heaven: muscular dark-skinned angels with wide, feathered black wings and mask faces like the crude female faces in Picasso's *Guernica.* Below, these mounds of corpses out of which jungle flowers spring.

The corpses are an untidy pile, like debris washed up on a beach. The hue of their skin not *white* exactly, but a pasty beige. And the faces smudged, indistinct.

L.K. tries not to feel shocked, wounded. She tries not to think—*But I am not "white"—not like that . . .*

The race hatred in this vision, so casually displayed on a tenement wall facing the John Lodge Freeway! Disgust, loathing, murderous fury from which L.K. turns her gaze, shaken.

At the height of the riot of July 1967 she and her husband had cowered in their house near Seven Mile Road. Hearing fire engines, sirens. Hearing shouts, screams, gunshots. Silently pleading—*But I am not "white"—not like our neighbors.*

Electric power was out. Phone lines were

inoperative. No TVs, radios. Martial law had been declared. Inside their darkened and barricaded house they'd been spared as marauding packs of young black men and boys surged in random directions like a furious stream overflowing its banks. What spared them: there were too many houses, too many buildings for rioters to trash and burn. Their most terrifying moments had been when Michigan National Guardsmen fired shots at looters in front of their house, chasing them down the street.

In a state of suspended emotion, she remembers now.

(Had any of the young black looters been shot? Killed? She and her husband had no idea; it was their own safety of which they thought at the time.)

Her face is wet with tears. Oh, that was— awful . . . And yet, how her young husband held her hands tightly to console her.

She'd loved him! His concern for her, his wish to protect her.

No one now in her life who would care for her like this. Who would wish to protect her.

"I am so lonely. I miss you, darling. I am so, so sorry."

Sometimes when she is alone, especially when she is driving a car, L.K. will speak in this way. It is a rare luxury she allows herself, knowing that no one else can hear, no one will know.

And she herself will forget as soon as she reaches her destination.

Exiting now at City Center, where (white) corporate America reasserts itself: banks, municipal buildings, the "heroic" statue known as the Spirit of Detroit, a fountain gushing water. A few blocks away, the city's showcase: a high-rise dark-tinted glass and aluminum monolith of swanky hotels, business and professional offices, and condominiums, quaintly called the Renaissance Center.

The Chateau Renaissance is not a hotel she knows. At least the pretentious name is not familiar.

Soberly she recalls her younger ghost-self, rising in one of the silent glass elevators of the previous hotel, on this very site.

Up, up, up—white numerals blinking above the elevator's door.

On the twenty-third floor, offering herself to the man who opens the door to her after she'd timorously knocked once, twice, a third time.

The affair had been deeply wounding to her, humiliating. Thrilling, profound. Scars from those perilous several months abide with her still, in obscure parts of her body.

The affair had not precipitated the end of her marriage. (Her husband had never known.)

Of course, the affair had precipitated the end of her marriage.

It is at the Chateau Renaissance that L.K. has made a reservation for just two nights.

Glittering opulence on the surface, the old structure beneath.

Yes, she is sure. It is the old hotel renamed, refurbished. Here is the old high ceiling of gilt squares, the old, quaintly trickling fountain, the row of gilt-embossed elevators.

On the twenty-third floor, the identical room awaits. Repainted, refurbished.

Except the Chateau Renaissance has made a concession to "resurgent" Detroit: in a corridor is an exhibit of paintings, collages, sculptures by local artists. Judging by the predominant imagery, most of the artists are African American. Many are female. This is not a subtle or meditative or minimalist art, but an art in the visually aggressive manner of Rauschenberg, Oldenburg, Warhol. Paint applied with a trowel, collages of Pop Art iconography, sculptures slung together out of scrap metal, plastics, Styrofoam. One of the sculptures is a pair of parted crimson lips, many times enlarged, on a phallus-pedestal; another is unnervingly realistic-looking hands and feet, with spikes hammered through them, on a primitive cross.

L.K. peers at the finger- and toenails on this sculpture, which are discolored with blood. Surely these artifacts are made of plastic and yet, how convincing . . .

The most lurid artwork, as it is the most riveting, is a collage titled *Blond Venus*. On a crude canvas sticky red paint has been smeared, and on the paint little black (plastic?) flies have been affixed; falling over this in a cascade of springy hair is an ash-blond ponytail of about thirty-six inches.

Is this human hair? L.K. knows better than to touch art, even such crude art, yet she can't prevent her hand from reaching out to caress the dry, brittle hair. Synthetic, she thinks.

Peering closely, she discovers that there are tiny roots to the hairs—stippled with blood. She stares, shudders, and backs away.

"Ma'am? May I help you?"—a uniformed hotel employee has been watching and quickly approaches.

Feeling faint. For a panicked moment, no idea where this terrible place is.

Then—of course. She has a reservation, she has come to check in.

Thinking—*If I vanish and am never again heard of, my signature here will be proof that I existed.*

4.

His name, he tells her, is Vann. He signs his work *Vnn*.

She tells him a name. It is not precisely her name, but the initials are identical to her own: L.K.

He is surprised (she thinks) that she has accepted his invitation to see his studio. Indeed, surprised and pleased.

A woman who looks like L.K.! In the company of Vnn.

In a bright, assured voice that suggests not the slightest unease, L.K. tells Vann that she has walked from the Renaissance Center to Belle Isle, she hasn't brought her rented car. She is happy to walk back with him.

Gusts of wind whipping her hair. Wind-roiled waves.

Crossing the bridge, L.K. sees in the river myriad scintillating eyes. Winking, glittering. In rough waves apparitions of swimmers, the agitated motions of their arms. It is painful to witness such struggles to keep from drowning . . .

Thinking—*Is not all of life a struggle to keep from drowning?*

"Vann" continues to eye her curiously. Greedily.

He asks: Is she (possibly) a journalist writing an article? A photojournalist?

No. She is not.

He'd thought (possibly) she had a camera in her bag.

But no. She does not.

Not with me. Not here.

L.K. is not a photojournalist, but she is a photographer, or has been a photographer. To be a photographer is not a matter of taking photographs but of having hope, purpose.

Her camera is back in the hotel room, unpacked. She has not yet had the energy to lift it in her hands.

Vann is telling her that she looks like the kind of person who is photographed.

She laughs, for this is flattering. It does not seem to her that this calculating man is likely to flatter without cause.

She says, "And you, too. You look like a person who is photographed."

This, Vann accepts with a shrug. (What does a shrug mean? Yes? No?) If L.K. is speaking ironically, Vann chooses not to notice.

Now he asks her, is she visiting someone in Detroit?

She doesn't reply at first. She has not intended to speak of herself except in the most impersonal terms. In her relations with men it is wisest (she has thought) not to give the adversary, that's to say the newly encountered man, any firm grasp of her. (The blunt image is of thumb and fingers thrust into a bowling ball, for a firm grasp of the ball.) Yet L.K. hears herself tell the man that she has come to visit a friend who is very ill. A friend she has not seen in years. A friend named Mia—they'd been college roommates, as close as sisters at one time.

Gravely, Vann nods, listening. She likes it that

she can so easily control the man's emotional connection with her by uttering the proper words in the proper tone of voice.

In this case, she is telling the truth. Nearly.

". . . Mia has been in remission, but now it seems that she is not in remission and chemotherapy doesn't seem to help any longer. And now—and now, it's—which is why I—we were very close once . . . It was awkward to decline the invitation from the family, not to stay with them, for I'd stayed in their house in the past and they have a big house—in Grosse Pointe . . . I couldn't bear it, staying there. Mia's terminal illness will pervade the household, there would be no escape."

Vann listens, his head inclined in sympathy. Gusts of wind stir the graying hair straggling from beneath the baseball cap.

She thinks—*Of course I know him! He is my friend.*

She thinks—*All a woman wants is for a man to listen like that. Any man.*

"I haven't—yet—seen much of the city. I want to see more. All I've done is drive from the airport and out to the hospice. I was so afraid, going into the building . . . I saw Mia this morning, and I stayed until the nurse asked me to leave so that she could rest. I'll see her tomorrow morning. Today I had to get away to Belle Isle. I didn't know how Belle Isle would be—if it would be—deteriorated and dangerous . . . Remember what they'd said, speaking of the 'race riot' in the 1940s, the 'grass of Belle Isle was red with blood' . . . I've always remembered that—those words. Maybe it isn't even true. Wasn't true. 'The grass was red with blood.' I feel that time is slipping from me. Through my fingers."

Why is she telling this stranger these wayward, rushing thoughts? She has not the slightest idea, except (perhaps) she wishes to throw herself upon his mercy.

A Detroit Police Department cruiser passes, headed out to Belle Isle. If she were in trouble, at risk, she had only to lift her hand, to wildly wave her hand to attract the police officers' attention; at once they would brake their vehicle, they would come to her assistance. A well-dressed (white) woman on the Belle Isle Bridge summoning help from Detroit police officers would not be ignored.

The fact that L.K. merely glances at the police vehicle, that she does not lift her hand, would seem to be evidence that she is not at risk.

Indeed, Vann and L.K. comprise a couple. To the casual eye, a slightly mismatched couple strolling together on the Belle Isle Bridge.

With a sudden thrill of happiness she thinks— *Now he will take my hand. He will hold my hand tenderly.*

Vann doesn't take her hand. Perhaps Vann

149

would like very much to take her hand, but he does not.

And when he walks close beside her, close enough to nudge against her, by accident or by design, L.K. eases away, clutching her canvas bag.

Halfway across the bridge. The police cruiser has vanished. Few pedestrians are crossing now. L.K. remembers: it is not the Belle Isle Bridge, but the MacArthur Bridge. Yet no one who lives in Detroit and visits Belle Isle is likely to call the bridge the MacArthur Bridge.

Vann is telling L.K. that he doesn't believe in extrasensory perception—"whatever the hell that is"—but he'd had a dream the other night in which there was a woman—"a woman like you, who came to my studio and wanted to see my new work and so I showed her . . ."

L.K. takes exception—*A woman like you.* How condescending! Insulting! Doesn't this arrogant man know that there is no woman *like her,* there is only *her?*

"Really. And what did 'this woman' think of your art, Vann?"

L.K.'s voice is so cold, Vann understands that he has blundered.

She is thinking she won't accompany him to the Durant building after all. She will say goodbye to him when they've crossed the bridge. She will walk away, quickly. He will not follow her. He will not dare follow her. She feels a wave of sexual disgust, repugnance for the man: the fleshy face, stained teeth, sour breath, layers of fat carried above his belt, misshapen toes. Who does he think he is, daring to approach *her.*

A would-be predator. Certainly a failed artist. A marginal figure in the no-man's-land of Detroit, Michigan, to which she has come by the sheerest chance and to which she will never return.

5.

Gently he takes her arm. "Here. We turn in here."

It has been a surprisingly long walk to a block of warehouses on the river east of Grand Boulevard. L.K. has not remembered that the Durant building is located on a short, stubby block called Durant, which intersects with Grand Boulevard.

She is feeling apprehensive. She could not have said why she has come into this desolate part of Detroit with an unkempt man who is a stranger to her.

In the distance are high-rise office buildings, incongruous in this setting. Smudged-smoky glass of the dagger-shaped Freedom Tower.

The April sky, so promising earlier, has turned gray and glowering. The temperature is plummeting. Yet L.K. begins to feel exhilarated, reckless.

He will offer me a drink. I will not accept.

151

The renovated warehouse to which Vann leads her is teasingly familiar to her, though it has been lavishly adorned with quasi-primitive mosaics. Here are the Found Object Sculptors League, the Blue Boar Gallery, the Durant Artists Coalition. Positioned on the roof is a triumphant mythological creature—part winged lion, part demon—a chimera with a fierce expression, bared teeth.

Your gaze just naturally lifts to the winged lion. Only belatedly do you see that the lion is surrounded by mounds of skulls amid crimson flowers shaped like tongues.

" 'To create is to destroy,' " Vann says, as if translating for L.K., "though to destroy isn't always to create."

Whom is he quoting? Is he quoting himself? L.K. supposes this is a remark she should know, attributed to Picasso, Kandinsky, Goya, Man Ray, she has no idea.

In the grassless front area is a ten-foot wind sculpture, whose blades, adorned with wan (white-skinned) human masks, are turning erratically.

Proudly, Vann tells her that the wind sculpture is *his*.

L.K. is subtly offended by the (white-skinned) masks. She wonders if Vnn is not himself "white," but a person of color, though light-complected.

L.K. tells Vann that the wind sculpture is "very striking"—she says nothing about the (white-skinned) masks, wanting to turn around and flee the warehouse even as she enters the building with Vann and feels a sense of immediate vertigo, as if the floor is tilting beneath her.

No. This is a mistake. Go back.

Recalling revelations of asbestos in many of the older buildings in Detroit. In the Durant and other waterfront warehouses, surely.

Recalls: asbestos fibers are thinner than human hairs. The cause of deadly cancers of the lungs, blood. Commonplace in buildings of a certain era, of a certain type. Roofing, insulation. Its lethal effects can take decades to emerge.

There'd been massive removals of asbestos-contaminated materials in the city, she recalls. Campaigns to clean up the despoiled environment. Raze the worst of the buildings. Local businesses had resisted initially. There had been litigation. Settlements. Numerous deaths.

On one side of the Durant is an abandoned warehouse; on the other, a rubble-strewn vacant lot.

Inside the Durant is a raw, open space, as if part of the ceiling has been removed; skylights let in glowering-pale light through panes of glass speckled with seeds and other debris. There is a second-floor balcony on which neon-flashing sculptures are displayed.

Interior entrances to the Blue Boar Gallery, the Durant Artists Co-Op, the Detroit Sculptors Coalition, Dequindre Rouge. Smaller galleries that open onto the foyer, exhibiting weavings, pottery, paintings, knitted things. Most of the galleries are closed, darkened. There are virtually no visitors or customers. Their footsteps echo distractingly. Yet, through the doorway of the Blue Boar, L.K. sees a woman—not young, though not exceptionally old—so familiar to her, she stops dead in her tracks, trying to recall the woman's name . . .

But she isn't alive now—is she?

The woman she'd known, the woman whom this woman resembles, had died years ago of breast cancer. L.K. is sure.

No. Whoever she imagines the woman might be, this woman could not possibly be.

And again, as they pass another small gallery in which wheat-colored macramé sculptures are displayed, L.K. glances inside to see a figure—a white-haired woman—from just the back, who seems to her startlingly familiar . . .

"Is something wrong, dear?"—Vann asks, concerned.

Quickly L.K. tells him no.

"Is she someone you know, dear? Would you like to go inside and say hello to her?"

"N-No. Not now."

The very prospect frightens her. No!

In this place they are preserved. What is this place!

The Edelstein Gallery is a larger gallery that exhibits more sophisticated art, including even, L.K. sees to her surprise, lithographs and woodcuts by Rockwell Kent, Ben Shahn, Andy Warhol, Louise Nevelson, Philip Guston, Marsden Hartley. Hadn't the Edelstein Gallery once been located in the old, elegant Fisher Building?

At first it seems that the Edelstein Gallery is darkened, but when she looks through the window, she sees that it is open after all. Indeed, a very thin young woman in stylish black is sitting at a desk speaking on a phone: an old-fashioned rotary phone. She glances up, sees Vann through the window, smiles (slyly?), and waves as Vann (and L.K., whom she ignores) pass by. This face is certainly not familiar to L.K., for the girl is very young, with Asian features and very black sleek hair to her waist.

L.K. feels a stab of jealousy. The way the girl and Vann exchange greetings . . .

An older man, physically unattractive, yet he exudes a sexual aura rising from his sense of himself, his masculinity. A woman of the identical age is disadvantaged.

"We can visit the Edelstein later if you wish, dear. On our way out."

Dear. L.K. registers this, uneasy. But she doesn't object.

Telling him no. She does not care to visit the Edelstein Gallery.

Artists' studios are on higher floors, Vann says. Space is cheaper to rent there. Okay to take the freight elevator?

The interior of the warehouse is much larger than L.K. would have expected, or recalls; the farther walls are lost in shadow.

The freight elevator is not very clean. There is a smell here of dirt, grime. A badly soiled tarpaulin on the floor that looks, to the casual eye, as if it is covering something the size of a small child lying prone.

In such close, confined quarters L.K. feels self-conscious with her newfound companion, who whistles thinly as if he too feels awkward.

Above the elevator door there are four numerals—1, 2, 3, 4. Yet as the elevator ascends with creaks and clatters, none of the numerals light up.

With forced ebullience Vann tells L.K. about the Durant—how being able to work here "saved his life" when he'd been a young artist in his twenties, with nowhere to go, a succession of poorly paying part-time jobs, including, for a while, a nightmare time in his life after he'd dropped out of Wayne State, working as an orderly at Detroit General Hospital.

"The only good thing about the job," Vann says, "is I learned to see how life becomes death—that quickly. No mystery to it, just a switch turned *off.*"

But this isn't true, L.K. thinks. Death does not come that quickly. And the shadow of death does not fade quickly—it does not fade at all.

How slow the elevator is! She feels a frisson of panic that it will jolt to a stop suddenly; they will be stuck in it together, between floors.

The man's eyes drift to her. He sees that his words have upset her, perhaps. That was not his intention.

Walking to the Durant, he'd brushed against L.K. several times, accidentally, or so it seemed. Here inside the elevator he stands stiffly apart from her, as she stands at a little distance from him. Her heart beats quickly with exhilaration. Is he afraid of her?

He asks L.K. if she has a "family"—by which, she supposes, he is asking if she is married.

"No."

So blunt an answer, she feels the need to amend: "Not now."

Then, trying to keep her voice from breaking, "Not for a while."

He waits for her to ask if he is married or has a family, but L.K. fails to ask. Quite deliberately she doesn't ask, and why is that? (Does she not *care?* Or does she wish to give this man the impression that she doesn't care?)

And so Vann volunteers: he has lived with

several women in the course of his life, and he has offspring scattered in the Midwest—"probably"—but he has not been married, and no child has ever looked at him and called him Daddy.

L.K. laughs. But is this curious remark meant to be funny? Vann seems to be boasting of having children he doesn't know, who have never known him.

Should she say *Too bad, you would have made a wonderful father.*

Probably, this is not true. Artists do not make wonderful fathers, to the degree that they are serious, driven artists.

Presumably it's time for L.K. to reveal to her companion that her husband, that's to say her former husband, has departed from her life irrevocably. She cannot bring herself to say *My husband has died,* still less *My husband is dead.* Her lips turn numb at the prospect.

She cannot bring herself to say, with a sob of fury—*I am not a widow, don't condescend to me. I am not defined by any man living or not-living.*

Her lips tremble. She is frightened of crying. How humiliating, the infantile face of one about to cry . . .

Yet Vann persists: "Not for a while—does that mean that you aren't in contact with him?"

Yes. That is what that means.

"And you have—don't have—children?"

L.K. is irritated, embarrassed. It is the mere

question that unsettles her, that a stranger should feel he has the right to interrogate her so intimately.

A flush rises to her face. *No. None. And it is none of your business why.*

"I'm sorry if I—I've—overstepped . . ."

The voice trails off. L.K. is furious at *if.*

At last, in awkward silence, the elevator jolts to a stop. A clang, a clatter as Vann forcibly opens the door.

L.K. laughs aloud, she is flooded with relief.

Never again, that elevator. She will find a stairway when she leaves.

They are on the top, fourth floor. Here remodeling has been crude. Dirt like grit beneath her feet.

Vann leads her along a corridor past artists' studios, some of them open to view—smells of clay, paint, turpentine are strong here. In one of the studios a radio is playing staccato rap music. On an easel, a half-completed abstract painting like a superannuated Jasper Johns.

L.K. has been irritated with Vann, yet now she is thinking that she likes him. Or rather, she is attracted to him. *Vnn.*

(The name is vaguely familiar, she has seen it somewhere recently—has she? On one of the hideous collages exhibited at the Chateau Renaissance?)

It has been a long time since L.K. has felt

anything approaching sexual attraction for any man. That the man seems to feel an attraction for *her* is the excitement.

Vann is leading L.K. some distance, to a farther wing of the warehouse. Grit beneath her feet is more noticeable. Offhandedly telling her that you wouldn't think junkies could find their way into the Durant, let alone to the fourth floor, but they do—"We've all been ripped off at least once." Vann is both disgusted and rueful.

Junkies. A startling word, in the mouth of someone like Vann.

". . . sometimes they break in downstairs, spend the night, that's okay with most of us, but there've been fires started in the winter . . ."

He has become a property owner, L.K. thinks. A bourgeois. Concerned for the safety of his art.

Vann fuming about *junkies* endears him to L.K., oddly.

She is thinking that if he touches her, she will not draw away. Perhaps she will touch him, fingers brushing against his wrist, his arm. Allowing the man to know how she feels about him.

(But how does L.K. feel, exactly? Like a sleep-walker whose eyes are partly shut, uncertain where she is and where she is going.)

If Vann kisses her, a mist will rise in her brain. That mist of passivity, oblivion. A promise of oblivion.

160

She will respond to the man, blindly. She will kiss him in return. Instinct will take over, she will not be obliged to think.

The fade-out of the movie screen. The curtain lowered.

But life isn't aesthetic, like art. She will have to see the man, close up. And he will see her, unblinking.

Indeed L.K. feels a mild repugnance at the prospect of becoming physically—*sexually*—involved with this man. She has no wish to see him unclothed—*naked.* If they spend time together intimately, she will hear him coughing, clearing his throat. Breathing heavily. Grunting.

Bathroom noises, a toilet flushing. She has lived alone for so long now, being in close quarters with another person, with a man, will be lacerating to her nerves.

Vann has unlocked the padlock to the door of his studio. As she steps inside, L.K. is surprised—more than surprised, astonished—at the dimensions of the space, its high ceiling, skylights, buffed plank floor, floor-to-ceiling windows emitting an eerie incandescent light. The room is part living quarters, part studio. Very impressive.

L.K. feels a stab of chagrin, she'd underestimated the man. Not for the first time in her experience with strangers, she'd been condescending to him.

Clearly Vnn is a successful artist. Or Vnn has money from a source other than art.

Or, what is equally likely, the artist has very good taste and has made of a crude storage space something resembling a work of art in itself.

"It's—beautiful."

"Is it! I'm glad that you think so."

Vann's face is flushed with pleasure. He'd wanted to impress her, she thinks. And so he has.

The loft is a large open space with a fifteen-foot ceiling of metal girders. In the living area are a black leather sofa, several leather chairs, a low-slung table fashioned of a single piece of burnished redwood. There are lamps carved from wood, with translucent shades. Lights descend from the ceiling on narrow poles or rise from the floor. On the floor are scattered Moroccan carpets. In an interior alcove, what looks like a small kitchen. Behind black-lacquered Japanese screens is the artist's work area.

The rough walls have been painted a muted oyster white, ideal for displaying art. Bright, primitively executed canvases and collages predominate. Vnn is a prolific artist, an industrious artist, one can see. The largest canvas measures approximately six feet in length, five feet in height, a vivid, shimmering wash of colors in the mode of Morris Louis and Helen Frankenthaler. There are looming humanoid figures covered in white gauze, like bandages,

162

in the mode of George Segal, with pinched, anguished faces and sightless glass eyes. More original are kites hanging from the ceiling, spiky in design, also very colorful, in the shapes of gigantic bumblebees, bats. The most clever is a five-foot butterfly that, as you approach, is seen to comprise hundreds of small butterflies. (Are these real butterflies? Captured, embalmed? L.K. notes that many are monarch butterflies, an endangered species.) "This is ingenious," L.K. says of the giant butterfly, though she isn't sure that she approves.

"My dear, the butterflies are not 'real.' "

"I wasn't sure . . ." L.K. is doubtful, disbelieving.

"It would take me forever to capture so many butterflies," Vann says, wincing and smiling, as a naughty boy might do. "I would have to anesthetize them one by one with chloroform. And I would have to be very careful to keep from tearing the wings."

L.K. sees that some of the delicate orange and black spotted wings are indeed torn. She imagines that she smells something sweetly chemical. (Ether? Chloroform?)

L.K. has to concede, Vann's loft/studio is very striking. Not what she'd expected. (But what had she expected? Something smaller, less ambitious? A pigsty? Mediocrity?) She had expected his work to be clichéd and ordinary,

163

just another variant of Pop Art, but really it is far more subtle, and the paintings are intricately *painted*—brushstroke by brushstroke. She is not condescending to him now.

Like all genuine artists, Vann has hidden his deepest nature beneath a personality worn like old clothes—indeed, like an artist's work clothes. He is slovenly, but only in his being—not in his art.

Indeed, L.K. is drawn to this mysterious person. *Vnn.*

"Would you like a drink, dear?"

"I don't think so, thank you."

"Yes, a drink. To celebrate us."

Us. L.K. is touched by this, though uneasy. What does *us* mean?

She thanks him and tells him she prefers sparkling water, club soda. If he has it, ice.

"But don't go to any trouble, Vann! Please."

"Call me Vanny."

Vanny. L.K. feels a sensation of sudden weakness in the region of her heart. The wild thought comes to her—*He will be my lover. Vanny.*

While Vann whistles thinly in the kitchen area, pouring drinks, L.K. continues to look about the living area. The setting is a work of art in itself, objects on display. Art books, photography books, framed lithographs. (One of these is a Chagall lithograph, near identical to one owned by L.K. herself. Another is a Ben Shahn.) Pottery, weavings. An antique urn, badly cracked, very likely bought at auction at one of the great old Palmer Park mansions. Sculptures fashioned of burnt wood, painted cotton, and burlap, like oversized moths. Startling to think that out of his own work and the work of others that Vann has collected over time, the slovenly man has created such beauty.

L.K. thinks, rebuked—*Beauty can never be deduced by examining its creator.*

Could she live in such a loft? Or, could she live in close proximity to such a loft?

Her smiling host brings her a glass half filled with amber liquid. What's this?

Single-malt whiskey.

But no, she doesn't want *whiskey.* Not at this time of day—afternoon . . .

"Try it, dear. You'll like it."

Laughing, she protests. "No. I can't . . ."

"I said, try it."

"If you have sparkling water, club soda . . ."

"Sorry. I don't."

"Wine . . ."

"Try this."

Clinking his glass against her glass, which feels to L.K. unusually heavy.

Oh, this is annoying! This is pushy, aggressive.

Dislikes the man, this macho posturing.

Out of politeness L.K. takes a small sip. Isn't sure what single-malt whiskey is.

165

The sudden heat of it! Amber liquid seizing her mouth, her throat, in a rush of sensation.

"To us, dear. To meeting by chance on Belle Isle."

These words are ironic, are they? Or romantic?

Vann is regarding her with a smile. Is it a fond smile, a bemused smile, a smile of appropriation, a smile of sexual yearning? Desire? Aggression? Threat?

He is no threat to her, she is sure. He means no harm to her, surely quite the opposite. Now that they are out of the clanging freight elevator.

But did they meet *by chance?* L.K. isn't sure that she believes in chance.

What appears to be *chance* is just obscurity, perhaps. You don't know the connections between things, as a fly blundering into a spider's web has no idea what he is blundering into.

To the fly, *chance.* To the spider, *destiny.*

Vann drinks. L.K. takes another, tentative drink. She has not had anything so strong to drink in years and feels a sensation of sheer elation, recklessness. Why not?

Her dear friend in the hospice is dying. She has been terrified of seeing her friend die before her eyes. As she'd been terrified of seeing her husband, her husband's body, after his death, when he had needed her and she had abandoned him out of cowardice.

Vann is telling her about the history of the

Durant. The "mecca" for outsider art for decades.

(How old is Vann? How long a career has Vnn had? The man looks to be in his mid- or late fifties at least. *She* may be a decade older.)

The closer L.K. examines her genial host, the more it seems to her that the man isn't "white"— not altogether. Could he be (part) Hispanic? Middle Eastern? (There is a large Lebanese-Catholic population in Detroit.) More likely part African American, with murky brown eyes. That broad, flattened nose, sensuous sharp-chiseled lips . . .

She has been staring at those lips. Thinking— *If he kisses me, I will* . . . She has no idea what she will do. Her limbs feel weak in anticipation.

L.K. has had lovers of ethnicities other than her own. She has been *color-blind* all her life.

Trying now to remember her lover. The emotional young painter who'd later killed himself, possibly by accident, with a heroin overdose.

Almost, she can remember him. Was his name Lester? Esdra. His olive-pale face. Thick dark hair. Serious, somber manner. The hesitancy of his touch.

She had not heard of Esdra's death until months after. Somehow that had made the death seem less urgent, less real.

She'd wept, her heart had been rent. But then she'd dried her eyes and hurried out to her car . . .

For always in that phase of her life people had awaited her.

Hears herself ask if Detroit is still a center for drugs.

An annoying question, L.K. knows. When Vann has been regarding her with soft, solicitous eyes.

"Depends on which drug. No more than anywhere in the Midwest."

She doubts that that can be true. In its boom years Detroit was besieged by drugs: crack cocaine, a killer. And now, from what she has heard and read, methamphetamine, manufactured illicitly in the devastated inner city, indeed in old buildings like those surrounding the Durant, is the leading killer.

"Why do people insist upon poisoning themselves? I've always wondered."

"I don't." Vann snorts, laughs. He is the experienced one, knowing all the answers. "I don't wonder at all."

"Yes, but why?"—L.K. persists.

"When you're high, you don't *want*—anything. And when you're not high, you're waiting for the high, which is what you *want*—not anything else."

L.K. feels rebuffed by these words.

Words of wisdom, she supposes.

But yes. It is the great weakness of her life. *Wanting*.

A moment's stiffness between them: the woman and the man.

From a window L.K. can see the Detroit River, not so scintillate from this distance, lead gray. Belle Isle is obscured by buildings. Lake Saint Clair is invisible. But she can see something of the skyline of Windsor, Ontario.

Living in Detroit, she'd fantasized a parallel life in Canada. In the city so much smaller than Detroit she would live a smaller, more virtuous and saner life, a life of anonymity. A husband, a child or two. A life lacking in invention and novelty and for that reason a life of immense satisfaction.

Once, with Esdra, in his rattletrap pickup truck that had aroused suspicions at the border crossing, she'd driven into Canada, not to the small city of Windsor but to Point Pelee, a vast national park south and east of the city, bordering Lake Erie. Esdra had wanted to take photographs of migrating birds, but his heavy Nike camera had malfunctioned. (L.K.'s camera had functioned well enough.) She recalls crossing the windswept Ambassador Bridge, returning late to Detroit. Storm clouds overhead, flashes of lightning.

Determined to tell her husband yes, she loved him, but no she could not remain with him. Her soul had been lacerated, lashed. For she'd fallen in love with . . .

She shakes her head to clear it. Oh, where is she *now.*

So much of her life has been lost to her. Each day, more falls away. Tattered and unraveling. Her heart is beating hard in this unfamiliar place that smells of paint, clay, turpentine, whiskey. Sweet-rancid rot.

Vann sees. Vann understands. He has lost much, himself. The sag of his shoulders, the flaccid gut. Bloodshot eyes.

Not quickly, but carefully, he approaches her. As one might approach a butterfly lighted upon a flower.

"You seem upset, dear. Are you remembering something that makes you sad?"

"N-No."

Feeling compelled to add, as Vann observes her, "Not really."

"Your college friend who is ill. You said."

"My friend—?" But has she told the stranger about Mia? In her awkward flirtation with the artist who calls himself Vnn, has she really been so crass as to exploit Mia's illness? She doesn't think so.

Vann is determined to change the tone of their conversation. Telling her that the waterfront area is being developed. There will be a condominium complex on the river. Offices. A publication—*Art in Detroit.*

"A very good time for investing. For investors."

To this L.K. has nothing to say. (Does he want her to invest money in Durant artists? In *him?*)

"You might consider an article about the Durant. My friends and me. Take pictures—we're photogenic."

If this is meant as a joke, it is a clumsy joke. Offensive to her.

As if L.K. has nothing better to do, nothing of more significance in her life than to write about the local Detroit art scene. An older woman groupie attaching herself to avant-garde *artistes*.

It is true, in her past life she might have written about the "resurgence" of Detroit. Might've called it the *late, great American city Detroit*.

She'd done such work, freelance photo-journalism. She'd known everyone, she'd driven everywhere and had rarely been afraid or in danger, and if so, only fleetingly.

But now the local magazines that might have published such an article, part cultural criticism, part commercial promotion, have vanished. Shuttered years ago.

She'd left her camera at the hotel. Probably she would not remove it from the tote bag. Where once the camera had been an extension of her soul, now it has become mere equipment, an impediment that feels heavy in her hands, pretentious. Vain.

Still, the camera fixes her vision. Cuts her vision to size.

A visual artist cannot fathom eternity/infinity. The viewfinder makes art possible.

She comes to position herself before one of the kites hanging from the ceiling on a wire. Is this new? Is the artist working on it at the present time? Much of Vnn's art looks unfinished, raw. Canvases with absences, blanks. That which is unspoken, undefined. The sort of art that L.K. has attempted is overfilled: she has felt that she must explain too much. Her art has been choked, airless.

Nature abhors a vacuum. It takes a certain degree of audacity to leave much open, untouched.

"Would you like another drink, dear?"—Vann is smiling, a genial host. L.K. notes that he has never uttered the name she'd provided him, as if sensing that it is not her true name.

Without knowing it, L.K. has finished the single-malt whiskey in her glass. But—"No more, thank you!"

Vann pours another inch or two of the amber liquid into her glass.

It is maddening, the man pays so little heed to her wishes. All but winking at her, up close—*You know, dear. And I know.*

Leading her now into the interior of his studio. Beyond the black-lacquered Japanese screens.

Immediately the smells of clay, paint, turpentine are stronger. The odor of something sweetly rotten, rancid. Here, beyond the stately black screens, is far less order, coherence. Canvases lean against the wall, smudged watercolors. Sketches in pencil, charcoal pencil. The floor is frankly dirty. Wadded rags, tissues cast down. Behind the screens. The artist's truest life.

So this is where the artist *works*. That's to say, where the soul of the artist *lives*.

Some of this work is very good, L.K. thinks. She tries but cannot fasten upon Vnn's influences. Lucien Freud? Francis Bacon? Goya? Somewhat crudely mixed with primitive art, Warhol parody. An air of vehemence, recklessness—Pollock. The larger canvases of sprawling, quasi-abstract naked bodies, collages, sculptures—intimidating in their size.

A six-foot tree of birds—bird skeletons. Tiny eye sockets, empty.

"*Tree of Life*—it isn't complete." Vann frowns at his creation, as if seeing it through another's eyes.

The tree is, or was once, a "real" tree, a young birch. The birds?

L.K. shudders, contemplating the perfect little bird skeletons that by their size appear to have been sparrows, songbirds.

Seeing her reaction, Vann says again, "It isn't complete. All my work back here is 'in progress.' "

He is standing close beside her. His voice in her ear, intimate and mesmerizing.

Then she discovers, at the rear of the studio, a supply of mannequins. Some are leaning against a wall as if weary, some lie in a heap on the floor as if discarded. Several are hanging from hooks, pulleys—an unnerving sight.

Vann doesn't want his visitor to wander back here, it seems.

"Maybe you've seen enough, dear. We can return to . . ."

Even as she is appalled by what she sees, L.K. feels drawn to see more.

". . . these are works in progress. I've set aside for the time being . . ."

L.K. comes closer. She notes that the mannequins are all female. They have no genitalia of course, but they do have small, conical, perfect breasts, slender waists and hips. Their faces are smooth, seamless. Some are wearing glamorous wigs, others are bald. They are all "white"—"Caucasian"—a pale, pasty hue. Several have been despoiled: their skulls cracked open and sponges placed inside to suggest the human brain; through eye sockets, plastic flowers emerge. Through nostrils, mouths. Tentacles.

One of the mannequins sports a bleeding-red wound between her legs, framed by "pubic" hair.

L.K. is shivering. Of course it is a mistake to be here in this stranger's territory. She has known this since the freight elevator.

Hurry! Now.

174

Yet she asks coolly, like a true art professional, "What do these—sculptures—sell for?"

"These 'sculptures' are not finished."

"But if finished—"

"Prices vary. Wildly."

"This one, for instance. If you were to price it." A mannequin on a hook, one of those with a sponge for a brain. Between its legs a mock-bleeding wound. Both the "pubic" hair and the hair on the mannequin's head resembles L.K.'s own hair, though it is—of course—synthetic and not human hair.

Vann states a price. L.K. recoils in surprise.

"D'you really get such prices? For things like this?"

"Depends."

Things is deliberate. Vann must hear the contempt in her voice.

L.K. cannot look away from other works in progress, stuck back here in the shadows.

Canvases smeared with paint and adorned with "human" artifacts—finger- and toenails, earlobes, hair. Much hair.

Hair of all hues, textures. Wavy hair, glossy hair, frizzy hair, straight hair. Ashy blond, dirty blond, chestnut, mahogany, russet-red, dark hair threaded with silver.

Shelves of wigs. L.K. assumes these are wigs and not human hair in swaths.

(But how pungent these smell! A sort of

arrested rot, treated with a chemical solution.)

"I'd told you, dear. All this is work in progress. Not for viewing."

"Yes. I can see that."

Vann lifts one of the wigs from the counter. Playfully, perhaps just slightly meanly, he suggests that L.K. try it on.

"Thanks, no."

"But it will suit you. Try."

Vann hands the wig to L.K., who takes it from him hesitantly. It's a thick black wig, somewhat matted, lusterless. Its smell is pungent—indefinable. L.K. has no intention of fitting it on her head, but she examines it closely and sees, or thinks she sees, blood-stippled roots of hairs—actual hairs.

She drops the wig, appalled. She is trembling badly.

Vann laughs and picks the wig up from the floor.

"It smells. It's awful. Please—put it away."

In what appears to be a refrigerated display case L.K. sees bruised and battered heads, sallow-skinned faces. Heavy-lidded, bruised eyes. Matted hair.

There is a sickish, rank smell. A window has been opened partway to air out the loft.

Along a wall, a white porcelain freezer humming just perceptibly with electricity. L.K. thinks—*He keeps his captives there. His "art."*

Overhead the skylight is scummy, opaque. L.K. is feeling weak and uncertain. Vann leads her out of the workroom into the living quarters of the loft. L.K. stumbles and sits heavily in one of the leather chairs. She reaches into the canvas bag for her cell phone and sees that it has gone dark, it has lost its power.

It is formaldehyde she smells. She is certain.

6.

"You don't recognize me, do you, dear?"

Words you don't want to hear in a private and sequestered place on the fourth floor of a near-deserted building.

Faltering, she says no. She doesn't think so . . .

"Try. Maybe you will remember, dear."

Dear, reiterated. She wonders if *dear* is meant to be consoling or ironic.

Staring at him searchingly. The genial creased face, as big and round as a sunflower? The murky-brown bloodshot eyes?

Of course, this is a *person of color.* In ancestry, if not in the (obvious) hue of his skin.

He removes the Tigers cap. Graying-dark hair, oily. Receding from a blunt forehead. You can see—(L.K. can see)—that this hair had once been thick, wavy.

"Vanny was what people called me. Including you, dear."

"Vanny . . ."

Does the name sound familiar? L.K. remembers a man—a young man—named Vanbrugh . . . Is this *Vanbrugh?*

"And you, you were—Lavinia." In a flat, jeering voice he has named her, exactly.

L.K. is stunned by his hostility. Realizing too that she has had too much of the powerful drink, a mistake.

"Lavinia Kohl. Yes?"

How diminishing it seems. To be found out, *named.*

"Y-Yes . . . How do you know me?"

"How I know *you?* Of course I know you. All these years, I have known you—hated you."

"Hated me? Why?"

"You left me for dead. You assumed that I was dead."

"What? N-No . . . That isn't possible."

"You came to my studio, on the first floor then. You saw me collapsed on the floor, you ran away."

Vaguely L.K. recalls: the young artist with a studio on the first floor of the Durant. Her lover, briefly. One of her lovers. It had not been that important—had it? No one would remember such a fleeting relationship.

But this man—this middle-aged, heavyset man who calls himself Vnn—is not that individual, certainly.

"You arrived, Lavinia Kohl, you let yourself

into the studio, you saw me collapsed on the floor. You panicked and left and never called for help. You left me for dead, and in fact I did die."

Seeing the bewilderment in L.K.'s face, Vann laughs.

"But then I was revived. Because someone else interceded and called an ambulance."

Vann has come to sit beside L.K. Closer. She has not the strength to pull away,

"My heart had stopped and was shocked into beating again. No thanks to *you*."

L.K. looks at Vann pleadingly. Her nostrils pinch at his sharp, accusatory smell. What is he saying?

"You didn't want to be involved. You were married—you were thinking of your marriage. Your safe, 'white' life. You saw that I'd collapsed, you had no idea if I was going to die within minutes, you simply fled and told no one. I suppose you thought that I would never know, since I was unconscious, and if I revived—I wouldn't know what you had done. But I knew. I was told. By another artist on the floor, who'd discovered me. She'd seen you running out— she'd seen your face, she said. How frightened you were. How guilty."

It is a bad dream, this memory. Though perhaps not a memory, but only a bad dream.

"I thought I would never forgive you, Lavinia.

But today, seeing you, recognizing you—seeing how you too have changed—I do."

"You—forgive me?"

"In Esdra's place. In the magnanimity of Esdra's soul."

"But—Esdra? I thought your name is . . ."

"Esdra was my friend. My brother. I am acting in his place."

"But nothing like this ever happened. I—I never left anyone to die—I did not. You must be confusing me with . . ."

"Another Lavinia? I don't think so."

Vann laughs expansively, drinking whiskey.

On shaky legs L.K. tries to stand. "I want to leave now—Vann. I am leaving . . ." Her voice is plaintive, pleading. The whiskey has made her very weak.

"Leaving for—where? You couldn't possibly go alone—in this neighborhood. And how'd you get back to your hotel? It's miles away. You can't walk. There are no taxis here."

"I—I could call . . ."

"No cell phone service here even if your phone wasn't *dead*."

L.K. has not the strength to scream. If she ran to a window—the loft is on the fourth floor, she could not jump out. If she stood at the window and screamed and flailed her arms, Vann would easily overcome her within seconds.

"You can't leap from a window, it's four floors to the ground."

L.K. is dazed. Alarmed. (Drunk? Her senses are muddled.) Trying to recall the old Durant: the old, first-floor studios. A young man, a boy really: Esdra. Had that been his name? She'd known several artists. Possibly, one had been Vanbrugh. They'd vied for her favor, had they? Competed for her attention? Though possibly, she hadn't wished to think at the time, they'd laughed at her among themselves as they laughed at other privileged white women.

"Stay a while, dear. You're in no condition to venture out of here. Let Vnn take care of you."

Naïvely she wants to think—*He has forgiven me. He will protect me.*

Vann circles his stubby fingers around L.K.'s wrist. His fingers are strong. The nails are ridged with paint, dirt.

L.K. shudders. She would move away, but Vann holds her fast, and she knows that any struggle on her part will be met with force.

"Dear Lavinia, why did you come here? You've made a long journey just to come *here.*"

L.K. doesn't protest. For this is true, she sees in retrospect. Her journey began years ago.

"Of your own volition, dear. No one forced you. You've come back here with me."

He will protect her, she thinks. He has said he has forgiven her, he will have mercy on her.

181

Slipping his arm around her shoulders. His heavy arm, L.K.'s slender shoulders. If she can make herself small enough, L.K. thinks.

She is exhausted. Can't keep her eyelids open. What has he given her to drink! She will be one of thousands of butterflies, preserved in formaldehyde! Her ashy-blond hair, like metallic filaments, will be preserved for all to admire.

Together, she and her male companion will drift off to sleep. Whiskey has warmed them. Her hand clutches his. If she tried, she could not hope to close her fingers around his wrist.

The happiest she has been in her posthumous life.

7.

But no: there is no sleep.

Happiness, but happiness is fleeting.

No sleep beyond a few fluttering seconds, and when she wakes suddenly, her eyes fly open to see that Vnn has left her to bring some of his *art supplies* to the sofa.

Over his (unshaven) jaws the artist has affixed a half mask of white gauze, of the sort worn by medical workers at risk from contagion.

On his big-knuckled hands he has managed to force surgical gloves.

Out of a cloudy, quart-size commercial bottle he has poured a virulent-smelling transparent liquid onto a wadded white cloth of the size of a face towel. Frowning as the liquid soaks into the cloth.

Oh, what is it? Ether?

Chloroform.

The whiskey has made her sleepy. The smell of chloroform—harsh, heavy—makes her sleepier still.

Wanting to protest—*But I am innocent! Have mercy.*

Yet—what is most mysterious—L.K. does not really seem so frightened of what is about to happen to her. For perhaps it has already happened and she is only remembering.

Carefully the man in the white mask is speaking to her. Patiently.

His animosity toward her, that has so wounded her, seems to be past.

"Remove your ivory bracelets, dear. And the necklace."

Fumbling to obey him. Her face flushes with chagrin. She would protest—*But I did not buy this ivory jewelry new! It is all secondhand.*

Vnn takes the beautiful bracelets and necklace from her and sets them carefully aside. He has only to glance at her watch, and L.K. slips it off her wrist.

"Very good, dear! Now take this cloth. You will press it against your mouth and nose and hold it there for as long as you can. It may help to shut your eyes. Breathe deeply."

Handing her the wetted cloth, which she takes from him hesitantly.

What has he instructed? Press the cloth against her—mouth, nose?

"You are one of the rare subjects allowed to control her own fate. That is, you will be allowed to 'put yourself to sleep.' It is painless."

Vnn speaks tenderly to her. Despite his disheveled appearance and the winking gold stud in his earlobe, he is a gentleman and will not hurt her.

"You are not to blame for the shallowness of your soul—none of your kind are to blame. You must be extinguished, but it will not be punitive, only just. So, now—you may put yourself to sleep as prescribed."

Rare that a gifted, original, wildly imaginative artist is also a *gentleman*. L.K. is one of the fortunate ones.

"You will be 'immortal'—to a degree. Parts of you will be harvested for a Vnn collage."

L.K. stares at the wadded cloth, virulent-smelling, in her hands. What is she supposed to do with this? Her eyes are badly watering.

"My dear? Try to empty your mind of distracting thoughts . . ."

On a nearby table beside Vnn is a curious object: a box cutter? L.K. has but the vaguest idea of a box cutter but knows that its blade is extremely sharp.

Knows that the box cutter is not preferred by

the artist, for its results are very messy. The box cutter is but a useful alternative if chloroform fails.

But why should chloroform *fail?* It is the humane option.

"Your mind should be emptied, as a clogged, filthy pipe should be emptied. Your mind should be purified of all that is low, petty, debased."

Yes—she is nodding. *Purified* . . .

She has always wished to be *purified.* Yes. That has been a spiritual goal.

Her tongue is oddly swollen in her mouth. Awkwardly she licks her parched lips. So strange the lips feel to her, she might doubt that they are *hers.*

Has the artist has appropriated parts of her face already? Tongue, lips. Pert patrician nose. Eyes.

L.K. asks if Vnn will let her go? Though knowing the answer beforehand, yet she feels that she must ask, for it is expected of her.

". . . I never meant to hurt you."

"You have not hurt *me,* dear."

"Anyone whom I have hurt, in my carelessness—I did not mean to . . ."

"It was another you'd let die, my brother."

"But—I didn't mean to let anyone die! I was frightened, panicked . . ."

L.K. clutches the cloth soaked with chloroform in her hands. She is not certain what Vnn has been telling her.

Feebly trying to rise to her feet. Once on her feet, once strength flows back into her knees, she will be all right, she believes. It is all that she wants now, and nothing more: to be *all right.*

She will surrender all happiness. All meaning in her life. It is the wisdom of the insomniac: once you have traversed a cycle of twenty-four hours of sleeplessness, you understand that all meaning has faded from the world. And so, your greatest hope is simply to be *all right.*

Yet she hears a woman's voice begging. Pleading. No pride. Shame.

Oh, why had she not signaled to the Detroit policemen when the cruiser passed her on the bridge? So easily she might have saved her life, instead of throwing it away negligently, as a princess tossing gold coins into a river.

Wanting has doomed her. And yet, without *wanting,* what has been her life?

"You know that I can't let you go, dear. Even if I wanted to. We have passed that point. And that sort of magnanimous gesture isn't Vnn's style."

Matter-of-factly, solemnly, Vnn speaks. Inviting her to concur as a reasonable woman would in such circumstances. *We are beyond the gravitational field—we cannot retreat.*

L.K. has taken up the wadded cloth in both her hands to steady the trembling. The smell makes her eyes water.

Impulsively she asks if Vnn has been kind to the others.

"Others—?"

"Who have preceded me."

She indicates the mannequins, the canvases and collages. The artist's trophies.

Vnn smiles as if he has been caught in a mild deception. A lover, a husband, who has been unfaithful.

"Yes. I admit it."

Adding, "And now—if your mind is emptied out . . ."

L.K. lifts the wadded cloth to her face. Just to see if she can do it.

Will the chloroform be swift-acting, like ether? Or will she recoil from it?

"Good, dear! Continue."

"I—I can't . . ."

"Of course you can. Try."

"But—"

"Try."

Is she imagining it, or is Vnn becoming less patient?

Draws a deep, shuddering breath. The chloroform is so *sharp,* her senses recoil.

As a girl, she'd learned to dive: on the rim of the pool, bend your knees, position your arms, pointed hands, lower head, push off and down. Deep, deep breaths, for you don't know when you will be breathing again.

A childish stratagem comes to her: she will pretend to breathe the chloroform in deeply and to lose consciousness. The man who has taken her captive will approach her, and when he is close enough, she will flare up in fury and she will fight him. Her teeth will rake his exposed throat, her sharp fingernails will stab his eyes. She is prepared!

But no, she has breathed too deeply. The damp cloth falls from her fingers. She is unable to keep her eyes open. Her hands fall into her lap, her arms have gone limp, her heart is beating less rapidly, her fevered pulse slows. Her head has slumped forward onto her chest, as heavy and empty as crockery. Her brain, which has been a honeycomb of *thinking! thinking!* for a lifetime, is emptying out at last. Her shoulders collapse, she cannot remain upright but falls sidelong onto the sofa, which collapses beneath her, melts away, so that, through an opening in the grimy plank floorboards, she falls, falls . . .

By the time she has come to the end of falling, the terrible *wanting* has ceased.

PAROLE HEARING, CALIFORNIA INSTITUTION FOR WOMEN, CHINO, CA

Why am I requesting parole another time?—because I am penitent.

Because I am remorseful for the wrongs I have inflicted upon the innocent.

Because I am a changed person.

Because I have punished myself every day, every hour, and every minute of my incarceration.

Because the warden will testify on my behalf: I have been a *model prisoner.*

Because the chaplain will testify on my behalf: I have welcomed Jesus Christ into my heart.

Because I have served fifty-one years in prison. Because I have been rejected for parole fifteen times.

Because I am seventy years old, I am no longer nineteen years old.

Because I cannot remember who I was when I was nineteen years old.

Because I regret all that I was commanded to do in August 1969.

Because the person I hurt most at that terrible time was—myself.

• • •

Why am I requesting parole?—because (I believe) I have paid what is called my *debt to society.*

Because I have completed college while in prison. I have a community college degree, Chino Valley Community College.

Because I have taught generations of inmates to read and write.

Because I have assisted the arts and crafts instructors and they have praised me.

(I love the thrill of power, making lesser beings my slaves.)

Because I have goodness in my heart that yearns to be released into the world.

Because I would *make amends.*

Because I am an example to the younger women.

Because I am the oldest woman prisoner in California, and there is shame in this.

Because the other prisoners are all younger than I am, and they pity me.

Because I am not a *threat to society.*

Because I was a *battered woman* and did not realize.

Because all that happened in 1969 happened because of that.

Because it was not fair, and is not fair.

Because the person I hurt most was—myself.

• • •

Why am I requesting parole?—Because Jesus has come into my heart, and He has forgiven me.

Because Jesus understood, it was the Devil who guided my hand to smite the innocent with evil intent.

Because the Devil whispered to us—*Do something witchy!*

Because I had no choice, I had to obey.

Because *he* would have punished me if I did not.

Because *he* would have ceased to love me if I did not.

Because *he* has passed away now and left me with this (swastika) scar on my forehead.

Because, seeing this scar I have borne for fifty-one years, you will judge me harshly.

Because the person *he* hurt most was—me.

Because I was abused by others.

Because I was trusting in my heart, and so I was abused by others.

Because I was abused by *him.*

Because I was weak-willed. Because I was a victim of what the therapist has called *low self-esteem.*

Because I was starving, and *he* gave me nourishment.

Because he asked of me—*Don't you know who I am?*

Because I dissolved into tears before him at such words. Because all my life I had been awaiting such words.

Because the Family welcomed me, at *his* bidding.

Because soon they called me Big Patty. Because they called me Pimply Face. Because they made me crouch down and eat from the dog's dish.

Because they laughed at me.

Because *he* did not protect me from them.

Because I gave my soul to *him*.

Because I am begging understanding and forgiveness from you, on my knees.

Because I am a good person, in my heart.

Because you can see—can't you?—I am a good person, in my heart.

Because it was easy to hypnotize me.

Because it was easy to drug me.

Because I could not say *no*.

Because very feebly I did say *no, no*—but *he* laughed at me and made me serve him on my knees.

Because I was ravenous for love—for *touch*.

Because stabbing the victims, I was stabbing myself.

Because sinking my hands into the wounds of the victims, to mock and defile them, I was mocking and defiling myself.

Because tasting the blood that was "warm and

sticky," I was tasting my own blood that spurted out onto walls, ceilings, carpets.

Because, at my trial, prejudiced jurors found me guilty of "seven counts of homicide," not knowing how I was but *his* instrument.

Because you who sit in judgment of me have no idea of the being I am in my innermost heart.

Because you gaze upon me with pity and contempt, thinking—*Oh she is a monster! She is nothing like* me.

But I am like you. In my heart that is without pity, I am *you.*

Because it is true, certain terrible things were done by my hand, which was but *his hand.*

Because it is true, these were terrible acts and yet joyous, as *he* had ordained.

Because it is true, I showed no mercy to those who begged for their lives on their knees.

On my knees for all of my life, I did not receive mercy, and so I had no mercy to give.

Well, yes—it is true, I stabbed her sixteen times. The beautiful "movie star."

And it is true, each stab was a shriek of pure joy.

And it is true, in a frenzy I stabbed the baby in her belly, eight months, five weeks old. For a mere second it crossed my mind, I could "deliver" this baby by Caesarean, for I had a razor-sharp butcher knife, and if I did this and brought the baby to Charlie . . . But I could not think beyond the moment, I did not know if Charlie would bless me or curse me, and I could not risk it.

For the baby too, that had no name, I showed no mercy. For no mercy had been shown me.

Because for these acts that are so terrible in your eyes, I have repented.

For these acts and others, I have repented.

Because in this prison I am a white woman.

A pearl in a sea of mud. A pearl cast before swine.

Amid the brown- and black-skinned, my skin shines, it is so pure.

He entrusted us with the first battle of Helter Skelter.

He sent us on our mission, to pitch the first battle of the Race War.

He kissed my forehead. *He* told me—*You are beautiful.*

Because I had not known this!—in my soul I believed that I was ugly.

Because at school, in all the schools I had gone to—there were jeering eyes, cruel laughter.

Because, when I was not yet twelve years old, already dark hairs grew thick and coarse on my head and beneath my arms and at the pit of my belly. In that place between my legs that was sin to touch. On my legs that were muscled like a boy's, and on my forearms. Wiry hairs on my naked breasts, ticklish at the nipples.

Yet of my body Charlie declared—*You are beautiful.*

Except: blood, like sludge, oozed between my thighs. A nasty smell lifted from me.

Go away, you disgust me, Charlie said.

Because you are saying—*The poor girl!*—she *was abused, hypnotized.*

Because you are saying—*She wasn't herself.*

Because none of that was true. Because love is a kind of hypnosis, but it was one I chose.

Because Charlie favored the pretty ones, even so.

Because I hated them. Because I had always hated them—beautiful women and girls.

Because it is not fair that some that are sluts, are beautiful like Sharon Tate, and some are ugly like me.

Because when we were done with her, she was not so beautiful.

Because I would not do it again!—I promise.

Because I stuck a fork in a man's belly and laughed at how it dangled from the flab of his belly, but I can scarcely remember.

Because I have been washed clean of these sins through the grace of Jesus.

Because I am a Christian woman, my Savior dwells in my heart.

Because I was not evil, but weak.

Because I was a "criminal" in the eyes of the law but a "victim" in the eyes of God.

195

Because the swastika scar between my eyes calls your eye to it, in judgment. Because you think—*She is disfigured! She bears the sign of Satan, she must not ever be paroled.*

Because the scar is faded now. Because if you did not know what it was, you would not recognize it.

Because I was a *battered woman*—a therapist has told me.

Because my case should be reopened. Because my incarceration should be ended. Because I have *served my time.*

Because sin has faded in my memory.

Because where there was the Devil, there is now Love.

Because in the blood of the dying I wrote on the walls of the fancy house—DEATH TO PIGS HEALTER SKELTER.

Because it was not to be that I would have a baby—so it was fitting, *she* could not have her baby.

Such a big belly! Big white drum-belly! Screaming, like they say a stuck pig screams, and squeals, and tries to crawl away—so you must straddle it, knees gripping her slippery, naked back to wreak the greatest vengeance.

Because she was so beautiful, the sun shone out of her face.

Because she was so beautiful, she did not deserve to live.

All of them, strangers to us—they did not deserve to live.

Do it gruesome—Charlie commanded.

Because that was the address he'd given us on a winding canyon road in the night—*Leave no one alive there.*

Because we did not question. (Why would *we* question?)

Because rage is justice, if you are the meek.

Because it is said—*Blessed are the meek, they shall inherit the earth.*

Because when flames burst inside you, you know that you are redeemed.

Because it is time for my parole, Jesus is commanding you—*Turn my minion loose!*

Because you are fools who think you see a putty-skinned plain old woman in prison clothes humbling herself before you, a harmless old bag with a collapsed face and collapsed breasts to her waist—you have not the eyes to see who I am, as with his laser eyes Charlie saw at once—*You are beautiful.*

Because Charlie perceived in me within a minute of seeing me, I might be a sword of God.

Because I might be a scourge of the enemy.

Because I had wanted to be a nun, but the nuns rejected me.

Because you will all pay, that the nuns rejected *me.*

Because if you release me, I have more justice to seek.

Because you hold the keys to the prison, but one day you will suffer as we suffer, in the flaming pits of Hell.

Because you are trying to find a way to comprehend me. So you can pity me. So you can be superior to me. *She was brainwashed. She was not responsible. She was fed hallucinogens—LSD. She was weak-minded, under the spell of the madman.*

Because you are mistaken. Because you have no idea what is in my heart.

Because beside Charlie, who was our beautiful Christ, you are vermin.

He would grind you beneath his feet.

Because we made her famous—"Sharon Tate."

Because the slut would be forgotten by now if we had not made her famous.

Because I dipped my hands in her hot, pulsing blood. Shoved my hands into her big belly. *Eviscerate*—Charlie commanded.

Because you see?—I am meeting your eyes, I am not looking away.

Because I am not servile to the Board of Parole like others who appear meekly before you.

Because I am a woman of dignity. Because

prison has not broken my spirit, which is suffused with Charlie's love.

Because I can see, you are filled with loathing for me. As I am filled with loathing for you.

Because even in death her eyes were the color of burnt sugar, her skin flawless and so smooth . . . I thought that I would tell Charlie—*I will go back and skin her! Should I go back and skin her!*

Because I was sure that Charlie would laugh and say—*Yes! Go back and skin the slut and return to me wearing her skin, then I will love you above all the others because you are more beautiful than all of them.*

Because this did not happen, and yet it is more real to me than many things that have happened.

As Charlie is more real to me than any of you.

Because we would tear out your throats with our teeth if we could.

Because it is ended now—my (last) parole hearing.

Because I leave you with my curse—DEATH TO PIGS.

INTIMACY

No reason to believe that he wishes you ill. That you are in danger.

No reason to think that as you speak carefully to him, respectfully, smiling your *kind smile,* he is not really listening, but staring at the movements of your mouth with an expression of muted rage.

No reason to believe that he is carrying, inside his loose-fitting clothes, partially zipped parka, khaki work pants with multiple pockets, or in the soiled canvas backpack on his knees, any sort of weapon.

Yet: you are alerted. Vigilant. Even as you instruct yourself *No—of course not. Don't be absurd.*

You are an individual who prides herself on being enlightened. Calm, poised, inclined to compromise and arbitration. *Not* alarmist.

It's the intimacy of the situation that is unnerving.

Intimacy—two individuals, middle-aged (female) professor, (male) student-writer/U.S. Army veteran in his late twenties, strangers to each other, finding themselves sharing a cramped space of approximately two hundred square feet in a basement university office.

Intimacy enhanced by the hour, which is late afternoon of an occluded November weekday, so that by five fifteen p.m. it is dusk outside the scummy half window of the office and the austere old sandstone building known as the Lyman Hall of Languages is near deserted.

Intimacy so stressful to you, your heartbeat has quickened, pinpricks of sweat are breaking out on your upper body beneath your clothes, though the air in the office is cold from the drafty, ill-fitting window.

Yet: no reason to believe that G***n K***f (as he has identified his writing-self on his manuscripts) is hostile to you specifically, still less that he will act upon this hostility, though the prose works of G***n K***f you have seen are steeped in violence, cruelty, sadism, and he has hinted to you, in a previous exchange, not in this office in the basement of Lyman Hall but in the corridor outside your seminar room on the third floor, that he has *done some things, impulsive things of which I am not proud, Pro-fes-sor.*

Pro-fes-sor. Uttered in a low drawl, with a twist of his lips meant to resemble a smile and a belligerent shifting of his gaze to your face.

Sometimes adding, as if he has just thought of it—*Ma'am.*

• • •

Twenty minutes late for the scheduled conference. So that you have been thinking with childlike naïveté—*Maybe he won't come* . . .

Kroff has missed a previous conference with you, in this office. He has missed a recent class. He has hinted of a life of complications, responsibilities—(is Kroff married? Is it possible that Kroff is a husband, a father?)—from which he can't easily detach himself, for the fiction writing workshop in which he is enrolled meets on Thursday afternoons, which conflicts, to a degree, with something else he is doing, or should be doing, which might have something to do with his status as a veteran (VA hospital therapy? rehab?) at an overlapping time.

Why then is Gavin Kroff taking the workshop if it represents a hardship for him?

Answer is, bluntly delivered, bemused pale-blue eyes and twisty smile, *You, Pro-fes-sor.*

Sharp rap of knuckles on the (opened) door of the office.

"Hello! Come in . . ."

Your greeting is friendly, matter-of-fact. Crucial for you to maintain a distance between yourself and the aggressive young man, who has indicated in many ways that he wants nothing more than to collapse the protocol of distance between professor and student, annihilate borders, establish *intimacy.*

Yet Gavin Kroff lingers in the corridor, stooping and staring. Though he has knocked on the door and the door is open, as the door is always open during your office hours and you have greeted him and invited him inside, still he appears hesitant, diffident-seeming. His face, almost attractive at a distance, seen close up is creased, suspicious. As if he were thinking—*Am I too early? Is this the wrong time? Do you really want me?*

"Come in, please. Gavin."

Forcing you to speak louder. Smile harder. Utter his name—*Gavin.*

A name that is strange in your mouth, like a swollen tongue.

It is not an era in academic history when professors address students by their surnames: *Mister, Miss.* In this quasi-democratic era, first names are obligatory.

Assuring the frowning young man that yes, this is the time you'd set for your appointment. He is not early, nor is he (very) late.

Guardedly Gavin enters the office. He is tall, well over six feet, but moves with a slouch, head lowered and shoulders hunched, as if entering a force field that is intent upon repelling him, against which he must be vigilant.

(Because he is a war veteran? Because he

203

has not fully recovered from being in combat? Because it has become second nature to him to distrust and fear his surroundings? Unless it was always Gavin Kroff's nature to behave with such unease and suspicion, even before joining the U.S. Army and being shipped to Afghanistan.)

Muttering what sounds like, "Thanks, Pro-fes-sor. *Ma'am.*"

If this is mockery, you don't acknowledge it. Truly you are feeling hopeful, optimistic about this conference.

Conference is the preferred term. Students drop by an office, make an appointment with a professor for a *conference*. Pointedly, Gavin Kroff requested a conference with you this afternoon, following an awkward exchange with him in class the previous week.

A faint, hairline pulse of a migraine has begun somewhere in the cerebellum of your brain, triggered by the ugly fluorescent lighting you'd been obliged to switch on a few minutes earlier. Otherwise you and Gavin Kroff would be conferring in a shadowy office in the sepulchral quiet of a university building at dusk.

Clutching his soiled backpack (which appears to contain something heavy), Kroff comes to sit in the chair beside your desk. He sighs, as if releasing a burden. His uneven, discolored teeth are bared in an inscrutable smile.

So suddenly, so close—only a few inches from

you across the corner of the desk. Even as you shrink from seeing, you cannot help but see the young man's blotched skin, stiff, dust-colored hair receding at his temples, unshaven jaws, and brash, tawny eyes, like cracked glass.

To the left of his mouth, a thick white worm of a scar. Hard not to stare at this scar, which seems to be staring back at you.

In one of Kroff's prose pieces a child is mutilated and maimed by an elaborate piece of machinery into which he is pushed by an older sibling; especially, his face is mutilated. Though you know that you have no right to assume an autobiographical intent, you have assumed that this is more or less how Kroff's face came to be scarred.

Unless it is a scar from a war injury.

In which case, you wonder if Gavin Kroff is scarred elsewhere, inside his clothes.

And what of the scars hidden from sight?— these are the ugliest.

If the basement office were larger, the aluminum desk would be positioned differently: you would be seated behind it and students would be seated in front of it. A discreet distance of several feet between you. But the office isn't large, two bulky desks take up most of the space. Since you are a visiting professor, however *distinguished* the title a transient hire, your assigned desk is nearer the door; your students are obliged to sit in a chair perpendicular to the desk, facing you at a slant.

The full-time faculty member who shares the office, whom you have yet to meet, has the desk at the rear, a preferred space beside the drafty window. This individual has filled a bookcase with books relating to the Renaissance and stacks of printed university material, most of which is several years old. On a dusty windowsill is a bust of William Shakespeare of the sort one might buy at a cheap souvenir shop at Stratford-upon-Avon, of the size of a small cat, and on one of the walls a faded poster gaily advertising *Shakespeare in Love*.

Your workplace, you think. A seminar room on the third floor of the building and this bleak subterranean office to which you've been assigned.

Of course, you do no *work* in this inhospitable *workplace*. It is used for student conferences solely.

So far this semester, few of these. Except for Gavin Kroff, who seems determined to extract from his relationship with the university, and with you, as much as possible.

If it were daytime and not dusk! You would not be so uneasy. If Lyman Hall were not so quiet . . .

During the day the old building quivers with life, as a corpse may quiver with electric currents coursing through it: thunderous young feet on wooden stairs that tremble beneath so much youthful energy, weight. Upraised voices, laughter. At such times the bleak anonymity of the human race is muffled, the vanity of human wishes signaled here by the cheap, campy bust of Shakespeare and the faded poster kept at a distance.

As you wait patiently—(for what choice have you?—you are captive here)—Kroff has been rummaging in his backpack. His head is lowered, he is breathing noisily through his mouth. A faint sheen of perspiration on his blemished forehead.

You feel a thrill of apprehension—an absurd apprehension, you are sure: that in the backpack, or on Kroff's person, he is carrying a weapon.

Gun, knife. His knobby hands would be adept with both.

In one of his impressionistic prose pieces, a three-foot length of wire.

And what is the purpose of the length of wire?—you'd asked him.

Kroff had shrugged, laughed. A pleasurable flush came into his face, and his eyes filled with moisture.

What could possibly be the purpose of a length of wire, Pro-fes-sor?

Isn't the point of literature to inspire readers to imagine?

(This exchange had taken place in a previous conference, weeks before.)

Kroff will not intimidate you, you think. No.

Politely, with a *kind smile,* you ask the young writer what you can do for him—a formal question that seems to trouble him, as if it were a riddle.

"Thanks, *Pro-fes-sor!* But I think you know."

". . . think I *know?*"

This is a surprise. This is a thinly veiled threat. (Is it?) (Yet Kroff continues to smile at you.) In his perpendicular position at the desk, Kroff manages to twist his neck even further than necessary, as if indeed he were caught in some sort of crippling machinery. Still he is panting, breathing through his mouth. You wonder if he is medicated: if the medications have calmed him or heightened his intensity. Could he be on steroids? Cortisone? His skin looks heated, as it has looked in the seminar when his work is being (carefully, discreetly) critiqued by the other young writers and—eventually, when the others have spoken— by you. Boldly Kroff fixes you with his tawny cracked-glass stare, like the stare of a glass-eyed doll.

Brazen familiarity in the gesture, which you can only try to ignore; you can only tell yourself that Kroff isn't fully conscious of the way he looks, the manic fixedness of his stare.

Intimacy in the way he regards you.

Intimacy you are determined not to acknowledge.

Intimacy—knowing too much about the other while knowing nothing essential.

Indeed, Kroff had entered the office in the sidelong manner in which he enters the seminar room, as if he were looking in two directions at once, like a creature with eyes on either side of its head; you have wondered if perhaps he has some sort of neurological impairment, though it could also be just ordinary clumsiness, a kind of obstinacy. *Here I am! Take me or leave me.*

The sort of individual, prevalent (you recall) in high school, usually male, whose awkwardness spills over from him and onto others in his vicinity, as if he were carrying a bowl of something viscous that spills onto others' feet—or rather, for Kroff inspires in you such aggressive metaphors, he is like one who sneezes without troubling to cover his mouth and nose, sending an explosion of bacteria out into the air, infecting all within range.

A subsequent impression is that Kroff's very awkwardness is calculated, as he usually manages to enter the seminar room to arrive after the other (fourteen) students have taken seats around the long, oval table, and so the only available seat is the one nearest the professor, at the head of the table. (By some sort of consensus, students will not take seats close to a professor if they can avoid it. To come too close to the figure of authority is to violate a taboo—if but a minor one.)

Yet in his way that might seem, to the neutral observer, blundering and wayward, Kroff maneuvers to sit beside you for the three-hour workshop. Skidding a chair along the floor, beside your chair. (But not too close. Even Kroff doesn't dare intrude too obviously into the professor's private space.)

Three hours! In your worst imaginings, it's like elementary school—a jeering kid beside the teacher and just slightly behind her, making faces to provoke mirth in other students.

But Kroff isn't so crude. Nor does Kroff think much of his fellow students.

Nor would the other students—all of them quite serious writers, one or two genuinely gifted (you wish to think)—appreciate Kroff's misbehaving in this way.

More likely, he sits beside you because he wishes to share the authority you represent in the seminar room. Gazing toward you, the others must take note of *him*.

And though you are reluctant to acknowledge it, Kroff seems somewhat fixed upon you . . .

See? I sit beside you. Could reach out to touch you—your wrist, arm. Hair. Cheek.

And so Kroff sits beside you at close quarters, gazing, staring, blinking and staring at the side of your face for three hours each Thursday afternoon, as the year wanes, the sky darkens ever earlier, and it is dusk by the time the workshop disbands. Often, if you are speaking, he nods in agreement with your words, sometimes vehemently. Though occasionally (you surmise: you don't turn to look at him if you can help it) he shakes his head in disagreement. He may even mutter to himself and grimace, shift restlessly in his seat, take fevered notes as if your every remark is priceless, or, pointedly, cease taking notes. He may even lapse into a trance of seeming stupefaction, open-eyed, mouth slack. (Not boredom, he has explained. No! Sleep deprivation.)

While his work is being discussed, Kroff is very still. Even his restless legs become stiff. His gesture toward disguising himself—identifying the author of the manuscript as G***n K***f—is meant to be a joke. (Maybe.) (But is it funny? No one has smiled.) Once, you glanced sidelong at him as one of the student-writers was speaking in an earnest, pained way, trying to say *something nice, encouraging, and inoffensive,* and you saw that Kroff's face was taut with fury. You would swear you'd heard his back molars grind. The most intimate of sounds, you might hear a lover grinding his teeth in the night, his head on the pillow beside yours as you lie awake unable to sleep.

Unbidden the thought came to you—*He would like to tear out all our throats.*

It is an old (urban) university, by American standards. On the bank of a river that has become mythic—"majestic"—in the American imagination.

Of land-grant, public universities it is not the largest, but it is one of the most prestigious, or has been until recently. Now a Republican governor and a Republican legislature have cut the state education budget by millions of dollars, boasting of "holding professors' feet to the fire"—a metaphor the media finds amusing.

In the (approximate) middle of your life, you find yourself a visiting professor here for the fall term. Your title is Visiting Distinguished Professor in the Humanities.

Because you are new here, and because there are few creative writing instructors on the faculty, more than one hundred students applied for your Advanced Fiction Workshop, for a mere fifteen places.

Very carefully, you have read through these applications and their attached fiction samples. You've read, reread. Coolly professional, you ignored pleas by students claiming desperation if they were rejected, for it was their senior year, for instance, or they were longtime admirers of your work; you hesitated before accepting an older,

General Studies student named Gavin Kroff, whose writing sample verged upon the obscure, for you'd seen that he had identified himself as an army veteran, and you wanted to give him, as you might have said if queried, the *benefit of the doubt.*

And so now you may tell yourself—*You brought this on yourself. Indulging in a cliché. No one else to blame!*

Says Kroff in a quavering voice, he'd like to speak frankly.

So naturally you concur. Of course.

"What I think is—in our seminar—*Pro-fessor*—I am not being treated justly by the other writers. And by you."

To this blunt charge you can think of no reply. *Not justly!* The very words are unexpected.

It is true, you have withheld superlatives from Kroff. On principle you don't believe in lavishing writing students with excessive praise, though (you assume) it is not very difficult for them to determine whose work you think is superior; usually, it is the work others in the class believe to be superior. In Kroff's case, you are not condemning, for you never *condemn;* but neither do you praise his work. Your commentary is terse, diplomatic. You dwell on sentences, paragraphs. If there is praise, it is for a certain "originality" of language Kroff exhibits.

But now Kroff is incensed. Saying he'd been goddamned grateful to be accepted into the seminar with a *world-famous professor.* It meant so much to him he'd (almost) gotten down on his knees and given thanks—as if you'd reached out and touched his bare, beating heart.

Now he feels differently. He's disappointed—disillusioned. Since the first piece of writing he'd given to the seminar for criticism there's been a kind of . . . he'd call it a kind of prejudice—"Like *racism,* almost."

Racism?

"Like, I am a white man—a kind of minority right now in this country . . ."

Quietly you try to point out that in the workshop there is a majority of "white" students. Out of fifteen students, at least eleven.

But Kroff dismisses this with a wave of his hand. Frowning severely.

"Like, a 'white' woman takes their side, you can count on that. All of you ganging up against me."

Takes their side? Whose?

You tell Gavin that you don't quite understand what he is saying. But—"I'm sorry . . ."

"Don't tell me *you are sorry!* That is not enough."

"But—I'm not sure that I know what . . ."

"Then listen! Listen to what I am saying. Don't interrupt me *please, Pro-fes-sor.*"

Kroff's voice is quavering with—is it resentment? Rage? The white worm beside his mouth is writhing.

Very still, you sit at your desk, hoping the fury will pass.

If you are calm, this incensed individual will be calm. If you breathe normally, this individual will breathe normally. You tell yourself.

(Quickly your mind calculates: Could you get to the door before Kroff seizes you? No.)

(Is there anyone in the nearest offices? Anyone in subterranean Lyman Hall at five fifty-five p.m.?)

Hot-eyed Kroff relents. Seeing (possibly) your look of alarm, fright.

Saying, "Okay it could be unconscious. It's maybe not conscious. The ignorant, bigoted things they say about my writing, narrow-minded and banal, they'd say of the prose poetry of Rimbaud or Rilke. They'd say of William Burroughs. Wittgenstein. Because they are not themselves writers—artists. Except for three or four of them, they are all younger than me, and for a long time I was the one who was *young*."

Kroff makes a snuffling sound, indignant. "So I'm saying, what they say of my writing is maybe not fully conscious. Not knowing what real writing *is*."

In a raw, aggrieved voice Kroff proceeds to list examples of *bigoted criticism* leveled against his work in the class. He has recalled every remark, however hesitant or innocuous. No one has even tried to understand what he is doing, he claims. No one has been *sympathetic.*

"They think they're better than me—'cause I enlisted in the army. 'Cause I served my country and got shot up and that's for suckers in the U.S. now."

Quickly you protest. Try to protest. That is not—true . . .

Kroff shoves manuscripts across the desk for you to examine. The pages are crumpled and torn, as if they've been retrieved from the trash.

(Hardly any need for you to reexamine these prose pieces. You've read them more than once, more than twice, annotating them for Kroff's benefit, and that is enough.)

Prose poetry, he calls it. Not fiction, not poetry. Not real-life, not invented.

Difficult to determine if Kroff is genuinely incensed or coldly calculating. In the midst of a tirade he seems to draw back to observe how his words, his heated manner, are affecting you.

Pro-fes-sor. Ma'am.

Is he furious with you, does he feel betrayed by you? Is it—(though you are certain *it is not*)—some sort of sexual animosity? Or does Kroff simply hope to manipulate you?

Does he want something from you?—or does he want nothing at all?

(Yes, you have seen Kroff, or someone who closely resembles him, in Lyman Hall after class has ended. You have seen him at a little distance in the corridors, slyly observing you. Perhaps he hides in a men's lavatory on the third floor, and after you start downstairs, he descends behind you in no haste, noiselessly. You have seen: Kroff avoids others in the workshop after class, unless it is that the others in the workshop avoid him. Perhaps he dares to follow you into the basement of Lyman Hall, to this very office. And then perhaps he dares to follow you out of the building and to the parking lot, where lights glimmer at the tops of tall poles . . .)

(Perhaps all these sightings, if that is what they are, are but coincidences. Perhaps there is nothing to your concern, it is but the concern of a woman who is alone in a world not so very hospitable to a woman alone, as if *aloneness* were a brazen and unwomanly choice. You will not inquire, for it is not your way to be an alarmist.)

(Also, you believe that Kroff is enthralled with you. Despite his rudeness, arrogance. The fact that a work of fiction by you is included in a popular anthology of American literature you are using in the course—*very impressive!* Not that Kroff has read anything you've written or that he cares enough to consider the editorial criticism you've offered him attached to each of his compositions, but rather that he reveres the title *Visiting Distinguished Professor in the Humanities* and would hope that some of its luster might rub off on him, as your most talented and audacious student.)

In the workshop, Kroff is often isolated, silent. His height, his manner, his status as an Afghanistan War veteran, to which he has only peripherally alluded in his prose poems, has made the other students wary of him, respectful and guarded. If he were friendly toward them, they would melt, and exude friendliness toward him; they would ignore, or try to ignore, the nature of his writing, so different from their own. But unlike them and unlike their professor, Kroff does not readily *smile.*

When one of our kind does not *smile,* we are disoriented. We don't know where to look. We feel threatened.

In the workshop, Kroff rarely comments on others' work. His responses are lofty shrugs, indifference—*Okay. Not bad.*

Indeed, Kroll is one of the older students in the workshop and (so far as you know) the only ex-military service member; he is the only student not enrolled in the college of liberal arts, but rather in a heterogeneous division called General Studies, where admissions are open to state residents regardless of grades. You assume that as a war veteran, Kroff pays no tuition and may even have a scholarship.

Occasionally, for some inexplicable reason, Kroff will heave himself to his feet during class, mutter an inaudible excuse, seize his backpack, and stalk out of the seminar room—(for he would never leave the bulky backpack unattended; he appears to guard it with his life); he may be absent for as long as forty minutes, but he eventually returns, with another inaudible excuse, and reclaims his seat in the skidding chair. You are likely to think—*He is barely holding himself together.* And you think—*Post-traumatic stress disorder.*

Not that you would utter this phrase to Gavin Kroff, who sneers at what he calls *tired old clichés.*

(But is not *tired old cliché* a *cliché* itself, the more *clichéd* for being *tired* and *old?*)

At the first workshop meeting it was clear that Kroff was a serious writer, for unlike the others, he'd brought with him a swath of material that, he said, he carried around with him everywhere and never let *out of his sight.*

He slept with it, in its soiled and dog-eared folders. There had to be computer files of Kroff's work, for he handed in his assignments via email as the others did, yet to hear him speak of his *modus operandi* (his word), he could not trust the electronic world, he could only trust the world of *hard copy.*

Saying, "If there's a power outage worldwide,

some folks will be devastated, wiped clean. Others will have planned ahead, like squirrels burying their food. It will be *survival of the fittest*. I plan to be in that category—*fittest*."

Kroff seems never to be satisfied with the work he hands in, yet he is not receptive to criticism. From you, he will accept some editorial suggestions with grudging thanks; when others make suggestions, he becomes stony-faced, resentful. *Promising*—others have said, cautiously. *Strong material, hard to understand, "controversial"*—they have said uneasily, searching for the right words.

No one has said to Kroff what all of us are thinking—*Cruel, awful, obscene. Unreadable. No more!*

It's a *memoir* he has been assembling, Kroff says. But it is simultaneously fiction—his theme is the incursion of fiction into real life, and the incursion of real life into fiction. "When you are a soldier, there is half of you that is your old, *real self*—but there is half of you that is some other, *stranger self*." When the credibility of his prose has been questioned, Kroff says in triumph—*Sorry! It happened just like that*. Or he says in triumph—*Sorry!—it's fiction, see? Invented.*

Now he insists upon reading aloud from his most recent prose work, material taken up the previous week in the workshop. You are dismayed, near desperate. This is one of his least comprehensible pieces, breathlessly cascading stream-of-consciousness fantasy that appears to be evoking the futile struggle of an individual (child?) who is being strangled while at the same time he is being sexually assaulted(?). (None of this is definitive, for Kroff aligns himself with Rilke and Rimbaud and will not be *tied down to banal concrete fact.*) Quietly, stoically, you sit at the desk with your hands clasped tightly together; your head is slightly bowed to deflect the imminent migraine that radiates from the fluorescent tubing and to suggest the gravity with which you are listening to Kroff's agitated voice. Your facial expression doesn't yet show the pain you are trying not to feel—it is one of teacherly solicitude, attention. There comes, like a tic, the *kind smile.*

In truth, you are furious with him. You are frightened. You are hoping to stave off the migraine attack until you are alone. (The last thing you want is Gavin Kroff's pity, or even his sympathy. You are in dread of fainting, being dependent upon Kroff picking you up from the grimy floor.) It's as if he has given you a rude push with the flat of his hand, not hard, but hard enough to stun, baffle.

Kroff's major subject seems to be the protracted abuse of a child. There has been whipping with a leather belt, and there has been binding with wire, and there has been the elaborate machine.

(Sometimes the mechanism appears to be an escalator, with gears exposed, into which a child is pushed.) Sometimes it seems that Gavin Kroff is the abused child, and sometimes, more horribly, it seems that a younger brother of Kroff's is the abused child and that the abuse is not *past tense* but *present, ongoing.*

This evening in your office Kroff reads beyond the section with which you are familiar, which was taken up in a recent class and had not elicited much commentary from the other students. For what is there to say about a child being tortured, in such obscure "poetic" prose? No one can doubt the seriousness of the writing or the commitment to his subject of the writer. But no one knows how to respond except in terms already aired in the workshop—*Hard to understand, couldn't follow all the sentences, had trouble figuring out what was going on and who was who . . .*

The new material, which Kroff reads with breathless relish, is even more graphic and painful than usual: a depiction of a garroting, at poetic length, as if Sade, William Burroughs, and Jean Genet had collaborated. In the voice of the eight-year-old victim there is recounted a ghastly torture scene, strangulation by garroting. Each time the boy (Kroff?) loses consciousness, the strangler (Kroff?) releases the pressure of the garrot to allow him to regain consciousness; when the boy has regained consciousness, the strangler again exerts pressure . . . On and on this goes, in the most excruciating "poetic" language, so that after a time it isn't clear if there is an (actual) child being tortured or if the prose piece is sheer fantasy. Or (as Kroff has himself suggested) is it an exploration of *simile?*

It is pointless to inquire of Kroff if the material is meant to be interpreted as "real"—or "surreal"—for when he is asked this question, he is likely to say, with a scornful laugh, in reference to one of his idols (Wittgenstein, Derrida, Bernhard), that he has created a pseudonymous self—*G***n K***f*—in order to create a *text,* and that a *text* has no ontological existence apart from letters, words, sentences displayed on a page.

(But she feels so sorry for the little boy!— Caitlin, one of the young women in the workshop, has exclaimed. What Kroff has written might be merely a *text,* but it has the power to terrify her and to bring tears to her eyes.)

Of course, all this is true enough. As a writer, a creator of *texts,* you can't disagree. Kroff has a naturally analytical mind, it seems, along with a naturally perverse, sadistic, and masochistic imagination, and all that he claims is plausible enough, as his use of profanities, obscenities, and racially tinged insults in his prose is merely *textual.* His ecstatic flights of prose are *texts* primarily, assemblages of words. That the words are often impenetrable, and the material often discomforting, is also true, but perhaps not the primary issue.

How to "criticize" such a writer? If he wished, Kroff could (probably) write as clearly and engagingly as others in the class, on other, less upsetting subjects; but he seems to have no interest in replicating reality, and it has been a cause for wonderment in the workshop (expressed not to Kroff himself, but to you, by other students) that he has so little interest in writing about the army, his fellow soldiers, Afghanistan. Perversely, his prose is set nowhere recognizable, like the prose of Edgar Allan Poe, and his "characters" scarcely exist except as vehicles for impressionistic descriptions of mental states. All is (maddeningly, exhaustively) interior and introverted, lacking psychological depth and dialogue: there are screams, groans, sighs, and utterances in Kroff's prose, but no conversations. No discernible plots or stories in his prose, only dire existential situations.

Time seems never to pass in Kroff's writing, except as it is measured in the torture of a body or the fleeting emotions of a torturer. Indeed, in his typical work *time is flattened, stopped.* The worst has already happened: both child and torturer have ceased to exist while at the same time they are just about to begin their encounter.

The child is always eight years old. The torturer is of no fixed age, but from internal evidence seems to be in his late twenties and has been discharged from the U.S. Army after serving two deployments to Afghanistan.

When Kroff first presented his work to his fellow students, it was clear that they were shocked, discomforted. One of the young women writers excused herself and left the room, and returned an hour later, when it was safe to assume that discussion of Kroff's work was over. (No one in the workshop has complained to you about Kroff's writing, and so far as you know, they have not complained to your department chair or to the dean. Perhaps, you think, they are sympathetic with you as a woman professor, a visitor at the university.)

Yet you believe you can discern in the other students a measure of admiration for Kroff for having created so obsessive a counterworld. His prose is like no one else's—like a text that has been translated from another language. Words seem inadequate, the structures of sentences as finicky as a spider's web, requiring many commas, semicolons, and colons in the construction of a single paragraph. The prose is *exhausting,* like running up an escalator whose steps are moving down. (To borrow one of Kroff's tropes.) It is possible to make progress in such running, but it is not an easy progress, and as soon as you cease running, you are rapidly descending.

You have given much thought to Gavin Kroff, far more thought than you've given to any other student of yours through your teaching career of twelve intermittent years. You resent him for this reason, and you are not likely to forget him. He is not naïve, you think, but he is primitive. His brain is a sort of machine that has been misprogrammed. His insistence that readers should interpret his work as merely textual, and not "real," is maddening to you, though as a writing instructor, you are not sure to what degree you have the right, still less the obligation, to refute him.

"Ma'am?"

Kroff is looking at you expectantly. He has asked you a question or raised a query, you must respond.

"So you are saying, Gavin, that the subject of your work is—*simile?*"

"No. The *mode* of my work is *simile.*"

Looking at you with an air of disdain, disgust. As if (he knows) you are only pretending to be stupid.

"This disquisition on the torture of a child is—what? An examination of—"

(You are speaking without irony. The threat of migraine vanishes all irony.)

"—of *perception.*"

Kroff is smiling angrily at you. Or rather, his mouth is twisted in a grimace of a smile.

Kroff has become very warm and has unzipped his parka. You feel a thrill of dread. There wafts to your unwilling nostrils the thick, coarse smell of a male body, clothes not recently washed.

Intimacy—the smell of another.

Intimacy—all but unbearable when it is unwanted.

". . . like, scenes for a *memoir.* From real life I am drawing material, like van Gogh looking at a landscape and painting not what his eyes see, which is what any ordinary person's eyes might see, but what his van Gogh brain sees."

To this you have no immediate reply. It's a telling phrase—*van Gogh brain.*

(Does Kroff align himself with van Gogh? With genius? Or with the madness of genius, in van Gogh's case.)

"Look, *Pro-fes-sor*—I can accept that others in the class who are basically ignorant don't 'get' what I am doing—but you, *Pro-fes-sor*—*ma'am*—you should. *You most of all.*"

You resist the impulse to apologize. You have nothing to apologize for.

Telling Kroff that you will have to be leaving, soon . . . Glancing at your watch, signaling to him—*Please! Please leave.*

Yearning to be free of him. This terrible intimacy.

So that you can rush to a women's room nearby,

cup water in the palm of your hand, swallow two powerful migraine pills. Hurry!

"Okay, *Pro-fes-sor.* Guess I should leave . . ."

Roughly Kroff thrusts his manuscripts back into the backpack.

Slowly then, he rises. Now he is looming over you.

That smell of his body again. That strange grimace of a smile.

You are trembling. Not smiling, not even that weak, kind smile. Only just waiting for him to leave.

Please please please please. Leave me.

And then Kroff says, as if he has just thought of it, "What I'm thinking, actually, is—I might drop the course."

To this you have no reply. Your natural instinct is to protest—*No, but why?* But you say nothing.

"Yeh. That's what I'm thinking. Why I came to see you, actually, *Pro-fes-sor.*"

Looming over you. Knowing that he is intimidating you, threatening you, for how can he not know?—and you are on your feet also, desperate, though trying to remain calm.

"Whatever you decide, Gavin, that is—that is up to you to decide . . . But now I have to leave. I'm afraid that . . ."

Gavin. That name. Weakly your voice trails off.

"That's what you advise? That I drop the course? But I won't get the tuition back—will I?

228

It's too late. Too late to drop. I've been treated like shit. You can't just—civilians *can't*—treat us like shit."

Numbly you tell the aroused Kroff that you are very sorry. Perhaps you could intervene on his behalf, with the dean—

Kroff interrupts: "You told us on the first day of the workshop that we should try to write 'memorable work'—right? So that is what I have done, and nobody else has done—yet you are trying to tell me, I think you are trying to tell me, that my work is not—*memorable*."

"Well, no—I didn't say that, Gavin. I wouldn't say that. Your work is—it is—it is *memorable*. Yes."

"So—what's wrong, then? You don't—" (pausing, unable to blurt out the words of hurt, anguish: *You don't praise me*) "—'get it'—I guess?"

"Maybe I don't, Gavin. I've tried . . ."

"You have *not tried*. Did you think what I wrote about my brother was *real?*—or *wasn't real?*"

No idea what to tell him. This angry, incensed young man. (Had he killed in Afghanistan? Was that his secret, he has been a killer and can't bear it?) Wondering if there might be someone—anyone—in the corridor outside this office who might hear you if you called for help.

"He isn't eight years old. Not now. He's older, he didn't *die*. I've got him trained. If I raise my fist, he pisses himself, he's that scared. When he was a kid, I told him he'd never become courageous if he didn't stand up to me, but he never did, he can't. A beautiful baby, they called him. But no longer."

Kroff is on his feet, grinning. He can see that you're distressed by what he has said, which is either a revelation or a confession, unless it is a further obfuscation.

"His name is Luke. He's what you call learning disabled. He loves me, he's forgiven me everything. It's like a joke—I'm God to him."

Kroff pauses, breathing audibly. "Also, know what, *ma'am?*—I'm his guardian. Just nine years between us, but I'm his *guardian,* he is in my *control.*"

With a grunt Kroff slips on the backpack. Clearly he is enjoying your distress. "Did you think I was writing about myself, *Pro-fes-sor?* Me and my brother? Guess it's pretty convincing if you and the rest of those assholes believed it."

Waiting for him to leave. Calmly gazing at him, trying not to surrender to the pain gathering behind your eyes.

"Y'know, I don't think I will be returning to the 'workshop.' Fucking waste of time. Imagine Rimbaud in a workshop—Nietzsche! Fucking funny."

At the doorway Kroff lingers, as if he expects you to call him back.

". . . disappointment. Waste of time. *You've* been a disappointment. Damned glad I didn't run out and buy some shitty book of yours, *ma'am*. You and those assholes."

Waiting for him to leave. Waiting for this ordeal to be over.

Almost you are counting the seconds until he will have left.

Thinking, with a thrill of fear—*He still has time. Whatever he has in the backpack, he can take out to use against you.*

"Fucking *cunt*. Like all of them."

Kroff has stepped out of the office, but he pauses outside the door. You can hear him panting. You hold your breath, praying he will not suddenly turn back.

But after a moment Kroff walks away . . . You stand very still, listening beyond the pounding of your heart to him walking away.

It's a trick. He isn't gone. He is waiting.

In case he is listening, you take out your cell phone, pretend to make a call. In a loud, bright voice saying, "I'm leaving now, I've been delayed. No—fine. I should be home in twenty minutes . . ."

Hesitantly you approach the doorway. Peer out into the hall, which is dimly lighted. Your eyesight seems blurred, you can't see clearly. But thank God, no sign of Kroff.

And so you gather your things with shaky

231

hands, switch off the overhead light. Still, your heart is beating painfully.

Before you leave, you cast your eyes over the bleak, subterranean room. Two aluminum desks, books crammed into a bookcase, a faded poster for *Shakespeare in Love*. You will never meet the individual with whom you share this melancholy workplace.

A discomforting odor here of moldering old books, a young man's heated skin, your own animal panic. You will never return, you think. If you have office hours, you will schedule them for the seminar room, immediately following the workshop.

Shut the door, which locks automatically. Make your way to the women's restroom. Inside, trash containers are overflowing. There is a smell of drains. Timidly you cup your hand to a faucet, swallow two migraine pills. Ecstatic pain has already begun to blossom behind your eyes.

Soul sickness. The migraine deep inside the brain.

One day you will discover that Kroff is not a veteran. You will make inquiries, for he will have (soon) imprinted his fury deep upon your soul. Where no one else has entered, in that (secret) place of migraine pain, yet Kroff will (soon) enter. You will learn that he is thirty-two years old. You will learn that he did not serve two deployments in Afghanistan; he did not see combat anywhere. You will learn that twelve days after arriving at basic training in Columbia, South Carolina, Gavin Kroff was discharged for "medical reasons" and shipped back home to Minnesota.

But now: when you dare to leave the restroom, you hear footsteps on a stairway and recoil in fear, absurd fear (you are thinking), for it's only a young woman, a student, who takes no notice of you.

And voices elsewhere, for Lyman Hall is not entirely deserted: evening classes are scheduled for seven o'clock.

Not alone. Not at risk. You chide yourself.

The dilemma that is strictly a female dilemma: to be fearful, cautious, cunning, shrewd, and protective of yourself, if (sometimes) overprotective; or to behave as (you suppose) a man would do, not so much fearless as not requiring fear.

Yet, on the way to the parking lot, you are walking quickly. You are not afraid, yet—you are walking quickly.

In haste, you've left your coat unbuttoned. You are bareheaded, your eyes are wet with tears. You fight the childish instinct to run. For where would you *run to?*—your car is some distance away, you need to have your car key in your hand but don't want to take time to pause, to rummage through your bag to find it . . .

And there on the path, as if out of nowhere, the tall figure waiting for you.

"*Ma'am*—hi! I'll walk you to your car. I was thinking it might not be safe for you around here, a woman alone like you are."

THE FLAGELLANT

Not guilty, he'd pleaded. For it was so. *Not guilty* in his soul.

In fact at the pretrial hearing he'd stood mute. His (young, inexperienced) lawyer had entered the plea for him in a sharp voice, like knives rattling in a drawer—*My client pleads not guilty, Your Honor.*

Kiss my ass, Your Honor—he'd have liked to say.

Later, the plea was changed to *guilty.* His lawyer explained the deal, he'd shrugged okay.

Not that he was guilty in his own eyes, for he knew what had transpired, as no one else did. But Jesus knew his heart and knew that as a man and a father, he'd been shamed.

At the *crossing-over time,* when daylight ends and dusk begins, they approach their Daddy and dare to touch his arm.

He shudders, the child-fingers hot coals against bare skin.

Hides his face from their terrible eyes. On their small shoulders angel's wings have sprouted, sickle-shaped, and the feathers of these wings are coarse and of the hue of metal.

Holy Saturday is the day of penitence. Self-

235

discipline is the strategy. He'd promised himself. On his knees he begins his discipline: rod, bare skin.

(Can't see the welts on his back. Awkwardly twists his arm behind his back, tries to feel where the rod has struck. Fingering the shallow wounds. Feeling the blood. Fingers slick with blood.)

(Not so much pain. Numbness. He's disappointed. It has been like this—almost a year. His tongue has become swollen and numb, his heart is shrunken like a wizened prune. What is left of his soul hangs in filthy strips, like a torn towel.)

Lifer. He has become a *lifer.*

But *lifer* does not mean *life.* He has learned.

Shaping the word to himself. *Lifer!*

—twenty-five years to life. Which meant—(it has been explained to him more than once)—not that he was sentenced to life in prison, but rather, depending upon his record in the prison, that he might be paroled after serving just twenty-five years.

As incomprehensible to him as twenty-five hundred years might be. For he could think only in terms of days, weeks. Enough effort to get through a single day, and through a single night.

But it was told to him, *good behavior* might result in *early parole.*

Though (it was also told to him) it is not likely that a *lifer* would be paroled after his first several appeals to the parole board.

Where would he go, anyway? Back home, they know him, and he couldn't bear their knowledge of him, their eyes of disgust and dismay. Anywhere else, no one would know him, he would be lost.

Even his family. His. And hers, scattered through Beechum County.

Who you went to high school with follows you through your life. You need them, and they need you. Even if you are shamed in their eyes. It is *you*.

Problem was, remorse.

Judge's eyes on him. Courtroom hushed. Waiting.

What the young lawyer tried to explain to him before sentencing—*If you show remorse, Earle. If you seem to regret what you have done . . .*

But he had not done anything!—had not made any decision.

She had been the one. Yet *she* remained untouched.

Weeks in his (freezing, stinking) cell in men's detention. Segregated unit.

Glancing up, nervous as a cat, hearing someone approach. Or believed he was hearing someone approach. Thought came to him like

237

heat lightning in the sky—*They are coming to let me out. It was a mistake, no one was hurt.*

Or, thought came to him that he was in the other prison now. State prison. On death row. And when they came for him, it would be to inject liquid fire into his veins.

You know that you are shit. Ashes to ashes, dust to dust. That's you.

No one came. No one let him out, and no one came to execute him.

He didn't lack remorse, but he didn't exude a remorseful air.

A man doesn't cringe. A man doesn't get down on his knees. A man doesn't *crawl.*

His statement for the judge he'd written carefully on a sheet of white paper provided him by his lawyer.

I am sorry for my roll in what became of my children Lucas & Ester. I am sorry that I was temted to anger against the woman who is ther mother for it was this anger she has caused that drove me to that place. I am sorry for that, the woman was ever BORN.

Pissed him that the smart-ass lawyer wanted to correct his spelling. *Roll* was meant to be *role. Ester* was meant to be *Esther.*

The rest of his statement, the lawyer would not accept and refused to pass on to the judge. As if he had the right.

Took back the paper and crumpled it in his hand. Fuck this!

Anything they could do to you to break you down, humiliate you, they would. Orange jumpsuit like a clown. Leg shackles like some animal. Sneering at you, so ignorant you don't know how to spell your own daughter's name.

Sure, he feels remorse. Wishing to hell he could feel remorse for a whole lot more he'd like to have done when he'd had his freedom. Before he was stopped.

Covered in welts. Bleeding.

A good feeling. *Washed in the blood of the Lamb.*

He believes in Jesus, not in God. Doesn't give a damn for God.

Pretty sure God doesn't give a damn for him.

When he thinks of God, it's the old statue in front of the courthouse. Blind eyes in the frowning face, uplifted sword, mounted on a horse above the walkway. Had to laugh, the General had white bird crap all over him, hat, shoulders. Even the sword.

Why is bird crap *white?*—he'd asked the wise-ass lawyer, who'd stared at him.

Just *is.* Some things just *are.*

But when he thinks of Jesus, he thinks of a man like himself.

Accusations made against him. Enemies rising against him.

Welts, wounds. Slick swaths of blood.

Striking his back with the rod. Awkward, but he can manage. Out of contraband metal, his rod.

It is (maybe) not a "rod" to look at. Your eye, seeing what it is, would not see "rod."

Yet pain is inflicted. Such pain, his face contorts in (silent) anguish, agony.

As in the woman's sinewy-snaky body, in the grip of the woman's powerful arms, legs, thighs, he'd suffered death, how many times.

Like drowning. Unable to lift his head, lift his mouth out of the black muck to breathe. Sucking him into her. Like sand collapsing, sinking beneath his feet into a water hole and dark water rising to drown him.

The woman's fault from the start when he'd first seen her. Not knowing who she was. Insolent eyes, curve of the body, like a Venus flytrap and him the helpless fly: trapped.

Plenty of time in his cell to think and to reconsider. Mistakes he'd made, following the woman, who'd been with another man the night he saw her. And her looking at him, allowing him to look at her.

Sex she baited him with. The bait was sex. He hadn't known (then). He has (since) learned.

He'd thought the sex-power was his. Resided

240

in him. Not in the woman, but in him, as in the past with younger girls, high-school-age girls, but with her, he'd been mistaken.

And paying for that mistake ever since.

To be looked at with such disgust. To be sneered at. That was a punishment in itself, but not the kind of punishment that cleansed.

In segregation at the state prison, as he'd been at county detention, because he'd been designated a special category of inmate because children were involved, and this would be known. Because there was no way to keep the charges against him not known. Because once you are arrested, your life is not your own.

Surrounded by "segregated" inmates like himself. Not all of them white, but yes, mostly white.

Yet nothing like himself.

They'd come to search his cell. Again.

Because he could not prevent them. Because there were many of them and only one of him.

In his cell there was nowhere to hide anything. (So you would think.) Yet with sneering faces they searched the cell.

And inside his lower body with furious gloved fingers, bringing him to his knees.

Yet they could not discover contraband. For it was nowhere here.

Where're you hiding it, Earle?—fucker, we know you're hiding something.

Their exultation in torturing him. Flushed faces, shining eyes, his screams are joyous to them.

In this place they were confining him, but the man who is free in his heart cannot be confined.

No prison, no segregated unit. No cell, no restraints, no straitjacket, no drugs forced down his throat or injected into his arteries to bind him.

Left him where he'd fallen, moaning on the filthy floor. A metal instrument (might've been a spoon) they'd shoved up inside him, into the most tender part of him, had been so forcibly removed, ravaged tissue was carried with it, slick with blood.

Thank you, Jesus. Washed clean in the blood of the Lamb, which is the most shame you can bear on this earth before you are annihilated.

On his knees alone on the night of Holy Saturday, observing the seven stations of the cross, the flagellant begins his discipline.

Each stroke of the rod against his bare back bringing expiation.

Crawling on his belly. Tongue extended. Makes himself pencil-thin, slithering like a snake.

Yet: a snake that can control its size.

From the crevice to the concrete.

Scraped raw the skin of his hands, bleeding.

On Strouts Mill Road, where the guardrail has been repaired.

Returning to his (ex)wife's house, his house from which he'd been banished.

Fluidly he moves. He has the power to pass through walls. He has whipped himself into a froth of blood. He has whipped himself invisible.

(It has not happened yet—has it? He sees that it is waiting to happen.) And so this time it will happen differently. Jesus has escaped his enemies and will wander the world as free as he wishes, like any wild creature without the spell of a wrathful God upon him.

He will take Lucas and Esther with him, in their pajamas. Very quietly he will lift them in his arms. Daddy! Daddy!—the children are smaller than he recalls, this is startling to him, disorienting. The children smell of their bodies, their pajamas are soiled. Halfway he wonders if their mother has drugged them too, to make them sleep.

Seeing it is Daddy, they are happy. He will take them to safety. Except they are hungry—whimpering with hunger. The woman has put them to bed without feeding them. Daddy! To Burger King in the pickup. He will take them, he is their daddy. The woman has been left behind, unknowing. The woman is unconscious in her bed, sprawled in nakedness and smelling of liquor.

It will be his error to think that the woman left behind will not exert her power over him.

Pressing down on the gas pedal. Highway a blur, for Daddy too is ravenous with hunger. And thirst. Stops for a six-pack at the 7-Eleven. Pops a can open inside the store, cold beer running down his fingers. This will be observed on the surveillance tape. That Daddy has not eaten, and Daddy has not slept in forty-eight hours. Love for the kids is all Daddy has to nourish him.

Driving through stunted pines. Icy road. Slick pavement, black ice it is called. *Your mother is to blame. The lying whore has sabotaged our family.*

Until now the woman has been pulling the strings. They have been her puppets—the father, the children.

But no longer.

At the *crossing-over time.* At home in the dark.

As a boy, he'd been taught. He had not wished to know, yet he had been made to know.

The stations of the cross are seven. Christ must bear his cross. Christ must stumble and stand upright again. Christ is bleeding from his wounds: chest, back, head. Soon, spikes will be driven through Christ's hands and feet. It is supposed that Christ was made to lie down upon the rough-hewn cross upon which he was nailed. Christ will submit to his crucifixion, for it is written. Christ will die as a man and descend to Hell. And on the third day Christ will rise again to enter the Kingdom of Heaven, where he will dwell with the Father for eternity.

He can think of little else. Useless to try to sleep, he must do penance in the darkest hours of the night. Kneels on the filthy floor of the cell. As he has been instructed.

Flagellant is a word no one speaks aloud. Yet many are the *flagellants* seeking penance.

The children's faces! Lucas, Esther. You tend to forget, a child's face is *small.*

The heads of children are small. As fragile as eggshells. Their arms, legs are thin. As if their bones are composed of a material lighter than adult bones, easily snapped.

Lucas and Esther in their pajamas. Tenderly he lifts them from their beds. The shaking of his hands is steadied somewhat by the weight of the children; it is a good weight, like ballast.

Her fault, the woman's fault, that his hands shake, for it is the woman's fault that he can't sleep, he must self-medicate, the pills leave him dazed and groggy, and the other pills spur his heart to palpitations, cause him to break into oozing, oily sweat. The woman has cast him from her life, she has made him an exile from his own household. Hadn't he painted the interior of the little house, hadn't he laid the linoleum tile, ash falling from a cigarette in his mouth. He'd stooped, strained his damned back. He'd done a damned good job. Kitchen floor, bathroom floor.

He'd got the tiles at a discount and he'd laid them in and she'd said how beautiful they were, how she loved him for such care he'd taken with their home.

Tonight he lifts the children in his arms. Lucas first, then Esther. The little boy is three years old, the little girl is one year old. In that year, how much has happened! But he does not blame either of them, it is the mother he blames. Wrong for a mother to love her babies more than she loves their father.

Leaking milk through her clothes. Disgusted and excited him, the breast-milk smell that is like no other smell.

In his muscled arms he holds the children. He's proud of his body, or was. Working out, lifting weights, no screwing around at the gym, guys he'd known from high school were impressed. And these kids he'd loved more than his own life.

Christ, he has come to hate his own life.

He'd hated the mother more than he'd loved the kids. He did not deny it. Jesus understood. You could not look fully into the face of Jesus for the powerful light in his face, but you knew that Jesus understood.

Driving the sleepy children. The little girl in the back, the little boy in the front seat. No child-seat shit. No time to take the child-seats from her car and into the pickup. Lucas could sit in the front seat like an adult. Esther was asleep anyway, let her lie down on the back seat. Lucas was saying *Daddy where are we going?*—worried and confused and not knowing if he liked it. Until Daddy put out his hand to thump the little shoulder to explain.

Anywhere you go with Daddy, you are meant to go.

Daddy will take care of you and your sister. Already Daddy is doing this.

Driving faster. The woman's voice in his head, haranguing. Bitch nagging. Hail striking the windshield, pounding against his head.

Lucas is whimpering. *Daddy! Daddy . . .*

The skid. The truck goes into a skid on black ice. Slams into the guardrail, and the guardrail crumples like plastic. And now the truck has overturned, the children's screams abruptly cease.

He is crawling out of the truck. All his strength is required. Yelling at the children—*Come on! C'mon! Follow Daddy!*

Yelling for them, but can't get back into the fucking truck. Tries, but can't get back. Tugs at the door handle. Thumps the (cracked) window with a fist. A part of him knows it is hopeless.

It's over. No hope. You are fucked.

She'd been the one who'd wanted them. Sober, saying, *Kids will change us, Earle. Wait and see. Give us something to live for, not just us.*

247

She'd begged. She'd pleaded. Licking him up and down with her cool, wet tongue he would recall as hot, scalding.

Kids will be like Heaven to us, Earle. People like us, we won't get into Heaven, they will shut the door on us. But we can peek inside and watch them, see? That's the kids.

He'd never forgiven her for saying such things.

Like the two of them were not enough. The kind of feeling he had for her, which was unique in his life, like a river rushing through a desert, making the dead land come alive again—that meant nothing to her.

Calling after him. Stumbling in the dark. Half drunk, or high on pills. Lay down and couldn't lift her head. Ten, twelve hours. Through the morning and into the afternoon and into early evening. How she'd self-medicate when a migraine came piercing her skull.

Saying, *I can't do it anymore, Earle. The way you look at me.*

There's no oxygen for me to breathe. It's just—I tried—but . . .

The way he'd followed her around when he was supposed to be at work. Checked on her—if her car was parked in the driveway. Called her a dozen times a day on her cell phone. Calling their mutual friends. Guy she'd worked for, he'd suspected her of fucking before they were married and, more he thought about it, possibly after as well.

Sick, he'd felt. Fever in the blood. Infection like hepatitis C he couldn't shake.

Yet incredulous, hearing the woman's words, it was sounding like she'd prepared. Or someone had prepared for her. Asking her, what're you saying? Because it had to be a joke. Hadn't he just made a down payment on a Dodge SUV for her? Wanting to see her smile again. Smile at him. And the kids, taking pride in Daddy.

Driving them to school. Picking them up from school. Silver-green vehicle, classy. He'd gotten a bargain on it, pre-used, good as new, joked with the dealer he'd be making payments on it until he was fucking retired or dead.

Important to make the kids proud. Give them something to be proud of in their daddy.

And then, the woman undermining him. Betraying him. *Injunction*—that was what pushed him over the edge.

Forbidden to approach within one hundred yards of the house and forbidden to approach within one hundred yards of the children and forbidden to approach within one hundred yards of the woman who has requested the *restraining order.*

Wife, she was. *Former wife,* it would be written.

Daddy's secret, he'd never wanted kids. Your kids judge you. Your kid are too close up. Then they outlive you. They cry because of you or they disappoint you. In the boy's face a look like shrinking, drawing back from his dad, Christ!— all Earle could do to keep from grabbing the little bastard and shaking him so hard his brains rattled like marbles.

But no. No. He didn't mean it, Christ.

How he'd leaned down and shouted into the kid's (scared-white) face. Opening his mouth wide, feeling his face turn ugly, shouting. *Don't you try to get away from me, you little shit.*

Hadn't meant it. Any of it. Therapists sympathized. Everyone loses his temper. Parents lose their tempers. Nobody is perfect. A perfect dad does not exist.

Crucial to forgive yourself, the Catholic chaplain said. Between love and hate we may choose hate out of fear of choosing love.

Saying to him, how we don't want forgiveness for our sins when it is our sins we love.

He'd come close to crying, being told such a thing. For it was true, it's his sins he loves, nothing else has meaning to him.

No one but *her.* But *fuck her.*

Driving fast on Strouts Mill Road, and then faster. Eyes steady in their sockets. He was gripping the wheel correctly. He was gripping the wheel as you would grip it if it were alive and trying to get away from you.

He prayed with his eyes open. He had nothing to hide. His eyes took in all things. He did not spare himself. He'd loved his kids more than his own life, but he'd hated their mother more than he'd loved them or himself, and that was the truth he had to live with.

He was fearful of Jesus. The love in Jesus. The love of Jesus was a pool that could overflow and drown a man.

He could understand meanness. He could see why people were cruel to one another. But forgiveness and love he could not understand.

He was sorry for the crimes he had committed. He believed that Jesus would forgive him, but *Jesus would not forgive the crimes his (ex)wife had perpetrated against him and the children.*

She'd told him he would have to leave. They would all be happier if he left, she said. He'd said, *Happy! We are not on this goddamned earth to be happy.*

He had not struck her. He had never struck her. Not head-on, not deliberately. He had struck the air beside her head. He had struck the wall, maimed the wall beside her head, but he had never struck her.

Better for us all if we end it now. You, and me, and them. Now.

Shrinking from him, recoiling from the fist swung in the air beside her head, the woman had lost her balance, stumbled and fell—how was that his fault? Not his fault. Everyone knew she was a drunk. Junkie. Gained weight since the first pregnancy, thick ankles, aching veins, none of it his fault. Not the good-looking girl he'd fallen in love with and married. She had tricked him. The children were not *hers* to take from him. He was praying with his eyes open. He prayed to them, Lucas and Esther who art in Heaven. Innocent children are in Heaven looking down upon the rest of us. Our earth is actually Hell—you look down upon it from Heaven. In a dream this came to him.

Holy Saturday is the day of liberation. Whipping his back raw with the clumsy rod he has fashioned. Blood streaming, itching, like ants streaming in open wounds.

Thank you, Jesus!—forgive me.

Another time it happens, skidding tires on black ice, the crash.

Another time, there is no way to stop it.

The truck is flung over like a child's toy, tires spinning. Rolling downhill into the creek and into the litter sunk into the creek, and the children's screams and his own screams mixed together in the stink of oil, gasoline, urine.

Another time, the screams, and then the silence.

Well—the children never stopped loving their Daddy, he is sure of that. They have never blamed him. They are in Heaven now and would not cast the first stone. No child would cast the first stone. The woman, she has cast the first stone. She has cast many stones. She will go to Hell. They will meet in Hell. They will clutch hands in Hell. They will throw their wounded bodies together in Hell. Their eyes will burn dry, sightless, in Hell. Their souls will shrivel like leaves in a pitiless sun, these leaves blown together across a broken pavement.

At the *crossing-over* time, such thoughts come to him. Between daytime and night.

For at this time he is not incarcerated in a filthy cell, but free to make his way along Strouts Mill Road. He is not driving the pickup. He is on his belly in the wet grass. He has eluded his captors, he is not what they think. The cunning of the snake, which has been the female cunning but has now become his.

Strength will come to him, the promise is he will soon stand upright, as a man is meant to stand.

Sure he'd heard the term *lifer*. Hadn't known exactly what it meant until it was applied to him—in the way he wouldn't have known what *cancer* meant exactly until it was applied to him.

Even then it wasn't an exact knowledge. The charge had not been homicide, but manslaughter: vehicular manslaughter. Driving while impaired. Violation of a court-ordered injunction. Breaking and entering a residence. The bastards had tried to charge him with abduction of underage children as well, but that charge had been dropped.

To these he'd pleaded *guilty*. Not in his heart, but in the courtroom before the judge, who was gazing down upon him in scarcely concealed repugnance, as a man might gaze down upon a creature subhuman though standing upright.

Then his mouth twisted. Furious grin, baring ape teeth he'd liked to sink into the fucker's neck.

And so he was given the sentence *twenty-five years to life*. Which meant you could not say *I will be out of here in ___ years*. You could not say *This will end for me, I will be released in ___ years*. None of this you could say with certainty. For even dignity is denied you in the orange jumpsuit with shackled legs.

He has not seen the young lawyer in a long time. Last time, their exchange had been brief and their consultation had ended abruptly.

Raising his voice, threatening the lawyer provided him by the court.

Fuck the lawyer, what the fuck did he need that asshole for. He did not need him or any lawyer.

Not probation this time, but incarceration. One of the other inmates explained to him that when he applied for parole, which would not be for many years, the ex-wife could exert her influence if she wished, for she would always be consulted as the ex-wife and the mother of the child-victims. If there had been threats to her, these would be duly recorded in the computer and never deleted.

He foresaw: always the woman would poison them against her.

In this way, always they would be married.

Problem is, remorse.

Heartily sorry for my sins. Now and at the hour of my death, Amen.

He did not lack remorse. But he did not exude a remorseful air.

And so, in the courtroom, this was perceived. The judge had perceived. Even the asshole lawyer had perceived. If it was remorse, it was remorse for not having taken the woman instead of the children and murdering the woman when he'd had the chance. The two of them together in the truck hurtling along Strouts Mill Road.

In her bed upstairs. In her bed that had been his bed. His bed from which she'd exiled him. In this way dooming him and the children, and he had not even known it at the time.

Waking in this squalid place and not knowing if the woman was still alive, and if he was still alive. Or if both of them were dead already.

You are forgiven for the harm you have done yourself. But for the harm you have done the others, you will never be forgiven. Know that, forever, you are of the damned.

In the words of Christ this was explained to

him. Bloodied face and body of Christ and eyes resembling his own.

In Hell they are together. Grinding against each other's bodies once so beautiful and now no longer but in their memories, in Hell their beautiful, smooth young bodies are restored to them. As in a dream in which the most intense yearning is suffused with cold, sick horror they are tearing at each other with their teeth, their bodies writhe together like the bodies of coiled snakes. Never will they come to the end of their desire for each other, never will they be freed of each other.

In this, there is a feeling beyond happiness. In this, there is the flagellant's penance.

By now the flagellant has whipped his back raw. He is panting, exhausted.

Bliss of Holy Saturday. And the promise to him, it will never not be Holy Saturday.

VAPING:
A USER'S MANUAL

Six-forty a.m., first vape of the day.
Jesus!—your heart just *skids*.

S-L-O-W helping your mom down the
    brick steps.
Hate the way her fingers clutch—*Don't
    let me go, Jacey* . . .
Vaping makes it okay. Brain rush!
It's okay, Mom. I've got you.

Weird how it's still dark. Six fifty-five a.m.
Like, you'd been awake all night. Mom
in her room and you in yours. Eyeballs like sea
anemones floating in the dark.

Mom coughing, choking, gasping for air, could
hear through the walls.

Four a.m., brought her the asthma inhaler. Got
her sitting up, pillows behind her back so she
could sleep/try to sleep that way.

Attacks are getting worse. Since last April.

In the morning, helping Mom put on clothes.
Stumbling one slender leg into the black suede
trousers, then the other leg, Mom teetering,
panicked, grabbing your arm. (Jesus!)

Even going to the Oncology Center your mother has got to look good. Has got to *try.* Closetful of clothes, some of them never worn, expensive. Also, high-heeled shoes.

But not today. Flat-heeled shoes today.

Next, the (hateful) walker. Foot of the stairs. Have to position it for Mom, she's scared as hell trying to use it. Hey look, Mom, you can't hang on to *me.* We're both gonna fall.

Doesn't trust the fucking walker since the time she fell. Fell hard. Looked away from her for one minute out in the driveway, fuck she fell.

Okay, Mom, it's steady.

Okay, Mom, you can *let go* of me.

Wouldn't know that Mom used to be a beautiful woman. Just a few years ago.

Used to be chic, blond-streaked hair. Now white-streaked and thinning.

White of her eyes showing over the iris like a thin crescent moon.

(How old is Mom? Fuck, not *old.* Forty-three?)

Appointment is seven forty-five a.m., but we're leaving early. In case something fucks up. As Dad says *Always keep in mind the fuckup factor.*

Last time you took Mom for her infusion, there was an accident on the turnpike—traffic backed up for miles. Oil in skid-streaks across the highway, gleaming like fresh blood.

The sky is lightening, like cracks in a black-rubble wall. Sun at the horizon like the damn city is on fire!

What vaping does to the brain: makes you *see*. All kinds of weird, beautiful shit you'd never *see* in your ordinary brain.

S-L-O-W driving to the Oncology Center. Three point seven miles to the Mercer Street exit. Already seven ten a.m., traffic backing up like a shit-blocked gut.

Mom sitting stiff beside me. Staring ahead. (Seeing—what? And what is she thinking?)

Before last April, Mom would be talking. You're not even in the room, your mom is talking to you, casting her voice out like a spider's thread—making sure you are there, you are *connected*. Kind of exasperating, expecting you to be listening and to reply, but now she's silent, like her mouth has been sewn shut, you miss it.

And if you look at her, she won't be smiling at you like she used to—might not even look at you at all. Panicky, staring inside herself.

Does divorce cause cancer?—or does the (undiagnosed) cancerous condition cause the divorce?

Clickbait on the internet. Crappy article in one of Mom's magazines.

Okay, I'm gonna take a chance. Passing on the right to get to the exit. Assholes gaping at me humping along the turnpike shoulder, must be passing ten, twelve vehicles. Fuck, it's an *emergency situation.* Gotta get my mom to the clinic.

Running over debris, part of a rusted fender, broken glass. Mom gives a scream like a little killed mouse. Me, I just laugh.

Juuling is cool-ing. You just laugh.

Each Thursday first week of the month early a.m. my mother has three hours of infusion—gamma globulin. Have to laugh thinking—*Gamma goblin?*

Because something is wrong with Mom's white blood cells: immune system.

Best fucking thing vaping does for you, makes you *immune.* Best damn infusion.

Special permission for me to come to school late on those days. Primary caretaker of my mother. *I need you Jacey, please. Don't abandon me.*

Christ! Embarrassing as hell. Mom pleading for me not to abandon her like her damn husband did. Somebody should shoot *him.*

First hit of the day, best hit. Press your hand against your chest feeling the heart pound pound pounding inside the ribs like a fist.

Feeling good in the car. Terrific sensation behind the wheel. The Lexus Dad left for Mom, I'm driving.

Asshole'd have a meltdown, he knew who's driving.

Mom has the driver's license, I've got a

learner's permit, it's cool. Nothing illegal. Good I remembered to grab Mom's purse on the way out. Wallet, driver's license. Credit cards. Cash.

(Loose bills in Mom's wallet. Last time I looked, twenties, two fifties. Tens, fives. Helped myself to one twenty and one fifty, and guess what?—on painkillers Mom never had a clue.)

Start off on a high. Wild!

Brain buzzing, hive of bees. All good.

Okay, Mom. You can open your eyes, we're here.

When the high wears off, feeling like shit. Air leaking out of a balloon.

My size balloon: five feet eight, one hundred twenty-three pounds, shoulder muscles, arm muscles okay. Swim team, track team, JV football, but like the other guys vaping, kind of short of breath these days.

Like, *fucking panting.*

Coach stares at us, disgusted. Steve, Carlie, Leonard, Jacey. Coach hears us panting. Maybe Coach can smell us. (But you can't smell e-cigs like you smell fucking cigarettes—right?) Like, Coach isn't going to accuse anybody of anything. Even if he guesses what we're doing behind his back. Knows he could get his ass sued by *irate parents.*

Defamation laws. Slander, libel. Lawyers for the school district.

So fuck Coach, who gives a fuck. Mom is in no condition to come to our meets anymore, Dad stopped coming years ago. And when Dad came and I set a county record for the four-hundred-meter sprint, he was on his fucking cell phone most of the time.

Hey kid. I'm proud of you.

Yeh okay, Dad.

I am! I goddamn am.

Okay, Dad. Cool.

Like I gave a shit. Like I'm panting and wagging my tail like some sorry-ass little mutt for Dad to pet.

That sprint was my best time. Still the county record.

Why vaping feels so good. Turns them all *mute.*

Why e-cigs are the greatest invention. Nothing like fucking tobacco cigarettes that stink and stain your teeth and you can see the damn smoke.

Only (old) assholes *smoke.* Dad boasts how he'd quit, but he's such a fucking liar, who can believe him.

Have to laugh seeing teachers' mouths move so seriously, but you can't follow what the fuck they are saying. Fun-ny!

Jacey, what's so funny? Would you like to tell us?

Trying to keep a straight face. Sputtering, hot. Friends in the class turning to grin at me behind their hands.

Nah. I'm okay.

You're—"okay"? Are you?

Let adults get the last word, that sarcastic tone, that's cool. Like anybody gives a fuck what they think.

Joke's on them—teachers. Don't know shit.

Every few years they vote to strike. But then some shit happens, they don't strike. Chump change they make for salaries, they deserve.

In the beginning, last year, there were just a few kids vaping. And not in class.

Now it's right in class, and half the kids doing it. (Including girls.) Teacher turns his back, you take a quick hit.

Inhale. Exhale. Cloud: chill. Laugh. Cough. The surprise of that head rush, so sweet.

Almond nicotine. Good shit!

Whatever it costs, it's worth it. Clears the sad, sick crap in your head like Power Wash.

Vaping Alert.

Soon as you step into a building. Quick-scope where you can Juul without being detected.

Any medical facility, NO SMOKING signs everywhere.

Like at the Oncology Center.

Nothing about e-cigs. Nothing about Juuls, vaping.

Number one: restroom in the corridor (single occupant).

Number two: men's restroom, stall.

(Yeah, I brought the Juul with me. Not intending to use but, like, to test my willpower.)

Goddamn: the infusion nurse can't find a vein in Mom's arm. Tightening a tough rubber band around her upper arm, palpating her forearm, looking for a vein. A sight I hate to see. Makes me feel queasy. Shivery. Shaky. So fucking sorry for Mom but disgusted with her too. You end up blaming them—*victims*.

Girls at school that guys have treated like shit. Should feel sorry for them, but fuck it, you do not.

Mom's trying not to whimper. Trying not to cry. Arms bruised, they're looking for a vein in the wrong damn place. *Try the left arm. Jesus. By the elbow.* Young nurse keeps poking her, apologizes, only makes things worse.

In vain, seeking a vein.

They sought a vein, in vain.

Yeh, I should exit the infusion room. Right. Should get out. There's nothing for me to do but watch. I'm getting upset, telling the nurse to get somebody who knows fucking what she's doing, which doesn't help. My voice is loud, everyone is looking at me. Other patients in their chairs having their infusions. Other nurses. If I say fuck you, Goddamn fucking fuck all of you, the security guard will peer in the window, glaring like he did last time. If I don't calm down, they will eject me from the Oncology Center. Then what will happen to Mom?

Okay, it isn't Mom's fault. None of it is Mom's fault.

Still, I resent her. Leaning so heavy on me. Wanting to protest, I'm only fifteen!

Three fucking years before I can leave home. If I'm lucky. If I can get into college, and if Dad will pay for it. Fucking *if.*

Then it sweeps over me like dirty water in my mouth—*What if Mom gets really sick, what if Mom dies?*

Lucky there comes another infusion nurse to the rescue. A guy, big, soft-bellied. Andy, his badge says. Weird, male nurses! But some of them are pretty good.

Clumsy-seeming Andy, but he's guiding the needle slantwise into Mom's arm at the elbow. Just a pinch, ma'am. Sor-ry. But Andy gets a vein on the first try, which is pretty damn impressive.

By this time my heart is beating so hard, it's an adrenaline rush without vaping.

When I return to the infusion room two hours later, the oncology doctor is waiting for me. Seems that Mom is *in discomfort.* Face white, wizened.

It's explained to me: your mother's blood pressure is *dangerously low.* Her blood work is showing *abnormally high white blood cells.*

Oxygen intake abnormally low—eighty-three.

Christ!—eighty-three out of one hundred?

Also, Mom has been complaining of *lower right abdominal pain.* So the oncology doctor is saying he is going to call the ER, prepare for Mom's being brought to the ER, which he recommends immediately. Don't go home first, go to the ER, and the office here will fax over the blood work, vitals, infusion record, etc., but Mom is pleading no, please no, she *does not want* to go to the ER. She is just agitated, she says. Gets high blood pressure in the infusion room, she says. Her pulse is high, she doesn't breathe correctly in the infusion room. Once she gets outside in the fresh air, she'll be okay. Mom pleads.

Yes, but there're markers in the blood work. Renal failure? Creatinine level high.

How high?—I'm asking.

Three point something. Shit—that is *high.*

Mom refuses an ambulance. Mom walks leaning on me, then on the walker, swerving and skidding through the plate-glass automatic doors like a drunk woman.

Just take me home, Mom says. No ER!

So I'm saying okay, Mom, but first you need to get checked out at the ER, then if it's okay we can go home. So I'm able to get her over to the medical center, checked in at the ER, start the process going. Turns out Mom's blood work is pretty bad. Anemia, plus other shit. *Chronic abdominal pain*—the oncology doc has recommended a scan.

While Mom is being examined by a (young, Asian-looking) doctor in one of the cubicles, I'm starting to feel really anxious. Maybe it's withdrawal—(already?)

What I'd resolved was not to Juul for, like, twelve hours.

Problem is, when you're *high,* you forget what it's like to be *not-high.*

When you're *high,* no thought in the world for dickheads that *crash.*

Don't ever smoke, Jacey. Promise me.

Yah okay, Mom. I promise.

. . . the things it does to your lungs, your heart, makes you short of breath, plus your breath smells, teeth stain. Plus it's expensive. Plus it's disgusting, sucking smoke into your actual body, exhaling it to pollute the air for others.

Okay, Mom. I get it.

Last week at school. Decided to test my willpower, leaving the Juul at home, hidden in my bureau.

Like, I am *no addict.* (I just like how e-juices taste.)

First hit of the day, early morning in the bathroom. Fantastic!

It's the chill cloud, the *chemical fruit* smell. Like some kind of sci-fi.

Actual fruit—strawberry, pineapple, melon—has a sickish smell, like rot. Like, you can smell the rot to come.

But vapor, fruit-vapor, that's pure. No rot, ever.

But then by noon fucked-up and feeling like shit. Staring at the classroom clock. Mouth so dry, compulsively swallowing. Fuck fuck fuck *fuck*. Instead of going to lunch had to bicycle home from school, sneak into the house so Mom didn't know, take a hit, one two three, savor the high, return on my bicycle to school at top speed, Spider-Man fast, but fuck it, ran out of breath on the Cedar Street hill, vision blotched and reeling, but made it, walked into geometry class while the fucking bell was ringing because of course I was going to get back in time, flying high.

All that week I left the Juul at home. Goddamn determined not to bring it with me to school. Goddamn determined to exercise *willpower.* And all that week, middle of the day feeling so fucked had to bicycle back home two point six fucking miles and having a hard time pulling uphill.

By Friday I was too fucked, tired. Just borrowed Carlie's Juul.

Hey okay. I owe you—okay?

That's cool, Jacey. No problem.

The guys are, like, *bemused* with me. Everybody knows e-cigs are not addictive, so what's the big deal?

Not like we're *junkies*. Pathetic loser *addicts*.

First, kids at school that vaped were creeps.
Losers. Then later, kids I knew, and some of the
guys I hang with. Then, guys on the team.

How I was turned on, last summer. At the pool
with the other lifeguards. Observed them taking
hits, e-cigarettes, weird concoctions—nicotine
and fruit flavors—Christ! Sucking strawberry
mist, not smoke, then exhaling—evaporating.

That's so cool, like magic, the way the smoke
evaporates before your eyes.

And Ben Marder says hey Jacey, want to try?—
and I kind of sneered *Nah. Why'd I want to do
that shit.*

You'd tried cigarettes, your dad's butts he'd
left in ashtrays. Never got any *nicotine rush* but
choked and coughed and felt like puking. Nasty-
tasting tobacco shit.

But then later, Carlie offered me, saying how
cool it was, so I said okay, by that time I'd been
smelling the chemical cloud a lot and was kind of
envious, I guess. Figuring just one time.

Carlie shows me how the e-cig works. You don't
"light" it—it's battery-operated. Like, cutting-
edge technology. Not crude shit like tobacco.

Very simple, actually. One two *three.*

Jesus! What a brain-fuck . . .

Guys laughing at me. Must've been a weird
look in my face. *Je-sus!*

How I discovered there's nothing like vaping.
Nothing so cool, by far.

Better than sex. (Everybody says. Not like I'd know.) Way easier than sex. And way cooler than sex—you don't need another damn person.

Whenever you can eliminate the *other person,* anyone you depend upon, anyone you need, that's a bonus.

Why vaping is so cool: makes you strong like Spider-Man.

Why vaping is so cool: undetectable.

Not like sloppy-ass cigarettes. Adults can smell the smoke on you across the room—breath, hair, clothes. Can't keep cigarettes secret like you can vaping.

And Juuling is best. Way cool.

How much?—you don't even think to ask.

Because whatever it is, it's worth it.

Because whatever it is, if you can afford it or not, there's ways of acquiring the means to afford it, like (for instance) your mom's credit card she isn't going to be using (much) anyway, sick as she is in the hospital now. Seventh floor.

Notified me on my cell phone, your mother is being admitted to the hospital. Brought by gurney to the seventh floor, room 7731.

So at reception I'm like, hey why's there an extra *seven?*—and the receptionist looks at me like I am the weirdest white boy she's ever seen.

Tried to explain, see there's an extra *seven*

in the room number, shouldn't it be just *seven hundred,* not *seven thousand?* So finally she got the joke, sort of, and laughed, like women laugh when they see you're trying to be funny in some dumb-ass way. Because (maybe) (they can sense) you are a little nervous, anxious, and a woman or a girl will feel sorry and play along with you.

Especially nurses, nurses' aides. Jesus!—they have got to see *everything there is to see.*

Who is the patient to you, are you a relative?— (eyeing me, like there could be anyone else my age and looking like me who'd be visiting my mom except a relative).

Yes. She is my mother.

(Weird that you would never naturally say *Yes. I am her son.*)

(Because you only have one mom. While a mom could have more than one son. Is that it?)

Handing me the ID badge, saying *Have a good day.* Like, if I didn't know better, I'd think the receptionist was laughing at me.

How I discovered that with an ID visitor badge you can wander through the hospital. As long as they see you have an ID, nobody looks at it closely or questions you. A hospital is a crazy busy place, especially in the morning.

Depressing as hell in Mom's room. Though it's a single room with a view from the window of the city skyline. Also the sky—clouds to watch.

271

Poor Mom with IVs in both her arms, scheduled for a kidney biopsy in the morning.

Didn't leave the Juul home today, figuring the stress would be such, in this place, I'd need to score a hit. Or two. There's a lavatory in the room I can use, slide the door shut. No smoking in the hospital but—no vaping? Would they kick me out if they knew?

Lucky, no smell that lasts beyond a few seconds. No ashes!

Nurse enters my mom's room, pushing a little cart to check her vital signs—(oxygen intake, blood pressure, pulse)—but I'm in the bathroom grinning at my face in the mirror and the smoke has evaporated and when I come out, I am ultra-normal, I am sure.

So high, I don't even hear what the nurse is saying. Is the oxygen intake improved or worse. Is the pulse fast. Blood pressure low? High? Mom's hurt, scared eyes looking at me, but I don't even see.

On some doorframes, white sheets of paper with autumn leaves printed on them. Meaning?

Hanging out in the visitors' lounge, far end of the corridor by the elevators. Three, four people in the lounge and one of them crying, two of them crying, someone with a deep, gravelly voice trying to console a child, none of it makes the slightest impression on me, like, could be TV. Admiring the fantastic view of the city, late-afternoon sun like a broken egg yolk. My head is feeling dry like bone, but the taste in my mouth is good.

Staring out the window toward the turnpike. S-L-O-W rush hour traffic moving out of the city like zombies. Land of the dead. Jesus!—it's good not to be one of those zombies but Spider-Man, flying high above.

Flying high. Above.

Vaping Dreams.

Long-term plan is: buy an assault rifle, online. Mom's Visa Explorer.

Scope out where Dad is living. Google Maps: 54 Roslyn Circle, Bay Ridge, NJ. Follow Dad to, like, the Bay Ridge mall. Asshole has got to drive to the mall sometime.

Well—if he saw me in the Lexus. That'd end it.

(If he saw, like, the license plate he'd recognize. I'd be wearing a hoodie, dark glasses.)

If the kid is with him, the new wife's kid with the asshole name Tyler, eight years old, or so Mom says, too fucking bad—*collateral damage.*

Telling Mom, who told me, your father feels he has failed you, honey. He feels he cannot *reach you.* But with the new son, he's gonna start over again.

Mistakes he'd made when you were young because *he* was young, a young father, didn't have the perspective he has now.

Fuck him! The look in Mom's face. I stomped out of the room.

(Yeh Mom liked to hear it. Sure she did.)

(Any bad-mouthing of my dad in Mom's presence, if it's her relatives, some friends, or me—Mom won't seem to agree, but for sure, Mom is cool with it.)

Plan is: no fucking camouflage gear. Hoodie, backpack. No black trench coat, etc., like those Columbine assholes. Baseball cap pulled down low over your eyes. Red joke cap—MAKE AMERICA FAKE AGAIN.

Plan is: get high. Super high. Deep inhale, slow exhale. Brain buzz. Feel the strength surge through you like every pore in your body is on fire.

Get into position. Sight your target. Quick then, before your dad sights *you.*

One-two-*three,* spray the crowd with bullets. What's it you have in your hands—AK-47. Kalashnikov rifle—cool! No one will figure out that one person in the crowd was the designated target. If you can mow down, like, thirty people—*Benjamin Fowler, forty-seven, Roslyn Park CPA* is just one of the fatalities.

Assuming you don't get caught, identified. No connection between *mass shooter* and *victims.* Quick-spray the scene with a "fusillade of bullets," rapid retreat, follow your designated escape route, discard incriminating evidence, disappear.

Perfect high: *disappear.*

No more *you.* Just—fruity chemical smell,
moist cloud
  e-vap-or-at-ing
  before your eyes.

Where can I buy a gun (legally)?

Internet guns for sale. *ArmsList, Craig's List,
GunsAmerica, Cheaper Than Dirt.* Got to figure
that undercover cops are trolling these sites like
they do, looking for pedophiles. So, maybe not a
great idea.

Asking the guys, did they know where I could
get a gun?—*I mean, like, legally.*

And the guys kind of shaking their heads, not
looking at me. Like, they know about my dad
leaving my mom and me, and (maybe) they've
been hearing me say things about what I'd like
to do to that asshole. So they kind of say they
don't know—*Unless online? eBay?*

Like hell. Easy way to get caught. State
requirement is you're eighteen years old or
more. If you have no record. Type in AK-47
and you're fucked. Like typing in *kiddie
porn.* Which is why I've given up asking. If
I'm high, I feel like tearing out their fucking
teeth, laughing in their faces, but if I'm not
high, if I'm crashing, feel so shitty-low strung
out, the wish is somebody would tear out my

throat with his teeth and put me out of my misery.

Would you live with your dad, then?—the guys ask. Meaning, if something happens to your mom.

Yeh. Guess so.

Where's he living now?

Shrug your shoulders, like fuck you want to talk about it. Fuck!

Why vaping is cool. Assholes ask you questions, you don't give a shit, just roll with it like *Sure, okay, any kind of shit you say. Sure.*

Problem is, the highs don't last like they did. Just a few weeks ago. Slow, deflating like a balloon, almost you can hear the fucking *hissing.*

Yeh it's kind of expensive. E-cigs and apparatus, not cheap.

One pod is equal to one pack of cigarettes. Or is it one hundred cigarettes. But how long would it take you to smoke one hundred cigarettes? Like, e-cigs go much faster.

Nicotine is much concentrated. Fantastic!

One of the guys, his dad is also moved out of their house, so you can talk to him, kind of. Saying *My father doesn't give fuck-all about me. Got to face it. He's married again, he has a young kid, my stepbrother, his wife has two kids of her own. I'm out.*

He says *Yeh. I guess.*

What I'd like is, to kill him. Just—wipe him away.

Yeh. Me, too.

But he doesn't sound interested. Like, he'd like to *wipe away* his old man if it wasn't too much fucking effort.

The single time I visited them in Bay Ridge, the hot new wife complained that I "smelled"—my underarms, crotch. Didn't like the way I dressed, including my running shoes that she said were "rotted."

Just that I was trolling her. (Joke!)

Didn't get all the soap out of my hair in the shower (I guess), so I looked like a "banshee."

(Fuck the bitch knows what a *banshee* looks like.)

(Maybe kill all of them, including piss-pot Tyler. *Collateral damage.*)

Hid in the fucking bathroom getting high on spearmint e-juice. Like, my eyes were crossed by the time I was finished, and fuck eating with them, no appetite for anything to be shared with them and anyway too excited to sit still.

Well—maybe some things got broken. Maybe precious little a-hole Tyler got scared and started crying. By the time I got home (via Dad's Uber account) my mouth was so dry, couldn't swallow. Chest weird-feeling, like something was inside clawing its way out.

Next time, you will know what to do. Bring the AK-47 with you, asshole.

One morning returning to Mom's room to discover autumn leaves posted outside the door.

Ask a nurse what's it mean and she tells you—*Patient is in danger of falling.*

Meaning, patient cannot be trusted to get out of bed unassisted. Patient *should not try* to get out of bed unassisted.

So, Mom is getting weaker? Fuck them.

Anything I can do for you, Jacey. Let me know.
Please! Your mother is such a lovely person.
Their mouths are sad. Their eyes are pitying.

First you just thank them—*Yah. Okay.* Like you're embarrassed they know about your mom and (you think) they care about her, and you.

Anything I can do for Lilian, Jacey. Let me know.

Then one day outside school, where she's come to pick Billy up after practice, you ask Billy's mother could she drive you to the hospital tomorrow morning—and she hesitates and says she will summon an Uber for you, because she has an appointment in the morning, on the farther side of town.

Let me know what I can do, Jacey—Len's mother says, so you tell her that your mother would appreciate a visit from her sometime, and

Len's mother says quickly yes, she would love to visit Lilian, she will try to get to the hospital tomorrow or the following day, but so much is happening in her life right now—*It's kind of crazy. Frankly.*

Still, your mom receives cards, flowers. Potted wax begonias from the ex-husband.

On the card—*Hope you will have a speedy recovery. Yours, Ben.*

Speedy recovery!—like, is this a joke?

Yours. That is a joke.

So furious, pulses are strumming in my head. Dying for a hit!

But shit, I'm short of cash. Like somebody is turning me upside down by my ankles, shaking out money from my fucking pockets.

Bad dream: a vampire bat is sucking my throat. Carotid artery.

Except, suck-suck-sucking my blood, the bat is also regurgitating into my blood sweet fruity-chemical taste and releasing a chill cloud to conceal us.

Funny sensation in my chest. Lungs? (Bubble lung? Sounds like a scare tactic/fake news spread by the tobacco industry.)

(Whatever I spend on vaping isn't as much as you'd spend on cigarettes. And there's no tobacco. *No cancer.*)

Dad would be furious with me if he knew about the vaping. If he knew my track performance isn't so great. Fuck Dad, what does he know.

Calling and asking *How's it going, Jacey?*—in this guilty-sounding voice, and I say, kind of mumbling, *Okay.* (Not calling him Dad. Not calling him anything.) And there's silence, so he says in the fake-Dad voice *You okay, Jacey?* And I say *Yeh sure.* And he says *How is your mother, Jacey?*—which is a trick question, so all I say is *Mom's okay.* Like rolling my eyes. The asshole hasn't got a clue what he sounds like, but this time I'm still high, still feeling good and not like shit, which is what Dad makes you feel like, except not now, now I am inside the Spider-Man costume, laughing in his face—*What the fuck do you care?* And Dad's so shocked, he can't even answer at first, then finally sputtering—*Don't talk to me like that, goddamn you. Who the hell do you think you are! I am serious. I care about your mother, and I care about you.*

Laughing at him, saying *Fuck all we care about you. And Mom too says—Fuck him.*

So Dad is shocked. Like he couldn't believe that his wife/my mother would say such words aloud is ridiculous, but he will talk himself into it, and the new wife will believe him. Sure.

Turn it all inside out to justify his behavior.

Sure. I know.

Why, you are gonna die, asshole. Spider-Man is closing in on you!

• • •

Prowling the hospital. Gliding like Spider-Man on invisible threads. No one does more than glance at the ID on your shirtfront. Not a glance at your bloodshot eyes, your zombie grin like a crack in concrete.

Running out of cash. Restless sensation, like you're crazy hungry—but not for food.

Floor below, take the stairs. Easy access. Carrying a tray, like from the cafeteria downstairs. Bustling hallways, staff change, seven p.m. Mingle with visitors, enter a room, and if there're people inside back out, honest mistake, easy to make in the hospital. ("Hey sorry—I guess I'm on the wrong floor!"), but if there's nobody in the room except a sleeping/comatose patient, go to the bedside table, see if there's a wallet in a drawer, glasses, hearing aid, quick remove the wallet, quick remove the cash, replace the wallet, nobody knows.

Heart pounding like an e-shot to the chest: cool.

Scored seventy-three dollars, first time.

Vaping gives me the courage. Brain rush. Running up the stairs two, three at a time—then flying. *Spider-Man!*

To be able to afford *vaping,* you need to prowl and scavenge. But to be able to prowl and scavenge, you need to *vape.*

Second time, one hundred ten. Plus some old

guy's fancy wristwatch in the bedside drawer along with dentures, hearing aids. (The patient's in the bed, sprawled, with his mouth open, skin like yellow leather, IV fluids dripping into his bruised arms.)

(Trying not to look at him. Turn your eyes away, quick.)

Another time, on the fourth floor, no money in the drawer. (No wallet.) But a rosary you snatch up and stuff into the backpack.

(Glance at the figure in the bed. Jesus!—a pixilated face you can't tell is female or male.)

No fear. Cool. Quick escape like Spider-Man.

The trick is looking like you know where the hell you're going. Nobody gives a shit about visitors.

Except: *Excuse me. Who are you, and where are you going?*

Female in dark blue uniform, must be a nurse. Middle-aged, hatchet-faced, no smile, and no bullshit. Staring at you suspiciously like with X-ray eyes penetrating your backpack, seeing exactly what you've scavenged tonight.

Trying not to stammer. Saying you are visiting your mother in room 7771.

Well, this isn't the seventh floor. This is the eighth floor.

Express surprise: eighth floor! You'd thought it was the seventh . . .

Got off at the wrong floor, you guess.

Smiling, not sweating. E-juice cool: tincture of lemon.

But the nurse isn't persuaded. Husky arms, taller than you. Looks like she could hoist you over her shoulder. No bullshit kind of (dark, almond-skinned) female squinting at your ID. Pretending she is memorizing your name, face. You are sure she's bullshitting. If she wasn't, she'd ask you what's in the backpack, what's in your pockets. Could summon security guards. But maybe, since it's late, past eleven p.m., she doesn't want to get involved. Might be she'd have to report you to the police, file an actual complaint, show up at a court hearing. Might be, it isn't worth it for her. If you have stolen cash, cash isn't traceable. A wristwatch, could be yours. There'd have to be a search of the hospital room by room to determine if the watch was missing from that room, plus isolated bills. Fuck, she's thinking, just fuck, it isn't worth it to burn this white boy's privileged ass.

So the nurse glares at you, disgusted, in a snotty voice saying she will have to escort you to your mother's room.

So you say okay, affable and unguilty. And the two of you take the elevator one flight down and she escorts you to your mother's room (with the fucking autumn leaves posted outside the door), which is as dim-lit at this hour as a wake. And there's your mother in her bed, IV fluids dripping into her battered arms. An attendant is checking her vital functions, heart, blood pressure, oxygen intake, so she's awake, if slightly dazed, but a smile lights up her tired face when she sees you—*Jacey! You didn't go home, you're here* . . .

First time since the infusion room, your Mom has smiled at you.

In this way you escape detection. The nurse melts seeing how Mom reaches for you like a sleepwalker. Seeing how you take her hand, you don't shrink away as another kid might do, embarrassed and scared.

Yeah, okay. Though you'd been ready to strangle her, the nurse, not your mom. Stuff her lumpy body in the utility room with the sign SOILED LINEN.

Alone in the room. With your mom. Blank black windows reflecting only the room as in a concave lens, subtly distorted. But safe!

Clutching your mom's (chilly, limp, thin) hand though she (still smiling, wanly) seems to have drifted off to sleep. Jesus!—the wild plan comes to you, you will activate the Juul in your pocket, bring the e-cig to your mom's mouth, give the patient a jolt to the brain like an electric shock.

Wake up, Mom! You're too young to die, and I am the one to save you.

Here's the deal: Mom lives, Dad lives.

Mom dies, Dad dies.

Think I can't do it? Watch me.

Jesus!—the kid put together a perfect crime.

Got to hand it to the kid, would've never thought he had the brains. Or the guts.

Yes-s-s—I am impressed. Guess I never gave him credit . . .

No. I don't know how he did it. Had to be high, I guess.

Goddamned vaping! These kids, today.

All I can figure: he must've bought an assault rifle online, used a fake ID or—whatever . . .

No, I wouldn't be surprised, he'd used his mother's credit card. (Wouldn't be the first time, d'you think she'd discipline him? N-o.)

Next thing, must've followed me in my car, Saturday morning. Headed for Otto's Discount Electronics at the mall, and at the first escalator going up, jammed with people, there's this explosion of sound—"fusillade of bullets"—"scene of terror"—people screaming, trying to get off the escalator, someone has fallen, another person has fallen, spurts of blood, jets of blood, crazy terrified wounded crawling over one another, I'm at the foot of the escalator on my knees, shielding my head, trying to crawl to safety behind a wall, but there's other people cutting me off, disbelieving that this is happening to me, victim of a "mass shooter," as bullets whip into my body, severing my spine in seconds, causing me to dance like a puppet cruelly jerked on strings, and then the back of my head explodes . . .

Okay, something like that.

Then the kid escapes.

So high, maybe the kid just flies away. Dad below, drowning in his own blood and skull burst like a pumpkin leaking brains, how'd Dad have a clue what the kid does next?

NIGHT, NEON

1.

Dusk, the heartbreak time. Slow-waning light falls upon the river like melting snow.

The hour when *neon* begins. Sudden, subtle. Few notice except those who have been waiting through the long, glaring day.

And of *neon* it is *blue neon* that most excites.

Driving past the Blue Moon Café. No reason to be driving past the Blue Moon Café, for she is due home within the hour . . .

Except: *blue neon* has entered her bloodstream like a powerful stimulant. Her senses have become alert, alive to the point of pain. She feels the quickening heartbeat, the pleasure of anticipation.

A rush of sensation, a profound thirst. And the anticipation of quenching that thirst.

"Just one. To celebrate."

Though (surely) it would be better to celebrate with Patrick, who is her coconspirator in this venture.

Though (certainly) it would be wiser not to celebrate alone.

"Just once."

Blue Moon, blue neon. Just the sight of it, a shot of adrenaline to the heart.

She won't stay long. She won't make it

287

complicated. No glancing up. No locking eyes.

If asked *Are you alone?*—the reply is *Yes. Until my husband joins me.*

Good to be a stranger at the Blue Moon Café. Always easier to navigate neon if you are not known.

Always easier if you don't make eye contact. Even in the mirror behind the bar, where (you'd be inclined to think) eye contact doesn't count, exactly.

In the funny, funky-glamorous sequined bag she carries into the café—oversize handbag signaling *girl with a sense of play, doesn't take herself overseriously*—she has secreted an instrument of self-defense.

Not *offense.* Never would she strike the first blow. Rather, *self-defense,* which would be, however, as swift, unerring, and lethal as if it were a calculated *offense.*

In this sequined bag, in which her wallet, car keys, cell phone, iPad and ear buds, lipsticks, hairbrush, tissues, and much other miscellany have been crammed, at the very bottom, wrapped in gossamer-thin fabric, is an ice pick six inches in length, its point kept very sharp, sparkling clean, for though Juliana has been carrying it secretly with her for months, possibly years, it has yet to be used.

And Juliana's other secret: she is pregnant at last.

A secret less than an hour old. A secret clamoring to be shared.

At last—this is triumph, the fairy-tale ending. Juliana, who has been reluctant to be married to Patrick, who has been hurt, wounded, baffled that Juliana has been reluctant to marry him even as she has insisted that yes, she does love him, careful to keep (secret) the distinction between *loving a man* and *being in love with a man*— well, now Juliana will rush at Patrick with the good news, she will embrace him, giddy and careless with joy, not a drunken joy, but (perhaps) a drunken-seeming joy, the lanky-limbed, funny- funky Juliana, whom Patrick adores for her honesty, her frankness, her sunny good spirits that lift his when he is, as Patrick sometimes is, in winter months in particular, inclined toward depression.

But no: *not depression.*

Juliana insists: *melancholy.*

For Patrick is, both agree, the more compli- cated, the more *convoluted* of the two of them.

Kissing her lover hard on the mouth, she will laugh at his look of utter astonishment—*Guess what! Fantastic news!*—and Patrick will squint at her uncomprehending—*What? What? What are you saying, Juliana?*

Maybe then whisper in his ear. Teasing words— *Due date guess when?*

Already Juliana is carrying herself with dignity,

precision. She knows that there are individuals in her family, and among her relatives, who have never predicted happiness for her; and now she will refute them. Her body will refute them.

Luminous, lighted from within, like one of those fleshy apricot-colored candles whose wicks, as they burn, descend inside the waxen candles, exuding a warmly mysterious, beautiful light. Taking care driving home from the clinic, braking at yellow lights she'd have blithely ignored the day before. Stopping at stop signs on residential streets with no traffic, which she'd certainly have ignored.

Never what you'd call a fleshy girl, lanky-limbed, tomboyish, now she imagines that she can feel her body becoming *womanly*. Small breasts becoming heavier, swollen and tender, and the nipples exquisitely sensitive, she hears herself laugh wildly in embarrassment.

Oh—is this me, Juliana? Not remotely me!

She will overwhelm her lover with love. Unneurotic, forthright, mammalian love, which Patrick has wistfully hoped for from Juliana, which Juliana has not been able to provide, not quite yet.

Pregnant women are the most beautiful women.

I am the happiest man alive.

Almost, Juliana can hear him: exactly Patrick's manner of speaking.

In his mouth, the most familiar, banal speech is given a new meaning, for Patrick speaks only what he believes.

Unlike (most) other men.

(Most) other men whom Juliana has known.

Oh, she is excited! An excitement shading into anxiety, so keen.

The way, on Front Street, ordinarily a street of no distinction, darkened store windows are reflecting the sun, about to disappear at the horizon in a watercolor wash of exquisite red-orange, as in a painting by Winslow Homer.

And the first headlights! And lights coming on inside buildings, houses. And the sky still glowering bright overhead. *L'heure bleu.*

Blue neon at the shadow end of a block—*Blue Moon Café.*

By day, neon is cheap, sleazy. You don't give neon a second glance by day.

But it's dusk now. Dingy blue neon in a café window competing with cruder neon signs advertising beer is a hook in the heart.

"Oh, God."

Her mouth has gone dry, she feels such yearning. She realizes, she has been so lonely.

Living with Patrick, who is so good to Juliana, who has no idea who she is, so lonely.

What has she done?—she has driven around the block.

She has not *driven past* the Blue Moon Café,

she has *circled the block* to approach the Blue Moon Café a second time.

But no, better not, wait to celebrate with the baby's father. That is the sensible thing to do, and Juliana is a sensible young woman.

Front Street is a part of the city still new to her. She and Patrick had moved into an old redbrick row house on Mill Street, on a partially gentrified block, just one month before.

Derelict waterfront area on the Delaware River. Warehouses, small, shuttered factories, mills. Abandoned freight cars covered in graffiti, like filigree. Yet on South Main and Front Street there are refurbished brick row houses—millworkers' homes back in the early twentieth century. There are antique shops, secondhand furniture stores, clothing consignment shops, Goodwill, a framing shop, art galleries.

Juliana is more adventurous than Patrick. Roaming through secondhand furniture stores, fabric shops. Even among the castoffs of Goodwill, her taste is exquisite, Patrick marvels at the bargains she has discovered and brought home in triumph to sand, repaint.

A small upstairs room adjacent to their bedroom. They will paint it rosy-pink (if a girl), robin's egg blue (if a boy).

Stars on the ceiling Juliana will paint. Maybe a few sparkly sequins embedded in the stars, like the sequins on her tote bag.

How good Juliana is at small, tender, caring tasks: she vows.

She'd suspected that she was pregnant of course. Has known, the drugstore test twice taken in secret, *positive.* But needing a confirmation, a proper examination, and a *due date: July 11.*

Until she tells Patrick, it is not quite real to her. *Guess when it is—our due date!*

Something with which to surprise others.

Juliana is feeling dry-mouthed, edgy. Can it be—already her clothes feel too tight? Beside her on the passenger's seat is a bottle of Evian water, but it isn't water she craves. Nooo.

Startled eyes in the rearview mirror. Juliana is surprising herself now, as (she thinks with satisfaction) she will surprise her mother and sisters, who'd predicted unhappiness for her, unable to be faithful to a man, unable not to lapse into her bad habits . . .

Astonishing to her, the birth date has been established. An actual date noted by the nurse-practitioner at the clinic. The child-to-be is the size of a comma . . .

It has been largely unspoken between Patrick and Juliana, they will be married if/when she becomes pregnant. They are deeply in love— (at least Patrick thinks so)—and Patrick wants children, he has said. And Juliana too, of course Juliana wants children. She has heard herself say.

Marrying is only logical, practical. Neither is so young—Juliana is twenty-nine, Patrick thirty-one. Juliana thinks of thirty as a kind of waterfall: once you plunge over those falls, you are gone. On your way to *gone*. Badly she wants the firmness, the security of marriage. Knowing that as you descend a flight of steps, each step is firm, will hold your weight and not collapse beneath it.

The next step in their lives, indeed. As moving into a ruin of a town house was the next step. Debris they'd swept from the upstairs rooms, down the steep staircase in a flurry of dust that set them sneezing, laughing. Stained tumorous wallpaper they'd stripped and flung into piles peaked like tents. Tearing up faded and filthy linoleum in the kitchen. Dangling electrical cords, broken wall switches, hardwood floors looking as if someone had dragged barbed wire across them. A kind of madness had come over them, a fever to strip the house of its former tenants, who'd let the property lapse into such decay that a practically penniless young couple could acquire it with a loan from relatives and a mortgage.

Watch us! We own this.

Last winter she'd ceased using birth control. Must be, then, she tells herself, she wants a child. Since she has given up drinking, she has been so lonely, it's a loneliness that begins in the mouth, a terrible thirst and a hunger, of which it is impossible to speak to anyone who doesn't understand.

It isn't that you yearn for a *child,* nor even to be *pregnant,* but to accomplish a feat small enough to have been accomplished by so many without effort at all through the millennia—in short, the history of the world: *increase and multiply.*

It's not quite six o'clock. She is not late returning home, will not be *late* for another hour at least. And if Patrick is not back, she will not be late until he is there, in the kitchen, preparing the evening meal, always something of an improvisation, a joint project that has become a nightly ritual: rich Italian sauces, special olive oil, capers, fine-cut onions, fresh tomatoes, fresh-made pasta from the Italian food store.

Blue Moon Café. All neon by night is exciting to Juliana, but blue neon most.

The earliest neon in Juliana's life. When she'd been a young girl.

That café, too: *Blue Moon.*

Ridiculous, of course. Juliana isn't a senti-mental person, Juliana knows better.

Really, she hasn't time to stop for a drink. She has the (secret) ice pick with her of course, but she no longer has any wish to use it.

Her old life, her life *then*—she has finished that life.

She is with Patrick now. She is pregnant now.

Still, since moving into their new home a few

blocks away, Juliana has been curious about the Blue Moon Café. You wonder if a place like this is an authentic bar, an old neighborhood tavern refurbished, or if it's a shallow, improvised place selling endive salads, sautéed tofu, kale smoothies, sparkling water, a few wines and novelty beers, no hard liquor.

If the atmosphere inside is high-polished hardwood floor or old scuffed tile, linoleum. If there's dim lighting, but not candlelight. Bright or shadowy, just enough neon, not overbright.

In a proper bar there's a balance between *bright* and *overbright*.

There's another bar, or tavern, on the Delaware River, a mile or so away, that has intrigued Juliana, but (of course) she has never investigated it. To do so would mean going miles out of her way.

The Blue Moon Café is *on her way.* Driving home on Front Street.

Juliana recalls having heard, something had happened to a woman in that other tavern recently. Nineteen years old, disappeared.

Not the Blue Moon Café, however.

In the street, Juliana has paused, car engine idling. The interior of the café appears to be dim, smoky. Yes there is a bar, just visible. Working-class place, neighborhood tavern, unlike the Blue Moon Café in her hometown, which was located in a strip mall on a state highway at the edge of town. And smaller than that café and not crowded, though (she's thinking) it's a weekday evening, still early. By eleven p.m. the air will be dense in the Blue Moon, thrilling.

By eleven p.m. she will be asleep. Her days begin early, before dawn in this season. Her work is erratically scheduled, unlike Patrick's; he is a full-time attorney in a suburban firm across the river, Juliana works part-time at the State of New Jersey Legal Aid office.

Both Patrick and Juliana have law degrees from the same law school: Rutgers-Newark.

He has the full-time job, a strong promise of permanent employment. Juliana has something lesser, but she has no complaints.

Parking on Front Street would be difficult in any case, vehicles on both sides of the narrow street, no parking lot (that she can see) beside or behind the Blue Moon Café.

Driving on. She isn't tempted. Buoyed by happiness, like one borne along by a swift current, unable to register where she is and who she is and why—as when she wakes from troubled dreams to take solace in the knowledge that she is finally with a man, a companion, who adores her without needing to know her.

Thinking—*It is all that I want. Nothing more.*

She is feeling proud of herself now. Not giving in, no drinking. Not a single drink in—how long?—almost eighteen months. And now that there's an official *due date,* certainly not.

2.

Blue Moon in another state: Pennsylvania. Another lifetime. She'd been a high school kid, sixteen. Try to tell Juliana Regan anything, wouldn't listen. Monday mornings you'd hear wild tales of the Blue Moon, which wasn't any kind of café, just a roadside tavern out Route 33. Dreamy with envy hearing of girls her age who went out with guys in their twenties at the Blue Moon and other taverns by the lakes.

And then, one summer night, a Saturday night, Juliana was one of these.

Not that it had been planned, it had not. More like an accident, where one thing happens and then another, and then another. But you could not guess how the first thing that happens could lead to the last in a succession of things that happen. In any case Juliana wasn't one to plan, had no car of her own and no way to transport herself. She had (girl) friends who had cars, or rather access to cars, but sometimes it happened that her friends drifted away and Julie (as they called her) was left behind. Or in her heedlessness Julie drifted away and was left behind. At the Blue Moon Tavern there was a parking lot of coarse gravel, she'd recall stones in her sandals, between her toes, hurting like hell. Doors of vehicles slamming, car radios abruptly silenced. It was August, she'd been at one of the lakes with her friends. In a halter top, short shorts, bare midriff, sandals. Chestnut-brown ponytail straggling down her back. Older guys, graduated from the high school a few years before, she knew their names and faces, but they didn't know her.

A boy named Carson, who went to Colgate. Sleek as a seal, his hair combed back from a high, blunt forehead, wet-flashing incisors, his fraternity at Colgate was Deke. Julie was too young to drink even beer, but in the confusion no one seemed to notice, or to care.

Too young for the crowd at the Blue Moon, but Julie knew to be impressed by *Deke.*

Talk of guys at Colgate inviting girls from the high school for fraternity weekends. Dazzling tales, dreamy tales, Julie was sick with envy, lavishing red lipstick on her mouth, critically eyeing herself in a restroom mirror.

Also they were smoking dope. In the parking lot, but (for a while) in the tavern, too. She wasn't accustomed to smoking anything stronger than cigarettes. She was dizzy, excited. What's meant by *high?* Dreamy/sleepy feeling. Wanting to snuggle, kiss. Wanting to feel a guy's arms around her. Strong, protective. Her face was flushed, sunburnt. Damned sunscreen had washed off, she'd been in the water. Two beers, lukewarm. Trying not to belch, giggling.

Ticklish!—where Carson was trying to carry her, "walk" her, gripping her underarms. He'd brought her somewhere, vaguely she'd let him kiss her. Some privacy they needed, he was saying. The other girls were older, indifferent to Julie. Not her friends. Resenting her. Where were Julie's friends—brought her to the Blue Moon and ditched her. No more idea how to kiss than a baby, just let whoever it was, the Deke, or anyway said he was Deke, kiss and suck at her mouth, try to stick his beery tongue into her mouth, but she balked, giggling and gagging. Outside in somebody's car, she'd felt his hands on her, hard. Saying *Just cool it, okay. Nothing to panic about, just cool it Junie.* Her name in his mouth a wrong name, though uttering *Junie* as if he didn't think much of the name, or her.

Then he was trying to straddle her in the back seat of the car, yanking at her shorts, beer breath in her face. How quickly this was happening. Julie panicked, pushed away his hands, crying. Managed to get the door open, half fell out of the car, and ran, ran the way a child might run, wet-faced, nose running, he'd run after her, furious and disgusted, cursing, chasing her through the parking lot, one of her sandals lost. Oh, her wounded foot! Panting, crouching beside a stinking Dumpster. An alley behind the Blue Moon Tavern, she ran to hide, like a terrified animal behind a garage, shivering and trying not to sob.

Behind her, the boy was calling in a lowered voice of drunken exasperation—*June! Ju-nie! Hey c'mon, nobody's gonna hurt you Jun-ie.*

His friends were following him, telling him to cool it. Shouts were exchanged, profanities. Like a rabbit she waited, very still as the predator sniffs the air. But she was upwind. He couldn't smell her. Not her panic sweat, the reek of her underarms. In crazy exhilaration her heart beat. Thinking—*If I can get back home. This once. If You will let me, God.*

She would tell herself later—*I had no weapon. Not a thing . . .*

Long after the guys had driven away, yelling and jeering, she'd remained in hiding behind the Dumpster. All the while squatting. Her body was covered in a cold, oozing, oily sweat of shame, her legs ached painfully. And finally she limped back home. Two miles. One shoe on, one shoe off. Adrenaline coursed through her veins, Goddamn she would do this. She would get back home, she would save herself, and no one would know, or almost no one. Managed to slip into the house by the back door. They were watching TV downstairs in the basement. Upstairs in her room, panting and reeling with exhaustion, shame. Bathing in a hot bath. Which was not some-thing Julie ever did—run a bath. Showers, maybe three times a week. Save on water, save on shampoo, d'you think we're rich? Out of the tub and taking care to clean it so that no one would know. No one would guess. His hands on her breasts had hurt, bruises were emerging in the pale skin. Staring at herself in the mirror with a kind of longing, trying to recall what she'd looked like earlier that day, the quick, bright smile, hopeful smile, always so hopeful, naïve. Recalling that afternoon when her friends had come to get her, the car at the curb, horn tapped. Or maybe they weren't her friends. If she could be that girl again. But no, could not. But the guy, the Deke from Colgate—he hadn't raped her. Though he'd boast—something. Grabbed at her between the legs, she'd kicked out fiercely and frantically. He'd had to retreat, cursing. Earlier, crowded into the booth, he'd been laughing at silly things she'd said, high on dope and beer, in her high-pitched little-girl voice that made her daddy love her, but when guys laugh, you know they are going to hurt you. Guys' laughter was like barking. Hurts your ears, it's a kind of warning. She'd been shrewd taking alleys home. Desperate not to be seen. Not hitching a ride. Saturday night, disheveled and dazed and hoping to hitch a ride, cops might've picked her up too. *God, if you spare me. I promise . . .*

A wild fantasy, she'd had something with

her. To protect her. A knife, an ice pick. Even a screwdriver, sharp at the end.

Something from the house. Kitchen, toolshed.

Static in her head, as in the house. Like silence that has been roughly shaken. Her mother and her father not speaking to each other at this time, and the silence between them sharper than the voices of her friends' parents. Her father's drinking, that was the quarrel. Or maybe not the drinking, but what the drinking meant, that her mother had to contend with. So (maybe) Daddy wasn't home. Just her mother and her younger brother, and (maybe) her brother wasn't home either, probably with friends playing video games.

So it was her mother and her sister watching TV downstairs. Her mother hadn't heard her return, but eventually her mother came upstairs, surprised to see her daughter with sleek wet hair, fresh-bathed, not sunburnt and disheveled and smelling of her body as you'd expect. And Juliana tells her mother she'd come home early, explaining that she hadn't felt so good at the lake, thought it might be cramps starting (which is so, so embarrassing), lucky that her friend Irene didn't want to stay longer at the lake either, the girls got a ride back home, glibly the lie comes to Juliana, that's why she is home early, she's taken ibuprofen (which is what her mother always gives her for cramps), sort of collapsed on her bed and slept and only just woke up. She's had a bath, she'd felt so filthy from the lake and sand, sweating in the sun. The mother sees the dilated pupils (maybe) but can't smell the Deke's sweat, which has been scrubbed away. If the Deke had (what was it called?—some ugly word) ejaculated on the daughter, can't smell that either. Can't see bruises beginning to emerge on the daughter's shoulders, arms, thighs. The daughter is in her pajamas, kitten-print cotton pj's cool against sunburnt skin. The mother sees the baffled hurt in the daughter's face but decides to believe the daughter claiming to have been home for hours on this Saturday night in summer.

The father would not have believed for an instant. The father would not have needed to smell the Deke's sweat or any other odor of a young male body. The father would not have needed to see the emerging bruises, he'd have understood how boys put their hands on girls like the daughter if they can. But the father was not home. Not that night and not other nights. The father had begun to keep a distance between himself and the children, it was not understood why. *Why* did he not want them nearer? *Why* did he not love Juliana so much any longer? Because she was sixteen? Because she wasn't a little girl any longer? The mother was drinking, too. Cold beer out of the refrigerator. Saying *It's kind of a lonely life after you're married. You don't really*

have your girlfriends then—they're all married.
They've got husbands, kids. In-laws. They can't
see you when you need them or even talk. If you
were close to a sister or a cousin, that's basically
over. You can't go out in the evening like guys
do after work, hanging out in a tavern getting a
load on. You do that, the marriage is over. They
fuck you, then they fuck you over. The mother
hiccupped, as if her own words had startled
her, shocked her. Juliana was pretending to be
falling asleep, no need to register hearing. In the
darkened bedroom the mother sat on the edge
of the bed, the bedsprings creaking beneath her
weight, until Juliana really did fall asleep.

All night long against her smarting eyelids,
flickering blue neon . . .

Blue Moon   Blue Moon   Blue Moon

Not long afterward the bad thing happened to a
girl, but not to Juliana.

Seventeen-year-old girl badly beaten, raped,
left unconscious at the edge of the Blue Moon
Tavern parking lot, local media never named the
girls, underage girls, but it was known that this
girl was from the next town, not from Juliana's
high school, no one Juliana or her friends knew.
The name, they would know, for it was a name
passed about, sullied and scorned, disdained,
even laughed at, her clothes torn from her, dis-

covered unconscious, naked, no memory of what had been done to her, no arrests ever made.

The Blue Moon Tavern was shut down pending an investigation into charges of serving alcohol to minors, eventually reopened under new management and a new name, but Juliana did not ever return.

3.

Pulsing red neon—THE SAND BAR.

Cruising the strip. Ocean Avenue, at the Jersey shore. The summer before her sophomore year at the university. After dark a glittering succession of bars, lounges, cafés, motels. Flashing neon: red, blue, purple, green, stretching for thirteen undulating miles south to Atlantic City. Just to see the Harbor Island strip at night, nearing midnight, ceaseless headlights like a waterfall, blaring of car radios, slapping of waves on the beach, and the sky above the Atlantic ridged and rippled with translucent clouds through which a drunken moon sailed . . .

After her employers' children were in bed, her duties for the interminable day completed, she'd hurry out, eager to spend time with new friends at The Sand Bar.

Mostly girls like herself. Sometimes, guys. Sometimes, older men.

Gradually she'd become accustomed to living away from home and from her mother's scrutiny.

(Her university was Rutgers-Newark, to which she commuted with several others in a car pool.) She'd had enough of being *mothered*— couldn't breathe. Daddy had moved out of the house. Juliana missed no one there, had become negligent in calling her mother. Nothing so boring as being *missed*. What could you say if you didn't miss another person in turn?

The new mother-presence in Juliana's life was Mrs. Hermann, who'd hired Juliana as a live-in nanny for three small children but expected other work from her as well: meal preparation, kitchen cleanup, housecleaning, hauling trash to a Dumpster thirty feet away. Something about Mrs. Hermann was grating to Juliana, the very composure of the woman's voice, low, assured, the voice of female complacency, self-satisfaction. Mrs. Hermann was accustomed to giving orders, you did not want to disappoint her, for instance taking a ridiculous amount of time to wash by hand, delicately by hand, "until they sparkle," expensive wine and water glasses Mrs. Hermann would not allow in the dishwasher.

"You wash delicate glasses by hand at your house, don't you, Juliana?" Mrs. Hermann pointed out, as if it were at all probable that the hired nanny lived in a household in which such expensive, delicate glassware was likely, smiling sternly at Juliana, meaning no irony, certainly not taunting her, taking for granted what was preposterous, and so forcing Juliana to smile and nod foolishly yes, *yes, of course, Mrs. Hermann.*

Juliana's room was a maid's room on the first floor of the Hermanns' tri-level house on one of the most beautiful Harbor Island canals, so close by the ocean you could, at night, if you lay very still and listened hard, hear the slapping of the surf. In the room were two doors, one of which opened directly outside onto the canal, no need to make her way through the house, and so in the later evening, after nine p.m., giddy with freedom, Juliana hurried breathless and excited to Ocean Avenue to meet her new friends, like Juliana hired by well-to-do summer residents who owned property on the island. This was happiness! This was *possibility.*

Quickly changing her clothes, tank top, shorts, or jeans, putting on makeup, examining herself in a mirror, and liking what she saw, or almost.

Exhausting to be responsible for young children. Juliana's face hurt with smiling hard, never losing her temper, never a sarcastic remark of the kind she'd be making at home; here was another mother's territory, *she* was a provisional member of the family who could be dismissed at any moment on any pretext. And so she tried, tried very hard; truly she liked the little girl, but truly she'd come to dislike the spoiled older boy who sometimes swiped at her with his fist, actually daring to hit her, and once he'd spat at her like a TV brat, what was his name?—Brad Simpson?—even as Mrs. Hermann blamed *her* for squabbles among the children and Mr. Hermann, aloof and indifferent, pressed his hands over his ears, blaming them all.

Yet hurrying to Ocean Avenue, Juliana is suffused with happiness, hope. Glittering waterfall of headlights on the avenue, seductive neon signs identifying bars, taverns, lounges, and the favorite of these was The Sand Bar, where dark-tanned men who'd been sailing or fishing off their yachts stayed until the bar closed, at two a.m. Often, by magic, drinks would appear at the girls' table—"All paid for"—courtesy of these men.

Mr. Hermann was a Philadelphia businessman, Juliana knew little more of him and his wife except that they had money, they had *things.* You could be scornful of the Hermanns' *things,* but only if you were not up close to see them and appreciate their quality: classy, steel-colored Mercedes, dazzling-white yacht, the "summer place" that must have cost two million dollars, Juliana calculated. Being a nanny for such a couple was a fluke—Juliana had been recommended by a friend of a friend, what was said of her must have been good, for the job paid twice as much as any other summer job she'd been able to find in Asbury Park. And it was the Jersey Shore, affluent Harbor Island.

The Hermanns were attractive people, though brusque, bossy. Both were short, compactly built. Mr. Hermann no more than five foot seven, Juliana's height. She thought of them as hard-shelled beetles, shiny on the outside, alert, wary, insecure in their wealth; something vulnerable about them, yet dangerous, as an overturned beetle, belly exposed, might be vulnerable and yet dangerous, venomous. Mrs. Hermann's hair was expensively styled, "frosted." Her fingernails were perfectly manicured, her makeup flawless, Juliana came to dread the woman's shrewd beetle eyes fixing upon her, tensing of the tight fore-head as briskly she gave Juliana orders—*Now what I'd like you to do, Juliana, this morning, is . . .*

In the woman's mouth the name *Juliana* sounded like a taunt, mockery—*Juli-an-na.* The wide, hungry mouth was a crimson slash in the heavily made up face. But always Juliana smiled. Juliana had become practiced at smiling to signal to older women that she was a good girl, not a sarcastic or cynical girl, a girl to be trusted.

A girl to be trusted with children. A girl to be trusted with a husband.

Except Juliana had no real power, only respon-sibility. The children knew, even the little girl knew. Juliana acquired a way of laughing that was a substitute for swearing, for never was she heard swearing by anyone in the household—

not even sighing loudly, sucking in her breath in disgust. She was uneasy in Mrs. Hermann's presence, yet she melted visibly when Mrs. Hermann praised her to her friends, which Mrs. Hermann had a way of doing, lavishly, like one waving a flag or tossing bills onto a table for a craven waitperson. Mrs. Hermann may even have been boasting of Juliana to the others, attractively groomed women like herself, in their forties, lolling beside the turquoise pool at the Harbor Island Yacht Club, or when Mrs. Hermann turned the crimson-slash mouth upon Juliana at close range, smiling unexpectedly like a generous TV host.

"Well, Jul-i-an-na! Quite a day we had, didn't we. You must be wrung dry. You're looking kind of peaked. You can take the rest of the day off, we've got a big day tomorrow . . ."

Juliana had much less to do with Mr. Hermann, fortunately. Such a busy man, such an *important* man, if you overheard Mrs. Hermann's boastful complaints, it seemed that her husband couldn't trust any subordinates to oversee his business, which was why he had to spend four nights in Philadelphia through much of the damned summer, driving out to Harbor Island late Friday and returning to Philadelphia very early Monday morning.

Mr. Hermann's name was Irving: June had not known any *Irving* before. There had been no

Irving at her high school nor in her hometown. Juliana was sure.

Irving Hermann was swarthy-skinned, darkly tanned. His dark, wavy hair was coarse yet fussily barbered. His eyes glowed with an indefinable intensity. He had the ebullient bossiness of the very fit shorter man who resents having to look up to meet another's gaze. His white shirt—(often, Mr. Hermann wore white shirts)—seemed to glow. Oddly too, Mr. Hermann wore long-sleeved shirts even in the heat, cuffs with gold cuff links, a signet ring in the shape of a pyramid, hairs on the backs of his fingers. He was a fastidious dresser, self-conscious, vain. His trousers were seersucker, he might wear a seersucker jacket to the yacht club. White with dark blue stripes. No necktie, the white shirt open at the throat and a spigot of dark hairs showing. He had a way, fussy, particular, of rolling up his shirtsleeves to the elbows, exposing muscled forearms covered in dark hairs, which drew Juliana's attention as if with a pang of nostalgia (though she didn't recall that rolling up shirtsleeves had been a habit of her father's or of any man she'd ever known). It seemed to be more and more frequently that Juliana happened to see Mr. Hermann, or a man who closely resembled him, at The Sand Bar in the later part of the evening: not in the bar area, which was likely to be rowdy and loud, patronized by younger customers, but in the lounge, in one of the candlelit booths where Juliana might glimpse her employer, or someone who resembled him, in the company of a woman, often a quite young woman, no one whom Juliana knew.

(But was it the same woman or several women? Juliana knew better than to stare.)

How it happened that Mrs. Hermann remained in the house on the canal on these nights, propped up in the king-size bed, sipping wine and watching TV on an enormous flat screen, in a silky nightgown from which her melon-breasts spilled abundantly—this was a mystery. Most nights when Mr. Hermann was on Harbor Island were spent on the yacht, or on friends' yachts, or at the yacht club, and Mrs. Hermann dressed for these occasions, made up her face extravagantly, and seemed to be enjoying herself; but other nights, inexplicably, Mrs. Hermann remained at the house while Mr. Hermann turned up at The Sand Bar sometime before midnight in the company of—someone . . .

As if entrusted with a precious secret, Juliana did not tell the friends with whom she was drinking. When their conversations swerved onto their employers, Juliana did not volunteer that her employer, Mr. Hermann, or someone who closely resembled him, was in The Sand Bar at that very moment.

Nights at The Sand Bar—good memories for

Juliana. Learning to appreciate high-quality beer, wine spritzers, acquiring certain tastes in wine, even "cocktails"—practice is needed, a degree of poise.

Drinking with her newfound friends, who were all very funny. And Juliana too, hilariously funny. Girls her approximate age from backgrounds not so different from hers, working-class girls, girls with divorced parents, like herself needing money for college, not above menial labor (laundry, scrubbing toilets), but what the hell, had to be done. They told tales, they laughed riotously. Determined to have a good time on Harbor Island after work hours. The atmosphere was festive, like a tilting deck. Juliana wasn't old enough to drink legally in New Jersey, but with a borrowed driver's license she was rarely questioned, most of the bartenders were her friends, also it was a fact that in Harbor Island everyone looked younger than their actual age, middle-aged women like Mrs. Hermann looked a decade younger at least. Especially in dreamy-dim neon-lit places like The Sand Bar.

Guys often joined them, easing companionably onto bar stools. Guys their own age or older who had summer work on Harbor Island: lifeguards, waiters, marina staff, gas station attendants. Some helped out on yachts, sailboats. Some were personal drivers. The more desirable were SAT tutors, paid lavishly for summer employment.

Some few were computer techs, also lavishly paid. Like jellyfish drifting in the currents of summer beside the Atlantic Ocean, these young men seemed slippery and indefinable. It would be a mistake to place any hope in their excited but ephemeral interest, you could not take them seriously—their names, like their faces and hometowns, were interchangeable.

Then there were older men, married men. Many of these.

The wedding band was a giveaway—of course. Flash of gold, like the flash of gold cuff links. Sexual thrill, like neon.

Bills negligently dropped onto the bar at The Sand Bar, a glimpse of a twenty-dollar bill, even a fifty-dollar bill, purchasing for the girls not beer or spritzers, but gaudy fruit concoctions with exotic names—Balinese Sunrise, Strawberry Martini, Kiss Goodbye, El Dorado Vodka Fizz, Atlantic City Blast. Sometimes there were surf-and-turf platters. Onion rings, cocktail olives. One August night, making her way to the women's room at The Sand Bar not so steady on her feet, Juliana found herself staring at a man in profile, familiar-looking, in one of the dim-lit booths, in the company of a sleek blond female with a showgirl look, tight black spandex top, glitter-dust sprinkled on her eyelids—a face you'd see magnified on an Atlantic City billboard advertising casino gambling. The man turned, glanced toward Juliana; unmistakably, it was Irving Hermann, frowning at her, a grimace of a smile, a warning—*Hey. You didn't see me and I didn't see you, sweetheart.*

The glamorous blonde was drinking something that resembled a daiquiri. Fruit-colored, peach? Mr. Hermann was drinking a martini.

In the women's room Juliana waited several minutes before emerging, making her way back to her friends at the bar like one walking a tightrope, straight and unerring, glancing neither to the left nor to the right.

She wasn't drunk, nor with drunken companions. Had to hope that Irving Hermann noticed her good-girl sobriety.

Soon then leaving The Sand Bar. Not yet seeing Mr. Hermann and his woman friend leave, which was good—possibly, neither had actually seen the other.

At about two a.m. that night, when she'd been deeply asleep in her bed in the maid's room, there came a rap of knuckles against the outside door. Juliana woke in alarm, knowing immediately who it was, had to be, rising groggy and apprehensive from her bed and with pounding heart crouched before the door, saying in a pleading voice *Who is it?*—explaining that she could not open the (locked) door because she was in bed, she wasn't dressed—*Please go away!*—but Mr. Hermann had a key (of course: among myriad keys on his key chain) and simply unlocked the door despite Juliana's pleas. Rudely he switched on the bright overhead light, staring at Juliana, not smiling, but then laughing, at her frightened face perhaps, in a slurred but affable voice saying *Sweetie you know that wasn't me tonight you didn't see me, right? And I didn't see you, Julian-ya.*

Juliana brushed her hair out of her eyes. Feeling the risk, the coercion in the man's gravelly voice, a playful sort of threat and yet an actual threat, the shiny-beetle carapace as hard as steel, yet Juliana managed to sound flirtatious, defiant— *Oh it wasn't? Not you, Mr. Hermann?—nooo?*

Her employer was no taller than Juliana but loomed above her as she stood barefoot a few feet away. Staring frankly at Juliana, as if he'd never really *looked at* the nanny before and seeing her now, exposed in the too-bright light, flimsy T-shirt and panties in which she slept, no cotton pajamas imprinted with kittens but fabric so thin her taut nipples were visible, pale patch of pubic hair visible, and her naked feet, curling toes, the staring man had to laugh at the cringing girl, a sort of chiding affection, a Daddy sort of affection, reached out to seize the damp nape of her neck, squeezed hard—*No, sweetie. You are correct—it wasn't me.*

Suddenly, no joking. Suddenly, Mr. Hermann was hurting her.

Instinctively Juliana fought back, squirmed out of the man's grip. Pushing against him, daring to touch him, her employer, *Mr. Hermann,* whom she'd never previously confronted in any way, would never dream of touching, suddenly everything was changed, and Mr. Hermann was pushing Juliana back, glaring at her, his breath coming quick.

Knocking Juliana off balance, onto the bed. Sprawling on her back, helpless and astonished on the bed.

His hand over her mouth, hard. Gritty flat of his hand.

Stop! Shut up! I said—shut up.

Juliana hadn't realized she was screaming, or trying to scream. So quickly this was happening. Desperate thrashing to throw the man off her, smelling liquor on his breath, still astonished, stunned, how abruptly the playfulness had ended, still Mr. Hermann's face was contorted in a grin, she heard a grunting kind of laughter as he straddled her, pushed up the T-shirt, tore at the panties. *Was* it play? (Irving Hermann sometimes tickled his children like this, or almost—rough-playing to make them shriek with laughter, kicking wildly.) Juliana tasted acid at the back of her mouth, panicked threat of vomit even as she tried to draw her (naked) knees up to shield herself from Mr. Hermann, propel him from her, but the man was too heavy, too determined.

318

Grunting atop her—*Oh!—uh!—uh* . . .

For a panicked moment Juliana couldn't breathe. Crushed by the man's weight that was dense, compact, like clayey earth. Then like a frantic animal she managed to squirm out from beneath him, yanking down the T-shirt, with outspread fingers trying to shield herself where he'd torn the panties, but by this time Mr. Hermann too was on his feet, chagrined, backing off, dazed, muttering to himself words Juliana could not decipher but understood were not directed toward her. With both hands he brushed his unkempt hair back from his forehead, panting as if he'd been running, angry-sounding, unable to catch his breath.

Juliana stammered for him to leave her alone, please go away and leave her alone, she wouldn't tell anyone Juliana promised, begged, by *anyone* meaning only just *Mrs. Hermann* of course and so hearing this Mr. Hermann laughed harshly, as if Juliana had said something meant to be funny, or so stupid that it was funny.

Hesitating, then deciding. Deciding *no,* not worth the risk.

Adjusted his clothing, gave another brisk swipe to his hair, lurched to the door, and was gone.

Soon then, Juliana heard footsteps directly over her head, heels coming down hard on the low ceiling.

Gone! It was over as swiftly as it had begun.

She was weak with relief. She was smiling, a sick sort of smile, with relief. Looking then for a way to secure the lock at the door, but there appeared to be none, nor was there a double lock at the door leading into the interior of the house, so Juliana dragged a chair to this door, hoping to secure it, like a character in a movie. To secure a door with a chair like this was somehow funny.

Trying to comprehend exactly what had happened, and what it meant, what had happened.

Juliana would be most struck by how quickly the assault had happened, how rapid the transformation from playfulness to actual hurt and a threat of greater hurt, recalling the ordeal in the college boy's car behind the Blue Moon Tavern years ago, exactly that, and then too the smell of the other's breath, hot, hissing breath, drunkenness.

No way to protect herself. If she'd screamed . . .

Something with which to strike him. Hurt *him.*

Something sharp, a knife. A tool of some kind, like a screwdriver.

But then reasoning: How could she? How, hurting *him,* would she not be hurting herself?

The heavy footsteps above her head faded. Mr. Hermann was ascending to the upper floor of the house where (probably) Mrs. Hermann had fallen asleep watching TV, wine bottle and glass on her bedside table.

He was drunk, he didn't mean it—he likes me . . .

Juliana lay awake through the remainder of the night. Telling herself that Irving Hermann did like her, at least when sober, Irving Hermann liked her, he'd always smiled at her in an affable sort of way, never had she noticed her employer really seeing *her*, not in any overtly sexual way, until this night.

Awake, she lay hot-skinned beneath the sheet that felt coarse to her sensitive skin, aroused in a way she could not understand was sexual, or rather knowing it had to be sexual, yet could not understand such arousal, such yearning, a wish to plead to the man for him to forgive her, no, for him to apologize to her, to beg her forgiveness for how he'd touched her, he'd hurt her, did he not understand how he'd *hurt* her?

In the morning her employer would apologize to her, Juliana thought. The prospect excited her, for it was rare in her life that any adult apologized to her or seemed even to have noticed that she had been insulted.

Hey. Sorry.

Okay.

Is it—okay?

Yes.

But next morning Irving Hermann didn't come downstairs for breakfast while Juliana was there, taking care of the children. Mrs. Hermann, too, came downstairs late.

Scarcely did Juliana glimpse Mr. Hermann

321

at all that day, hearing footsteps on the stairs, muffled voices at a distance.

There were just a few bruises on Juliana's face, forearms, wrist, and these were easily hidden. Makeup, sleeves. Hair combed slantwise across her forehead. Mrs. Hermann's sharp eye saw nothing, Mrs. Hermann suspected nothing. In the maid's room, when she returned at noon from the beach with the children, Juliana was surprised, though not terribly surprised, to see several bills slid partway beneath the pillow on her bed.

Fifty-dollar bills, unique in her experience. How many?

Five, no six. Six!

He would never approach her again, Juliana knew. Never would he enter the maid's room again.

Still, Juliana found a screwdriver in one of the kitchen drawers and hid it in her bureau. Clumsy weapon, not really sharp, but if she ever needed it, it might save her life . . .

But soon then, as if the encounter in the maid's room had been a turning point and not—as Juliana should have presumed—irrelevant to her employers' marriage, the couple began to quarrel openly.

Not just muffled voices behind shut doors. Now wicked exchanges like TV dialogue. Escalating profanity, shocking to Juliana's ear, in the mouths of the well-to-do adults who were her employers.

Abruptly, Irving Hermann appeared at the house on the canal at times unpredictable to Juliana. No longer did he drive out from Philadelphia for the weekend; now he might appear midweek, not to stay in the house, but (evidently) to stay in a motel nearby in order to see the children, whom he took out for meals or onto the yacht or swimming at the club. There were phone calls, muffled pleas of Mrs. Hermann.

Renee was her name: Renee Hermann. Juliana thought it was a sad name, not a name she'd have wanted for herself. And never *Mrs*—Juliana did not want *Mrs*.

Mrs. Hermann began to have difficulty waking in the morning. Half dressing, dragging herself from bed, her face not yet made up, pale, flaccid, accusing. When Mrs. Hermann finally entered the kitchen—(long after Juliana had fed the children)—there was the risk of objects clattering to the floor, cutlery, glassware. Plates slipped from Renee Hermann's fingers, shattered on the floor. Mrs. Hermann cursed, as crude and swift as any man, any of the guys with whom Juliana drank in the late evening, as furious and despairing as Irving Hermann himself.

The little girl cried petulantly, the boy ran wild, crazed. Their mother screamed at them but otherwise made no attempt to discipline them; that fell to Juliana, the older sister, the stepsister, whom no one had to obey or respect. Juliana was cautious of chasing the boy, fearing that he would turn and pummel her with his hard, little fists, he'd bare his glistening incisors at her, eyes flashing white-rimmed above the iris, like Mr. Hermann's eyes when he'd straddled Juliana in triumph, flat on her back in the bed.

More often now, Mrs. Hermann drank during the day, not just at the yacht club (where all the wives and mothers drank, no harm to it), but by herself, in the house. In the kitchen. In the bedroom. Carelessly Mrs. Hermann swallowed pills and sent Juliana to the drugstore to pick up more pills. With unseemly haste all this seemed to be happening, the Hermanns' marriage breaking up like ice melting, breaking into chunks, and these chunks melting. Of course the fissures had been there previously but not visible (to Juliana's eyes); even Mrs. Hermann had not seemed to know, to be genuinely surprised, out-raged. Juliana tried to feel sympathy for the woman, though impatience too—*What did you think was going on? Couldn't you guess?*

She could not comprehend the sexual nature of a marriage. She had no idea, totally she was mystified. Would not Mrs. Hermann have sensed—*something?*

Maybe the Hermanns hadn't made love in years. Maybe not since the little girl was born. Maybe that was it. If she'd had a baby, Juliana thought with a little shiver of disgust, she

324

wouldn't want to *make love* again for a long, long
while.

The kind of lovemaking Juliana had experienced, somewhat rough, tentative but rough,
inexpert, thrusting, a kind of pummeling, had
left her insides chafed and raw; imagining the
bloodied state of the uterine canal, the vagina,
after childbirth, left her faint-headed. Just—
no.

Hardly the nanny's fault, her employers'
melting-away marriage, yet Juliana felt obscurely
to blame. She wasn't the showgirl blonde with
the glittering eyelids in The Sand Bar, but—
almost—she could imagine that she was that
girl, a version of that girl. And maybe Irving
Hermann—"Irv"—had been one of those married
men who brought drinks for Juliana without
Juliana's realizing; sometimes in the febrile
night she felt the man's fingers at the nape of her
neck, stroking and kneading. Started off gentle,
teasing, then turned hard, hurtful. She heard his
low, teasing, bemused voice. *Sweetie!* She heard
the guttural moans, grunts. She felt a rippling
sensation pass through her body in the region of
her groin, a sharp sensation in her breasts, a sort
of misery, an anguish that left her weak, faint.

She'd secreted away the (six) fifty-dollar bills.
She would tell no one, for who was there to tell?
No one.

Frequently, by day, Juliana encountered

325

men—to her, "older" men—who resembled Irving Hermann: not tall, compactly built, dark-tanned, in white polo shirts, white cord trousers, shorts, prescription sunglasses, so that their eyes were hidden. Once, on a gusty stretch of ocean beach where she was walking alone while the children were (in theory at least) taking their late-afternoon naps and Mrs. Hermann was drinking in her bedroom and watching daytime TV, Juliana stammered—*H-Hello? Mr. Hermann?*—but the man in T-shirt and shorts passed by, arrogant and indifferent to her, not hearing.

After a long day of telephone calls, Mrs. Hermann drew Juliana aside from the children to ask bluntly—*Did my husband ever touch you, Juliana? Did he ever come into your room? Did he say—things—certain things—to you? You can tell me now,* but Juliana shook her head *no,* certainly *no.* A guilty flush came into her face, but Mrs. Hermann did not seem to notice.

These days, the household so unsettled, it would have been natural to ask Mrs. Hermann where her husband was. Yet Juliana could not ask.

At The Sand Bar she saw such men, these were older, married men, possibly they were divorced men, in their forties, fifties, even older—men older than Juliana's father, older than Irving Hermann. Perhaps she was attracted to them, but only "attracted"—she knew to avoid them, she would not accept drinks from them, shaking her head, laughing *Nooo. Don't think so.*

Like sharks they waited. Out in the waves, dark fins obscured by the froth.

Rumors you'd hear . . .

But no: not in Harbor Island, an affluent, upscale town on the Jersey Shore.

Elsewhere, farther south in Atlantic City, that was where the murdered women began to be found that summer, dumped bodies naked and partly decomposed, banner headlines in local newspapers—*prostitutes.*

In all, eight *prostitutes* discovered in a marsh behind a notorious motel in a derelict neighborhood of Atlantic City.

Are you certain, Juliana? My husband—Irving— did not? Ever?

Pleading with Juliana *Say yes! Tell me.*

Pleading with Juliana *Say no! Spare me.*

Juliana repeated the words she'd rehearsed. Stammering out of what might be interpreted as embarrassment, avoiding the woman's angry, blood-veined eyes. *No, Mrs. Hermann.*

But Mrs. Hermann persisted: *Did you see him with other women? Don't lie, don't you dare lie to* me.

Finally, beginning to be nasty—*Did he pay you off? Did you take money from him? Do you think I'm a fool? You—and him . . .*

Soon after this, the summer ended for Juliana. Three weeks before Labor Day.

Mrs. Hermann *gave notice* to Juliana: her employment was ended, she would receive one more week's salary, that was all. Her transportation home would be provided.

No, Mrs. Hermann said, waving her beringed hands, *no no.* There was nothing to discuss.

Juliana was disappointed, wounded. Her wonderful job on Harbor Island!

True, she'd disliked the job. She'd disliked the people. (Except for the little girl, but there were times when she disliked the girl, too.) She'd loved Harbor Island, though.

The Sand Bar. Absolutely, red-flashing neon in the windows of The Sand Bar.

She was losing about half her salary, but she'd gained a (secret) sum from Irving Hermann, of which Mrs. Hermann could not know.

So quickly everything was ending!—what to tell her friends? Her mother?

The beautiful summerhouse was being shut up. Weeks ahead of time. The children were dismayed, unhappy. Grimly Mrs. Hermann spoke on the phone about putting the house *on the market,* not to rent but to sell. She never wanted to return to Harbor Island. She and the children were returning to Philadelphia at once, she'd hired one of the young men to drive them.

Seeing Juliana standing uncertainly, Mrs.

Hermann might say—*Oh, you! Are* you *still here?*

Packing her things in the cramped little maid's room that overlooked the canal. Trying not to cry, rubbing her neck. By now, no bruises remained.

Close up, the canal was less beautiful than she liked to recall, oil spills marred the rippling surface, droppings of gulls were everywhere on the boardwalk, but Juliana would long remember the slapping of waves at the wide beach at Harbor Island, the sky at the eastern horizon lightning at dawn, that foolish tremor of hope in the heart at the sight of the red neon sign—THE SAND BAR.

So quickly Harbor Island had ended, and what had it *meant?*

4.

MONEY BAR in flashing red neon. In fact the name was Monkey Bar, but the *k* had burned out.

Here too were tropical drinks, gaily colored cocktails with little fluted umbrellas, cinnamon sticks, lime slices, grapefruit. Gin, vodka. Tequila, she'd never tasted before. Licking her lips, waiting for the rush she knew would be coming.

Each time, the rush is a little less. Like caffeine in the morning. Nicotine. Still, the promise of flashing neon was an unfailing summons to her blood.

At the Mon ey Bar, where the walls were covered in glossy posters of tropical/jungle scenes. Cavorting monkeys with curlicue tails. Monkeys in red livery busboy costumes. Monkeys upright, drinking toasts to one another, paws white-gloved and so resembling hands. A mirror running the length of the bar all but hidden by glittering bottles so that it was an achievement to locate her own face there, a small but essential piece in a jigsaw puzzle.

Juliana liked the raffish Mon ey Bar because it was far downtown, miles from campus. A place where you understood you would be lonely, because you were alone. Other bars, taverns, places nearer campus, you'd be jammed at the bar with many others shrieking with laughter and so your loneliness would seem more unnatural. More acute. Stuck listening to some guy speaking loudly into your face, spilling beer on you, glancing and grinning at his guy friends. Ramshackle houses on Fraternity Row, deafening rock music and drunk guys, girls careening in high heels, hours from wondering how they will get back to their residence halls. Sickening smell of vomit discovered on the front of your own clothing . . . By the end of freshman year, Juliana had had enough of *that*.

There was kid drinking, binge drinking, and there was serious adult drinking. *She* wasn't interested in kid stuff.

Strange how all her life, after the Blue Moon Tavern, she'd never been a kid again. If a kid is trust, if a kid is naïve and stupid, Juliana wasn't one of those.

At the Mon ey Bar, patrons were older. Never any guys Juliana's age—a relief. She liked being the youngest person in the bar. That was a distinction, flattering to her. Men were protective of her, if indeed they noticed her. The Mon ey Bar was attached to a staid old hotel called the Commodore, which gave it a classy air. The taciturn bartender came to know Juliana by name, but greeted her with only a curt nod when she entered the bar. He was her father's age, thick, dark, oiled hair like an actor in a 1950s movie.

Worse comes to worst, he'd protect her. She knew.

At the Mon ey Bar her senior year, she'd had good times. Basic premise of a bar like this is that no one knows you, judges you. And usually you don't pay for any but your first drink, sometimes not even that. Being so young, reasonably good-looking, Juliana never had to worry, she could arrive with just a few dollars and never reach for her wallet. Older men felt privileged to buy her a drink—"no strings attached"—which wouldn't have been the case with asshole frat boys.

No strings attached. The phrase made Juliana smile. What did it mean? She didn't like *strings attached* to anything.

In the Mon ey Bar she met interesting people: "characters." Not exclusively men, one or two fascinating women, but usually men of course. Once, an older, white-haired gentleman with soft, shadowed eyes, alone at the bar nursing a drink when Juliana arrived, his eyes moved upon her at once, not smiling but staring, as if he might stare at her with impunity but she couldn't see him; when Juliana glanced at him he remained stiff and unsmiling, observing her intensely. Juliana hadn't felt frightened by the man but somehow privileged, honored. *As if he knows me. Even if he doesn't.*

She was drinking gin and tonic. Cool, clear. Left her clear-minded. She'd arrived at the Mon ey Bar at about ten p.m., a weeknight. She would leave by eleven thirty. She measured her drinks, took care not to drink too much. Girls she knew at the university came back from dates drunk, slurring their words, stumbling, clothing disheveled and faces swollen, God knew what had happened to them, had been done to them. Juliana felt pity for girls who couldn't drink, contempt. If they'd been forced to have sex while drunk, it was (technically) rape, but they would never acknowledge such an incident, pretend they didn't remember. Or, indeed, they didn't remember. Juliana would never find herself in such a situation; she knew how to drink.

Returning from the restroom to discover that

the white-haired gentleman had left the Mon ey Bar. Adjacent to the bar was a hotel restaurant, a dim-lighted steak house with leather-cushioned booths and plush crimson walls, out of curiosity, Juliana went to the doorway to look for the white-haired man, but she didn't see him. The Commodore Steak House was expensive, pretentious, the only good restaurant in town, to which visiting parents took their undergraduate offspring when they stayed at the Commodore.

She'd felt the loss of the white-haired man, strangely. He'd have smiled at her, she was certain, if she'd been friendlier to him. If she'd approached him, not discouraged by his blank expression, his rude stare. *Hi. Do I look familiar to you?*

She might have done that. Juliana sometimes surprised herself, speaking boldly to strangers.

Next morning a call came from her mother, informing her that her father, from whom her mother had been estranged for years, had died "suddenly" of a massive heart attack the previous night . . .

Juliana listened, stunned. Her temples felt as if a vise were tightening against them.

The parents had been separated for years but had not divorced. The mother, the father. Couldn't give each other up because it would be (Juliana guessed) giving up their shared past. But much of the time Juliana hadn't known where her father was living. He'd rarely called, he'd become sensitive to slights, self-defensive, quarrelsome. He would mail her a check now and then and became furious if Juliana never got around to cashing it.

Told of her father's death, she was taken utterly by surprise. Rocked back on her heels. "What am I going to do the rest of the day?" she asked her roommate, who winced and laughed.

No funeral, Juliana's mother said. Isn't that just like him.

Her father had willed his body to a medical school for dissection. Therefore no funeral, not even a cremation. No commemoration. Leaving his "earthly remains" to a medical school had been Juliana's father's plan for years; it should not have been a surprise to anyone and yet Juliana was surprised. Called back her mother to say, sobbing—*But we didn't think he was serious, did we?*

After Juliana had called to ask the question several times, Juliana's mother said irritably—*Yes. I did.*

It was at the Mon ey Bar where Juliana met Nathan Gertler, a visiting professor from UC-Berkeley, gaunt, bearded, polysyllabic, a film scholar who published criticism in *The New Republic*. He'd been attracted to Juliana's sunny, uncomplicated manner, her resolute good cheer, sweet but knowing smile; he'd initiated her into a new drink that quickly became her favorite: vodka seltzer with lemon.

Gertler was amused by Juliana. Entertained by her. Doris Day chirpiness, Ava Gardner eyes. When she told him that she rarely saw movies, he'd been genuinely shocked: "Good God, girl, what do you *do?*"

Juliana had wanted to lift her glass, to hint. But Doris Day would never so expose herself. Nor would Ava Gardner.

Gertler complained to Juliana that his students, who were graduate students in film, lacked "visual" eyes. They reduced art to clichés, they stared without seeing. They could sit through an entire film and not once "hear" the musical background, let alone describe it. Gertler told Juliana of the films of Jim Jarmusch, about whom he was writing a book for Yale University Press; soon then, he took her back to his apartment, sparely furnished, university housing, an address Juliana would not recall afterward, where they saw *Down by Law*, *Night on Earth*, *Mystery Train*, *Broken Flowers*, and *Only Lovers Left Alive* on Gertler's console computer, in a blurred marathon of days blending into nights and nights into days, punctuated by red wine, bourbon, dope, sleep on a rumpled bed, but not lovemaking—not exactly.

Waking to discover her wrists, ankles bound with twine. Laughing though she was frightened, telling Gertler this wasn't funny, she wanted to be released, she had to leave, but Gertler shook his head—*Sure. But not so soon.*

Misunderstanding, possibly. Too much dope. (What smoking dope does to the temporal lobe Juliana had learned in one of her psych classes, or maybe it was crack cocaine, so potent you were better off not ingesting it at all.)

Gertler fed Juliana by hand, fork, spoon, a paper napkin neatly at her throat, pungent dark wine lifted in a glass for her to swallow, dared not *not* swallow, the front of her shirt would have been wetted. Juliana did not beg, did not cry, did not betray fear, did not betray outrage, allowed Gertler to bring marijuana cigarettes to her mouth, pretended to be inhaling, thinking—*Daddy help me. Daddy, I'm sorry.* In Juliana's bound state she and Gertler watched films Gertler predicted she would love—"screwball comedies"—by Preston Sturges. Though paralyzed with fear, Juliana managed to laugh at young, slender comedienne Barbara Stanwyck in *The Lady Eve*—a little spasm of laughter that seemed to convince Gertler that Juliana wasn't unhappy with him, it wouldn't be a mistake to let her go.

Eighteen hours, captive in the sparely furnished apartment in a seedy university residence. Eighteen hours, just a single glass of tart red wine in all that time. Why he'd decided to let her go, Juliana never knew, unless that had been his plan all along, a plan he'd executed previously with other undergraduate girls. Just joking, Gertler explained—"kidding around." Laughing heartily, as in a screwball comedy, and Juliana was able to laugh too, probably yes it was just funny, most things were funny when you examined them closely. And this, a scene out of a film. (Wasn't Gertler working on a film script of his own? Of course.) Juliana went away by herself, grateful to be alone, thinking that she'd liked Gertler well enough, wouldn't report him to university officials, she wasn't a *snitch*. He hadn't actually *harmed her*, what the hell.

Now Juliana could speak knowledgeably of Jim Jarmusch, what she could recall of the films was dreamy, seductive, and then startling, unpredictable. Her favorite?—*Only Lovers Left Alive.*

5.

And again in the Mon ey Bar. Juliana's final evening there.

Strange and unexpected: in the blurred spring of her senior year at the university she'd become engaged. It seemed to have happened in a dream. But not a *neon dream*, just an ordinary dream.

The fiancé was several years older than Juliana, graduating from the university's business school with a master's degree in corporate finance. Juliana had no idea what that entailed, and not much interest. Money in itself held no interest for her, except the Mon ey Bar intrigued her as red-flashing neon words.

Mon ey Bar. Juliana had no doubt, these words had entered her sleep.

Out of nowhere Gordon Kechel seemed to have come. Someone told Juliana he was the son of rich parents. Why he liked her, Juliana had no idea. Doris Day sunny smile? Ava Gardner sexy-sloe eyes? In his presence Juliana smiled often, no reason not to smile, she scarcely heard what Gordon was saying, but she found his sand-colored hair attractive, wavy, always combed, the serious eyebrows, tawny, intelligent boy-eyes.

Juliana knew she could trust Gordon. She could trust Gordon not to know her.

Though older than Juliana by six or seven years, Gordon was an anxious lover, inexperienced, grateful (it seemed) that she didn't ever suggest that she was less inexperienced than he, that she expected anything of him or by him other than what he did, or tried to do; she anticipated nothing beyond what *was.*

Essentially she was untouched, uninvolved. Lying with the panting man in her arms, so grateful for her, the most mild of kisses, the gentlest of murmurs, of the sort one might make to a child to placate him—*Yes. I love you, too.*

Though Gordon and Juliana had known each other only a few months, Gordon soon began to press for an engagement. He needed the *steadying* of a permanent relationship, he said. Juliana was touched, and slightly embarrassed, that any man should speak to her so candidly, acknowledging his weakness.

Gordon was distracted, beset by worries having to do with his academic work and his relations with his father, as by gnats fluttering about his head. Juliana had never met anyone so obsessed with family and family history. His litany of worries, resentments. His hopes, plans. His jealousy of an older brother. His preoccupation with grades. (Unlike Juliana, Gordon could not bear any grade lower than A minus. And even an A minus, he confessed, made him feel as if he was slipping down a rock face, desperately grasping at the rock with his fingertips, tearing his nails.) His anxiety about the future had much to do with the fact that after he graduated, he would be working with his father in the Kechel family business, subordinate to his brother.

"But why?"—Juliana asked.

"Why—what?"

"Why should you work with your father? And why would you want to be 'subordinate' to your brother? You don't get along with your brother."

"Because—that's how it is."

"How what is?"

"How—how my life—the business . . . How it *is*."

Juliana was touched, if mystified, by the rich

man's son, so dependent upon his father's opinion of him. Often entire evenings of their lives were devoted to Gordon compulsively repeating his father's remarks, and Gordon's replies, whether from telephone conversations or from emails; always Gordon was anxious to know how Juliana interpreted certain remarks, indecipherable to Gordon.

Juliana perceived early on that Gordon's father was a cruel master, manipulating both his sons into rivalries that fed his ego, but Juliana was too shrewd to tell Gordon anything like this. Instead she said, "It's very clear, your father is impressed with you. He trusts you. That's why he seems to be critical sometimes—he wants to motivate you."

"Is that it! I see."

And Gordon really did see, once Juliana pointed out to him a possibility that was not exactly a probability but that strengthened his dependence upon her as well as upon the father.

Lazily Juliana thought—*If I try, I can become the wife of a rich man.*

Smiling to herself—*But do I care enough? Is it worth it?*

It remained a mystery to Juliana why Gordon cared so obsessively about his father's good opinion. He didn't really care about money, he had no reason to care whether his father hired him in the family business. Gordon was an impressive young man; in fact, all his grades were high, he could get work elsewhere, perhaps where he'd be more valued. Nor did he care about social standing, whatever that was.

Clothes, possessions—not of much interest to him. Most of his clothes were purchased at Brooks Brothers, not because they were fashionable and attractive in a preppy way, but out of a failure of imagination. He didn't own a car, he took taxis when needed. Why he had fallen in love with *her*—Juliana could not fathom.

Well, to the superficial/male eye, Juliana was highly attractive. Chestnut hair, wide-spaced eyes, strong cheekbones, even, white teeth. Her laughter was startled-sounding, childlike. Nothing particularly amused her, and so everything was funny. Though she was not an alcoholic (she was certain) she'd acquired the blurred affability of the alcoholic, to whom not much other than alcohol matters, an air both self-reliant and seductive. Juliana could not become emotionally involved with anyone; thus it seemed to others that she was no risk, she exhibited no needs, hunger. She would not break down in tears over a misunderstanding, she would not demand more than another could give, she would not succumb to *moods*. Other young women, recognizing Gordon Kechel's (literal) worth, had pursued him; Juliana had not.

Though she did not love her fiancé, still less was

she *in love* with him, Juliana had come to depend upon Gordon Kechel. He was one of those who would never discover her secret, essential life— he wasn't that perceptive, or curious; certainly, he wasn't possessive. And Juliana was flattered by his interest in her, his apparent devotion. The rich man's son, interested in *her.*

She did not want a relationship that was emotionally draining, with a more vital, inquis- itive man. She did not want a profound sexual experience. Why was *wanting* a desirable state?— Juliana could not comprehend. But she was happy in Gordon's presence, as in the presence of a protective older brother. She felt elemental, less duplicitous. He would never even notice alcohol on her breath, if she had time to disguise it. *He takes me for what he thinks I am. He doesn't look further.*

She told her fiancé neither truth nor lies but what he wanted to hear, and what he told her, she scarcely heard except to murmur *Yes! I see.*

"My father wants to meet you, Juliana! He's making a special trip."

Juliana smiled as if happily. Telling herself it was only natural, no need for alarm.

And inevitable. Inescapable.

Mr. Kechel was staying at the dignified old Commodore Hotel downtown. A suite, for two nights. He wanted to take Gordon and Juliana to dinner in the hotel, meeting them for drinks at the hotel bar beforehand.

This would be the Mon ey Bar. Juliana felt a moment's panic.

Gordon had never been to the Mon ey Bar. Gordon never heard of the Mon ey Bar. Gordon rarely drank, he had no interest in bars, student pubs. As an undergraduate at a small liberal arts college, he hadn't belonged to a fraternity. Juliana would not have thought to mention the Mon ey Bar to him, but Gordon's father had stayed at the Commodore previously, and he insisted on having drinks in the Mon ey Bar before dinner.

Steeling herself for entering the Mon ey Bar with her fiancé and his father and being greeted by the bartender in a way to embarrass her, but— of course—Juliana's bartender-friend knew to betray no recognition or surprise at seeing her with them, as if Juliana were a total stranger.

Thinking, with relief—*Invisible in the Mon ey Bar!*

For wasn't that the promise of all such neon-lit places?—*invisibility, anonymity.*

As a previous guest at the Commodore, Mr. Kechel was familiar with the campy, crude cartoon monkeys on the walls of the Mon ey Bar, which he identified as thinly disguised representations of African Americans and found amusing; Juliana was shocked by the matter-of-fact remark, as by the amusement, and looking

343

now at the cavorting monkeys, thick-lipped, with nappy hair and bulging eyes, she saw that Mr. Kechel was surely correct. Except these were ugly, racist caricatures, not amusing. (One of the grinning baby monkeys was even eating a large slice of watermelon . . .) Juliana felt a retroactive shame, so long she'd patronized the Mon ey Bar oblivious to the demeaning cartoons.

"You seem disapproving, Julie—that is, Juliana. Are you a civil rights person?" Mr. Kechel asked with exaggerated politeness.

If Mr. Kechel was being ironic, Juliana chose not to react.

"I am, I guess. Yes. That seems only common sense."

"*Common* sense? How so?"

"Civil rights means 'rights for all.' Protecting us, too."

"Us? Who is 'us'?"

Juliana paused. A demon urged her to say *white folks*. Instead she said, with schoolgirl earnestness, "All Americans. All of us."

Juliana's earnestness was a rebuke to Norman Kechel's playfulness, and momentarily dampening.

It was a surprise, and not an unpleasant surprise, to see that Mr. Kechel was nothing like his son. In the first instant you detected something playful, mirthful, unyielding in his manner, in the very ease of his smile. Here was a success-

344

ful man. Here was a man who thought well of himself, who radiated an air of equanimity, secure in the knowledge that no one would contradict or oppose him.

He wore expensive, well-cut clothes designed to flatter his thickened body—by their look, Brooks Brothers. He was carefully groomed, with impeccably barbered hair, a smooth-shaven heavy jaw. White shirt, white cuffs. Cuff links. Not a handsome man, with a blunt face, large nose, close-set eyes, yet in his presence you looked at no one else; you wanted only to impress such a man, to make him smile, laugh, appraise you as a man appraises a woman—frankly, appreciatively. "You didn't tell me, Gordon—she's gorgeous. And the name is—Juli-ana?"

As if Juliana were not there, hearing such extravagant words. Mr. Kechel took her hand in his, squeezing hard enough to make her wince. His gaze level with her own. Juliana felt a thrill of weakness, passivity. That flash of cuff links!—a muted sexual charge. Reminding her of Irving Hermann, of whom she had not thought in years.

Juliana wondered why Mrs. Kechel wasn't accompanying her husband, for wouldn't Mrs. Kechel want to meet her son's fiancée also?—but Juliana would never have asked.

Gordon was both embarrassed and flattered by his father's manner. He laughed as a child might laugh, teased, even ridiculed, yet grateful for the attention of an elder. His drink in the Mon ey Bar was a single beer that he scarcely touched. His father ordered Johnnie Walker Black, straight. "And what would you like, dear? Lime daiquiri? Strawberry?"

Juliana meant to smile and decline an alcoholic drink—*No thank you.* But heard herself say uncertainly, "Well—I could try that. Strawberry daiquiri?"

She'd have preferred a gin and tonic. But *strawberry daiquiri* sounded (and looked) more feminine.

As they drank, Mr. Kechel asked Gordon perfunctory questions about his coursework and pretended to listen to Gordon's answers, sipping at his drink and devouring nuts. He was far more interested in interrogating Juliana, in a manner both intrusive and playful: what was Juliana's college major, what did Juliana plan to do after graduation, where had Juliana been born and where did Juliana live, who were her parents?

None of your goddamned business, mister— she'd have liked to retort.

Instead Juliana stammered answers of a plausible nature, as a naturally shy girl might stammer. In fact she hoped to interest, intrigue the man. She hoped to forestall the glaze of boredom in his face when he listened to Gordon.

And his gaze dropping as if incidentally to her

346

bare arms, her small but distinct breasts, slender waist. Like a child roughly tickled, Juliana blushed with pleasure. In the months she'd known Gordon intimately he had scarcely questioned her at all. He had never looked at her as Mr. Kechel was openly looking at her. However ordinary, even banal, everything Juliana told Mr. Kechel seemed to fascinate him.

He even asked what were her favorite films. Imagine Gordon asking Juliana such a question!

"Oh, I guess—mostly films by Jim Jarmusch . . ."

"Who?"

"Jim Jarmusch."

"Jar-munsch?"

"Jarmusch."

Juliana laughed, as if she were being tickled.

"What's his nationality, this Jar-musch?"

"American."

"Yes, but what kind of American? Semitic?"

During this exchange Gordon was quiet. Excluded from the conversation, from time to time checking his cell phone.

Not checking for email, Juliana knew. Checking the time, the weather, the constellations. News bulletins.

Oh, why wasn't Gordon more *assertive?* Juliana was feeling vexed with her fiancé. How readily he'd surrendered her to his domineering father, as if out of spite.

"My dear, I see that you are not—yet—wearing an engagement ring. Is that deliberate?"

"Is it deliberate? I think—I don't think—we've been thinking about it . . ."

Juliana turned to Gordon, who was staring at his cell phone.

". . . we aren't conventional, I guess. We haven't discussed it."

"Bullshit, my dear," Mr. Kechel said affably. "You don't believe that yourself."

"Believe what? That we aren't conventional?"

"If you are to be married, you must be engaged. That is the *convention*."

Then, with a wide smile: "Why don't we look for one tomorrow? I'll be staying over, you know. There must be a decent jewelry store in this hick town."

Juliana laughed again, not certain what to think. *Was* Mr. Kechel serious? Gordon seemed scarcely to be listening.

"Do you like diamonds, my dear? Emeralds? Sapphires?"—it wasn't clear if Norman Kechel was teasing.

Juliana had no idea how to reply. The rich man's self-confidence was intimidating to her, unsettling.

Their table was booked in the hotel steak house for eight p.m., but Mr. Kechel was in no hurry to curtail the levity of the Mon ey Bar, where more patrons, mainly men, were entering, seating themselves at the bar, facing the glittering wall of bottles.

How like an altar, such a wall of bottles. Juliana had not so clearly noticed in the past.

Wishing she were alone, in the Mon ey Bar. So much easier in life, alone.

Most of the patrons of the Mon ey Bar were men of Mr. Kechel's age, social class. They were possibly businessmen. Travelers. This was his kind of bar, Norman Kechel told Juliana— "Somewhere between classy and sleazy." Overpriced, to keep out riffraff and frat boys. High-quality whiskey, scotch, bourbon. Impressive. Like the dour old Commodore Hotel, with fifteen-foot ceilings and cramped bathrooms, old-style bathtubs with dripping showers. Marble floors, antique chandeliers. The hotel was the real thing, even if nobody much wanted the real thing any longer.

"My room smells like somebody blew out his brains there. Not recently—nineteen twenty-nine."

Juliana laughed, though the humor of this remark was lost upon her. Was nineteen twenty-nine the stock market crash? The start of the Great Depression? How old was Norman Kechel? She liked the man's low-keyed, deadpan humor. He could be on late-night TV, muttering innuendos out of the corner of his mouth. Unlike his earnest son, he liked to drink and made no secret of it.

Indeed, Norman Kechel was a *drinker.* Must have made his money as a younger man, when he took that sort of thing seriously, and now he was happiest in a dim-lit neon place like the Mon ey Bar, sipping a whiskey and chewing stale nuts that left his fingers covered in salt. In the long, horizontal mirror behind the bar his blunt face bobbed, as flushed and amorphous as an under-sea life-form.

That the man was a drinker, Juliana understood. She knew Norman Kechel intuitively, from the inside. Yet it was crucial to her that Norman Kechel not quite guess how kindred the two of them were.

Counting each sip of the strawberry daiquiri. Calculating when she might plausibly order another.

But no, maybe not. Maybe wait for dinner in the restaurant, have a glass of wine then, or two. Mr. Kechel would insist upon excellent wine, a treat for Juliana.

When Gordon excused himself to use the men's room, Mr. Kechel shocked Juliana by laying his hand on her hand and pressing it firm against the tabletop. "How on earth did you meet my son, dear? You're far too beautiful for him."

Juliana laughed, blushing.

"You're far too *sexual* for him."

Wanting to yank her hand away from beneath the man's hand but not wanting to offend him or draw attention to herself. The taciturn bartender, keeping an eye on their party, would notice.

"He's a very lucky young man, my son. Oblivious as all hell."

Juliana had no idea how to reply, though no reply would seem to mean acquiescence.

"You love him, eh? You're sleeping with him? Since when?"

Juliana shook her head. This was going too far. Now she did extricate her hand from beneath his as he murmured an (insincere?) apology—"Hey, sorry. Didn't mean to offend."

Juliana, flush-cheeked, made no reply.

"*Did* I offend? That was not my intention."

When Gordon returned, it was nearly eight thirty. The young couple had to convince Mr. Kechel that they should move into the dining room now, before the restaurant kitchen closed.

Mr. Kechel agreed, reluctantly. A waiter carried their drinks to a table in the adjoining room, as stately and dour as the Mon ey Bar had been raffish and rowdy.

"Okay, kids. Order anything you like on the menu, within reason. The old man's paying the bill, right?"

Juliana ordered filet of sole, daintiest of white fishes. Mr. Kechel, "rare" plank steak, and Gordon a turkey platter with stuffing, mashed potatoes.

"More drinks, kids? No? Just me? Hey."

At dinner it was decided, by Norman Kechel,

351

that the three of them shop for a "suitable" engagement ring the next day. Of course, Norman would be paying for the ring.

"The least I can do, welcoming such a fresh-faced young woman into our family."

Fresh-faced. These words seemed vaguely mocking, silly. Were not all faces of the living *fresh?*

Plans were imprecise and improbable, and Juliana was hardly surprised when in the morning a text came to her from Gordon; he wouldn't have time that afternoon to look for a ring, they would have to postpone. Of course, it was a school day: Gordon had a three-hour graduate seminar in international finance that afternoon. Juliana had two classes, which she didn't mind missing: art history and psychology, both lectures. No sooner had Juliana agreed to a postponement than she had a call from Norman Kechel, who informed her that their plans had not been postponed—"Not yours and mine."

It would be a surprise for Gordon, Norman Kechel told her. Choosing a beautiful ring by themselves. Of course, Juliana would select the ring. He, the father of the groom, would merely purchase it.

Juliana was uncertain how to reply. She hadn't given much thought to an engagement ring until Mr. Kechel had brought up the subject, and now she'd begun to anticipate a ring . . . Mr. Kechel was sounding jaunty, ebullient at eleven a.m. Juliana wondered if the older man had had his first drink of the day. His voice was as smooth as the smoothest whiskey poured over ice, and there was no hint of the preposterous nature of what he was suggesting.

When Juliana offered the weak excuse of having no way to get downtown except a city bus, Mr. Kechel arranged for a taxi to pick her up at her residence and bring her to the Commodore, where she was to meet him, not in the lobby, but in his room on the fourth floor. "In your room? Really?"—Juliana laughed at the man's effrontery. "I'll leave the door ajar," Kechel said, "just in case." *Just in case—what?* Juliana had no intention of going to Kechel's room, she would call him from the lobby. She dressed carefully in a white linen jacket, red-striped scarf, pressed dark slacks, and good sandals. She did not look like a college girl, rather more a young professional woman or a model. Brushed her chestnut hair until it shone and bristled about her head with static electricity.

Juliana was curious about what would happen between her and Kechel. She did not really believe that anything would happen. Through their strained dinner Kechel had cast bemused glances at her, and she'd tried to ignore the intensity and hungry intimacy of his gaze. He'd overridden her choice of filet of sole and insisted that she order filet mignon—"A women's meat."

He'd all but cut pieces of the meat for her on her plate. Several times he'd called her "Princess." He'd ordered a second glass of wine for her, over her protests. (Juliana did not drink this second glass. Pointedly.) At the table with them, Gordon sat silent, sullen, eating his bland turkey dinner and affecting an air of indifference, unconcern; on the table beside him he'd set his cell phone, which was registering notifications, at which he did little more than glance.

Afterward Juliana asked Gordon why had he ignored her at dinner, and Gordon said she'd seemed to be enjoying herself pretty much. Why'd she require *him?*

"Your father talked to me, mostly. I had no choice. But you didn't talk to either of us. Why was that?"

But all Gordon could do was repeat, Juliana had seemed to be enjoying herself pretty much. He hadn't wanted to interrupt.

This new edge to her fiancé. Juliana felt a stab of dismay, dislike.

Next day, Juliana arrived at the Commodore Hotel in the early afternoon and, as Mr. Kechel had suggested, called his room from a phone in the lobby. After three rings Kechel answered and told Juliana in his bright affable voice—"Come right up, dear! I've been waiting."

Juliana demurred. Why didn't he come down to meet *her.*

"A drink is in order, dear. We have privacy here."

"If you want a drink, Mr. Kechel, we could have a drink in the Monkey Bar."

Juliana had meant to sound playful. Realizing belatedly that Mr. Kechel probably had no idea that the hotel bar was called the Monkey Bar.

He'd prefer up in his room, Kechel said curtly—"I'm waiting, dear."

Juliana laughed, annoyed. *Why* should she come upstairs?

There was a pause. Had Kechel hung up the phone? He had!

Juliana felt her cheeks smart. She would take an elevator to the fourth floor, but maybe, just maybe, she wouldn't go shopping with the old man for an engagement ring after all.

Upstairs, Juliana saw that the door to Kechel's room was ajar. On the doorknob a sign—DO NOT DISTURB.

"Hello?"—Juliana pushed the door open. She was prepared to be amused, to laugh.

The room was indeed spacious, with a small adjoining sitting room, a wainscoted ceiling. The blinds had not been opened. The furnishings were opulent, stately; the look of the room slovenly. The king-size bed was enormous; a heavy satin bedspread had been pulled up negligently over rumpled bedclothes. Breakfast things on a tray, and on a sideboard an opened bottle of whiskey. From the minibar, Juliana supposed.

From the left, as Juliana entered the room, Norman Kechel approached her quickly, silently. Without a word of greeting, he gripped her shoulder, pulled her farther into the room, shut the door. His mouth plunged at hers, hard, sucking like a pike's.

Kechel was unshaven. Shoeless, barefoot— shorter than Juliana recalled. His breath tasted of whiskey but was sour, not sweet.

"Good morning, Julie—Juli-*an*-ya!"

Pushing her against a bureau. Juliana's back against the bureau. She was laughing, trying to laugh, this was so absurd, such an assault, a man so much older than she, what was he thinking? She did not actively resist, though she was certainly not compliant. Thinking—*I am not really here. Does he think that I am* here? *Not me!*

She felt both incensed and yet gay, giddy. She might have been drinking with the old man, just the two of them, through the morning. She might have been explaining herself to Gordon, or to any observer. The raffish atmosphere of the Mon ey Bar had spilled out into daylight and prevailed now everywhere: nothing mattered, or could be made to matter. Monkeys cavorted, monkeys were laughable. Against the insides of her eyelids, a seductive-red glow of neon.

She'd wakened that morning with a faint, dull headache. The *hanging-over* it was, of a pleasurable high.

What is a *hangover* but a kind of memory, deep in the brain.

Kechel seemed to be assessing Juliana with a low growl of approval. He was one who liked to bestow such words upon women—*beautiful, gorgeous.* Juliana understood that it was thrilling to him, the man, the elder, doling out such compliments, assessing. For he was the one to assess others, he himself would not be judged. He gripped Juliana's shoulders harder, taking possession. He began kissing her, harder. This time he forced her mouth open, the intention was to overcome, to hurt. She might have shoved him away—an elbow in the fatty chest—in the very heart that is the heart of the beast—but she did not.

They would search for a ring together, and it would be a beautiful ring. How many thousands of dollars would the groom's father pay. Gordon would be impressed. Gordon would be jealous. Juliana felt a shudder pass through her, contempt for the weak son who could not stand up to his father. In that instant Gordon Kechel disappeared: disintegrated.

If I marry the son, Juliana thought, this *will be the understanding between us.*

A wild sort of gaiety came over her. A gaiety of desperation, profound loss.

She felt powerless before him. The authority of the older man. It was privilege he exerted, this authority. She, the son's fiancée, was part of his privilege.

His hands clutched at her hands, she could not push him away.

He was walking her somewhere. As you'd help a child walk. But Juliana did not need *help*. She was not *drunk*. Her breath came quick, in anticipation. Apprehension. She'd kicked off her shoes. She was shorter than the man, this was good. He would not be threatened by her, he would not be tempted to hurt her. He could lean over her, commanding her. She instructed her-self—*I can slip away from him at any time. This is just a game. This is not serious.*

They were at the enormous bed. Juliana was curious now, what would happen. She was *not drunk* but was feeling giddy-gay, drunken. Her heart raged in contempt of the weak, younger man who might have been observing the scene with horror. Too late now, too late to turn back. No choice but to loosen her clothes before the impatient, fumbling man could tear them.

Kechel had been drinking, she recognized him as a *drinker.* He would be her father-in-law, they would be drinkers together. Except she would keep her secret from him, if she could. For as long as she could.

In his vanity Kechel turned from Juliana,

removing his clothes, or most of his clothes, self-conscious of his body, the body of a man of late middle age. Juliana caught a glimpse of a fatty-muscled chest, a broad chest covered in gray hairs, pale, flaccid skin, loose flesh at the waist.

She felt a thrill of superiority. She was *young,* the man was *not young.* Though Juliana did not much value *young,* she understood that the older man did.

Her own body was smooth, slender, as supple as a dancer's body. Her breasts, her waist, the curve of her thighs—graceful, desirable. There was something mocking in the young female body, its negligent beauty. Kechel was the witness. Kechel was strongly attracted to her, yet Juliana could sense his resentment of her. Flesh quivered at his belly and at his groin. The fat slug of his groin was slow to thicken with blood. Kechel urged her toward the bed and onto the bed, and Juliana did not resist. A kind of paralysis had overcome her, a kind of anesthesia. Her body was something she merely inhabited; she could not defend it from harm.

With little ceremony Kechel parted her legs, her beautiful, slender legs, scarcely was he aware of Juliana now as he labored to summon hardness from some netherworld of the soul that he might ram himself into her. His grunting came more quickly. Perspiration from his straining face fell upon Juliana's face. And there was Juliana's head being pushed against the headboard of the bed. *Oh!—oh* . . . This was too raw, she could not bear such rawness without a drink. Drinks.

A vision came to her of someone listening in the adjacent room. A middle-aged woman, an embittered woman. Mrs. Kechel, Gordon's mother, forced to hear the mechanical rhythmic thudding, the panting of the male, impersonal, brainless . . .

Kechel groaned, falling on Juliana. His tensed muscles softened, collapsed. After a dazed moment he muttered something Juliana could not interpret, perhaps not meant for her ear.

Heaving himself, panting, from the damp, tangled sheets, staggering to the sideboard to pour drinks: straight whiskey. Juliana had no intention of drinking straight whiskey at this hour of the day. Juliana had no intention of drinking straight whiskey at this hour of the day in a hotel room with the (naked) father of her fiancé.

Somehow Juliana had become naked. She'd allowed the man to reduce her to himself—*naked*.

They were *drinkers* together. He'd seemed to know. The previous night, he'd known. But she could not acknowledge it, she would not.

The fat, hard slug had hurt her, she hadn't been prepared for its force. Misjudging the man because he was decades older than she and wheezed so piteously. But harder and rougher than she'd anticipated. Kechel was sitting on the edge of the bed now, still breathing heavily, stroking her thigh. There appeared to be a kind of delirium in his face, a flushed, dazed expression.

Wanting to ease away from the weight of the man's hand but not wishing to risk insulting him. Juliana knew from past experience that an affable man is likely to be the most easily insulted. No, you did not want to arouse the enmity of the affable man.

The fat, hard slug at his groin was soft and flaccid now, harmless. A sort of oily-milky secretion had been released from it. Taking the whiskey glass from Kechel's fingers, Juliana considered striking the ugly slug with something. Kicking with her foot. But Juliana's foot was bare, the bare sole of her foot would not seriously injure the fat, thick thing. Better not try to injure it if you could not destroy it altogether. Juliana laughed, for this is the wisdom of the ages.

Not intending even to taste the whiskey, Juliana found herself sipping it. She wasn't an expert in hard liquor, but she guessed that this was good, expensive whiskey. Out of the minibar, double the usual price.

Kechel was saying how beautiful Juliana was, how beautiful her body, her eyes, her hair—"Yes, but you know that, dear, don't you? Of course you do."

Was the old man besotted with her? Juliana

laughed, uneasy. She must calculate her escape. She must leave soon.

But no: they were planning to shop for an engagement ring. Of course. That was why Juliana was here, in this sour-smelling bed.

Let the old man spend money on her, it was what she deserved, Juliana thought. She'd earned it. She would marry Gordon, or possibly not marry Gordon, but she would keep the engagement ring, for she'd earned it.

"You do know the effect you have upon men, Juli-an-ya, don't you. Of course, you aren't a child. You know."

Almost wistfully Norman Kechel spoke. Juliana wondered if, in some wild flight of fantasy, the father of the fiancé might take the fiancé's place: divorce the old, worn-out wife, marry the beautiful young fiancée. A preposterous turn-about, but not impossible.

It's up to you—Juliana told herself. *No one else!*

The smooth apricot-colored liquor had gone to her head, very pleasurably.

Stroking her thigh, leaning down now and then to kiss it, his wet lips against Juliana's shivery flesh, Kechel was telling Juliana about his business in Kansas City. She'd missed the part where he'd identified a product. Or possibly there was no product, just a service of some kind. He spoke of his wife's family—"Pioneer stock." *He* was immigrant stock, second generation.

In that wistful yet somehow reproachful tone Kechel spoke of his children, sons. He did not speak of Gordon by name. *My sons. Good kids. But needing guidance.* Juliana had resolved as an adolescent to have no children of her own. Not ever. Children are the disappointment, always falling short. Always, strings attached. No. Already too many of them inhabited the world, choking and smothering one another.

Juliana was becoming dizzy. She'd had only two, three mouthfuls of the exquisite apricot-colored liquor. Had to lie back on the bed, against the headboard, one of the pillows crooked and uncomfortable beneath her. Eyelids heavy. Had she made a mistake? Had she miscalculated Norman Kechel? Had the man drugged her? Poisoned her? Confusing Kechel with the visiting professor in film studies who'd also drugged/poisoned her.

Whiskey wasn't her drink, whiskey was a man's drink. Straight whiskey. Still, the taste was good. Soothing. You could not deny that.

No, no more! Thank you but *no more.*

Her eyelids were heavy. A hand removed the whiskey glass from her hand, gently.

Must've slept. Time was confused. Was she alone? Or—

Not Gordon. Vaguely she understood—*Not the film professor and not Gordon.*

Whoever this was beside her, a heavy, humid

weight. And now he was standing above her. A kind of triumph, heaved to his feet. Vaguely she could see the face, not a familiar face. Not a kindly face. Not a fatherly face. In that heavy-jawed face, disapproval and dislike.

Wearing a white terrycloth bathrobe out of the hotel closet, the man stood above her swaying, gloating. The terrycloth white was bright and potent and hurt her eyes.

What was the man doing? Taking pictures of her with his cell phone? As she lay sprawled and helpless? Tried to shield herself with her arms. Naked arms, naked torso. Breasts, belly. Seeing the contempt in the face that should have been a kindly face, the blood-darkened rage. Quivering jowls. She was trying to hide, as a child might hide, curled up, knees to her chest. She hoped he would not strangle her in this bed and pull the cover over her. She hoped he would not leave her for dead. Drag her into the bathroom, her life-less body hauled into the bathtub, an old, heavy porcelain bathtub of another era, as large as an Egyptian sarcophagus.

Those many years, the rumors you hear. Girls, women, raped, strangled, beaten to death, left for dead in their own vomit, excrement. The kindest of these (you might tell yourself) was the *body never recovered.* For then the *case was still open.* A possibility that the victim is *still alive.*

"Evidence. My naïve son needs to know the kind of slut he's gotten involved with."

The voice was slurred, elated. The voice went on to inform Juliana that he had a plane to catch, six p.m. that evening. He had no intention of taking "the slut" on a "shopping spree." He was going to take a shower, Kechel said, to wash the smell of her off his skin, and when he came out of the bathroom, he wanted her gone.

Throwing her clothes at her. The face bloated with gloating, fury.

Juliana pulled a sheet over her stricken body. It was what you did—cover a body. Her reactions were slow, as if underwater. She'd been thinking at first that Kechel was joking, for his manner was often jocular, not serious; yet he did not seem to be joking now.

"Get dressed. Get out of here. Get out of my son's life. If you try to see him again, I will show him this evidence, what you are . . ."

He was laughing at her without mirth. He was triumphant, gloating. She was stunned, she'd so miscalculated. The shame of it . . .

He left her, she could hear the shower in the bathroom. Still, Juliana wasn't certain what had happened. *Was* Norman Kechel joking? He'd seemed so smitten with her.

Stricken with pain. Shame. She was whispering to herself—*It will be all right. It will be all right. He didn't hurt you, you are alive.*

Her fingers fumbled to dress herself. The clean, chic, attractive clothes on the sullied, smelly body.

No one to observe how she managed to button her jacket, pushing pearl buttons through tight, embroidered buttonholes.

The room swirled about her. She struggled to remain on her feet. He must have put something in her drink—a sleeping pill, possibly. How naïve she was to have accepted that drink from him—how vain she'd been to think that her will was stronger than the man's.

Recalling now, though with difficulty, how he'd hurt her, making love to her. The excuse of—"making love." His roughness, clumsiness. He'd even closed his hands around her throat, in play. Teasing. But serious. Oh certainly—he'd have enjoyed strangling her. All that talk of *beautiful, gorgeous*—just means that they resent you, would love to strangle you.

And as Kechel strangled her, he'd have rammed the hard, fat slug-thing against her faster and faster until it burst.

She loathed him. She would have to kill *him*. That way Gordon would never know. The shame of this, this humiliation, would be erased.

But killing the man, the physical bulk of the man, the weight, the *will* of the man—how could Juliana do this? She wasn't prepared. She wasn't strong enough. Even with a knife, a weapon—not strong enough.

On a bureau lay the man's wallet, in plain sight. This was too obvious. *It's a stupid test. He knows I won't dare take his money.*

She took his money. Just larger bills, fifty-dollar bills, twenty-dollar bills. The smaller bills she left in the wallet, out of contempt. The several credit cards she rearranged in the wallet so that Kechel would assume they were missing. The large-denomination bills she folded into small, tight wads and placed in the pockets of his trousers, which were neatly draped across the back of a Queen Anne chair.

These wadded-up bills the man would discover in his pockets, though not immediately.

By then Juliana would be gone from the Commodore Hotel. Never again would she see Norman Kechel. Never would she see Gordon Kechel. Never again would she return to the red-neon Mon ey Bar, with its crude racist caricatures that she'd mistaken, in her ignorance, for innocent cartoons.

6.

Wild Goose Tavern. Where in the front window neon cascaded in emulation of a waterfall, bright blue, cloudy blue, dark blue advertising a Canadian beer.

Where, six years later, Juliana met Ned Spires.

Or, Ned Spires met Juliana.

Working as a paralegal, part-time. Telling herself it was good work, necessary work. As many hours of her (daytime) life devoted to the cause of social justice as she could manage.

Twenty-six years old. Life just beginning!

Twenty-six years old. Christ, how long has her life been . . .

Drinking vodka now. Savoring the many facets of vodka. Invisible, no-taste, low-calorie.

Juliana had gone through a (perverse) phrase of whiskey—apricot-colored, smooth-burning, potent. In the wake of the fiancé's father, a trance of self-loathing.

Following that, a phase of rum and Diet Coke.

But best of all, vodka, seltzer, and lemon. Dreamy waterfall neon captured the taste, the tone. Like something glimpsed through swirling, frothy water.

On the grandiloquent old jukebox with flashing colors, Johnny Cash. Sexy-deep baritone voice of the dead.

At the Wild Goose Tavern those many nights they'd talked earnestly of life, death, poetry, music. The films of Jim Jarmusch, which Ned Spires too admired: not surprisingly, his favorite was *Paterson*. (Though his favorite filmmaker was Andrei Tarkovsky.) Is there God, is there an afterlife, is there *meaning* in life. What do we owe one another, how do our lives intersect? Can we love, deeply, more than once? *Must* we love, deeply, more than once?

Unexpected, absurd—Juliana was entranced by Ned Spires. His skin was pocked with ancient acne scars, his eyes were often haggard. Merriment lay over his face like a cobweb, there were deep frown and smile lines beside his eyes. Ned too was a drinker.

In the Wild Goose Tavern, which was near a large urban university, Ned Spires reigned over the bar, in his hoarse-mellifluous voice reciting poems by W. B. Yeats, Seamus Heaney, John Berryman. Surprising how many drinkers at the Wild Goose listened to poetry, enthralled by Ned Spires's voice.

He'd been born in County Galway and was brought by his very young parents to the United States, to Boston, as a child of three. After four decades in the States, his accent was still Irish-inflected. His preferred drink was Irish whiskey straight, but for most occasions Guinness Extra Stout from the tap.

Juliana was acquiring a taste for the dark, bitter ale. You had to swallow hard once, twice, to get a mouthful down. That taste at the back of the tongue like a dark spreading stain.

So much in life is negotiable, Juliana came to see. What she'd disliked and disdained she might learn to like very much. Under the proper tutelage.

Her first glimpse of Ned Spires, he'd been unprepossessing. Subsequently she'd come to see that if you looked closely and if you listened to Ned, he was really a beautiful man.

She'd come to love the very sound of the name: Ned Spires. Confused with the waterfall neon in the Wild Goose, glimmering lights reflected against the man's face and her face and in the mirror behind the bar behind shelves of bottles.

And in the front seat of his car the first night they were alone together. Drawing her fingertips over the warm, blotched skin of the man's face as a blind woman might draw marveling fingertips over Braille.

Ned Spires's poetry was the poetry of celebration but also, being Irish, the poetry of privation. Deprivation. Bitter loss, stoic resignation. He hadn't ever believed he deserved to be happy, Ned told her.

Ravished by her. He said. His eyes on her, worshipful. But she was too young, or was he too old? (Only forty-three. Not *old*. Except for his thinning coppery hair and bruised eyes, he'd have looked years younger.)

By this time Juliana had begun taking night school courses at a branch of the John Jay College of Criminal Justice. By day she worked as a paralegal. She was often on the phone, she was often sifting through records. She was a researcher, she accumulated data. She'd acquired computer skills beyond those of her (male) superiors, whom she had to instruct even as they disdained such skills. She understood that until she had a law degree and passed the state bar exam, she would not be taken seriously by any of these individuals; she would not be eligible for any job she might believe worthwhile.

In telling Ned Spires a selective account of her day-life, she felt a small thrill of pride. That life, a life she wore casually, as one might slip on a stylish jacket, was in fact a life of work, effort. Trying to reverse unjust convictions. Investigating corrupt police officers, perjured testimonies. What was required was the most stubborn idealism. You had to be made of something like the roughest rubber. Yet the life seemed often, to Juliana, to belong to another person.

Oh, why did she torment herself—*thinking*. In a man's arms not needing to think. That is the point of *in a man's arms*.

That is the point of the *Wild Goose*. Voluptuous night, neon.

A fact: after drinking, lovemaking is possible. Your brain is not loose-rushing like a runaway cog. Your brain is numbed, unresisting. Your brain is *childlike*. How simple and without complication is your life at such times.

Ned was kind to her. Vowed he would not *lie*.

Saying—Well, look: she was *young*.

"And I am *worn*."

Ned Spires was a man set apart. Even before Juliana learned that he was a poet, an acclaimed poet, with several books published by a distinguished publisher. Professor of Romance languages at the Jesuit university.

Eagerly Juliana read the poetry of Ned Spires. Seeking some tracery of herself in the man's life. Some prophecy.

Not *her* so much as a premonition of *her.* The poet's yearning for the not-yet-known, the poet's guilt over betrayal.

Of course, Ned Spires was married. Twice married. Almost twenty years married, in all. Near-grown children from the first marriage, young children from the second. Are your children *the light of your life?*—Juliana had not meant to sound mocking, jealous.

If she loved a man too much, toads leapt from her mouth. Vodka released them.

In fact yes. "Light of the life"—the child bearing life into the next generation. In their eyes, the original light, which some of us have lost.

With a strange fatality the poet spoke. A luminosity in his blemished face. Juliana had to look away.

Well! She'd been rebuked. No one had spoken to her in quite this way, a knife to the heart.

She despaired, she would not see this man again. He was so very superior to her, secure in his love for his children, basking in his poetry. Beyond his own poetry was the world of poetry itself—he'd memorized countless poems, the most beautiful and profound lines of others were always at his fingertips.

His favorite line was from a poem by Elizabeth Bishop (of whom Juliana had heard but had never read): "The art of losing isn't hard to master."

How true, Juliana thought. The art of losing, *she'd* mastered at a young age.

Why vodka was so soothing now. Originally a way of numbing hurt, now a pleasure in itself, like a sparkling waterfall.

By day, work: her hands began to ache, sharp, shooting pains in both hands, typing for so many hours on the computer keyboard. Her forehead crimped like paper crushed in the hand. At last released at six thirty p.m.

Running through rain to the Wild Goose Tavern, where he might be waiting for her, a drink on the bar before him.

Or in one of the favored booths, waiting for Juliana. Already a vodka for her, or a tall glass of pale ale.

If Ned wasn't there, it might mean that Ned wasn't coming that evening. No excuse, no reason. He wished not to be *expected*.

Juliana knew. Juliana understood. Indeed, Juliana felt the same way herself. *I hate it, where I am expected.*

Yet if Ned wasn't at the Wild Goose, possibly Juliana would walk a few blocks or take a taxi to the Shamrock Inn, where she was also known, welcomed. These were neighborhood bars near the university, like home to her. The bartenders knew her and liked her. Home is *where, when you go there, they have to take you in.*

And beautiful to Juliana, mysterious—the waterfall sign in the front window as she approached the Wild Goose. Or the flashing gold sign in the window of the Shamrock Inn. Red neon, blue neon—the several dreamy blues of neon.

Night, neon. Neither possible without the other.

The Black Rooster: farther away, on the state highway. She'd have to take a taxi.

Red scripted neon, advertising a German beer. Faint with relief, the simplest happiness, at last seating herself at a bar, this bar, elbows on the bar, rain glistening on her face and in her hair, seeing herself in the eyes of others as in the mirror behind the bar, attractive young woman, still a young woman, first name only—*Juliana.*

But few patrons knew Juliana at the Black Rooster. Bartenders recognized her, but were not especially friendly. Ned Spires wasn't likely to come here, the Black Rooster wasn't one of his places.

In a way, Juliana was relieved that Ned Spires wouldn't come to the Black Rooster. Relieved that no one knew her here. Except she'd been hearing tales of an unidentified man in that area, reported at the Black Rooster and at other taverns, stalking women, lone women, women with long hair, like Juliana. And all of them young, with girls' faces.

Not so comfortable a place, a different vibe here. No Johnny Cash—no old-fashioned juke-box. TV could be tuned to sports or to Fox News. Raucous, rowdy. Clientele younger guys, truckers. And a bare plank floor, blank ceiling that failed to soften and blur voices.

Red neon in the window at the Black Rooster. The small trip of the heart that is hope.

If, when she wished to be unfaithful to Ned Spires. Unfaithful to Wild Goose. Drinking at the Black Rooster for the night.

Stricken with guilt over his young children, Ned Spires stayed away from the Wild Goose for five, six days. Juliana had nearly given up hope, but then he'd unexpectedly returned. A drinker will always return, you have only to wait. And that night in Juliana's studio apartment, in Juliana's thrift-shop brass bed that winced beneath their weight. Juliana's hair spilling around the man's face, onto his shoulders. Lifting herself above him, he'd gripped her hips. Big-knuckled hands, surprisingly strong.

Could he lift his youngest child in one hand?—Juliana marveled.

Once, her father had lifted her in one hand. She

could swear. She could recall. Lifted toward the ceiling, like an offering to the gods.

Above Ned Spires, lowering herself onto him, gently. Their lovemaking was tender, even contemplative. Juliana did not want to think that their lovemaking was like poetry, a rueful past tense.

The skin of her face was drawn tight to bursting. Her eyes rolled back in their sockets, blind. Her brain was struck blind, she could not bear it—such sensation, and the fleetingness of such sensation. All her bones turned to water. A convulsion in her loins that went on and on and on, leaving her faint, exhausted.

. . . love you. Love love love you don't leave me . . .

There were no words that were genuine, the poet had said. Because all words have become worn, as pebbles worn smooth by the tide.

As worn as stone steps. So many have trod upon.

She'd protested, these words were genuine. For her. It was the first time she'd loved anyone. Truly loved a man.

Pleading with this man with the sad-skeptical eyes, to believe her.

Reciprocated desire is the risk. Juliana had grown to desire men at a distance. To experience herself as the object of desire: a figure in a mirror, unattainable.

You see, hear yourself through a scrim of

alcohol. Otherwise life is too raw. Touch blundering and too raw.

She'd confided in Ned Spires that she'd once been engaged. In the spring of her senior year of college. Like a dream it had been, she'd been a fiancée and had had a fiancé. Like a dream, it faded from memory as soon as she'd wakened.

And you didn't love him? The fiancé?—with gentle irony Ned Spires spoke, like one teasing out inaccuracies in a child.

No. I didn't know what love was.

And now—you know what love is?

Are you laughing at me? That isn't nice.

Am I laughing at you. Darling, no. But I am wondering if you are laughing at me.

Ned Spires went away, his wife's mother had died. All the family was gone to Milwaukee, Wisconsin, for eight, ten, twelve days.

In the Wild Goose, she'd waited patiently at her place at the bar. Drink before her, vodka on the rocks. A pack of cigarettes. (But she rarely smoked, allotting herself only seven cigarettes a week.) Shutting her eyes, loving the guttural Johnny Cash voice, words directed to her. *Turn, turn, turn.*

Wheel of fire.

Ned returned from the ordeal of death, burial. They saw each other again. He'd missed her, he said. His life was being torn in half.

She'd gone away, angry and hurt over a slight.

No more than an intonation in the man's voice. He had not pursued her into the parking lot and beyond, and so in desperation late that night she dared to call him at home—*I think I love you. We've gone too far. You have caused this, Ned.* The words were astonishing to Juliana, purely invented words, like froth on her lips. No idea what she was saying. Why she was even calling Ned; she'd promised she would never call him at home and only on his cell phone if the call was urgent.

How many times had she ever called a man, any man, at his home?—not ever.

Hearing Juliana's voice, Ned was not so welcoming as she'd expected. Not so consoling, confiding. In a lowered voice cautioning her—*I can't talk now, Juliana. This isn't good. Don't call this number again, please. I thought I'd told you.* Juliana was shocked by such a rebuke, she could not reply. In silence like a gaping wound, she broke the connection.

Had she been drinking—well, of course. But not *drunk.*

For hours then, the man would worry, lie awake and worry that Juliana might have injured herself. Done some violence to herself.

Some violence to herself that might involve him.

In her heart she hated the man. Had not the slightest intention of seeing him again, calling him again. Not the slightest intention of respecting his wishes, his marriage. Returning to the Wild Goose the next night, where she used a public phone so that he would not block her call.

Not that she cared about Ned Spires, she did not. Not really.

But her pride, her soul. As if he'd spilled a drink carelessly, making a joke of it.

Again the lowered voice. Chastised, frightened when he realized who it was.

. . . *begging you Juliana, please don't. I love you—I will always love you, but—you must know—this is a very difficult time in my marriage . . .*

Juliana laughed. It was not her, this was not Juliana Regan, this furious person.

. . . *your marriage! How dare you speak of* your marriage! *What of the marriage between us—you and me? We are married too . . .*

For it was true. Ned Spires knew it was true. Hadn't he said it so many times. Hadn't his poetry claimed this.

It was a desperate fact, Juliana loved Ned Spires deeply. It was a sudden fact, a surprise to her. Like being shown a lab report—*yes, a malignancy.*

Unexpected, yet as soon as you see it . . . Of course.

Juliana could not bear to live without Ned

Spires. Her very soul, her pride had been ravaged by the man.

But she would not call him again. If he tried to call her, she would not answer. Calmly counting two, three, four nights, he would be lying awake and anxious and (just possibly) he'd left the phone off the hook. And let his cell phone lose its power so that she could not call his cell phone either. (She'd tried. Once.) But Juliana was patient, she could wait. Patient, cunning, intent upon revenge.

It mattered to her that her daylight self, her professional, paralegal self, was an admirable person. Everyone agreed: Juliana was *wonderful*. Juliana was *fired with idealism*. All the lawyers liked Juliana, knew they could rely upon Juliana, admired her for her intelligence, idealism. All of them knew that she was taking night courses at John Jay. But after dark, another Juliana emerged, of whom they knew nothing.

She was not responsible, Juliana thought. It was the condition of the human soul. This revelation of the daytime self, the nighttime self. The perfect clarity that vodka best provides.

And so, she calls his number just one more time. The forbidden number.

Having poured herself a drink. A full-size glass, but only half full.

This time the wife answers, hesitantly. Fearfully. *Yes? What? Who is this?*

Juliana has not heard this voice before but recognizes it immediately.

Calmly asking if Ned Spires is there, she needs to speak with Ned Spires, she is one of those whom his poetry has touched.

A former colleague at the university, an adjunct instructor.

In fact she is in danger of her life, she must speak with Ned Spires, it is an urgent matter . . .

(But why has Juliana said this? She has no idea, the unexpected words have sprung from her mouth.)

At the other end of the line, the receiver clatters onto a surface—slipped from the woman's fingers.

Quickly Juliana breaks the connection.

She has gone too far. She has blundered, said too much. She pours another inch or two of vodka into the glass. Already her phone is ringing.

She sees, of course it's Ned calling her. She *has* gone too far, he will be vexed with her.

She'd been a reckless child. Lighting matches. Lighting matches, dropping matches. No intention of setting a fire. But the fire has happened.

Timorously, Juliana lifts the receiver. And there is Ned's voice, close in her ear, lowered, cautious.

Juliana? You just called—did you?
Don't do this to me, Juliana. To us.
My wife is not well—you know that. Please.

I think—we have to stop this. Whatever this is, it must cease.

Don't ruin my life, Juliana. Please.

If you love me—you've said—and yes, I love you—but—if you ruin my life—there will be no love . . .

Juliana has not intended to speak, only just to listen, to hear the voice of the man she adores. To hear him admit how he has wronged her, to apologize. She intended to listen to him in silence, in dignity, perhaps she would forgive him, but these words are not the words she wishes to hear, these are words that inflame, goad. She hears herself cry—*Your life? Goddamn you, what about my life? My life is in ruins.*

Breaking the connection, furious.

Following this, much seemed to happen.

Ever more swiftly, like the swirling of water into a drain.

Another night, waiting in a car borrowed from a lawyer friend, allegedly for a work-related errand.

Cannily, not in front of the Spire house (of course), but two houses away. Headlights off. Ignition still on. At midnight seeing a light in her lover's house upstairs. A single, weaker light downstairs. Like wildfire, elation overcame her. Flames licking at her hair, her fingertips. She'd brought a bottle of vodka with her. With defiant fingers she lifted the bottle, drank. Consoling herself—*None of this is real. This is just a test. I can stop anytime. I will stop.*

It was within Juliana's rights as the beloved of the man who lived in that house to approach the front door, to ring the bell. The lover's poetry often spoke of risk, daring. To gain life one must be willing to risk life.

Soon then, the upstairs light went out. The downstairs light remained.

Juliana thought—*He would come to me if he knew. He wouldn't let me suffer like this.*

Waiting for him to come to her, but he did not come, and so finally, feeling very tired, she decided to drive away.

Thinking that in a sense she'd triumphed over Ned Spires. He'd been reduced to begging her not to ruin his life, a coward's life. As Juliana's lover, he'd been ardent, ecstatic. He hadn't had a mind for his unhappy wife, then. And so now Juliana cared nothing for him. She pitied the man, a weak man finally, like Gordon Kechel, who'd given her up without a fight—who'd simply repudiated her without ever seeing or even speaking with her again.

How could Juliana have loved Ned Spires!— the acne-roughened face, shadowed eyes. The pathos of his poetry, about which (though he tried to disguise it) he was so vain.

Mere scribbled words, publications in magazines in which a poem was merely decorative amid a page of prose bounded by advertisements, a poetry prize or two—did the deluded man think such meager achievements would make him immortal?

He would beg Juliana to relent, eventually. He would beg her to forgive him and to love him again. She knew. *A drinker will always return.*

Yet when Juliana returned to the Wild Goose Tavern the next night, Ned Spires wasn't there. She waited at the bar in her usual place until eleven p.m. He'd let her down, she should have known. Weak, a coward! Acquaintances of his from the university stopped here, weeknights. Juliana knew them by their faces, not names. She'd never been good at names. Nodding at Ned Spires when she was with him, and at her. But when Juliana wasn't with Ned, not seeming to see her.

Bastards. She hated them all.

Into the Wild Goose in the later part of the evening came a familiar face, a white-haired older friend of Ned Spires, possibly a fellow poet, to whom Juliana spoke as a naïve young girl might speak.

Asking this person if he knew "Ned Spires"—if "Ned Spires" was to be trusted? A good man?

The white-haired man stared at Juliana in surprise.

Asking her, why did she want to know?

Juliana said that "Ned Spires" told her he was

separated from his wife and filing for a divorce and she was wondering was any of that true . . .

Seeing in the white-haired man's face an expression of doubt, dislike, Juliana ceased speaking. For she was not accustomed to men regarding her with such condescension, especially not older men who were (usually) grateful for her attention.

Carefully the white-haired man told Juliana that he "had not heard a word" about a separation, still less a divorce.

"But Ned Spires is a 'good man'—to be 'trusted'?"

The white-haired man frowned, for this line of inquiry was annoying to him. Pointedly he glanced at the bartender, who was eavesdropping from a few feet away, and so the bartender came to Juliana and told her politely that Ned Spires was an old friend and that she'd best return to where she had been sitting or, better yet, consider leaving, for it was after midnight.

Did Juliana need a ride home? Any kind of help getting to her home?

"No! I do not."

Juliana retreated, wiping at her eyes with her fingertips. She had not intended this harshness—this was *not her.*

Much of what she'd said was not Juliana speaking. Vodka, it was.

Meaning to leave the tavern, on her way out of

the tavern, but turning suddenly and returning to the bar to explain to the men. Their eyes shifting onto her in annoyance, dread.

"He has threatened my life. 'Ned Spires.' I mean—that was what I'd learned. But—I think—" Juliana's voice faltered, she felt as if she were grasping a rope, hauling herself up out of dark, churning water in which she might drown as the men stared at her. "I think I may have misunderstood. You are saying that Ned Spires is a good man. He *is* kind . . . I was one of his closest friends, we shared his poetry together. I don't wish him ill. Yes, Ned is a good man, he is to be trusted. I see that now. I'm sorry, I was misinformed. I've said the wrong thing. You don't need to tell him. I see now that I was wrong— he'd never said he was getting a divorce. He never said that to *me*."

Following this, Juliana avoided the Wild Goose. She did not telephone Ned Spires, she made no effort to contact him. And soon, then, she stopped drinking, or rather began the stages of *not-drinking,* which she envisioned as stone steps in a hill badly worn from many feet preceding hers, but Juliana too would ascend it, in time.

7.

But now, Blue Moon Café. At dusk, that heart-break time.

Blue Moon, blue neon. She won't stay long.

Taking pleasure in the anticipation. *Just club soda, thanks!*

Taking pleasure in slow-driving along Front Street. Passing darkened storefronts in this small town on the Delaware River that has become familiar and comforting to Juliana, like home.

Not home, not quite yet. But soon.

Much has changed in Juliana's life since the Wild Goose Tavern. Three years since Ned Spires. Shame and desperation, bad memories steeped in vodka.

Now Juliana no longer drinks. Certainly not vodka, which is lethal.

Not even beer, with Patrick.

Unknowing, innocently, Patrick has urged her. *C'mon, Julie! Just a sip, it's just beer.*

But now, since she has become pregnant, Patrick no longer urges her to drink. Instead, he fusses over the food Juliana eats, watches over her almost too carefully.

It has been just a month. Already Juliana feels changes in her body, she is certain she isn't imagining . . . Fascinating, though in a way frightening, for isn't this *her body?*

Exactly as she'd imagined, Patrick is in awe of her and of the pregnancy.

Pregnant women are the most beautiful women. I am the happiest man alive.

Soon Juliana will be thirty years old. By which time she and Patrick will be married.

A good man, a kindly man, reliable, intelligent—knowing little of Juliana's former, secret life before she'd met him.

Why is Patrick not more curious, Juliana wonders.

To Juliana, *curious* and *suspicious* are near synonymous.

In this lack of curiosity, this trustfulness, Patrick somewhat resembles Gordon Kechel.

Once a drinker, always a drinker whether drinking or not—Juliana understands this principle but has never considered herself a *drinker* in any clinical sense. Not an *alcoholic*.

Ned Spires had been an *alcoholic*. Not Juliana.

Life-saving to Juliana, she'd managed to escape the man. He'd pleaded with her to stay with him, to marry him, he'd divorce his wife of twenty-five years and marry her, but Juliana understood this was folly, she'd escaped with her life.

As Juliana is a good, steady driver, in control of her vehicle, so (she tells herself) she is in control of her drinking.

She has yet to visit the Blue Moon. Months living in this town, aware of the Blue Moon, which she passes frequently and which exerts no particular pull on her, except at night when the blue neon sign glimmers in the window and her heart is quickened to the point of pain.

So deeply moved sometimes, she has to brake

her car, park at a curb until the powerful emotion has passed.

All that I have lost. But—what is it I have lost?

Even if she were still drinking, Juliana reasons, she'd have stopped by now. Since learning she was pregnant. She'd have stopped on the very day she'd found out.

The pregnancy is still something of a shock to her. When she wakes in the morning and the realization sweeps over her. As if in her dreams there is no pregnancy, her body remains a girl's body, untouched.

Waking, she is stunned to realize her situation. Her condition. Not an idea, a physical fact. On the calendar there is marked the (probable) *due date*—July of next year . . .

So far away! Juliana feels a touch of panic that she will not be able to bring this pregnancy to term. Already she has found out, no reason except wishing to know, mere curiosity, how late in a pregnancy a woman can safely have an abortion.

She hasn't yet given much thought to childbirth, to an (actual) infant she will be nursing. She has thought fancifully of the upstairs room in the house on Mill Street, which she and Patrick will convert into a nursery.

At less than six weeks it's too early to determine the sex of the baby. An ultrasound has been scheduled for Juliana's eighteenth week. They will postpone painting the nursery walls—rosy pink for a little girl, sailor-blue for a little boy.

Since the pregnancy, there has been a renewed energy in their life together. Focus, Patrick has said happily. All lives require *focus*.

Each commutes to work, but in contrary directions. Juliana hasn't yet given much thought to what she will do after the baby is born, in what ways her life will be altered.

She hasn't informed her employers, not just yet. Possibly next week.

The Delaware River is the border between New Jersey and Pennsylvania. In this former mill town on the river a young couple can afford a down payment on a renovated row house (originally built in 1922).

Thrift-shop furnishings, wallpaper bought at a discount. An overgrown backyard they'd cleared of debris—children's broken toys, rotted lumber, even a pair of thigh-high fisherman's boots. It would be a forty-minute drive from this house to the Wild Goose Tavern, the Shamrock Inn. The Black Rooster, across the river in Bucks County, Pennsylvania, is slightly closer.

Since she moved to the former mill town on the Delaware River, Juliana has not returned to these taverns. Not since meeting Patrick.

Since she has ceased drinking, Juliana has lost interest in bars, taverns, cafés. Though, admittedly, the sight of neon is a strong attraction.

Especially, Juliana would never drive to the Black Rooster alone, without a companion.

Solitary women seem to be more at risk now than they'd been when Juliana was in her early twenties. Risks she'd taken walking alone late at night, those nights she'd returned at midnight from the Mon ey Bar, she would never take now.

Has the world changed, Juliana wonders. Or has her perception of the world changed.

Sober now, she perceives the world as a sober place. Not hills and valleys but a plateau.

Still, she carries her (secret) weapon with her wherever she goes. Even to work, in a run-down urban neighborhood in Trenton, and even in the daytime, for (of course) she doesn't remove the ice pick from the very bottom of her tote bag; most of the time she isn't aware that it is there.

Not long ago something terrible had happened to a young woman, employee of a local hair salon, who'd gone for drinks at the Black Rooster with coworkers, was followed out of the tavern by an unidentified male patron, who came up behind her in the parking lot, struck her on the side of the head with his fist, and knocked her unconscious. He'd dragged her into a wooded area nearby, cut her clothing with a shears, and torn off her underwear, slashed her skin, "tortured" her with the shears, and left her for dead . . .

This was the third or fourth sexual assault against young women in the area since Juliana and Patrick moved to the mill town eighteen months before.

Juliana has read of the incidents, fascinated and repelled. All the young women have survived the attacks, but none have consented to be interviewed. If Juliana had gone to school here she would have a circle of friends and acquaintances who would know about these attacks—she would know someone in law enforcement, or at the hospital—but she's an outsider, she has no access. All she knows is what the media has released.

Juliana does recall having read—*No arrests have been made.*

The cruelty of the world, to some young women. *She,* the pregnant fiancée, soon to be wife, is treated with tenderness by her devoted lover.

Patrick insists upon feeding her. In an iron skillet he sautés organic farm free-range chicken. Trout, salmon. Portobello mushrooms, red onions, peppers. He prepares rich soups—lentil, black bean, fish chowder. Juliana is ravenous with hunger when she sits down to eat, but after a few mouthfuls she has had enough, or more than enough.

Fatten her, stuff her. As if (in secret) Juliana is trying to lose weight, and so when they are together and Patrick is in charge, he must oversee her eating, make certain that she gains weight as it is normal for a pregnant woman to gain weight.

How many times this fall Juliana has driven past the Blue Moon Café on Front Street. Always slowly. It's a kind of test, she realizes. Like walking a tightrope.

Though there is no likelihood that after so many months, and in her new delicate condition, she is likely to lapse.

Seeing now through the window that the Blue Moon is becoming crowded. Thursday evening, nearing six p.m.

Friday evening would be too crowded, rowdy. Saturday would be impossible. And earlier in the week, not so convivial. Thursday is the ideal weeknight for Juliana; inside there will be a companionable din of voices, laughter. Mostly men. If there are women in the Blue Moon, they will be with companions. Rarely alone.

Eyes gliding over Juliana if she sits at the bar, curious. Do we know *you?*

It has begun to rain, suddenly. Neon in rain, dreamy and blurred, beautiful.

Patrick won't be home yet, probably. Juliana can be a little late returning. If he calls her worriedly, she can answer her cell phone, reassure him she's all right.

Thinking—*Just this once. No harm to it.*

Fated, without volition, seeing an empty parking space on Front Street near the Blue

Moon. If she'd had to park in the rutted-gravel lot behind the café, she'd have driven home without stopping.

Club soda, she will order. Slice of lemon. Over ice cubes.

Her mouth is dry. Her mouth is parched. Hours on the phone, bright fluorescent lights at the law office, exhausting.

Not vodka. (Never vodka!) Though maybe, if circumstances seem right, a single glass of white wine . . .

Just to celebrate. Her happiness.

That escape, from the poet. Finding Patrick, who adores her and trusts her absolutely.

And so it has happened, Juliana has parked the car on Front Street. As she enters the Blue Moon Café (for the first time), she feels her pulse quicken—recalling entering such cafés in the past (for the first time), she has embarked upon an adventure, the outcome of which she cannot know.

That is part of the happiness, the not-knowing.

In the window, blue neon, but inside on a wall, red neon lettering—MOLSON'S.

At once Juliana feels at home in the Blue Moon Café. There is even an old jukebox, she is sure that she can play Johnny Cash here. There are well-worn black leather booths, bar stools. The interior isn't too crowded. Yet not too empty. Another woman, perhaps two women, in one of the booths. Otherwise, all men. At the bar, all men. Eyes move upon her, alert with curiosity, not unfriendly. But no one Juliana will know, no one who knows her.

On one of the walls, framed photographs of high school sports teams. Football, baseball. Local kids now grown up, patrons of the Blue Moon.

No doubt some of these boys are in the Blue Moon tonight. Aging athletes bearing a residue of pride.

Juliana shakes rain out of her hair. Juliana feels ready to laugh, she has no idea why. Sitting at one end of the bar, facing the mirror behind the rows of glittering bottles. Her tote bag, faux gold-glittering, out of the way at her feet, between the legs of the bar stool where she can keep an eye on it unobtrusively.

Politely the bartender greets Juliana; warily he smiles at the solitary young woman who has entered the Blue Moon Café, no one he recognizes.

It is an entirely new place to Juliana—Blue Moon Café. Yet it is utterly familiar. When she uses the women's restroom, she will recognize the low ceiling, stained sink, exposed plumbing, and uneven tile floor. She will recognize the smells, the mild sour stink, not unpleasant, in an odd way comforting.

What will she have? Club soda to begin, with

ice. Then (she thinks) maybe, a (single) glass of white wine, depending . . .

Juliana is in no hurry. This (secret) interlude in her life, she deserves.

Like a rift, an odd tuck in wallpaper. A puckering, an incongruity. Hidden by furniture, no one ever knows. Not a blemish if invisible!

On the TV above the bar is the replay of a recent sports event, or highlights of that event. All is urgent-seeming, yet all is (merely) replayed, it has become history. The hotly contested game has been won and lost. The athlete interviewed before the game has been vindicated or has been humiliated. In the house on Mill Street, Patrick may be home after all, watching TV news, likely it is PBS. Likely it is urgent news of the day about which all informed American citizens should know. If Patrick calls her cell phone, Juliana may not answer, or if she answers, she may say quickly in a lowered voice—*Oh honey, we're on a conference call. Can't talk now. See you soon!*

Glancing around to see a man approaching her. Politely asking if the stool beside her is taken. Seeing that Juliana is alone.

Juliana laughs, pushing hair out of her face. Why does he need to ask permission to sit on the bar stool beside her? No need to ask, the bar stool is unoccupied, isn't it?

In the mirror behind rows of bottles Juliana's

face is blurred and indistinct, as if undersea. Barely Juliana can recognize herself.

Gripped in her warm hand, the glass containing her drink has lost its icy edge. Soon lukewarm liquid that has gone flat, from which romance has fled. Juliana is intrigued by the stranger, who has seated himself beside her with an almost formal deliberation—hands on the bar as if to steady himself as he sits on the stool, taller than Juliana, observing her sidelong. He is in his late thirties, perhaps. Fair skin, red-tinted hairs on the backs of his big-knuckled hands, thick wrists. A sulfurous smell—tobacco? Incongruous in this setting, he is wearing a white cotton shirt, long sleeves rolled to the elbow. His forearms are tight-muscled, covered in coarse red hairs. A wristwatch with a leather band, on his left wrist. And his eyes, crinkled at the corners like kindly eyes, or eyes with a habit of squinting.

Juliana feels light-headed, faint with anticipation. In that instant, suffused with a kind of joy.

The man beside her is asking what has she been drinking? Is she ready for something stronger?

Acknowledgments

Thanks and much gratitude to the editors of the magazines, literary journals, and anthologies in which these stories originally appeared:

"Detour" in *Harper's*

"Curious" in *Salmagundi*

"Miss Golden Dreams 1949" in *Collectibles*, ed. by Lawrence Block

"Wanting" in *Narrative*

"Parole Hearing, California Institution for Women, Chino, CA" in *Boulevard*. Reprinted in *The Best Mystery Stories of the Year*, 2021, edited by Lee Child and Otto Penzler.

"Intimacy" in *Vice*

"The Flagellant" in *At Home in the Dark*, ed. by Lawrence Block

"Vaping: A User's Manual" in *The Nicotine Chronicles*, ed. by Lee Child

"Night, Neon" in *American Short Fiction*

Center Point Large Print
600 Brooks Road / PO Box 1
Thorndike, ME 04986-0001 USA

(207) 568-3717

US & Canada:
1 800 929-9108
www.centerpointlargeprint.com